The Welcome Light

THE
WELCOME LIGHT
Jessica Stirling

St. Martin's Press
New York

Library of Congress Cataloging-in-Publication Data

Stirling, Jessica.
    The welcome light / Jessica Stirling.
       p.   cm.
    ISBN 0-312-06490-X
    I. Title.
PR6069.T497W4   1991   91-18107
823'.914—dc20   CIP

First published in Great Britain by Hodder and Stoughton.

First U.S. Edition: October 1991
10 9 8 7 6 5 4 3 2 1

Contents

The road to resolution lies by doubt:
The next way home's the farthest way about.

Francis Quarles: *Emblems*

One

Picking Up the Pieces

Two tiny silver buckles held the straps of the caliper brace in place. They jingled as Kirsty unfastened them but neither she nor her son paid any attention to the cheerful little noise. Clinging tightly to her breast Bobby watched his mother separate the straps and ease the iron splint from his calf. Fingers kneaded the material of her dress, knees dug into her stomach but he uttered no murmur of pain or protest as Kirsty drew the device away and pushed it under the chair out of sight.

"There now," she said. "All gone until tomorrow."

Bobby leaned his weight against her, cocked his head, rested his chin on her shoulder and, saying not a word, stared bleakly at the wall.

At first Kirsty had tried to make a game of the daily fitting and removal of the splint. Bobby would have none of it. He sensed that the brace signified weakness, something necessary but detestable. Its associations could not be disguised by baby talk any more than its hard metal frame could be softened by kidskin sleeves. It was her son's silences that Kirsty found difficult to bear. His determination not to cry seemed far too precocious for a child of not quite three. It was as if the paralysis had robbed him of his innocence and brought too soon to the fore the Nicholson traits of obstinacy and pride.

"It doesn't still hurt, does it?" Gordon said.

Kirsty glanced up at her brother-in-law who leaned against the kitchen sink by the window.

"Ask him yourself," she said.

"He's not speakin' to me these days," Gordon said. "I don't know what I've done wrong."

"He's not speakin' to any of us," Kirsty said.

"Maybe he needs fresh air," Gordon said. "You should take him to the park tomorrow."

"In this weather?"

"The weather's not so bad," Gordon said. "You can't wrap him up in cotton wool forever, Kirsty."

At twenty, Gordon was four years younger than his brother Craig. In the past few months he'd shed much of his boyishness. He was no longer light-hearted and frivolous and made no attempt to coax Kirsty from her dark moods. He was, she knew, the ambassador for Craig's estranged family and would carry news of Bobby's health and welfare back to his mother and sister in the big terraced mansion on the hill.

"When do you go to see Dr Anderson again?" Gordon asked.

"Not until March."

"I suppose we'll just have to wait until then to see how much damage has been done to the muscles and nerves."

"What do you know about infantile paralysis?" Kirsty said.

"Not much," Gordon admitted. "But I spoke to a doctor the other day an' he said – "

"Doctors! After what happened to poor Jen Taylor I've no great faith in the medical profession."

"It was Kelly who neglected Jen, not Dr Anderson."

"I don't care who it was. They're all the same," Kirsty said. "I keep wonderin' what would have happened if Bobby had contracted the disease first. He'd be dead now, wouldn't he?"

Night after night Gordon would stand edgily by the sink, arms folded, unable to relax with her, with Bobby.

"Why was Jen taken an' Bobby spared?" Kirsty said. "Can you tell me that?"

"Course I can't."

"At least you're not trying to palm me off with some sanctimonious rubbish," Kirsty said. "But I can't understand why it had to happen to Greta. I mean, she had nothin' to call her own except her wee girl. And look at me. I've got everythin' a woman could want – a nice house, a decent husband, my own business an' money in the bank."

"Ach, Kirsty, you shouldn't torment yourself with such mor-

2

bid thoughts," Gordon said.

"Somebody's got to think about these things," Kirsty said. "Everybody else just seems to want to sweep Greta under the carpet, to forget she ever existed. Good riddance to bad rubbish."

"That's not true."

"But I'm – I'm stuck with it."

Gordon shook his head but seemed at a loss for words, as if he too had lost the knack of caring.

For the past half year Gordon had been employed by Carruth's Brewery Company which was managed by his prospective father-in-law, James Randolph Adair. In June Gordon would step to the altar with young Amanda and fulfil the terms of their formal engagement; then he too would be gone from Kirsty's ken to reside in Adair's grand villa on the city's western outskirts.

The rise in Gordon's fortunes had been engineered by his stepfather, Breezy, oldest of the Adairs and chieftain of the sprawling clan. Breezy had dragged his brothers and sisters out of the black mud of a smallholding and by trading, dealing and manipulating had raised them all up in the world. It seemed as natural as breathing for Breezy to do the same sort of thing for his stepchildren. He would willingly have embroiled Kirsty's husband, Craig, in schemes for advancement if Craig had not resisted and remained loyal to his position as a constable with Greenfield burgh police.

Kirsty tugged Bobby from her shoulder and sat him square on her lap. "Bring me the basin, please, Gordon. An' make sure the water's not too hot."

She had no reason to be sharp with her brother-in-law. He had always been her ally and confidante. But she could not help herself.

Gordon sighed. "Blood heat, right?"

"Test it with your elbow."

"Oh. Sorry. I forgot."

She began to undress her son.

It was nine weeks since Bobby had been struck down. Christmas had come and gone uncelebrated and the New Year of 1900 had crept unheralded into the house. Canada Road had echoed with the skirl of bagpipes, the braying of bugles, toasts and songs

3

and drunken revelry. But the neighbours in No. 154 had restrained their enthusiasm for the advent of the twentieth century out of consideration for the sick child on the top landing. There was also anxiety that Bobby Nicholson's disease might spread, that their sons too would be crippled by the mysterious miasma or their daughters die of it like the poor bairn round in Benedict Street. By mid-January, however, community attitudes had changed. Superstitious wives put the particularity of the outbreak down to Divine retribution, punishment on Greta Taylor for her adulterous past and on the Nicholsons for their pride and presumption.

Kirsty remained unaware of the malicious stairhead gossip. Since Bobby had been released from the quarantine ward in Glasgow's Hospital for Sick Children she had remained locked in the house with him. She could not bear to have him out of her sight for more than a few minutes at a time. She would leave him in Craig's care only when necessity drove her out to buy provisions at the Buttercup Dairy or Mr Kydd's corner grocery. In spite of Craig's grumbling protests she'd even insisted on taking Bobby into her bed in the kitchen. There she would lie awake, not daring to move for fear that she'd hurt him, lying rigidly alert for a moan or whimper that might signify the onset of another calamity, waiting in fear for Bobby to be taken from her as roughly as Jen had been snatched from Greta Taylor.

Gordon filled the big brown baking bowl with warm water from the tap of the gas heater by the sink, brought it to the hearth and set it down carefully by the side of Kirsty's armchair. Next he fetched soap and sponge and an egg cup full of a soothing oil that Dr Anderson had provided for Kirsty to massage into Bobby's muscles. Gordon, Kirsty realised, had become almost as familiar with the evening ritual as she was herself. She watched him place the egg cup on the hob and then hold out the big towel towards the grate to warm too. She slipped Bobby, naked now, between her knees and supported his weakened right side with her forearm while she rolled up her sleeves and arranged the canvas apron as a splash guard over her knees and feet. Sullen but unresisting Bobby allowed her to sponge him down.

"I do believe he's put on a pound or two," Gordon said. "His appetite must be comin' back at last."

"He's still too fussy for my likin'," Kirsty said.

"Semolina puddin'," Gordon nodded. "Aye, whatever ailed us when we were young we were always stuffed full o' mutton broth an' semolina puddin'. How about it, son? Fancy some semolina an' a big dollop o' raspberry jam, hm?"

Bobby stared at his uncle, mute as marble.

Gordon said, "I reckon his tongue's still paralysed."

"Don't *say* that," Kirsty snapped.

"Sorry. Sorry."

Gordon backed from her, the towel held out like a flag of truce. It was on the tip of Kirsty's tongue to apologise for her rudeness but she stubbornly kept her mouth shut and expended her ire by scrubbing Bobby's tail with the soapy sponge.

Gordon was no dandy, not like his sister Lorna's young man. Nonetheless he was smartly dressed in chequered suit, stand-up collar and fashionable string tie. Kirsty supposed that as a representative of the management side of Carruth's it was incumbent upon him to impress the landlords and licensees with whom he did business.

She sniffed. "What's that smell?"

"Have a guess," Gordon said.

Proximity to the fire had brought from his clothing the faint but unmistakable odour of beer.

Kirsty said, "I thought you sold the stuff, not paddled in it."

"I don't even sell it, not really."

"What do you do for Carruth's then?"

"I collect the takin's from some of the city pubs," Gordon answered. "Check stock tallies, inspect lavatories an' cast an eye over the pumps – "

"What for?"

"To make sure the management's honest," Gordon said. "I spend a lot of time crawlin' about in cellars awash with suds."

"If you don't like it, Gordon, why do you stick it?"

He shrugged. "It's only temporary, a rung on the ladder. Anyway, I don't have much choice."

Kirsty dried Bobby with the warm, white towel then lifted him on to her knee. Perhaps he *had* put on weight. He had certainly grown taller, as if nature were hastening him towards boyhood to compensate for the ravages of the infection. She took up the egg cup and dipped her fingers into the warm oil. She hated the smell of it for it reminded her of the stench of the hospital ward where Bobby had been kept in isolation. She gripped Bobby's ankle and stretched his leg until she felt resistance. Her manipulations were practised and precise. She was sure that she caused Bobby no pain, that it was humiliation that made him to turn against her, and bump his head into her chin while she examined the lower limb.

Tibia and fibula: Dr Anderson had told her the names of the bones and had shown her how muscles and tendons were connected to them. He had also instructed her in basic massage and had given her a little pamphlet, with diagrams, for further study. She stroked away with a firm caressing motion, noted that the calf muscles remained flaccid and had lost bulk. She did not flinch when Bobby bored his head into her breast again.

Gordon lit a cigarette and stared from the tall window into the cold January sky. He could not bear to watch this part of a ritual which still seemed to him cruel. Strange that Craig found this procedure fascinating, would sit and watch her work without a qualm.

Kirsty said, "Have you heard any word from Greta yet?"

"Nothing." Gordon kept his back to her. "In fact, Breezy's about to put her house on the market. I told him I'd shell out the rent for the next half year but he wouldn't stand for that. Got quite shirty at the very idea."

"Surely it's no skin off his nose who pays the rent?"

"I think he wants me to get on with my life as if nothin' had happened. Mam, Lorna – they all do." He paused. "Perhaps they're right."

"You can't blame Greta for leavin' Glasgow."

"No, I'm not blamin' her." Gordon blew a little plume of tobacco smoke against the pane and watched it disperse. "The only thing that held Greta here was the bairn. It certainly wasn't that miserable job at the Irish Market or her connection with our lot. With Jen dead, though, it must have seemed – " He shrugged. "I miss her, Kirsty. Right or wrong, I miss her."

"We all do," Kirsty said.

"So," Gordon turned, "since there's nothin' I can do to change things, I've decided to accept them. How about you?"

"What's that supposed to mean?"

"When are you going to re-open the shop?"

"I'm not."

"What? Not ever?"

"No."

"Now that's daft, plain daft."

"It's my shop, my decision."

"But business was boomin'. An' you're still loaded with stock. I mean — "

"I don't want to discuss it."

"Suit yourself," Gordon said.

"For once," Kirsty said, "I intend to."

Twelve months ago she had inherited two hundred pounds from her friend Nessie Frew. At Gordon's urging, she'd wagered a portion of the money on a racehorse owned by Dolphus Adair and trained by his cousin Russell Smith. Gordon had hinted that the race had been fixed in advance and it was no real surprise when the filly brought home the bacon. With Gordon as a sleeping partner Kirsty had invested her capital in a general goods shop in Gascoigne Street and, in remarkably short order, had built up a profitable business.

Acquisitiveness and a desire for independence had not been Kirsty's only motives in taking on the shop, however. Craig had had a brief affair with Greta Taylor and it was to extract revenge on her husband that Kirsty had first persuaded Greta to come and work as her assistant in Gascoigne Street. Later they had become fast friends. Now Jen was dead, Greta vanished and a companionable sense of achievement that Kirsty had discovered in shopkeeping had been wiped away by the tragedy.

"I'll see that you get your money back, Gordon."

"I'm not worried about the money," Gordon said. "I'm worried about you. You can't spend the rest of your life cooped up in this kitchen like the bloody Prisoner of Zenda."

"I can't — I won't leave Bobby."

"Take him with you, like you always did."

"It won't be the same," Kirsty said. "Besides, he can't walk."

"'Course he can walk," Gordon said. "When you're not there to carry him he hobbles about on that brace thing well enough."

"I'm always there to carry him."

"Aye, well, when he's twelve or thirteen years old it's goin' to look damned funny, that's all I can say."

Kirsty bit her lip. "Did Craig put you up to this?"

7

"Put me up to what?"

"Persuadin' me to go back to work."

"Hell, no! If you ask me it would suit Craig nicely if you stayed right here and played at bein' a nice, dutiful wee housewife for evermore," Gordon told her. "It's me that thinks you should get back into harness."

"It's none o' your business."

"Damn it, Kirsty, it is my business. Once upon a time I came near to fallin' in love wi' you."

"Aye, when you were just a silly wee laddie."

"I'm no silly laddie now, Kirsty." He pushed himself away from the sink and flicked his cigarette end into the fire. "There are times when I wish none of us had ever set foot in Glasgow."

"If your mother hadn't brought you to Glasgow then you wouldn't have met Amanda," Kirsty said. "Think of that."

"I am thinkin' of that."

"I was under the impression that you loved Amanda."

"I do," Gordon said. "I suppose."

For an instant she felt a surge of affectionate concern but stifled it. Gordon's prospects were unchanged by Jen Taylor's death and by Bobby's illness and Kirsty was in no mood to share guilt with anyone, least of all her brother-in-law.

"You've made Amanda a promise, Gordon," Kirsty said. "If you had doubts about marriage you should have spoken up before now."

"Jeeze, you're beginnin' to sound just like my mother."

"I'm not flattered," Kirsty said.

"You've also managed to change the subject," Gordon said. "What about the shop, Kirst? Do you really intend to give it up?"

"I can't run it on my own."

"I'll buy it from you – as a goin' concern."

"What'll you do with it?"

"Make money," Gordon said.

"How will you find time to – "

"I'll put in a manager."

"A stranger?"

"Oh, yes," Gordon said. "It's safer with strangers. You know where you are with strangers."

"You just want to hang on to the shop in case Greta comes back, isn't that it?"

"Greta isn't comin' back," Gordon said. "You're right; nobody wants her. She's served her purpose an' now she's just an embarrassment to all concerned."

Bobby, who had fallen asleep in her arms, wakened and whimpered. She hugged her arms tightly about his naked body, hugged him as if he could defend her against unpalatable truths.

"Gordon, what do you *want* from me?"

"I want you to pick up the pieces, that's all."

"I can't."

"Damn it, you can."

"How?"

"Go back to Gascoigne Street, take down the shutters."

"Dust the cash register?"

"Aye, why not?" Gordon said. "There's nothin' sinful about makin' money."

"I – I can't," Kirsty said again.

Gordon plucked hat and scarf from the dresser top. "I'll have to go. I'm late for supper as it is." He coiled the scarf under his collar and tucked away the ends. "Think about it, Kirsty. If you mean what you say, if you really don't want to go back to Gascoigne Street, I'll buy the business from you at a fair price."

"Do you actually want it, Gordon?"

"Not particularly. I just can't stand to see a valuable asset go to waste."

"I'll – I'll let you know."

"When?"

"Soon," she said and let him find his own way out.

After he'd gone, Kirsty sat motionless by the fire, Bobby asleep in her arms. She thought not about Craig or Gordon or even Greta but about David Lockhart, whom she had loved once and who had left her to return to his father's Christian mission in China. David might have been able to explain why she felt so responsible for Jen Taylor's death, why she was afraid of going out to face the world again – but David was far, far away. The night express to Inverness trailed a long ribbon of sound along the Greenfield embankments and gently rattled the tenements to make sure that folk were still awake to mark its passing.

Kirsty listened, wistfully at first then with a sudden breaking in her heart. She lifted Bobby up a little, slid the soft cotton nightshirt over his head and settled him again in her lap. She blinked, listening still to the train's faint, far off echo, and then, for the first time in weeks, let the tears flow freely, not for Bobby, not for Greta, but for herself.

* * *

Constable Archie Flynn, big, amiable and none-too-bright, had grown weary of living in police barracks in Edward Road. He was envious of men like Craig Nicholson, men who had sweet and gentle wives to go home to after a shift. Archie had a terrible notion to find a wife for himself. He didn't want to wind up like Sergeant Drummond with nothing to call his own but three briar pipes, two pairs of boots and a cold bed in a boarding house. Archie made it known to all and sundry that he was scouting for a bride and, in consequence, deserved all that he got.

"How about her then?" Peter Stewart would say and point out wee Norah Barnaby, three feet dot and forty-five years old, as she shuffled down Riverside Road.

"Well – " Archie would say, dubiously.

"Hey, Norah," Peter would shout. "Hey, here's a fella fancies you, Norah."

Norah had nothing against coppers but, by God, she had plenty against men. She would yell out in a voice rough enough to scour barnacles off a dredger. "Him, is it?"

"Aye, this fine, well set-up young fella here."

"God, I wouldnae huv *him* in a bloody gift."

Archie, the fool, would indignantly enquire what was wrong with him. And Norah would tell the world at the top of her voice just what she thought of promiscuous youths who wanted nothing from a girl but a fleeting amour round the back of the wash-houses and what said promiscuous youths could do with themselves.

Peter, when he'd caught up with Archie, would pat his pal's shoulder and say, consolingly, "Well, I doubt she's not the one for you, Archibald. Pity that. You'd have made a lovely couple at the altar."

Craig had too much on his mind to join in the ribbing of Big Archie. He had been given a fortnight's leave when his son was critically ill and had returned to the roster so haggard that Lieutenant Strang had assigned him to permanent back shift.

10

On back shift Craig was so busy that he had precious little time to brood about Bobby's health or the state of his marriage. At the end of the working day, however, he usually managed to find time to collect Sammy Reynolds from the door of the People's Mission, where he worked as caretaker's assistant, and walk him home to the Claremont Model lodging-house in Scutter Street.

Daft Sammy had been the 'pet' of the officers and men of Ottawa Street station ever since Craig and David Lockhart had rescued him from the poorhouse and, between them, had found him work and a place to stay.

This past few months Sammy had sprouted into a great shaggy hulk, not tall but broad-beamed and bulky. His moon face, which had previously been a picture of bucolic innocence, was crossed by street slyness when he didn't get things his own way. He had recently been introduced to the joys of tobacco and would puff away in the lavatory with lads from the Boys' Brigade or Senior Bible Class and shamelessly cadge ciggies from anyone if he thought he could get away with it. Also, Sammy had acquired a gun; not a real gun, of course, but a wooden replica of the sort used by the Greenfield Volunteers on their street parades. The company were parading a lot these days, preparatory to shipping out for the Transvaal to fight the Boers. Sammy could mimic a soldier's strutting march to perfection, rifle sloped, broad bottom waggling.

"*Aaaeeez* RIGHT," Sam would bawl and snap a salute at Rab McKechnie who squatted drunk as a lord in the doorway of Slattery's pub or at Mrs Scott's greasy big mongrel which sprawled on the threshold of the Buttercup Dairy. "*Aaaeeez* FRONT."

Sammy's wasn't the only head turned by word of the war against the Boers. Many a small boy dreamed of little else but kilt and bayonet and finding glory on the veldt. Grown men too were possessed by patriotic fervour and a diabolical hatred of Kruger and his gang.

Craig kept abreast of the news from abroad but did not share the general air of jingoistic excitement. He did not quite approve of the wooden rifle that Sammy brandished with such glee or the way the boy would snipe indiscriminately at pigeons on the roof or pedestrians on the pavement and yell, "Gotcha! Lie doon. Ye're deid."

Craig could not help but contrast Sam's pointless energy with Bobby's weakness, the knowledge that his son would never be a soldier now, would never walk straight and manly in any sort of uniform, and to feel resentful.

Perhaps it was guilt that drove Craig to the corner stall at Banff Street that particular night to stand Sam a black pudding supper before he returned the boy to his lodgings. Perhaps it was a lingering hope that he might glimpse a light again in Greta's house in Benedict Street. Craig too missed the little black-haired street woman more than he dared admit. He had gone, with Gordon, to Jen's funeral in Wolfe Road cemetery. There had been no preliminary service in a kirk or the chapel adjacent to the hospital. The child's body had been boxed in some darkened basement below West Graham Street and transported directly to Wolfe Road from there.

Only Gordon had accompanied the coffin, had ridden in the hearse, for nobody had been able to find Greta to ask her what she wished done. Greta had been at the gates, though, standing back from the graveside in that new, raw burial ground which offered no comfort or catharsis for the pain of the loss of a child so young. He could not forget his last sight of Greta, in neat black coat and neat black hat, small as a child herself, loitering all alone in Wolfe Road while the tiny coffin was lowered into the ground.

When it was over, when Craig had turned from the graveside and looked towards the gates Greta was gone, and none of them had seen or heard from her since.

"*Ten* SHUN. *Aaaeeez* RIGHT."

"Sammy, for God's sake!"

"*Squaw-hod* SAAL-OOT."

"Sammy, will you shut your face. Do you want t'wake the whole bloody neighbourhood?"

"See but, there's Mr Flynn."

The last half inch of the Gold Flake that Craig had given him had popped from Sam's mouth into the gutter and the boy stooped and scrambled in search of the damp butt while Craig watched Archie Flynn, clearly harassed, hurry towards them from the tail of Benedict Street.

"Craig, thank God it's you."

"What's up, Archie."

"Somebody's in there, in number thirteen."

"Is it Greta? Has she come back?"

"God knows!" said Archie. "The door's locked fast an' I can't get in. But somebody's inside, I'm sure, somebody lyin' doggo."

"Ah wouldnae mind a doggie." Sam sucked noisily on the crumbs of tobacco he'd retrieved from the gutter. "Ah could look after a wee doggie fine. *Woof. Woof-Woof. Woo – "*

"Shut it, Sammy," Archie told the boy. "This is police business."

"Ah'll be in the polis soon, so ah wull."

"Aye, Sam," Craig said. "But only if you learn to do what you're told."

Benedict Street had always been the toughest part of Archie's beat but since the demise of hard man Billy King last year the citizens had seemed chastened and the district had become remarkably peaceful. Number 13, where Greta Taylor had lived, had been dark and empty for many weeks and to Archie, who was not alone in his superstitions, a sort of pall still hung over the close.

Grabbing the boy by the hand Craig set off towards No. 13 and left Archie to bring up the rear. Fortunately Sammy seemed to have grasped the importance of keeping silent and stood quietly by Craig's side at the close mouth while the coppers discussed tactics.

"I glimpsed a light in the bedroom," Archie said, "but when I went an' knocked on the door, nobody answered. But there *is* somebody in that house. I'll swear it."

"Did you check the back?"

"The blind's drawn an' the window's still shut."

"Did you use your lamp?"

"'Course I did."

"So whoever is inside knows you've spotted them?"

"I'd imagine so," Archie said.

"Go to the door again." Craig nudged Archie. "Challenge them again."

"Why don't you do it?"

"It's better if they don't know I'm here."

"Even if it's her? Even if Greta Taylor's come back?"

"Go on, Archie. You, Sammy, not a cheep out o' you."

Keeping the boy with him Craig crept into the close. He pressed himself out of sight against the stair wall and listened intently, his heart beginning to pound.

Archie knocked loudly on the door.

"Mrs Taylor, is that you?"

A thick, tense silence hung suspended behind the closed front door. Copper's instincts told Craig that Archie had been right; there was someone in the house. His mouth went dry. He saw, in his mind's eye, Greta gone mad with grief stalking the unlit kitchen, flinging back bedclothes and yanking open cupboards in search of the child she'd lost.

Shaking his head, Archie retreated again into the street and Craig and Sammy followed him.

"Nothin' doin'," Archie said. "Now what?"

"Take Sam to Banff Street, buy him a puddin' supper, then walk him round to the Claremont. I'm goin' to wait here."

"So you think I'm right?"

"Never doubted it, Archie."

"Once I've seen off his lordship I'll come back."

"No, Archie. Just sign off an' toddle home to bed."

"I should report it, you know," Archie said.

"No, don't."

Archie said, "You're hopin' it's her, aren't you?"

"Whoever it is," Craig said, "I intend to wait until they open that door, even if it takes all bloody night."

"Ah'll stay too," Sammy said, surprising the coppers by his apparent grasp of the situation. "Ah can shoot the bad man deid."

"You'll go with Constable Flynn," Craig said. "Do what he says, an' no nonsense. Right?"

Sammy glowered for a moment and then offered Archie his hand.

With some relief Craig watched the pair depart down Benedict Street. When he heard Sammy shout, "*Ry-hut wheel*," from the Banff Street corner, he slipped into the close once more and settled on the stairs to wait.

The intruder hadn't forced an entry. That in itself meant very little for there were plenty of locksmiths in Greenfield who'd carve you a key for the town hall clock if you had enough money to offer for it. Patience, however, was not a hallmark of the average criminal and Craig reckoned he would not be in for an all-night vigil. In fact, he'd hardly had time to smoke half a Gold Flake before a sound within the house brought him to his feet and he saw the door open an inch.

In the vertical crack he glimpsed a pale face, and knew, with a thump of disappointment, that it wasn't Greta's. An instant later, however, his mood swung to one of raw elation when he recognised the intruder. He let the man emerge, close the door and turn to relock it, then he stepped up behind him and said quietly, "Well, well, well! If it isn't Mr John Whiteside. Nice to see you again – old chum."

Whiteside started, spun round and flung up the leather brief-case to protect his head from attack.

"Have no fear, Johnnie. It's only the law."

Whiteside sagged back against the door with a muffled snarl of dismay and anger. "I might have known it would be you. God, Nicholson, you scared me half to death, damn you."

"So sorry," Craig said. "But if you'd opened the door to Constable Flynn when you were asked there'd be no need for me to search you now."

"Oh, come now. You know perfectly well I've every right to be here. Look, I have keys, keys given to me by the owner of the property."

"Do you have a letter of authority too?"

"Don't be damned ridiculous," Whiteside said.

"In that case how do I know you didn't steal those keys?"

Johnnie Whiteside was the oldest of Albert 'Breezy' Adair's nephews. He had baulked at following his father into the legal profession and, together with his cousin Eric, had thrown in his lot with Uncle Breezy. Currently he managed the family ware-house in Partick East and, over the years, had attended to many bits and pieces of Adair business of a less than salubrious nature.

"I'll start by lookin' in your case," Craig said.

John Whiteside squared up to him. They were both taller than average and each believed that he carried a weight of moral authority which gave him an edge in the superiority stakes.

"Lay a finger on that case, Nicholson, and I'll make sure it costs you your job."

"Naw, naw." Craig shook his head. "Even the great Breezy Adair couldn't pull that off. I don't care how much butter-money you've paid into the Police Benevolent Fund on his behalf, nobody's goin' to sack me for doin' what's right an' proper."

"The contents of this case are private."

"What's in there? Letters, personal letters?"

"Why in God's name should it be letters?" Whiteside said.

Craig shrugged. "I thought perhaps you, or Breezy, had somethin' to hide."

"No, I've nothing to hide. Nothing."

"Then why are you sneakin' into Greta's house at this hour of the night?"

"Because I've been working all damned day, if you must know," Whiteside said. "You aren't the only person who has to earn a livin', old son. I've been engaged in checkin' an inventory received from the agent's office against the contents of the dwelling."

"Why?"

"To see what's to be put into store." Whiteside smirked. "Didn't know that, Nicholson, did you? Yes, Breezy's decided to sell the house. Not the whole tenement, of course, just the ground floor apartment."

"Why?"

"Apparently he wants shot of it."

"What if Greta – "

"Greta's gone. Greta's taken a long walk."

"So you *do* know where she is?"

Whiteside's tone became suddenly placatory, almost sympathetic. "Believe me, none of us know where Greta's gone to. Breezy is just as concerned as the rest of us."

"Is she – is she dead?"

"Oh, good God!" Whiteside exclaimed. "Is that the copper's brain at work? Do you suppose that my uncle's had her murdered?"

Craig could not deny that some such suspicion had been preying on his mind of late.

"Naw, but – "

Though Whiteside had the upper hand, he chose not to exploit it. "I know what she meant to you, Nicholson. But in spite of your prejudice against us, we folk on the hill are not barbarians. We cared for Greta too – and her child."

Craig was on the brink of blurting out that he knew the real reason why the Adairs had been so interested in Greta Taylor and why they had cared for her welfare. Greta had been used to avert a nasty family scandal. The child now dead had not been Greta's at all. Jen had been fathered on Olive Carruth Adair by the sporting captain, Tom Wells. Greta had only been the foster mother. However, the fact that Whiteside was here to clear out the house, that Breezy was putting the apartment up for sale indicated all too clearly that Greta was not coming back to Greenfield, that she was gone for good.

"You do believe me, don't you?" Whiteside said.

"What option have I?"

"None at all, really," Whiteside said. "Now, if you don't mind steppin' to one side, I would be awfully grateful. It's been a long day and I am rather keen to get home to bed."

"When will the house be sold?" Craig asked.

"End of the month," said Whiteside.

"Good riddance?" Craig asked.

Whiteside gave one of those low, patronising chuckles that only the educated classes ever seemed to master to perfection and patted Craig very lightly and fleetingly on the sleeve as he stepped round him.

"I'm glad I'm not a cynic," Whiteside said. "Night-night, Constable Nicholson."

Craig followed the man to the close mouth and watched him hurry off in the direction of Dumbarton Road to find a cab to take him home – or elsewhere.

"Night-night, y'bastard," Craig muttered then headed down to Banff Street to buy himself a supper from the stall.

* * *

"Kirsty, Kirsty, are you awake?"

She lay asleep on top of the bed, one arm raised to keep the glare of the gas light out of her eyes, the other was curled protectively about her son. Craig stood looking down on her in a sort of trance, the parcel of chips and black pudding cupped against his trouser leg.

She was not so pretty as she'd been in the days he'd run away with her. The years had taken their toll. Somehow the freshness had left her. There were tiny creases that he hadn't noticed

17

before upon her brow and by her lips. Bobby was turned on his side under the quilt, nothing much visible except hair and brow and the tip of his nose. He seemed settled tonight, not twitching or whimpering as he'd done in the early days of his recovery. Craig was tempted to brush a hand over his son's head and tuck the quilt tighter about him but he resisted.

Black skirt stretched to show the shape of Kirsty's thighs, black stockings defined her trim ankles. She'd unbuttoned the collar of her blouse and he could see the soft flesh where her breasts began to swell. He took a deep indrawn breath. He had learned to stifle his need of her and no longer found it difficult to do. He did not imagine that she would resist or deny him; it was simply that the time was not ripe for love-making. Since they seldom shared a bed he could not take her quick and sudden under the covers like an ordinary husband might do. He had to wait, to court her, to gauge her moods and match them against circumstances and against his own longing. It had been different with Greta. Greta had always been ready for him and, after the first time, had never denied him.

Craig sighed, hoisted up the brown paper parcel and set it on a dinner plate which had been left on the table.

The kitchen's untidy state told him that Kirsty had not intended to fall asleep. Whatever her other failings, she had always been a neat, clean housekeeper. Exhaustion, not laziness, had persuaded her to lie down. He was tempted to wake her but did not. Without taking off his uniform he crept about the room. Cramped and crammed with furniture as it was, he managed to make himself tea and to set a tray all without disturbing her and, just after midnight, carried supper through to the front parlour.

The gas fire was another little luxury that Kirsty's money had bought. He was glad of its comfort tonight, though. Seated on a cushioned stool he balanced the tray on the side of the bed and ate and drank, bathed in the firelight's glow. Many a man would be glad of such comfort on a cold January night. But there should have been more – and there wasn't. How could you ever explain to old Hector Drummond or eager Archie Flynn? They'd think you were daft.

He missed Greta. He could not deny it. That part of his life was over, however. He was left with the job, with Kirsty, his imperfect son, and an untidy parcel of regrets.

He finished the meal, smoked a cigarette and then carried the tray through to the kitchen in the faint fond hope that Kirsty would waken, would welcome him with a sleepy smile, would open her arms and invite his kiss.

She slept.

Craig washed up, put everything neatly in its place, hooked the guard over the grate and turned out the gaslight.

He hesitated by the recess and, without expectation or excitement, whispered, "Good night, love," before he went quietly back to the room at the front of the house to climb into bed alone.

Two

Lorna in Love

Lorna Nicholson was bored. It was not in her nature to be bored and she was not actually sure that 'bored' was the right word to describe her present condition but no other seemed to fit the bill. She knew only too well what 'tedium' meant and all the ramifications of 'monotony' for, Lord knows, she'd learned to recognise those states of mind and matter only too well during her student days at Prosser's Commercial College. Especially this half year when she was stuck in a class with thirty-five gibbering girls and four sullen, weedy-looking boys to have the rudiments of Commercial French drummed into her day after dreary day, as well as having to keep up with typewriting, shorthand and advanced bookkeeping.

"*Fais attention, Mademoiselle Neeekolson.*"

"*Oui, Madame McGibbon.*"

"*Geeebon. Ma-geee-bon. Qu'est-ce que tu as aujourd'hui?*"

"*Je suis* BORED, *Madame. Je suis très, très* BORED."

She didn't say it, of course, not out loud. She would never dare talk back to the tyrannical old hen like that. But rebellion boiled in her more and more often and she was afraid that one fine day she might forget herself.

But was she really bored or was she, perhaps, suffering the unfamiliar pangs of love? Lorna did not dare admit that the only time she felt alive, *engagée*, was when she was in the presence of Mr Ernest Tubbs, salesman and gay Lothario. When Tubby wasn't around she was suspended in limbo, with nothing much to fill the void except memories of their last encounter and anticipations of the next.

Love, she couldn't possibly be in love!

Love was a joke on other people, something she teased Gordon with. Gordon *was* in love. And look at him, poor devil, mooning, moping, hang-dog and permanently po-faced. She didn't feel at all like that, not, at least, when she was alone with Mr Tubbs.

No, no, no! It couldn't be love. Tubby and she were having too much fun to be in love. They laughed a lot, ribbed each other mercilessly, kissed with a smack, hugged like bears, chased each other round lamp posts and up closes, and generally behaved like daft idiots. She'd observed her brother's courtship with Amanda Adair, noted how they hardly ever smiled, never deigned to laugh and took the whole business of being officially in love with great glumness. No, Lorna decided, she was not in love. She was just bored, bored every minute of every day when Tubby wasn't around to keep her stimulated and entertained.

Since Kirsty had been forced to put up the shutters on the shop in Gascoigne Street, however, Tubby hadn't been around all that often. He had a living to earn and, with G. A. Nicholson's closed, had had to extend his territory to sell his quota of goods for the warehousemen, Mathieson, Mullard & Milroy, by whom he was employed. Tubby didn't talk much about his home life. He had one brother, at least, and a widowed mother, and he lived with them in – Lorna gathered – near poverty in the Maryhill ward of Glasgow. She sensed that Ernest was embarrassed by his impecuniosity and she did not press him to discuss that distressing aspect of his life.

Being just sweet seventeen, Lorna lacked the perspicacity to wonder why a man so poor could dress so well. In fact Lorna was so fed-up with college and the stuffiness of her own domestic environment that her trust in Mr Tubbs would not have wavered if he'd turned up one day with cropped head in a suit stencilled with broad arrows.

The blossoming relationship with Ernest Tubbs protected Lorna against the gloom that had descended upon the rest of the family. She was worried, of course, about her nephew Bobby, particularly after the wee Taylor girl died. But she'd heeded her mother's warning not to visit Kirsty or Craig and risk contracting the infection. She got all her news about Canada

Road from Gordon. She was decent enough to wait until Bobby was well on the mend before she put to Gordon the selfish question that had been on her mind for weeks.

"When will Kirsty open up again?"

"I doubt if she will," Gordon had answered.

"But – but she must!"

"Why must she?"

"Because I want her to."

"Good God!" was all Gordon had said to that and had skulked off into his bedroom, shaking his head like some fusty old kirk elder.

Lorna'd had to be content with that unsatisfactory answer, at least for a while.

Somehow, the weeks had slipped away and she'd ceased to think much about Kirsty or the shop or Bobby's dreadful illness. She became too wrapped up in her own concerns and in Mr Tubbs to realise that Bobby was out of quarantine and that she could visit Kirsty at any time without risk.

Each week night, before the bell had stopped ringing, Lorna would whizz along the corridor and leap down the staircase that separated Prosser's classrooms from the street below. Curls bouncing, books thumping in the satchel at her side, eel skirt flickering about her trim ankles, out into the street she would eagerly rush. Shop windows gleamed in the cold air, lights shimmered, electrical tramcars spluttered and popped like fireworks at the junction; Lorna's excitement was immense as she flew across the road to the rendezvous spot on the corner under Rolleston's clock.

Most often Ernest would be there waiting for her. But sometimes he would not. Business would delay him unavoidably. On those occasions Lorna would hang about for an hour or so and then, almost weeping with disappointment, would catch a tramcar home. When he was there, though, the night would light up like a fairy-flash. She would suddenly feel as sparky and alive as an electrical cable and when he kissed her in greeting she would experience a tiny, inexplicable *phisk* between his lips and hers, the same sensation as you get by stroking a cat's whiskers on a frosty morning. Lorna would gasp, then giggle. Tubby would utter a long *oooooo* of sensual satisfaction before he linked his arm with hers and trotted off with her, like children playing ponies, to the Westminster tearooms.

Mr Ernest Tubbs was not at all tubby. He was, in reality, very tall and thin, and in consequence wore his fashionable clothes with dash and flair. Lorna never tired of admiring him. She particularly liked to watch him eat. He would devour pie and peas or a sausage hotpot with mannerly alacrity and great relish while Lorna sipped sweet tea and toyed with a coconut bun.

Meals at the Westminster tearooms were cheap and speedily served, which made the place popular with budget-conscious clerks and their salesgirl sweethearts and there was, in the midst of macaroons and mince rounds, a faint, erotic lovey-doviness that the young folk seemed unconsciously to share.

Lorna, however, was less fortunate than her salesgirl companions in love. She had a curfew upon her. Like Cinderella she had to abandon her Prince before the witching hour – not midnight but eight – struck on Rolleston's enormous overhead clock. She had to be home in Great Western Terrace in time for dinner or awkward questions might be asked as to where she'd been and who she'd been with. Lorna was in no doubt that her mother would read the riot act if it came to light that she was being wooed by a man with the inferior prospects of a mere commercial traveller.

Later, Lorna could never quite decide whether the idea had been foisted upon her by Ernest or if it had been born in her own mind out of desperation. Whatever its origins, by mid-January the idea had been discussed enough to have grown into a full-fledged plan. She took it first to Gordon, cornering him in the long brown first-floor hallway one night after dinner.

"Gordon, what *is* happening to Gascoigne Street? I really must know."

"Oh, must you?" Gordon said. "All right, I'll tell you. Kirsty's lost interest. She's goin' to sell out her share of the business an' give up."

"Oh, God, no!"

"You're makin' a heck of a fuss about a Saturday job."

"Can't you persuade her to think again?"

"No – why should I?"

"Well, you own the property, don't you?"

"I can lease the property no bother," Gordon said. "I can probably even chin Whiteside into takin' the stock off our hands at some sort of reasonable price."

"It's a waste," Lorna said, indignantly. "A shameful waste of an excellent commercial prospect. I think Kirsty should be made to put in a manager. She could then take a percentage of the profits against her investment and leave the runnin' of the business to folk who happened to be interested. What d'you think, Gordon?"

"You're barkin' up the wrong tree, Lorna," Gordon said. "If you think you're ready to manage a shop – "

"I didn't say that."

"Who put you up to this?"

"Nobody. It's my idea."

"Breezy'll never let you leave college without your certificates," Gordon said. "Besides, he has plans for you. I reckon he intends to put you into one of the big city counting-houses once you've finished your education."

"Well, he can get rid of that plan for a start," Lorna said. "Look, Gordon, I've done my stint in Gascoigne Street on Saturdays. I know the ropes. I'm a better bookkeeper than Kirsty will ever be." She hesitated. "In any case, I'd have professional assistance an' advice if I needed it."

"From me? No, Lorna, I'm not warehousin' any more. I've cut my cloth to a different shape. An' I doubt if Breezy will be entirely eager to help you disobey his – "

"I wasn't thinking of you or Breezy, matter of fact."

"Who then?" Gordon asked.

"Mr Tubbs."

The growl of the electrically operated dumb waiter that connected the kitchens with the dining room sounded in the panels close by the couple. Lorna started and glanced guiltily towards the corridor's end. Madge's voice, muffled but acerbic, drifted down to her, followed by a sort of *yawp* from Breezy that may, or may not, have been laughter.

"Ernest Tubbs!" Gordon said. "So it was Tubbs put this nonsense into your head, was it?"

"No, not exactly."

"Tubbs is a salesman, Lorna. He'll do anythin' to secure retail outlets for Mathieson, Mullard an' Milroy. That's all he cares about – sales an' commission."

"No, it isn't."

"Have you been seein' Tubbs on the sly?"

"No, of course not."

"Lorna?"

"Well, I have bumped into him now and then by accident, just by accident. Since the shop closed, that is."

"Be careful, Lorna."

"Why? Tubby's all right."

"He's a salesman, an' salesmen have no scruples. I should know. I was one, remember?"

"Huh! You're a fine one to talk about scruples, Gordon Nicholson. Givin' up your freedom to marry into money."

"That's quite enough o' that, Lorna."

He stepped away from her and retreated into his bedroom.

Lorna, however, was nothing if not persistent. She had no fear of Gordon. Even if he would not become her ally, he would never betray her confidences. She followed him.

He lit the electrical lamp on the dressing table. The bulb burned wanly, flickeringly, as if the intricate system of wires that had been fitted into the house's walls and ceilings was imperfect in its contacts and connections.

"Bloody thing!" Gordon exclaimed, weariness manifest in temporary anger.

"Look," Lorna said.

She stepped forward and tapped the base of the glass bulb with her knuckle and the light steadied at once.

"How did you – ?" Gordon said.

"It's the lamp. The screw fitment hasn't been properly moulded. Common enough."

"Huh!" Gordon said, ruefully.

Unlike her parents and even her brother Lorna did not consider the domestic application of electrical power as a mysterious phenomenon. She was a child of a new generation and had studied the wiring diagrams that the workmen had spread on the hall table during the days of the system's installation. It was all very logical and patterned, not at all strange. A trace of new-century meticulousness had crept into her dealings with her family too, though emotions could not be traced and printed as accurately as wiring charts, not yet. Lorna thought of things as easy, provided there was a plan, a diagram to follow. She was impatient with her brother who seemed to have lost all his

25

panache since he had started mingling with brewers, publicans and the like. He seemed, at times, defeated by the weight of responsibility that he had taken upon himself.

"Lorna, I'm tired. I really would like to go to bed."

Lorna said, "I'm not goin' to give up, Gordon. I want to be a shopkeeper, like Kirsty, an' this is a golden opportunity for me."

"You're too young."

"Too young, am I? Well, we'll just have to see about that," Lorna snapped. "For your information, I intend to pursue the matter further and without reference to you."

"God, you're beginning to talk like a circular letter," Gordon said. "When you're not spoutin' off like a termagant, that is."

"A what?"

"See, you don't know everythin', after all."

"It's nasty, isn't it? An insult?"

"Ask Kirsty."

"About 'termagant'?"

"About the bloody shop, idiot."

He had lighted a cigarette and was seated on the side of the bed, leaning on one elbow and pleasantly wreathed in faint blue smoke. The dullness had gone out of his eyes, she noticed, and he was observing her astutely but with some of the old, familiar warmth. Oddly, she was suddenly wary, unwilling to accept his concession at face value.

Gordon said, "You're absolutely right, Lorna. Why should Daddy Adair push you around too. Hell, I don't give a tinker's damn about the shop or who runs it. If you can get Kirsty to agree then I'll back you up."

"Why this sudden change of tune?"

"Aw, come on, Lorna!" Gordon exclaimed in exasperation. "Look, go an' talk to Kirsty."

"Mother says I've still not to go near Bobby."

"Bobby's better. He's not givin' off deadly rays or anythin'. He has a wee limp an' some wasted muscles, that's all. He keeps askin' for you, you know."

"Does he?" said Lorna. "Can I – can I touch him?"

"Good God!"

"All right," said Lorna. "I'll go an' talk to Kirsty."

Gordon rose and, like the gentleman he was struggling to become, opened the door for his sister.

"You will tell me what she says, dear heart, won't you?"

"Don't worry, sonny boy, you'll be the first to know."

*   *   *

During the long isolated weeks of Bobby's convalescence it seemed to Kirsty that some of the rifts in her marriage had begun to heal too.

Perhaps Gordon had been right in suggesting that Craig would only be content when she became a wife like other wives, a stay-at-home, humdrum, ordinary, devoted to and ruled by her husband. Certainly Craig had been quieter than usual, and quite attentive. Though he hadn't told her so in as many words she sensed that he had been hurt by Bobby's illness and the lameness that it had left in its wake. He was concerned for Bobby, of course, but he was also embarrassed by the defect in his son, as if somehow he had been saddled with goods that had turned out to be shoddy. It was not from the direction of Gascoigne Street, however, or from the Adair's mansion on the hill that trouble blew into Kirsty's marriage again but from much nearer home.

Constable Andy McAlpine had been courting disaster for long enough. Every man in Ottawa Street station knew that it would only be a matter of time before the roaring boy steamed right off the rails and got himself sacked.

The wives in the coppers' tenement were equally cynical about Andy's long-term prospects, for his wife, Joyce, had never been reticent about her trials and tribulations. She had never tried to pretend — as many a wife did — that hers was a model marriage or that her husband's drunken binges were nothing but an excusable male foible. In any case, it would have been exceedingly difficult for Joyce to disguise her hardships. Andy in his cups was indiscriminately violent and, short of sticking her head in a coalbag when she appeared out of doors, Joyce could not have hidden her bruises and cuts from her neighbours.

At first she had made an effort to be loyal, and would come up with all kinds of excuses for her injuries.

"Fell again," she would say. "Clumsy bugger, am I not?"

"Walked into a door in the dark."

"Slipped on the step on my way to the closet."

"Banged into a box in Mr Kydd's shop. But the doctor says it's not broke — my arm, I mean, no' the box. Ha-ha!"

27

Soon after Craig and Kirsty had arrived at No. 154, however, Joyce had run out of credible excuses and, given half a chance, would pour out the sordid truth to anyone who would offer her a little sympathy. There was more to it than anger, humiliation, the pain of her injuries or the perpetually straitened circumstances to which Andy's drinking condemned her. Joyce had, it seemed, begun to fear for her life.

"Mark my words, Mrs Walker, it'll happen one o' these days."

"What will, Mrs Swanston?"

"He'll do for her good an' proper."

"Then he'll swing for it."

"Aye, an' I'll dance for joy the day he does, believe me."

It was universally agreed, even by big, soft, good-natured Mrs Piper, that whatever end lay in store for Andy McAlpine hanging was too good for him. The coppers' wives were, however, bred-in-the-bone realists and knew only too well that what affected Andy adversely would affect Joyce and the children even more. If Andy lost his job, the family would lose its income and the roof over its head, and a policeman sacked for drunkenness would not find it easy to come by other employment.

Joyce might have allies in plenty in No. 154 but she had no close friend to whom she could blurt out all her woes and from whom she could seek practical support. Perversely an element of culpability attached itself to Joyce, as if the women blamed her somehow for marrying a man as bad as Andy or suspected that there might be an invisible flaw in her that had initially driven him to the bottle. So ingrained was their prejudice against their own sex that not a one of them could quite separate Andy's failings from those of his wife and read into the woman's despair a kind of collusion with her husband's sly brutality. For whatever reason, they offered Joyce collective sympathy but separately kept their distance.

Kirsty saw nothing at all of Joyce McAlpine in the weeks before and after New Year. She had been so inured in her problems that she had not even heard the gossip about the sudden deterioration in the already rotten relationship between Andy and his wife, and the consensus opinion that 'things down there' were reaching a head at last.

All that Friday, since he'd signed off day shift, Andy had been at the booze, whacking through what remained of the wage packet in a crawl from pub to pub. In the manner of certain habitual drunkards, though, he seemed by closing time to have tippled himself sober and he came down Canada Road walking brisk and straight. It was only when you passed him close that you could see how far gone he was. Tabs of foam were at the corners of his lips and his eyes were glassy red.

Precisely what happened between Andy McAlpine and Joyce remained obscure. There had been no great audible barney, no thuds or thumps or screams, no wailing of children, as there often was late after a shift's end. It was surmised that Joyce had heard her man coming, had put the children into the front bedroom to protect them and, showing her usual courage, had come out to take it on the chin. Andy had certainly struck her, no doubt of that. But then there had been something else, something different, some new variation on Andy's familiar sadistic repertoire, some act that lay below mere physical pain and touched a bright red nerve in Joyce. For whatever reason she'd found flint, and had finally and at long last snapped. She'd picked up a coal hammer, struck Andy on the back of the head with it and laid him out cold on the kitchen rug.

Seven hours and twenty minutes later, when Andy should have been standing tall in the morning muster, he was still lying like a corpse on the floor at home with a pillow and two newspapers tucked under his head and arms neatly folded across his chest where Joyce had arranged them. She'd done nothing else to succour her husband, though. She hadn't bothered to remove his collar, boots or even his cap. She and the children simply stepped over and around his body as if he'd been reduced to nothing more bothersome than a hole in the lino or a wrinkle in the rug.

Craig, in uniform, left the house a minute or two after midday. Back shift did not commence until three but a football match at Whiteinch had necessitated some doubling of duties and blue uniforms and big brown horses would be much in evidence along the Dumbarton Road for most of the afternoon.

Seconds after Craig stepped out of the close and strode away up Canada Road, Kirsty's doorbell rang.

"Aye, who is it?"

"Me, Mrs Nicholson. It's Joyce, from downstairs."

"What do you want?"

"Some words in private, please, if you can spare the time."

"Joyce, I'm awfully busy. Can you not come back later?"

"No, Mrs Nicholson. It's now or never."

Hoisting Bobby into her arms, Kirsty fumbled with lock and chain and opened the door. She was astonished at the sight that met her eyes. This wasn't Joyce McAlpine all haggard and harassed and come to beg a pinch of tea or a half cup of sugar for her man's supper. The small, scraped, fair-haired woman was dressed in Sunday best, down to a black straw hat with two trimmed orange feathers protruding from the band like horns. Apart from a fresh blue bruise on her left cheekbone she showed no evidence of abuse but her complexion was bloodless and her eyes circled with grey, like charcoal dye. She had her children with her. Fair and pale, they were small-scale versions of their mother. They too were dolled up in their best clothes and, also like their mother, were tearless but tight-lipped. By Joyce's side, resting on the landing, were a bulging carpetbag, a bonnet box and a dented tin travelling trunk.

"Are you – are you goin' somewhere, Joyce?"

"I prefer not to discuss my business on the landin', Kirsty, if you don't mind."

"But you can't bring the children in here," Kirsty said. "Bobby might still be infectious."

"I think I'll risk it," Joyce McAlpine said.

* * *

Craig had only struck her once and, on that occasion, had been immediately full of contrition. Tonight, however, he was in such a glowing rage that Kirsty feared he might forget himself and abuse her just as Andy McAlpine had done Joyce.

"What the hell do you mean – you gave her money?" Craig shouted.

"She asked for a loan. I gave it to her."

"Did she tell you what it was for, eh?"

"To buy railway tickets," Kirsty answered him.

"To help her away?"

"Yes," Kirsty said.

"Did she tell you *why* she had to run away?"

"To – to escape from him."

"Aye, damn it. An' *why* she had to escape from him?"

"She was frightened for her life."

"So that's the bloody story, is it?" Craig shouted. "How the hell could she be afraid o' Andy when he was lyin' battered an' bleedin' on the bloody hearth rug downstairs."

"Lyin' drunk, more like," Kirsty said.

"Where did you get the money?"

"From the bank."

"On a Saturday afternoon?"

"All right," Kirsty said. "That's not the whole truth. The truth is that I had some money of my own hidden here."

"How much?"

"Five pounds."

"How much?"

Kirsty bit her lip. She realised that she had been foolish to try to deceive him on small points but she had not anticipated such a violent reaction from her husband. He had trapped her in a lie, though, and now he would make it seem as if she'd plotted with Joyce McAlpine not just against Andy but against all the men in Ottawa Street, all the errant husbands in Greenfield.

Kirsty said, "I gave her every penny I had. Twenty-three pounds, if you must have it exact. Twenty-three pounds, seven shillings and sixpence."

"To help a bloody fugitive."

"He bashed her, Craig. God, everybody knows he used t' bash her. Well, he did it once too often, that's all."

"That's all! That's all, is it?" Craig mimicked her clipped and prissy manner of speech, then shouted again. "Jesus, Kirsty, she assaulted him wi' a deadly weapon."

"The coal hammer, I know."

"Aw, so *you know*, do you? Well, I've seen what a coal hammer can do an' I can tell you she's damned lucky she's not bein' hunted for murder."

"He was drunk, Craig. That's why he stayed out cold for so long."

"She could have killed him, this pal o' yours," Craig roared. "An' you helped her escape. My big-hearted wife's the one who finances a flight from the law."

"Keep your voice down, Craig, you'll frighten Bobby."

Craig did not so much as glance at his son who had dragged out the heavy cardboard box in which his toys were kept and had

31

begun to take inventory of them. Bobby's posture was odd, like that of a cat engaged in washing its tail, one leg stuck out and balanced maintained by a stiffened arm. Wooden blocks, wooden animals, crayons, blobs of wax and lumps of chalk, odd nuts and bolts and bits of string were spread out on the carpet and seemed to engross all Bobby's attention, rendering him oblivious to his father's fury.

"Where did she go?"

"I'm not tellin' you," Kirsty said.

"*Where?*"

"Where he can't get his hands on her."

"Crawlin' back to her Mammy, I expect."

"For your information, when she was daft enough to marry Andy McAlpine her Mammy threw her out."

"So you do know where she's gone?"

"Last I saw of her, she was headin' for Dumbarton Road."

"With the children?"

"Of course, with the children," Kirsty said, testily. "Do you think she was goin' to leave her bairns to *his* tender mercies?"

Craig moved before she could react. She did not even have an opportunity to flinch. He grabbed her by the shoulders and thrusting his face close to hers, told her, "They're Andy's children too, in case you'd forgotten. Now he's lost them. Legally, she'd no damned right to take them away without his consent."

"He should have thought o' that when he was knockin' lumps out of their mother," Kirsty said.

"He never laid a finger on those bairns."

"I never said he did."

She had expected a measure of disapproval, a reprimand, some cloth-mouth tittle-tattle about her willingness to help Joyce run off with a gift of money, but not this irrational interrogation. She knew fine where Joyce had gone; she'd gone to catch a train to London, to Hammersmith, where she had a cousin who she thought might take her in until she could find work and a place of her own to stay. Twenty-odd pounds would provide Joyce with a nice buffer against penury and keep her going for a while. Kirsty had no regrets at all about what she'd done or about the speed with which she had reached her decision to help the desperate woman.

In fact, in helping Joyce McAlpine, in being a party to a

supreme act of defiance, she felt as if she'd brought a little colour back into her own life, colour that had been absent since that November afternoon when Jen had been buried and Bobby had been fighting off fever in the quarantine ward. Now Craig was telling her she'd been wrong. Black-and-white wrong. Indignation burned away her guilt like a match put to tissue paper. She jerked her forearm up between Craig's wrists and broke his hold on her.

"An' where's *he*, Craig? Supposin' *you* tell *me* that?"

"What?"

"Where's the conquerin' hero, the injured party? Is he at death's door in the Western Infirmary?"

"Naw, he's — "

"In the morgue, hm?"

"Don't be bloody daft, woman."

"Aw, I thought by the way you were goin' on that Joyce had done him terrible damage."

"I never actually said — "

"So," Kirsty went on, "where is he? Is he out searchin' the streets for his poor lost bairns?"

"Well, I — "

"Is he down at the station swearin' out a warrant for Joyce's arrest?"

"Naw, he wouldn't do that."

"Then where is he?" Kirsty demanded. "Where is our poor heartbroken old Andy right now?"

"How the hell do I know."

"I tell you where he is, Craig. He's down the damned pub, that's where he is. He's proppin' up the bar in Slattery's or weepin' into his beer in the Vaults right this very minute."

"What do you expect him to do?" Craig said. "Sit in an empty house, starin' at blank walls?"

"If he'd sat in the house a bit oftener before it was empty he wouldn't be in this predicament now," Kirsty said. "Still, it's too late for Andy McAlpine."

"Too late? What d'you mean?"

"He's done for, Craig. In three or four weeks he'll have drowned himself in a mixture o' whisky an' self-pity."

"Aye, an' it'll be all your doin'."

"*Damned* if it will," Kirsty snapped. "It won't be my fault, nor

Joyce McAlpine's fault, nor the fault o' the Burgh council.
Andy'll have nobody to blame but himself."

Her retaliation had mollified Craig a little.

He said, reasonably, "All right, Kirsty, just tell me where she
went an' we'll say no more about it."

"Let *him* ask me," Kirsty said.

"Who?"

"Constable Andy McAlpine," Kirsty said. "Let him come upstairs an' ask me straight to my face."

"God, Kirsty, Andy would never stoop to that."

"Then he can whistle for an answer," Kirsty said.

* * *

Saturday night passed into the first hour of Sunday and the
tenement was quiet. Kirsty, with Bobby snuggled against her,
had finally drifted down into deep sleep and was not the first to
hear the commotion in the close. It was only when Bobby tugged
her hair and muttered sleepily, "Doggie, Mammy? Hear the
doggie?" that Kirsty came fully awake.

She soothed her son, stroked his hair, and listened to the
sounds in the close below, a howling: "*Joooyce, Joooyce, Joooyce.*"

She slipped out of bed and opened the kitchen door. Craig
was already in the narrow hall, struggling into his trousers.

"It's him," Kirsty said.

"I know it is."

"*Joyoioioioisss.*"

"He'll waken the whole close," Kirsty said.

"He probably has already."

"What are you goin' to do, Craig?"

"I dunno. Put him t' bed, I suppose."

Craig opened the door to the landing and found Calum Piper
already out there, tousled too, nightshirt tucked into trousers, a
pair of carpet slippers covering his big naked feet.

"Is his wife not back yet, Craig?" Mr Piper said in a stage
whisper that could be heard two floors down.

"No, I doubt it."

"We canna just leave him," Mr Piper said. "Listen, there's
Sergeant Walker's voice. Och, he'll take care o' it."

"He might need some help," Craig said. "We'd better go
down, Calum."

"Aye, I suppose you're right."

Kirsty stood behind the door for three or four minutes, shivering in her nightgown, listening to the little drama being played out below. She heard Andy kicking woodwork, Mr Walker's uncertain reprimands, more maudlin howling, scuffling, male voices, more scuffling, the slam of a door – then silence. It seemed that it took three burly policemen to do the work of one wee wife. Kirsty gave a wry little grunt, went back into the kitchen, put on the kettle and made herself a pot of tea.

She was seated on the edge of the armchair by the fire with the cup in her hands when, some ten minutes later, Craig returned. He was cold and came at once to the grate, hands fanned out to catch the warmth of the coals.

"You'll be happy now, I suppose," Craig said.

"Why should I be happy?"

"He's in a hell of a state."

Kirsty sipped tea, said nothing.

"He was sick," Craig said.

Now she knew why Craig was so subdued. He'd had a glimpse of the real world and it hadn't proved palatable.

"So, did you wash him before you put him to bed," Kirsty asked, "or did you just leave him lyin' on the floor?"

"Huh!" was all the answer Craig gave her.

"Do you want tea?"

"Aye."

She rose, poured a fresh cup for her husband and handed it to him. Hunched over the fire, cradling the cup in his palms, he said, "Andy hasn't twigged yet it was you gave her the money."

"I suppose it'll be 'your duty' to tell him," Kirsty said.

"Nah," Craig said. "There'll be plenty o' folk only too eager to do that for me." He glanced at her. "Ach, Kirsty, you should never have interfered."

She was too tired to argue, too tired and too sure that she'd been right to do what she did. The twenty-odd pounds she'd given to Joyce McAlpine had been money well spent. She had gained from it too, had realised that she was suddenly, overwhelmingly bored with guilt.

"I'm goin' to bed, Craig."

She eased herself into the bed in the recess and settled herself beneath the covers, all without disturbing Bobby who slept now, thumb in mouth, in a soft, comfortable ball against the wall.

Craig lit a cigarette and sighed. "You know, Kirsty, I don't think you've heard the last of this."

"No, I don't suppose I have," said Kirsty and, without another word, reached out and closed the curtain on Craig, the kitchen and the dregs of the day.

* * *

Sunday trains to Balfron Station were few and far between. Gordon had had to drag himself early from bed and, at journey's end, square up to a hike of a mile and a half to reach Russell Smith's racing stables at Bree Lodge. He did not grudge the effort, however. He'd liked Bree since the first day he'd set foot on the place and had taken to horse riding like a duck to water. Mainly he headed out into the country to escape the oppressive grey atmosphere of winter Sabbaths in the city and to shake off, if he could, the strange grey melancholy that had taken possession of him of late.

He was no longer an invited guest of the Smiths and did not hang about the Lodge in the hope that he would encounter Amanda. He simply paid his hire fee like any other gentleman with an interest in riding, changed his clothes and shoes in the locker room and went out to wait for one of the lads to bring him a mount, usually Dandy, a cob of sufficiently passive temperament to suit a near-novice.

Gordon would mount up and let Dandy amble down the track that led across Buchanan to Loch Lomond's discreet tree-lined shores. Later he would return to the Lodge to share a spot of dinner with Russell Smith, Breezy's cousin and a trainer of considerable reputation in the racing game. Sinclair Smith, Russell's bookmaker brother, had been conspicuous by his absence of late. There was no sign either of Captain Tom Wells. No information had been volunteered as to why the Captain, a famous amateur jockey, was not in training for the spring season and Gordon did not have the gall to ask.

In fact, Gordon was heartsick of the Adairs' dark secrets. He journeyed to Bree not to seek their company but to escape from it. He told nobody where he spent his Sundays, not even Amanda.

Wintry mists and rain clouds locked out sight of the lochside mountains and distant heights of Argyll. A farm boy born and bred, the climate held no fears for Gordon. He rode out under an oilskin cape without pace or fervour whatever the weather and always found the smell of fresh dung and wet pine preferable to that of stale beer, and the croaking of rooks and keening of buzzards more soothing than publicans' arguments and complaints. That day Gordon was in relaxed mood, a jogging frame of mind until, on an undistinguished spit of land separated from the loch by scrub alder and stunted birch, he encountered, unavoidably, the Adairs' old shooting brake and in it three Adair women.

The brake was not the usual conveyance that Olive Carruth Adair used to skip about the countryside. As a rule she preferred a fast-running little dogcart that she could drive herself. Today, however, Olive was not alone. Amanda and Phoebe were with her and the driving seat of the brake was occupied not by one of the familiar servants but by a big, knobby-cheeked woman dressed mannishly in greatcoat and half-top hat. For a fleeting moment Gordon felt quite guilty, as if he had no right to be there, then he realised that it was Dolphus's women who were out of their natural habitat, seven or eight miles north of The Knowe, at a time of day when decent folk were snug in front parlours or slotted into pews for Sunday worship.

The track was rough and narrow and the two-horse brake filled every inch of space between the shrubs. Indeed, when it rocked on its heavy wheels the vehicle's sides tore twigs and papery leaves from the branches and left a trail of debris in their wake.

Gordon's initial impulse was to drag on Dandy's rein and crash the cob off into the jungle. Too late: he'd already been spotted, not by Amanda, but by sister Phoebe.

"Look, look, it's Gordon," Phoebe cried, more in alarm than delight.

Gordon raised his cap and meekly steered the cob to the side of the track. When the brake groaned to a halt, he bowed and said, "Well this is a pleasant surprise."

The three Adairs were dressed in sombre, fur-trimmed garments that seemed too opulent and mature for the girls but suited entirely their grief-stricken mother. Amanda was attempting to comfort Olive whose oval face was laved by tears, whose eyes were cleansed of guile and mischief so that she appeared as ingenuous as a child and even more beautiful as a result. Lace handkerchiefs were spots of snow against the funereal fabrics. Olive hid her face with one while Amanda waved another in Gordon's direction as if to shoo him off like a bothersome horsefly.

"What are you doing here?" Amanda demanded. "Have you come to spy on us?"

"What?"

"Has Daddy sent you to spy on us?"

"No – he – I mean, I only came out to Bree t' ride."

"How dare you follow us!"

At that moment Phoebe, at sixteen, seemed the most mature of the females in the back of the brake. She said, "I'm sure Gordon did not expect to meet us under such circumstances, Amanda. Nor can he know where we have been."

Olive swayed and leaned for support against her eldest.

"Drive on," Amanda cried, imperiously. "Drive on, Aggie. Do as I tell you."

"Ah canna, Miss. Him's in the way."

Aggie, the servant, met Gordon's eye. She cocked an apologetic brow then cracked her whip above the horses' ears and urged them forward with a hoarse shout, leaving Gordon no option but to back Dandy, rump first, into the alders.

In some astonishment, Gordon watched the brake trundle past him. In spite of Amanda's rudeness, he could not simply let them depart without another word. He filed his mount behind the conveyance and followed, followed, really, Phoebe's pale, anxious face as she alone turned to acknowledge his presence.

"Go away, Gordon," Amanda shouted.

"Oh, don't say that to Gordon," Phoebe told her sister. "He's your intended husband, after all."

Amanda wore black gloves so that he could not see the ring with which he had symbolically plighted his troth and that had cost him a deep dip into his savings, even although Breezy had got it at discount. He supposed she would be wearing it under the kidskin, however, and a certain proprietorial instinct steeled him to continue his pursuit.

Leaning forward from the saddle, he called, "I didn't know you'd be here, Amanda. Honest! I only came out for a breather.

What in God's name's goin' on? Is your mother ill?"

Olive had remained in a sort of swoon, supported by her daughter's shoulder. Now, however, she chose to recognise him, show gratitude for his solicitude and, perhaps, even absolve him from intentional interference. She dispatched a limp little wave, rotating her wrist and fluttering her lace, while Phoebe, more practically, leaned over the back of the padded seat to talk to him.

"It's all so sad, Gordon. So very, very sad."

"What is?"

"Phoebe," Amanda warned. "Don't you dare."

"Why shouldn't I tell Gordon? Gordon won't clipe to Daddy. Gordon doesn't like Daddy either."

"This has nothing to do with Gordon," Amanda said. "Gordon is a man and men do not understand these things."

While the brake ground up a shallow hill towards the broad estate road that would lead to the public highway a half mile on the sisters then fell to serious squabbling. Gordon sighed and sat back.

For the first time he felt not just equal but superior to Amanda. He had experienced a certain detachment before but not the feeling of quiet arrogance brought on by observing the rich, spoiled children of a spoiled, rich woman quarrelling in the back of a shooting brake. He followed solemnly, smoking a cigarette, while Amanda tried to box her sister's ears and in the process knocked askew all three elegant hats.

"Stop it, stop it, do," Olive protested, weakly.

But Amanda paid no heed to her mother's request and the girls continued to flap and slap at each other until the high road hove into view and Aggie reined the horses to ease the brake through the estate's old stone gateposts.

Gordon tossed away his cigarette. He brought Dandy up to the side of the brake. As if offering respect to mourners in a cortège he plucked off his cap and held it down by his flank, kept his bare head bowed as the brake wheeled out on to the open road and turned right towards Strathblane. From the midst of tousled finery, Olive, regal and doleful as Victoria, gave him a signal of farewell while her daughters continued to roil and squabble beside her like mink in a basket.

Then Amanda's head popped up over the upholstered leather

and she called out, "Forgive me, darling, Forgive me."

Gordon waggled his cap and nodded.

"Come to see us at The Knowe. Come next Saturday." She blew a kiss from her fingertips and mouthed the words, "I love you."

Gordon smiled, nodded, waggled his cap – and the instant the brake was out of sight, pulled Dandy's head round and set off at a gallop for the lochside to see where the hell they'd been.

*   *   *

Only a chap as long and slender as Ernest Tubbs could have got off with sporting a three-piece suit of houndstooth check on a dank afternoon in February and, for the sake of sartorial elegance, deny himself the consolation of a topcoat. Lorna felt quite drab by comparison, though Tubby assured her that she looked stunning and that if he hadn't just had lunch he'd have gobbled her up on the spot.

The spot was the gate of Dowanhill Tennis Club where the couple met for an arm-in-arm walk down the hill to Dumbarton Road and Greenfield. It was the sort of weather that drew out the bored as well as the brazen and the Sunday streets were crowded with honest citizens on the stroll as well as young folk showing themselves off to each other.

Canada Road was busy too and it was only by chance that Lorna and Tubbs arrived at No. 154 just as Kirsty, holding her son's hand, emerged from the close. It was Lorna's first sight of her nephew since his illness and the ugly caliper clamped to his little leg made her gasp and cling tightly to Ernest's arm.

"Oh, God!" she exclaimed, beneath her breath.

Ernest transferred a hand from her waist to her shoulder and, as a soft dry sob escaped her, murmured, "Easy now. No undue fuss, remember."

Lorna stooped and received Bobby as he hurled himself into her. He had grown taller but his face was pinched and pallid, the iron brace bumped and banged against her when she lifted him and it was all she could do, for a moment or two, to hold back tears.

"Haven't you got a kiss for your old Auntie, then?"

Bobby smacked his lips sloppily against her cheek then, wriggling, addressed himself to Ernest over Lorna's shoulder.

"I gotta bad leg, see."

"Never!" Tubby said.

"Have. Have. See. See."

"That's not a bad leg," said Tubby, straight-faced. "I've seen a lot worse legs than that in Auchenshuggle."

Bobby grinned coyly. Obviously his memory had not been impaired by his illness and he recalled Mr Tubbs' eccentricities all too well.

"Nah!"

"True." Gently Ernest Tubbs lifted the limb and inspected it. "You'd get no sympathy for a leg that *good* in Auchenshuggle."

Bobby settled against his aunt's breast and watched Tubby to see what would happen next. Kirsty had joined them now and watched too, unsmiling, as Ernest Tubbs lifted off Bobby's tartan tammy, tickled his fingers down his coat buttons and finally, from the top of the long stocking that protected his wasting limb, produced a tiny figure of painted lead.

"This," Mr Tubbs declared, "is a real bad leg."

The warrior was black and naked save for a fringe of grass about his waist. He had a bone in his nose and brandished a long red-tipped spear. Tribal ferocity always went down well with small boys but this unfortunate native, like all the others in the flat box in Mr Tubbs' pocket, had been patiently doctored, a tiny pin of brown-painted metal soldered on to his calf.

"Told you," Tubby said.

"Awww . . . " said Bobby, agog.

"Aw-shen-shoo-gal," Tubby prompted.

Bobby giggled, lifted the lead warrior from Mr Tubbs' palm and inspected it closely. He touched the spear with the ball of his thumb. "What's 'at for?"

"Oh, that," Ernest said, innocently, "is for pickin' his nose, a habit common to all Auchenshugglians."

"Enough, Tubby," Kirsty said, but in a tone that indicated to Lorna there was still sufficient warmth in their relationship for her outrageous proposal to stand a chance of being listened to, if not accepted.

"Where were you off to, Kirsty?" Lorna asked.

"Oh, just to the park."

"The park, dearest?" Lorna enquired of her beloved.

"Suits me fine," said Mr Tubbs and, taking Bobby from the

girl's arms, lowered him to the pavement to walk unaided by his side.

* * *

When there was nobody around with whom he could discuss the minutiae of racing then Russell Smith stayed, for the most part, silent. To Gordon's relief, however, the trainer was still at the dinner table in the lodge's big stone-flagged kitchen when Gordon arrived back from his exploration of the lochside. The grooms had eaten and gone and once she'd served him with a plate of stew, the cook-housekeeper also departed, providing Gordon with an ideal opportunity for a little private conversation.

Russell Smith was eating treacle tart. He ate like an amputee, the spoon in his right hand, the left folded out of sight below the level of the table. He was a small, compact man, dressed in expensive tweeds, a cravat held by a stickpin in the collar of his shirt. His hands were tiny, like mouse paws, and his eyes, a faded blue, never left the pudding plate or the tumbler of whisky and water beside it, not even when Gordon addressed him.

"Who lives in the cottage down by Innis Bay?" said Gordon.

"Why do you ask?"

"Does it belong to Tom Wells?"

"It did," Russell Smith answered. "I assumed you knew that, bein' one of the family an' all."

"It's not his permanent home, though?"

"No," said Russell. "The family pile's over at Gravelston, in the Pentlands. The cottage is just a little country place, convenient for Bree."

"I was down that way this morning," Gordon said. "The cottage gives every appearance of bein' deserted. Would I be right in thinkin' that Captain Tom's gone off for a while?"

"Didn't your lassie tell you?" said Russell Smith. "Tom Wells has resumed his commission in the Lancers. He's sailed off to South Africa to fight against the Boers."

"At his age?"

"Tom's not so ancient," said Russell Smith. "In any case, I hear they're desperate for mounted officers on the Veldt."

"When did he leave?"

"The first day o' January," said Russell. "No tearful farewells

42

for the captain, though. He simply sent me a letter tellin' me to dispose of his horses come the spring sales."

"So he doesn't plan to return?"

Russell Smith shrugged his shoulders. "Not to Bree, apparently."

"What about the cottage by the loch?"

"Rented from the Duke."

"How long's Tom Wells had a foot in there?"

Russell Smith looked up. His faded pupils were hardly visible at all amid the wrinkles. For a moment it seemed that he might be about to break off the conversation, then he said, "Five or six years."

Gordon said, "That's where she met him, isn't it, Russell? Down in the cottage by the loch shore?"

"Among other places."

"Did Dolphus know? I mean, surely Dolphus didn't know?"

"No, Dolphus thought it was some other man."

"Who?"

"Och, nobody of any consequence." Russell Smith pushed back his chair and got to his feet. "Are you ridin' again before dark?"

"No, I have to get back to Glasgow," Gordon said. "I'm grateful to you for tellin' me the truth."

"It isn't the whole truth, son, only a bit of it," said Russell Smith. "How did you find out about the cottage?"

"I met them, met Olive, on the track this mornin'," said Gordon. "Pure chance."

"She didn't know that the Captain had gone?"

"I don't think she did," Gordon said. "She was fair upset. He obviously wasn't gentleman enough to tell her to her face that he was leavin' for good."

"What do you know about gentlemen, son?" said Russell Smith.

"Not much," Gordon said. "But I'm learnin', by God I am."

"When's the train from Balfron station?"

"A quarter to three," said Gordon.

"I'll have Gabe fetch out the dickie and drive you down there."

"Don't put yourself to bother on my acount," Gordon said.

"It's no bother, son," said Russell Smith. "We'll be seein' you again soon, I hope."

"Next Sunday, I expect," Gordon said.

But he didn't mean it. Somehow the Adairs had tainted his pleasure in riding out on a Sunday too.

In fact at that moment he doubted if he would ever set foot on Bree again.

*   *   *

Forrester Park had been gifted to the community by the family of the burgh's most famous son, a shipping magnate of disgustingly humble origins who had made a fortune by engaging in the kind of commercial piracy that either got you hanged or knighted; in Sir James's case, mercifully, the latter. Over the years the modest fifteen acre endowment had acquired battalions of trees and regiments of shrubs, a bandstand, a little boating pond and a full-length statue of the burgh's benefactor which stood on a plinth of dark mildewed marble and stared disapprovingly at the Merkland dock and Clydeside's modern riggings.

The park was mobbed that calm, dank Sunday afternoon and, with untypical foresight, the public works department had even put out an extra keeper or two to make sure that louts from Riverside or the Windsor Road did not steal the seats or bruise the tender herb by playing football on the grass and that the groves of evergreen did not become shelters of iniquity for drunkards or disreputable women.

It was here in the Forrester, in the course of a summer that seemed very distant now, that Kirsty had walked Bobby in his new perambulator, had picnicked with Nessie Frew and, later, had met with David for sunny strolls around the pond, and had been, albeit fleetingly, content. She could hardly call herself content now. The argument over Joyce McAlpine had soured her once more and brought to the surface many of the tensions that lay beneath her relationship with Craig.

Nonetheless she was pleased to be out and about once more and not displeased to share the afternoon with Ernest Tubbs and Lorna. It was heartening to see Bobby play again, though the protective instincts of the past months did not fade easily and she kept a weather eye on her son when Tubby took him off a little way to play leap-frog over the iron hoops that bordered the paths.

Lorna too had changed. She hadn't become glum like Gordon. Rather the contrary; she had acquired a gaiety of manner that seemed too forced to be natural, that had in it an element of callousness. It did not take Kirsty long to realise what the changes indicated. Lorna was in love, thoroughly and irrepressibly in love with Ernest Tubbs, a fact that softened Kirsty's attitude to her sister-in-law and which explained the waywardness of her behaviour.

It was not by chance that Lorna's conversation drifted round to the matter of the shop in Gascoigne Street. Fresh air had sharpened Kirsty's wits, had lifted the cloud of apathy that had hung over her for too long.

"Out with it, Lorna," she said. "Enough of the hintin'."

"Oh, right!" Lorna said. "Gordon tells me you want to give up the business."

"I haven't time to devote to a shop . . . "

"That's what we thought," Lorna interrupted. "Why not put in a manager, let somebody else run it for you? You'd have a stake in the profits but none of the bother."

"I'm not sure I want to – "

"I mean me, of course. I could manage it fine."

"You're too young, Lorna."

"Good God! *Everybody* says that. I thought you'd be different," Lorna said. "I thought you'd understand. I mean, when you were my age you were married."

"That's different."

"How's it different?"

"To look after a shop you have to be – well, responsible."

"An' you don't have to be 'responsible' to look after a house an' a husband?"

"It's different, that's all," said Kirsty, lamely.

"If you don't want to give up Gascoigne Street," Lorna went on, "then why don't you take me on as your assistant? I mean, you know fine I could cope with that."

"Yes. Yes, but – "

"Now that Greta's gone you'll have to find somebody."

"Did Gordon put you up to this?"

"Not him," said Lorna.

"Who then – Breezy?"

"God, no. Breezy would have a purple fit if he knew I was

thinkin' of leavin' college before I get my certificates."

"I think I agree with Breezy on that score."

"Aye," said Lorna, "but it's what will happen then that worries me. Breezy plans to stick me into some mouldy old counting-house somewhere in Glasgow."

"Have you talked it over with him, sensibly?"

"Sensibly? You don't talk sense to stepfathers. Especially step-fathers like Breezy. His word is law."

"Well, when the time comes you'll just have to dig in your heels, Lorna."

"The time *has* come," Lorna said. "I'm diggin' in my heels right now."

Mr Tubbs had taken both Bobby's hands and was swinging him, brace and all, back and forth over the high iron hoops, risking the wrath of the park keeper who glared at them from across the pond. Bobby loved it, of course. He giggled loudly and shouted, "Hup, hup, hup, Tubby, hup, hup."

Kirsty sensed in Lorna an eager desperation that hinted that Lorna was growing up and straining to be free of childish restraint. Kirsty was not so old or set in her ways that she had forgotten what that mixture of excitement and frustration felt like, how girls as young as Lorna saw the future shining before her, beckoning her to enter like a welcome light above a door. There were no shadows in the future for Lorna, no clouds on the horizon. All her troubles were contained in the present. After a month or two behind the counter in G. A. Nicholson's Domestic Emporium, however, would Lorna's enthusiasm for shopkeeping wane, would she hanker again for change? It was a risk she would have to take if she was to accept Lorna's offer and return to business before all her trade was lost.

From just behind her shoulder Kirsty heard Ernest Tubbs enquire, "What's the problem, Mrs N? You look fair perplexed."

"Kirsty won't take me on as a manager," Lorna put in.

Ernest had Bobby by the hand and the wee boy was chatting away happily to the lead warrior with the spear, holding the figurine up close to his nose.

"I – I didn't say that, Lorna," Kirsty put in.

Ernest said, "Is your stock-in-hand all bought an' paid for, Kirsty?"

"Yes. I settled the outstandin' bills through Mr Marlowe, my lawyer."

"Is Gordon still a sleepin' partner?"

"Yes. He owns the shop. I lease it from him."

"How long does the lease have to run?"

"Over a year," said Kirsty.

"May I ask what percentage of invested capital Gordon put up initially?"

"I don't think that's any of your – "

"Would he sell out?" said Ernest.

"Ernest, what – " Lorna began.

"Hush a wee minute, sweetheart," Ernest told her.

Kirsty said, "What do my financial affairs have to do with you, Mr Tubbs?"

"Do you really want to let the business go, Mrs N?"

"I – I haven't made up my mind."

"Because if you don't," Ernest said, "I'd like to buy into it. Half shares. Fifty-fifty."

"You!" Lorna could not contain herself. "You don't have two brass farthin's to rub together. How can you afford it?"

"I can't," said Tubby. "But my brother can."

"Your brother!"

"What do you say, Kirsty?" Ernest asked her. "Is this a proposal that might interest you, in principle at least?"

"There's more to this than meets the eye," Kirsty said.

"What brother?" said Lorna.

"What you need is an active partner," Ernest continued. "When Gordon was in the wholesale trade it made sense to have him as a sleepin' partner. Now he's out. Now he's of no practical use to you, unless, that is, you plan to turn the shop into a beer hall."

"An' what would you turn it into, Mr Tubbs?" said Kirsty.

"A goldmine," said Ernest Tubbs with such sober sincerity that Kirsty was almost tempted to believe him. "What do you say, Mrs Nicholson? Is it somethin' worth discussin'?"

After a moment's hesitation, Kirsty answered, "Yes."

*　　　*　　　*

Night fell stealthily across The Knowe. It came early into the hollow at the bottom of the knoll where the Greek-style villa was situated, stole up through the trees and then seemed to consume

47

the house at a gulp. So dim were the pedestal lamps that flanked the doorway, so wan the chandeliers within, it appeared that to endure such cheerless gloom at all the house's inhabitants must have no more substance than ghosts.

Dinner had been disposed of by half past eight. By nine o'clock the shivering servants had crept off to their beds leaving James Randolph Adair back where he had been all afternoon, sprawled in the scruffy armchair in the library with his legs stretched out to the little wigwam of green branches that smouldered in the grate. He had been at the bottle all day, near enough, knocking back not beer or sparkling lager from his own vats but a whisky of such dubious origin that few distillers would have recognised it as a potable commodity at all.

As a rule Dolphus had no tolerance for spirits and a mere snifter of Royal Deerhound would have knocked him skew-whiff. Such was his anger that day, however, that when he walked into the dining room for dinner, he was as cold and sober as a martyr's headstone. He seated himself at the head of the table without a word; not that there was anyone to say a word to, except McKenzie, the latest in a long line of child-servants to come and go from The Knowe. Dolphus did not enquire as to the whereabouts of his family. The youngest would be incarcerated with Nanny in the nursery but he had expected Amanda, Phoebe or Olive to be present and had screwed himself up to demand – yes, demand – answers to certain of the questions that had plagued him all week long. But there wasn't a trace of the womenfolk at the dinner table and he'd be damned if he'd make an ass of himself by sending McKenzie to fetch them. He ate swiftly, drank more whisky and hastened back, fuming, to his lair in the library.

In due course, after the servants had gone to bed, he finished the last of the Deerhound and climbed the stairs to the villa's upper floor. He crept along the long corridor, listened at the door of the nursery and heard not a whisper, not a whimper from there. He went then to his own bedroom, entered and lit the gas lamp by the door. No fire in the grate; the room was icy cold. McKenzie had put a hot pig into his bed, however, and Dolphus, shivering, fished out the stone bottle and hugged it to his chest in the hope that it might thaw the lump there.

Olive's suite was next to his own, connected by a stout oak

door. Still hugging the pig he stooped and put his ear to it. Mysterious and somehow taunting, the butterfly-soft flutter of female voices beat against the masculine fabrics of the house. He tried the door handle, found it locked, locked as it had been for the past decade.

Dolphus stepped stealthily back and, turning, was confronted by his reflection in the mirror of the huge, double-fronted wardrobe. He peered at his image in disbelief. With the stone pig clutched to his heart he looked so weak and so cowed, so old too as if he had already begun to pass into the house's history, leaving hardly a ripple on its varnished surfaces.

Breezy would not be sleeping alone. Breezy would be spooned against the flanks of his big, warm bosomy wife. When the lights were out it wouldn't matter a jot that Madge was coarse and common.

Dolphus dumped the pig on to the bed. He undressed. Normally meticulously tidy, tonight he tossed his clothing everywhere and let it lie where it lay. He climbed into his nightshirt. He put on the old viridian smoking jacket that served him as a dressing gown and studied himself in the mirror again. His thinning hair stood out in an unholy corona and he crammed on his cotton nightcap to cover it.

Laughter, faint and fluctuating, drifted through the oak.

Royal Deerhound, perhaps, gave him Dutch courage.

Bare-calfed, barefoot, the nightcap's tassel whisking behind him, he charged along the corridor and yanked open the door of Olive's bedroom.

"What is this?" he shouted. "What is going on, hah?"

The sight that greeted him was like a painting of a scene in a seraglio. Dolphus had never seen his grown-up daughters so revealed, nor his wife, tear-stained and dramatic, in a pose of such abandon. All three were sprawled on Olive's bed. Olive was in the middle, propped up by bolsters, hair unloosed, gown hitched carelessly high about her thighs, breasts exposed. Phoebe and Amanda too were in a state of unpardonable dishabille. Their pink nun's-veiling nightgowns were unribboned at the collars, trailing and diaphanous about their legs. To his horror, Dolphus realised that his daughters were as shapely and shameless as the woman who had given them birth.

Never in his wildest dreams, his most tormented nightmares,

could Dolphus have envisaged such intimacy between Olive and her girls, such an extravagantly feminine conspiracy. Evidence of their profligacy was everywhere. Hissing white gas lamps, blazing coal fire. Wine bottles, plates of cold cuts and winter salad were strewn on stools and among the powder pots and paints on the dressing table. If this was heartbreak and suffering then it was heartbreak suffered in outrageous comfort and style.

Dolphus stood at the door in flannel nightgown and threadbare jacket, nightcap dangling over one eye. He had but a split second to absorb the import of the tableau before his daughters reacted to his sudden appearance. Phoebe screamed as if he were an apparition. She screamed again and rolled away from her mother, screamed with laughter. Amanda was not amused, not in the least. She bounced on to her knees and yelled at him. "How dare you come in here without Mother's permission! Get out, I say, get out."

Phoebe stuffed her knuckles into her mouth to stifle hysterical guffaws and kicked her feet in the air. She had just enough sense of propriety left to thrust an arm between her knees and stretch her nightgown tight. Dolphus didn't care if Phoebe found him risible. He had always known that Phoebe would grow up to be a ninny. It was Amanda's reaction that stunned him. The daughter whom he had loved best had been transformed into a fishwife before his very eyes. She screamed at him, *"Leave Mama alone."*

Dolphus obeyed instantly. He stepped into the corridor and swept the door closed behind him. For a full minute he stood before the blank wall, eyes like moons, then he grunted, "Hah?", swung about, flung open the door again and plunged headlong into the bedroom.

Olive was weeping. Cheeks scarlet with rage, Amanda was trying to console her. Sore and groaning with laughter, Phoebe had rolled back against her mother's haunch like a little piglet. And into Dolphus, unbidden, stole a weird desire, the like of which he had not known in umpteen years, a thin red thread of lust for the wife who had spurned him. He came to the bed end and leaned on it.

"Why is she crying, hah?" The tone of his voice silenced even Phoebe, caused her to hug closer to her mother's knees. "Is she *sick* again, hah?"

Amanda's anger was brighter, more youthful and virile than his own. She gave him answers, more answers than he'd expected, or wanted. "Mama's poor heart is broken," Amanda cried. "Captain Wells has gone to fight the Boers."

He had known about the bastard child, had even persuaded Breezy to farm it out. He knew that the child was dead and had, oddly, felt a pang of regret at its passing. But the emotions that had so changed Olive, had reduced her to a flabby sac that floated about the upper floor of the house, that would not eat or drink, had seemed to him excessive mourning for a child she had never nursed, had never even known.

"He may die in South Africa." Without conviction Olive endeavoured to make her daughter be still. "And it will all be your fault if he does."

"Who?" said Dolphus.

"No, Amanda. Don't," said Phoebe. "Don't tell him."

"Captain Wells, Tom Wells. He loved Mama, and you drove him away," Amanda cried with all the reckless passion of a true Carruth. "Now she may never see him again, not in this world."

"What does Tom Wells have to do with us?" said Dolphus.

"Captain Wells," said Amanda, "was my sister's father."

"What sister?" said Dolphus, stupidly.

"The sister who died last year."

Dolphus was motionless for two or three seconds then he took off his ridiculous nightcap and dropped it softly to the carpet. He took a pace or two back into the room and removed plates from one of the velvet stools and seated himself, slowly, so slowly. He stooped over, rocking, and stared at the fragments of cold tongue and chicken breast that remained unconsumed on the plates.

He said nothing for a while, while the women, silenced by his silence, cowered together against the bedhead.

At length Dolphus spoke. "Go to the nursery."

Fear not anger kept Amanda's tongue loose. "It's too late, Papa. He's gone. He's taken up his commission again and is out of your reach."

"Will you get out," said Dolphus, evenly. "Leave your mother and me alone."

"No, you'll – "

"Please, dearest. Please leave us," said Olive.

"Come on, Mandy," said Phoebe. "It's time to make ourselves scarce."

Phoebe clambered from the bed, smoothed down her nightgown and then offered a hand to her sister who reluctantly slid from her mother's side and planted her bare feet on the carpet too. Colour had drained from her cheeks and her face was as white as the sheets that dragged in tortured knots after her.

"You won't – won't hurt her?" said Amanda, just beginning to cry.

Dolphus said, "No, I won't hurt her."

"Promise?"

"I promise."

He opened his hand as if to touch her, then paused, then let the hand drop. His shoulders sagged. He gestured to Phoebe to take her sister away.

The room still blazed with white light. The coal fire's glow was rosily reflected on the knobs and rails of the bedstead where Olive squatted, knees drawn up and heels tucked in against her bottom. She was crying in harsh, dry little sobs but when Dolphus approached she looked up at him with huge, moist eyes and blinked, and blinked, and blinked. He saw that her unpowdered flesh was lightly lined with the first signs of advancing age. Her beauty and breeding offered no defence against inevitable decay. He touched her almost tenderly, and the booming, arrogant voice that he'd acquired just to impress her slipped back into a soothing modulation tinged with the vulgar accent with which he'd once been burdened.

"So Wells, poor devil, was the father all along."

"Why, Dolphus, why do you say 'poor devil'?"

"You lost the child. Wells, in consequence, lost you. Is that not the way of it, Olive?"

"Yes."

"Did you love him very much?"

"Yes."

"Did he abandon you?"

"Yes – latterly."

"Where did you meet? At Bree Lodge, was it?"

"Nearby. Tom had a cottage by the loch."

"So," said Dolphus, "there never was a groom, a common-or-garden lover?"

"No others – only Tom."

Lightly he touched her cheek, fine bones under smooth skin, and pinned her head lightly against the bolster. He had not broken her after all. She had broken herself. It was not his failure but hers that had led them to this narrow pass.

"What will you do to me, Dolphus?"

"Nothing," he said.

"Will you not send me away?"

He answered by kissing her, by crushing his lips to her mouth and by caressing her breast beneath the fluid fabric of her nightgown. He did not resent the fact that she did not respond.

She whispered, "Do you still want me, Dolphus?"

He was perspiring heavily and the backs of his legs trembled. He had to force himself to stand up, step back from the bed.

She had the guile to lower her lashes. The feint, the coy manoeuvre that had once upon a time so captivated his heart did nothing for him now. She had not simply had a fling with some low-life Irish groom. She had betrayed him with another blue-blood, with one of her own kind. He could never forgive her for that.

She was tearful, remorseful, willing to surrender to his punishments. In the sweet, tremulous, little-girl voice that he had not heard her use in ten years or more, she asked him again, "Do you not still want me, Dolphus, dear?"

"No, Olive. I don't want you – at any price," he answered.

Then, leaving her where she was, he returned, quite composed, to his cold and sombre room next door.

Three

The Facts of Life

Traditional Scottish pessimists – at a conservative estimate about half the population – were happy at last. Their apocalyptic predictions that the winter was bound to have a sting in its tail had finally been borne out. Sleet and snow flurried on a wind that would cut you in half and, just a week to the day after Kirsty's Sunday outing, you could count the folk in the Forrester Park on the fingers of one, gloved hand.

Greenfield's streets were almost deserted and even Dumbarton Road contained only a few drippy-nosed pedestrians and the inevitable company of Boys' Brigade boys being drummed to a church parade like so many human sacrifices. Kirsty took care to dress warmly. She had shopped in Glasgow that week and wore a brand new costume of smooth Cheviot coating with lined saddle sleeves and a trimming of black Russia braid on the bodice. She'd lost weight since Christmas and made the most of it by nipping in her waist to show off her bust and to let the narrow skirt swell at the hips. Underneath, though, she wore the most unfashionable combinations and an extra vest, and her stockings were so thick and long that they seemed to be gartered just under her heart.

Lorna had plumped for a loose, youthfully-cut outfit that, Kirsty suspected, covered several layers of lambswool. Even Ernest Tubbs had forsaken colonial lightweights in favour of something he called 'a mad alpaca', an overcoat of such length and density that, when topped with a black Homburg, he looked like the Prince of Wales' umbrella.

It was not just the cold that made the girls tense as they boarded the tramcar for the journey to Maryhill. This was a 'state occasion', a first meeting between Lorna and Ernest's families and both she and Kirsty were nervous about it.

"Mother's not an ogre," Tubby had said. "She's not goin' to eat you."

"But what if she doesn't like me?" Lorna had cried. "What if she hates me, in fact?"

"Course she won't hate you," Tubby had said. "She'll love you, like I do."

Ernest, it seemed, had been exceedingly niggardly with information about his family. Even after three months of serious courtship, Lorna knew little about her beloved's domestic situation. Kirsty had been invited along not only to meet Frank Tubbs, her prospective business partner, but also to represent Lorna. She had been appointed, by default, as a dependable female relative who must break the ice for an eventual parley between Tubbses and Adairs. Kirsty was experienced enough to realise that the gesture was bound to be interpreted as 'interference' and that her stock with the Nicholsons, Craig included, would fall further because of it. She had told Craig nothing of Ernest's proposition or of the real reason for her visit to Maryhill. It would have been useful to have Gordon's advice but Gordon seemed to have disappeared from the face of the earth, as far as she was concerned.

Craig was still angry with her for helping Joyce McAlpine. And not only Craig; all the coppers' wives had turned against her. Indeed the tide of ill feeling ran so high that Kirsty was cut dead by everyone in the close including Jess Walker and the amiable Mrs Piper.

Matters had not been helped when, on Tuesday of that week, Andy McAlpine had been removed from his house by order of Lieutenant Strang and put into barracks in Edward Street. The fact that Andy had not been sober since the night of his wife's departure did not enter public account. Suddenly Kirsty was to blame for it. Suddenly she and Joyce McAlpine were being classed as two of a kind. This unjustified deterioration in domestic relationships had one positive result, however; it steeled Kirsty in her resolve to return to trade and commerce. Whatever transpired that Sunday afternoon, with or without a partner she was determined to reopen the shop in Gascoigne Street.

Even Ernest couldn't find breath to prattle over the rattle of the new-style tramcar and Kirsty realised that the young man too was nervous about the visit. Eventually he gave them a nod and, with Lorna hanging on to his hand like a child, they descended from the vehicle and set off into the hinterland of old tenements and recently-built terraces to the west of the thoroughfare. It was even colder here. The sky seemed big and broad, filled with slate-grey cloud torn from a great black bank of the stuff that hung over the horizon.

Lorna's nose had turned white as candlewax and, between funk and cold, she seemed struck dumb as Ernest guided her along the street towards Lindenhall Gardens.

Lindenhall Gardens was shaped like a gin bottle and curved at the throat into a flight of shallow stone steps flanked by stone balusters and topped with gas lamps.

This was not the sort of middle-class ward that Lorna had had in mind when she visualised Tubby at home. Kirsty too had created a picture of some older, more battered neighbourhood, a street down on its uppers, not a quiet, spacious enclave with a fenced private garden in the middle and plane trees growing out of the pavement.

Linden Vale church looked down on the gardens, its classical simplicity in sharp contrast to the ornamental extravagance of the new architecture.

"See," said Ernest. "That's the way the good folk walk to heaven. Fifty steps an' there you are."

He led them to the gate of a main door apartment, part of a double-drummed corner building, complete with massive bow windows, conical black-slate roofs and, over the doorway, a sandstone balcony.

"The humble abode." Ernest opened the front door with a flourish and called down the long, long hallway. "Mother, we've arrived."

The hallway was so long that it gave back a little echo of Ernest's voice and a faint ring too, off the parquet and radiator screens. The house had the hot-toast smell of good gas heating and a rich, underlying aroma of roasting coffee beans. The Tubbs, it seemed, enjoyed their creature comforts. When, as a young girl, Kirsty had dreamed of a proper home it was something akin to this that she'd had in mind, not Walbrook Street or Breezy's grand mansion.

"Ernest, is that yourself?"

"Ah, Frank!" said Tubby. "It is. It's us at last. Why don't you pretend you're civilised an' come out of your lair to greet our guests?"

The man who emerged from the shadows at the far end of the hall was a good fifteen years older than Ernest. He was quite different too in gait and build, clean-shaven, with a broad, open face and thick silver-flecked hair.

"Who's that?" Lorna whispered.

"My big brother, Frank," said Ernest.

Frank Tubbs was awkwardly pulling on a jacket over a waist-coat and cream linen shirt. Kirsty glimpsed armbands and cellu-loid cuff protectors before he shook the latter off and stuck them into his trouser pocket. She noticed too that his fingers were ink-stained and that he had about him the not unpleasant smell of cigar tobacco.

Ernest made the introductions. Frank Tubbs shook hands with Lorna first. He did not bow. There was in him none of that impudent self-mockery which was Ernest's stock-in-trade. Next he offered a broad hand to Kirsty and gave her the trace of a smile. She could feel strength in the hand and, though he might appear shy, even diffident, he did not avoid Kirsty's eyes.

"Miss Nicholson," Frank said, "do let me take your coat."

"No butlers in this domicile," said Ernest. "Day servants only, and they have Sunday off. On Sunday we fend for ourselves, for the good of our souls an' all that. Anyway, since my brothers Willy and Roy departed, there's only the three of us here."

"And your hats, ladies." Frank said. "Is that the way it's done, Ernest?"

"Yes, yes. Hats too."

Lorna had not, as yet, uttered a word. She seemed struck dumb again, by the house's taste and elegance. Kirsty wondered what on earth Tubby and she had talked about during their hours alone. It couldn't all have been affectionate insults and sweet nothings, could it?

Frank Tubbs had a gentle way with hats. He was not so inexperienced in *politesse* as Ernest's banter had suggested. He went off towards a door at the end of the corridor then paused and called out. "Show the ladies the offices, Ernest. I think that would be wise."

"Offices?"

"I think he means the water closet," Lorna said.

"Oh! The bathroom."

"Yes, daftie, the bathroom."

"Good notion," Ernest said. "Step this way, please, then we'll all go in for an audience with mother. How's that?"

"That's fine," Lorna said.

Kirsty, however, wasn't listening. She was watching Frank Tubbs put away the coats and hats.

*　　*　　*

Morgan's Bar was down in Brandling Street in one of the long, old buildings that burrowed through a warren of ramshackle tenements to the high, weedy bank that supported the North British Railway's mile-wide shunting yards and goods depot. On pay-nights Brandling Street was no place to wander alone. It was a haunt of dockers and riverboat men, tank drivers, stokers and broken-nosed labourers from the repair sheds by old Stobcross, forbidden territory for clerks and journeymen, the meek and the mild. If you came down to Brandling Street you came to drink and, if the fist was offered, to fight. Morgan's was a low-order, high-yield pub, a tied house that had turned a pretty penny for Carruth's over the years. Morgan's customers had no palate for new-fangled lagers or clean, bright beers. Only big, old, black-banded fifty-four-gallon hogsheads of traditional heavy brew crashed down the barrel runway from the double-doored delivery hatch in the building's side wall and crates of bottled stout, a favourite carry-out for firemen and dockers.

Gordon had spent an unconscionable amount of time in and under Morgan's Bar in the past week or two. It was one of his regular ports of call – he made collections there every week – but he had been sent back several times not to check the takings but to account the stock-in-hand. Some managers went quite daft when Gordon hinted that their arithmetic might require examination. Tom Jarrett and his burly wife, Ruby, landlord and lady of Morgan's Bar, were not of that stamp, however. They made young Mr Nicholson most welcome, fed him a substantial second breakfast and a fair-to-middling dinner and even sent their eldest daughter, Minerva, down to the cellar to keep him company while he prowled about the barrels and crates. Minerva had proved more of a hindrance than a help. She was too winsome to ignore, especially when she sat on top of a hogshead, paddled her legs and showed Gordon a lot more girl than a virtuous young man had a right to see. He'd had a lot of trouble with his calculations that afternoon and had had to rework them all again at home in the evening. Next morning, however, he'd dropped his sheet of figures into the Accounting department in Bishop Street and thought no more about it.

On Friday afternoon, though, Gordon was summoned to Accounting and informed by Mr Friendship that he would be required to attend a meeting with the Jarretts at Morgan's Bar on Sunday afternoon.

Gordon had learned not to question authority, especially Mr Friendship's authority. He had arranged to call on Amanda at The Knowe on Sunday afternoon but had no hesitation in posting off a letter of apology to his fiancée; business came first.

At two-thirty on a raw, windswept Sunday afternoon Brandling Street was deserted. Essential crews manned the rail yards behind the raddled tenements but the wee shops were all closed and public houses shuttered, Morgan's included.

Gordon had never seen Mr Friendship, Carruth's chief accountant, out of his natural habitat before. He was surprised at the width of the check on the man's raglan and the jauntiness of the little trilby on his balding pate. Mr Friendship had always seemed such a leathery and severe man that Gordon had somehow expected him to dress like an undertaker. Veteran traveller, Gerald McDade, on the other hand, was as drab and shabby as ever. He was not ill-groomed – no commercial gentleman worth his salt was ever that – but he was somehow as lacking in colour and distinction as the average dockside pigeon.

The men were waiting in a close mouth some fifty yards from the pub when Gordon arrived. Mr McDade nabbed him and drew him in out of sight of the Jarretts' windows, for the landlord and his family lived in rooms above the premises.

"Do you know why we're here, Gordon?" Mr Friendship asked.

"No," Gordon answered.

"Well, you'll find out in due course," said Mr Friendship.

The Welcome Light

"Now, lad, I don't want you to say a word unless I ask it of you. Betray no surprise at anything that may transpire."

"Right," said Gordon.

"Have you got the keys, Gerald?"

"Here in my hand, Mr Friendship."

"Very well. Let's get on with it."

Gordon followed the men as they slipped out of the close and sidled along Brandling Street. By now it was obvious that the Jarretts knew nothing of the visit, that no 'meeting' had been arranged. For a moment or two Gordon shared a sense of power as he trailed his superiors into the lane that flanked the pub and watched McDade unlock the padlock on the cellar's double doors.

One by one the men slithered down the runway into the pitch-black cellar. McDade produced a candle which was duly lighted and placed on a barrel and then, from his overcoat pocket, brought out a plan which showed the building in all its elevations. Heads together, Mr Friendship and Mr McDade pored over the document as if it were a treasure map.

"What," Gordon whispered hoarsely, "are we lookin' for?"

"To see just what the Jarretts are up to, lad."

"How do we know they're up to anythin'?"

"Stock sheets," said Mr McDade. "There's a leak in the profits an' we're here to find out why."

"Why don't you just ask the Jarretts?" said Gordon.

"Hoh!" Mr Friendship glanced at Mr McDade and shook his head. "What a boy this is, hm."

"Lot to learn, son. Lot to learn." McDade picked up the candle and handed it, all sticky with tallow, to Gordon.

"This way," said Mr Friendship. "I want a look behind those racks."

"It's only bottles back there," said Gordon. "Empty bottles awaitin' collection."

"We'll see." Beckoning to Gordon to follow him, Mr Friendship set off towards the cellar's nether end.

Tallow dripped on Gordon's glove. No matter how he angled the candle the flame wavered and threatened to go out in the dank draughts that wafted about the cellar. He could not understand quite what was going on or what his bosses expected to discover behind the rack of empties that backed on to the gable

60

wall. The bottles were mostly Carruth's own labels, stout bottles with vulcanised stoppers set with springs like mousetraps. It wasn't up to Carruth's to make collection. This was done by a carrier from the contract bottlers near Glasgow's High Street.

Gordon, with McDade's assistance, moved crates and loose quart bottles out of dusty racks while Mr Friendship, hands in pockets and trilby pulled low on his brow, watched as a low door in the short-end wall was exposed to view.

"Thought so," he grunted.

"What's in there?" said Gordon.

"That's what we'll have to find out, son." McDade reached through the rack to try the door's rusty latch.

"Locked?" said Mr Friendship.

"'Fraid so, sir."

"They'll have the bottler hidden in there, I expect," said Mr Friendship. "If that's what their game is."

"Shall I kick it open, Mr Friendship?"

"No, Gerald. Time to let the landlord have his say," said Mr Friendship. "Gordon, cut upstairs and fetch Tom Jarrett for us, will you?"

"Me?"

"It's what you're here for, son," said McDade.

"To learn how things are done." Mr Friendship gave Gordon a little nudge in the direction of the stairs that led to the ground floor bar. "No time like the present, is there, Mr McDade?"

"None, sir," the traveller answered.

*   *   *

Phyllis Tubbs was the smallest woman that Kirsty had ever seen. She was no dwarf, however, but as dainty as a porcelain figurine. Hands in her lap, she was seated by the fire in a low satin-lined tub chair, her little gilt slippers a good three inches from the floor. She had been brown haired once and a trace of the original colour could still be seen in the silver. Her complexion was smooth and sallow like a country egg and her eyes so alert that Kirsty fancied that inside the tiny, ageing body a quick and nimble-witted child was trapped.

"Mother," said Ernest. "I've brought my friends to see you."

"Glad to hear it," said Phyllis Tubbs in a voice as clear as a silver bell. "Now, perhaps, we might have tea."

61

"Frank's just gone to make it," said Ernest, not at all put out by his mother's acerbity. "Before we throw ourselves on the trolley, however, may I present Mrs Kirsty and Miss Lorna Nicholson."

"Which is the one, Ernest?" Phyllis Tubbs enquired.

Without hesitation Lorna said, "I'm the one, Mrs Tubbs."

"Are you, indeed?" said Mrs Tubbs. "I hope you're fond of muffins?"

"I love muffins."

"Plain or toasted?"

"Toasted."

"Well," said Mrs Tubbs, "that's an interesting start."

"Mater, behave yourself," said Ernest.

"Nonsense," Lorna said. "Why shouldn't we start with muffins? What about a favourite jam, Mrs Tubbs? I'm for raspberry."

Mrs Tubbs shook her head. "Plum."

"An abyss opens up," said Lorna. "Perhaps Ernest should take me home now."

Phyllis Tubbs smiled. "No, I think we can settle by arbitration. What do you say, Mrs Nicholson?"

"I take what I'm given," Kirsty answered.

"Very wise," said Phyllis Tubbs. "Now we've sorted out our differences perhaps you'd be good enough to ring the bell, Ernest."

"Ring the bell! Mum, it's Frank out there, not a galley slave."

"Ring it anyway," said Mrs Tubbs. "It'll give him something to grumble about. He just loves to grumble, does our Frank."

Kirsty studied the woman with interest. She was dressed in an up-to-date sunray skirt and bodice blouse. Her hair was arranged in loose curls at the forehead, and held by fillets of ribbon at the neck. The styling was youthful and yet, because she was so petite, Mrs Tubbs did not appear silly. She was, Kirsty guessed, about sixty.

Obediently Ernest tugged on a tassled cord hidden by the long velvet drapes at the bay window and from far off down the corridor came the jingle of the kitchen bell.

The sound was immediately followed by a gruff bellow from the hall, "Stop that, old woman."

Phyllis Tubbs winked at Lorna. "Keep them on their toes, dear. Isn't that the motto?"

"Absolutely," Lorna agreed, and laughed.

The girl sat back against the gigantic tapestry cushions that strewed the chesterfield. She seemed completely relaxed now and at home in the bosom of Ernest's family. Kirsty was less sure, less yielding. She could not put aside a suspicion that Phyllis Tubbs' easy, teasing manner had an element of calculation behind it.

Frank appeared with the tea trolley and, instructed by his mother, duly did the honours while Ernest added a few more lumps of coal to the fire with tongs and then settled himself, saucer and cup in hand, on the padded fender. Kirsty noticed that Frank Tubbs did not join the circle by the fire but took himself to a chair near the windows. She had to turn her head to see him there but she was aware of his scrutiny and felt herself reddening a little. Lorna was recounting her version of the capture of Austin Whiting, the famous forger, which had taken place in Gascoigne Street, an incredible event in which she and Ernest had been the heroes of the hour and which had not seemed quite so funny at the time. It was towards the climax of Lorna's tale that Kirsty became aware that Frank Tubbs was no longer behind her but had moved his chair closer to her own.

He leaned forward, hands on knees, and said quietly, "Will you take my brother on as full partner, Mrs Nicholson? Have you given the matter any thought at all?"

There was sudden attentive silence from the group by the fire. Lorna and Ernest were hanging on Kirsty's answer but she was most aware of Phyllis Tubbs' shrewd, brown eyes on her.

"Yes, I've given it a lot of thought."

"If it's a question of financial assurances," Frank said, "I may be able to put your mind at rest here and now."

"In what way?" said Kirsty.

"I'll guarantee to underwrite the first full year of the partnership at any figure you deem fair."

Lorna had lifted herself up on the cushions. She darted a glance at Kirsty and then, questioningly, at Phyllis Tubbs who made a little gesture as if to indicate that the fun was over and it was time for adult conversation.

Kirsty tried to gather her wits. Warmth and friendliness were, she knew, part of the tools of the trade for confidence tricksters and fraudsters. She had heard lots of stories from Craig, including the classic chestnut about the young Englishman who'd been persuaded to buy Jamaica Bridge. She was not about to allow herself to slither into a quagmire of gullibility.

She said, "I'm not the sole owner of the business."

"No, I'm aware that your brother-in-law has a financial stake, in addition to being owner of the property itself. He'll be recompensed for giving up his holding, of course."

"What if he doesn't wish to sell?"

"Oh, Gordon will sell," put in Lorna. "He's not interested in cheap commerce any longer."

"I doubt if we could see our way to actually offering for the property, for the building," Frank said. "But the lease has some months to run, does it not?"

"Almost two years."

"And the annual rent is fifteen pounds?"

"Yes."

"Gordon will be happy to extend the lease at that price, I'm sure," said Lorna.

"Hush, dear," said Phyllis Tubbs in her little bell of a voice.

Kirsty realised that the Tubbs family knew a great deal about her business. She could only assume that Lorna, who had access to the books, had betrayed confidences which Ernest had carried back to his brother. The odd thing was that she felt no resentment towards the Tubbses because of it.

"You appear to have it all cut and dried, Mr Tubbs," she said.

"No, not at all," said Frank. "But surely an arrangement between us can only be to our mutual benefit."

"Tell me how that will be," said Kirsty.

"I'll buy out Gordon's share in Gascoigne Street and put the balance, to the equivalent of your share, into stock," Frank Tubbs said. "The investment of additional capital will increase the turnover and the return. Ernest will buy stock – he's ideally placed to do so – from Mathieson, Mullard and Milroy."

"I thought the idea was that Ernest would manage the shop?" said Kirsty.

"In due course," said Ernest. "Once we're better established, then I'll give up representing the Ems and take over full managerial responsibility."

"In the meantime," Kirsty said, "who's goin' to serve behind the counter, do the books, wash the windows?"

"Me, of course," said Lorna.

Kirsty frowned and said, "Alone?"

"You an' me together, that's what I mean," Lorna replied.

"Does Ernest get paid for doin' two jobs?"

"No," Frank Tubbs said. "Until such times as he gives notice to his present employers I'll remunerate Ernest from my own share of the profits."

"The thing is," said Kirsty, "that you seem to know a great deal about my affairs but I know nothin' at all about you."

Phyllis Tubbs said, "We don't have any secrets, Mrs Nicholson. Frank will be pleased to tell you what you wish to know."

"What is it that you do for a livin', Mr Tubbs?"

"I used to be a teacher."

"A master at Lauder's Academy," Phyllis Tubbs added, "like his father before him."

"Used to be?"

"My sons all became teachers," Phyllis Tubbs went on. "Roy has a post in Perth; Willy in Dundee. They're married, of course, and have children of their own now."

"You're not married, Mr Tubbs?" said Kirsty.

"Not I."

"Old Frank's far too sensible to fall to Cupid's arrow." Ernest seated himself on the arm of the chesterfield and put a hand on Lorna's shoulder. "It's the wherewithal, Mrs N., ain't it? You're wondering where our money comes from?"

"In fact – yes."

"Frank writes," Mrs Tubbs confided.

"Writes?" The fleeting image of Frank Tubbs, chalk in hand, standing before a blackboard, came into her mind.

"Textbooks for students," said Ernest.

"And other things too," added Phyllis Tubbs.

Frank Tubbs cleared his throat. "Mother, there's no need to bore Mrs Nicholson with all this."

Lorna dug an elbow into Ernest's ribs. "You sly devil! Why didn't you tell me you had a famous brother?"

"We're a modest lot," said Ernest. "Frank doesn't like it discussed. But it's a plain fact that those dull old textbooks my brother wrote do coin in the pennies."

"Now the schoolteacher wants to own a shop?" said Kirsty.

"I've no ambitions to build a commercial empire, Mrs

65

Nicholson," Frank Tubbs said. "I'm doing it to give my brother a start in life. It's strictly for this black sheep's benefit. My father would turn in his grave if he thought one of his offspring had eschewed an honourable profession like teaching to become a salesman."

There was just sufficient levity in Frank Tubbs' voice to take the sting out of the remark. Kirsty sensed that mother and brother were as proud of Ernest as they were of the scholars in the family.

"What do you write about, Mr Tubbs? Commerce?"

"History."

"Same thing, really," Ernest put in. "Old Frank might want to write about it but I want to make it, so I do."

"Oh, you dolt," said Phyllis Tubbs. "Isn't he a dolt, Lorna?"

Lorna squeezed her sweetheart's hand to show solidarity both with his philosophy and his cause.

"Not in my book, Mrs Tubbs," she said.

*   *   *

Mr Friendship's autocracy had insidiously communicated itself to Gordon. As he crept up the twisting wooden staircase from the bar, he realised that he too now thought of the Jarretts as criminals. He moved warily along the corridor towards the kitchen door as if he expected to be greeted by brigands armed with swords and knives. It was soon obvious, however, why the Jarretts had heard nothing of the intruders in the cellar. Gales of laughter shook the kitchen door, children's laughter punctuated by Tom Jarrett's booming bass. They were playing a card game of some sort. Gordon listened to their chanting – "Wan, twa, three, fower," a collective breath, "five, six, *knave*," for a moment then rapped loudly upon the door.

Instant silence: a boy of about six dragged open the door and glowered up at him.

"Who're you?" the wee boy demanded.

Gordon gave the door a gentle push and, as it swung inwards, found himself confronted by all nine Jarretts, including Tom, Ruby and the winsome Minerva. They were gathered round the kitchen table under a ceiling gas light. The room was more like a farm steading than a Glasgow tenement. It had panelled walls, shelves, and an oblong window through which Gordon could

The Facts of Life

just make out hazy daylight. A blazing coal fire in the grate made the temperature uncomfortably hot but the Jarretts seemed to like it that way.

A cotton cloth, strewn with playing cards, covered the table and Gordon had a faint recollection of having played the family game with his Da a long time ago on Dalnavert. It wasn't a game for serious gamblers but provided fast and furious fun nonetheless. The Jarretts were playing for nuts. Hazels, brazils, walnuts filled a shallow brass bowl before Minerva who, in her role as banker, had position at the head of the table. Small Jarretts kneeled on chairs, clung to Mammy's broad lap or stood by Pappy's side, noses on the table's edge, and glared at Gordon through a forest of pop bottles and glasses of brown ale.

"Come awa' in, Mr Nicholson." Ruby Jarrett gestured with a fat hand. "Never thought a chap like you wad be workin' on a Sunday."

"I – "

Tom Jarrett dumped a youngster from his knee and got to his feet. "Is somethin' wrong, Mr Nicholson?"

Gordon did not have to devise a diplomatic answer to the question. McDade had arrived and, edging Gordon to one side, answered for him. "Aye, Jarrett, somethin' is very much wrong."

"I'm not aware that anythin's out o' order, Mr McDade."

"It's the books that are out o' order," McDade said.

"Och, no, no, no," said Ruby Jarrett.

"But aye, aye, aye," said McDade. "Now we've got to find out what you've been up to. I'll require you t' step downstairs wi'out further ado, an' bring your special set o' keys with you."

"My what?"

"You heard."

It was all over in twenty minutes.

The speed of judgement and punishment made it seem as obscene as a public hanging but Gordon was too confused to utter a word in defence of the Jarretts. One minute, it seemed, the family was happily gathered round the table in the cosy kitchen, and the next it was shivering in the night wind that whistled down Brandling Street.

Clothing had been hastily bundled into shawls, crockery and ornaments stuffed into wicker baskets and the Jarretts' few sticks of furniture carted down from the first floor, through the bar and out on to the pavement where they waited, forlornly, to be piled on to a handcart as soon as one could be found.

As far as Gordon could see, there was no reason for evicting the Jarretts without recompense, ceremony or apology. What stilled his tongue, however, was the stoicism with which Tom and Ruby Jarrett accepted their fate. Perhaps, Gordon told himself, Mr Friendship was right and the landlord was guilty of some clever fraud.

In due course two of the older lads appeared with a handcart. It had been hired, not borrowed, from the yard of a local chimney sweep. The family's possessions were flung upon the cart, the youngsters piled on top of them and, with Tom and his eldest heaving on the shafts, the cart was swivelled around and pointed down Brandling Street towards the heart of Glasgow.

"Where will they go?" Gordon stood helplessly outside the pub and watched the exodus.

"Lodgin's, I expect," McDade answered. "Their kind won't wind up in the gutter. Their kind never go cold or hungry for long. They'll have money, don't think they won't. They'll have what they stole from Carruth's for a start."

"But – but we didn't find any evidence of theft."

"'Course we didn't," said McDade. "Their kind are far too clever for that."

A handful of men from the railway yard had dawdled out of the sheddings to observe the Jarretts' misfortune. They did not, however, offer condolences or even bid the family farewell, just stood well back as Tom and his boys hauled the handcart past them and slewed it to take the corner into Chiselhurst Road.

As Gordon watched the Jarretts trudge away into the winter dusk, he could hardly believe that it had happened at all, let alone that he had been a party to it. The last thing he heard from the Jarretts was a girning cry from the youngest child and the last thing he saw was flossy-haired Minerva, loitering behind the rest, raise her fist in a gesture so obscene that even McDade was black affronted by it.

"Good riddance to bad rubbish." Mr Friendship delivered his verdict, turned up his coat collar and, for a moment, seemed about to depart.

"What about the pub?" Gordon said. "I mean, won't it have to be closed until another landlord's found?"

Mr Friendship and Mr McDade exchanged another of those patronising glances then Mr Friendship patted Gordon's shoulder.

"New staff," he explained. "Already hired, already on the way here to take over."

"What!" Gordon exclaimed. "When?"

"Any time now." Mr Friendship consulted his pocket watch and swung the key-ring on his forefinger. "Six o'clock I believe they're due. Isn't that right, Gerald?"

"Spot on, sir," McDade answered.

And Gordon muttered, "Jeeze!"

*   *   *

Ernest Tubbs and Lorna parted from Kirsty at the tram stop at the top of Kingdom Road. Tubby would walk Lorna up the long hill to Great Western Terrace where he would leave her, with a kiss to keep her going, just out of sight of the mansion's windows.

It was after six o'clock and Craig, Kirsty imagined, would be champing at the bit. He was not due on his first night shift until eleven o'clock but, obsessed with punctuality, he would expect supper by seven, and his uniform, freshly pressed and brushed, to be laid out on the bed by half past. She would manage all that on time but it probably wouldn't be enough to appease her husband.

Ten minutes at this stage would make no difference to Craig's mood. She had so much tumbling in her mind that she braved the cold wind and set off for a quick walk to Gascoigne Street before she returned home to face the rigours of the evening. For some reason she was bursting with energy. She felt more alive than she had done in months. She wondered at this side of her that seemed to demand the leading of a double life. Was it a reaction to the harshness of her childhood or disappointment with her marriage to Craig? She was not so vain as to imagine that she'd been a perfect wife. As she walked along Dumbarton Road that bitter Sunday evening, she tried to weigh and balance the little sins of omission and commission which she had committed, to find the measure of truth for who was really to blame for the threadbare marriage.

Churches and mission halls were lighted now, doors thrown

open for the evening's services. Children and women were braving the chill that had kept them by the fire all day. Though they knew Kirsty only by sight, men done out in sober suits and polished boots tipped their hats as they hurried past, for she was young, well-groomed and sprightly and the cold air had tingled their blood as well as hers. The new organ in Greenfield West kirk uttered the deep, profound notes of a Voluntary as Kirsty approached the doors. She paused to listen for a moment or two before she crossed the road. It was strange to think that the good folk of Walbrook Street were winding their way towards St Anne's just as they'd done when Nessie was alive and David was still in Scotland. She missed David far more than she would admit. She had tried so hard to release him from her heart, to acknowledge that yearning for David was like yearning for the past – the worst kind of unrequited love. All that she could do to free herself would be to do what she had done before, replace him with activity, keep herself so busy that she did not have time to think of him or pine for what might have been.

G. A. Nicholson's Domestic Emporium: Gordon's name but not Gordon's shop. The shop front's sloping ledges were thick with street dust and the gilded letters above the doorway had begun to fade. Even so, just looking at the building, Kirsty felt again the pleasure of possession. Perhaps this was what the orphan in her demanded, ownership in lieu of love.

It had always been her place, her mark, even if she had first taken it on out of bad faith. Now the Tubbs family wanted to share it with her, to make it bigger and better. She knew why she had wandered round this way. It was to reach a decision, to make up her mind.

Time was when she'd have been overwhelmed by Frank Tubbs, when a man of that age and position in life would have intimidated her and she would have surrendered to his will at once, without a struggle. But not now. Oh, no, not now. If she took them on at all, it would be on her terms.

Later that night, after Craig had gone on duty, she would fish out pen and paper, would write to her solicitor, Mr Marlowe, and instruct him to draft letters of partnership with Mr Frank Tubbs but to leave them undated and, as yet, unsigned.

*   *   *

The wind had had the temerity to find a way into Albert Adair's mansion on Great Western Terrace and was playing fast and loose with doors and sashes and the expensive Persian carpets that covered the marble of the hall. The paintings that flanked the staircase sighed wistfully in their great gilded frames as if they longed to be sails and not mere dead canvas smeared with oil and glazed with varnish; and, though it was built of stone thick as a castle, the house too seemed to groan in dissatisfaction as if it were made of galleon timbers that hungered to return to the river and the sea. It was no wild gale that strode along the terrace, just a keen whistling westerly that had found the key to Albert's house and entered to make a restless mischief there. It grated on Albert's nerves, however, and caused the depression that had been haunting him for weeks to drift down again like mist across a mountain.

Madge had been laid up all afternoon with one of those headaches that Breezy could not dismiss as a female wile. He knew it was the genuine article for the simple reason that it had robbed his dear lady wife of the power of coherent speech. She did not blame him for her pain, bully her maid or whine for sympathy but just lay on her back, first on the chaise and later in bed, with a cold compress on her brow and her eyes covered by a black lace. Breezy was worried. He vowed to himself that if she had not improved by midnight he would personally go round the corner and pull Dr Galway out of bed to attend to her. Meanwhile he fed her Belladonna pills and, when they proved ineffective, succumbed to her plea to let her take a Daisy Powder which, even at seven pence for ten, guaranteed absolute miracles of healing.

By the time Lorna arrived, plain phenacetin had done its work, the blinding pain had eased and Madge slept.

"Will I pop in an' see her?" Lorna asked.

"No, let her rest."

"You're the boss. What's for supper?"

"I don't know," Breezy said. "Ring for Miss Rowland. See what she's got in the pot."

"I'll pop down, shall I? What about you?"

"Never mind me. I'm not hungry," Breezy growled. "An' don't eat in the kitchen. Cook doesn't like us bein' down there."

"Aw, cookie doesn't mind me," said Lorna. "Saves the maids

71

settin' and servin'. By the way, where's the lord of the manor tonight?"

"He's been out all afternoon."

"Gone a-wooin', perchance?"

"I think it's brewery business," said Breezy.

"Workin' on the Sabbath: how vulgar!" said Lorna as she bounced out of the room again. "Old Dolphus don't half get his money's worth from my poor brother. Jam tomorrow, though, what!"

Breezy was relieved to see his stepdaughter depart. Lately Lorna's bubbling energy had become wearing, made him feel old and lacking in resilience. He hung around the hallway for a minute or two but when Lorna did not return from the house's lower depths he wandered into the front parlour and poked the neglected fire into a semblance of life.

It was a weird, disturbing night. He could see the bare branches of trees across the road writhing and tossing dementedly and yet he could hear no sound, not a whisper of the wind that tormented them. Perhaps, to add to his other woes, he was going deaf too. He lit a small cigar, supped whisky, rocked on the balls of his feet before the flickering fire and, like many an ageing pragmatist before him, dwelled gloomily on death, taxes and undiscovered crimes. Thus Gordon found him some ten minutes later.

"Ah, Breezy," said Gordon, without preamble. "I'm glad I caught you alone."

"Oh?"

"Yes, I rather want a word with you."

Breezy's heart sank at Gordon's ominous tone. He wasn't really in the mood to play the role of stepfather these days. Nonetheless, he motioned Gordon to a chair by the fire and poured him a glass of Glen Grant.

Gordon's dander was well and truly up, though. He refused the whisky and the chair, paced about the window bay, glowering.

Breezy's spirits continued their downward spiral.

"Well, son, what's on your mind?" he forced himself to say with a brightness that was entirely false.

Breezy listened patiently while Gordon poured out the story of his afternoon's excursion to Morgan's Bar and its conse-

quences.

"The cupboard was empty," Gordon concluded. "There wasn't one single piece of evidence to prove that the Jarretts had been fiddlin' – yet out they went. Turfed out without redress."

"How did Jarrett take his dismissal?"

Gordon scowled. "He didn't say much."

"Have you asked yourself why Jarrett didn't protest?"

"Because he *had* been up to somethin' fishy?"

"That's certainly how I'd interpret it."

"Would you fling a family of nine into the gutter at five o'clock on a cold winter night without a shred of evidence to justify it?"

"Without a qualm," Breezy said.

"What!"

"If I had a Chief Accountant like Jimmy Friendship in my employ and he smelled somethin' fishy down at Morgan's Bar I'd have the staff turned over before you could say 'knife'."

"Mr Friendship isn't God, you know."

"No, but he's the next best thing."

"Jeeze!"

Breezy felt his patience dry out and become stringy, like yesterday's mutton. He tried to control his temper, reminding himself that the boy was young and still inexperienced.

"Listen, son," he said, evenly. "Listen very carefully. I don't think you've realised yet that Chief Accountants in the licensed trade are men apart. They hover over stock sheets like mothers over cradles. They can spot a single point variation in the rate percent of gross profit at a thousand yards. And when they do they don't rest until they discover the reason for it."

"There *was* no reason," Gordon insisted.

"None that you could see, maybe, but leakage isn't just a matter of rusty pipes or sprung barrels. Leakage is a kind of theft, one that every brewer dreads."

"I know what leakage is," Gordon said.

"When your Chief Accountant comes to you an' whispers the dread word, you don't hang fire, believe me. You jump. You act. You get rid of the culprits."

"If Mr Friendship was so sure of his ground why did he have to involve me?"

"The lesson was for your benefit, Gordon. I doubt if there was any need for you to be crawlin' around the cellars at all. Jimmy

Friendship was probably just puttin' on a show to impress you, to see if you have the grit to manage Carruth's one day."

"Did Dolphus tell him to do it?"

"I wouldn't be surprised."

"Are you tryin' to tell me it was my fault those poor devils got flung out of house an' home?"

"'Course not," Breezy said. "Jarrett went quietly. He probably knew he'd been tumbled by Jimmy Friendship."

"If Jarrett was really guilty of theft, of embezzlement, why wasn't he charged?"

"Bad for business," Breezy said.

Gordon glanced at the tumbler of whisky on the side table, lifted it and drank.

Breezy said, "How about a spot o' supper, son? You must be famished?"

Gordon ignored the attempt to withdraw from discussion.

He said, "Would you really have pitched the Jarretts into the street, Breezy?"

Breezy got to his feet. He was resigned but, oddly, he felt a little better now. He did not, however, put an arm about Gordon's shoulders; he, of all people, knew the difference between affection and patronage.

"What you mean is, would I have served them notice and let them stay on until morning?" Breezy said. "Absolutely not."

"But why?"

"Because I might have arrived the next day to find my barrels seamed, my wines salted, my beer engines filled with sand," Breezy said. "Now, yes, I know you think that Tom Jarrett wasn't that kind of man but no brewer can afford to take a chance on it and lose two or three days trade if he's wrong."

"I must admit," said Gordon, "I never thought of that."

"The lesson Jimmy Friendship gave you today was simple: When you have to strike against an employee, strike fast and stand firm."

"And that's ethical business, is it?"

"It's *practical* business," said Breezy. "All those top-hatted, upright gentlemen you see strollin' about St Vincent Street an' Exchange Square would applaud Jimmy Friendship for what he did today. Oh, aye, they might be honest, charitable, God-fearing citizens at home, kind to children an' animals an' generous to

the poor and needy, but there isn't one of them wouldn't have flung Jarrett out on his ear. When it comes to protectin' profits we're all tarred with the one brush, Gordon, whether you like it or lump it. Do you understand?"

Gordon pursed his lips, paused then said, "Yes, I understand."

"Good," said Breezy. "Another whisky then?"

"No thanks. I've had enough," Gordon said. "Where's Lorna, did you say?"

"Downstairs."

Gordon placed his empty glass carefully on the side table, crossed to the door, opened it and went out without another word.

Breezy watched sadly. He too knew what it meant to learn to stomach disillusionment and felt more sympathy than anger for his stepson. He poured himself another finger of whisky and stood by the window, listening to catch the drone of the wind in the bare, tossing trees but hearing nothing but the infernal flapping of carpets and creaking of panels as if, for no reason, the whole damned house was swaying and shifting on its broad, imperishable foundations.

"Oh, hell!" said Breezy and, after knocking back his drink, trudged upstairs to offer comfort to his ailing wife.

* * *

Amanda said, "I really shouldn't be here with you, Gordon. Alone, I mean."

"Why ever not?"

"An unmarried girl and a handsome young man, un-chaperoned, at an intimate dinner."

"Hardly intimate." Gordon gestured towards the thirty other diners who, that Saturday night, had piled into Milngavie's Black Bull Hotel to escape the dismal weather. "Besides, we're engaged."

"Mother said it would be all right."

"And Dolphus – Daddy?"

"I don't think he knows where I am."

"Or cares?"

"What on earth do you mean? Of course Daddy cares. He loves me very much and is concerned about my welfare."

"Oh, come now," Gordon said. "It hasn't been a happy family of late, Amanda. How can you pretend that it has?"

"I don't have to pretend."

"What would have happened to you," Gordon said, "if Olive had run off with her lover? How would you have felt about that?"

The question was direct and cruel but Gordon had been shedding his illusions about a lot of things lately and Saturday dinner at the Bull was just part of his scheme of adjustments.

Amanda picked at a fragment of smoked mackerel and was, Gordon realised, confused by his directness.

In the diffuse light from the Bull's new electrical lights Amanda seemed to have lost some of her intimidating gloss. She was still, of course, incredibly beautiful. Gordon had not been impervious to the envious glances that were directed his way by the other men in the room. Yes, Amanda Adair was the Belle of the Ball. You couldn't take her out, even for a discreet little dinner in a local hotel, without it becoming a show.

He pushed away his plate with his fingertips. "You haven't answered my question, Amanda."

She was definitely agitated. She picked at the pearl buttons of her fawn silk dress while a serving girl removed the dishes and a waiter scampered forward to pour more wine into Gordon's glass.

"I've – I've forgotten what we were talkin' about," Amanda said, when the table had been cleared and set again for the next course.

She wanted him to change the subject but Gordon pressed on. "If your mother had scarpered with Captain Tom wouldn't you have felt abandoned?"

"No, I don't think so."

"Oh, so you knew about the affair, did you?"

"Gordon – "

"The scandal would have ruined our wedding, you know."

Foolishly Amanda sprang at the bait. "No, Mother wouldn't have left until after our wedding."

Gordon sampled the wine. It was a fragrant little Meursault with a dry undertaste. Breezy had recommended it and it seemed fitting not only to accompany fish but also to endorse his mood.

Amanda said, "I – I mean *perhaps*. Perhaps she'd have gone after our wedding. I mean – I don't know. Gordon, it's none of your concern anyway."

"None of my concern? Dearest, I'm soon to be your husband, an' there can be no secrets between a wife an' her man."

Amanda retaliated. "*You* don't tell *me* everything."

"What don't I tell you?"

"How can I tell you if you don't tell me what I don't know."

"Pardon? I don't think I quite got that."

"Gordon, why are you behavin' like this towards me? I've apologised for being rude to you that Sunday morning."

Gordon did not relent. "Mummy would leave? Daddy would stay? Was that the arrangement?"

"There wasn't any 'arrangement'," Amanda said. "Daddy didn't know about – "

"Oh, wasn't it inconsiderate of Captain Tom to hop off to fight the Boers just when he did?" Gordon said. "Quite spoiled all the plans."

"Stop it, please."

Tears rimmed her eyes. For an instant he felt almost sorry for her. But that didn't hinder him.

He said, "I've taken a room upstairs."

Surprise dried her tears before they could trickle on to her cheeks. "But why? If you don't want to go home tonight you can stay at The Knowe."

"The Knowe isn't very private."

"Gordon, what is this? What are you – ?"

She was pleased that he had turned the conversation from awkward matters to a subject on which she felt more at home.

"If I asked you nicely, Amanda, would you come to my room after supper?"

"I couldn't possibly spend the night."

"I'm not askin' you to spend the night."

"Gordon, it would be far too risky. I'm known here. Someone would be sure to tell Daddy."

Gordon nodded. It was as he'd expected. She did not protest at his proposal out of modesty. Her only concern was whether or not she could get away with it without being found out.

He said, "There's a back stair. Very discreet."

"When I got to your room, sir, what then?"

77

The old Amanda was back, bright, confident and flowing. It was bred in her, he reckoned, to take the upper hand at every possible opportunity.

"What do you suppose?" he said.

"I think, sir, you might try to take advantage of me."

"Oh, aye. You can bet on that."

Amanda drew back, pert but proper, as a waiter guided a serving girl towards their table.

"Beef, sir?" the waiter said.

"Here," said Gordon.

He watched Amanda go through her pretence of being utterly enchanted by every potato and pea, thrown into ecstasies by every slice of roast beef that slithered on to her plate. Even while she was performing her practised dining-room charade, however, she was rubbing her ankle against his calf beneath the table cover. When waiter and girl had gone, Amanda glanced at him expectantly.

Gordon held her gaze for a second then lifted his fork and speared a potato, put it in his mouth and through it said, "No, you're right, of course."

"Am I?"

"It wouldn't be proper."

"Gordon?"

"What?"

"I – I really wouldn't mind."

"No?" He paused, hot beef poised on his fork. "No. But I would."

She blinked, bewildered. It was all too easy to play games with the likes of Amanda. He felt no remorse. Before the nuptials and the bridal night he would have Miss Adair eating out of his hand. When she rubbed his calf with her ankle once more Gordon jerked his leg away and frowned his disapproval.

"Amanda, please, remember where we are," he said and, to celebrate the first little victory in his war with the upper classes, snapped his fingers loudly to summon up a bottle of *vin ordinaire*.

*   *   *

Once, not so long ago, she'd come along Dumbarton Road, on a morning much like this one, burdened with pails and brooms to

78

meet with Greta Taylor and set to upon the grubby interior of
the shop in Gascoigne Street. Today, though, Kirsty had no
burden but Bobby; and he was no burden at all. He had come to
terms with the caliper. He ignored the ring of soft bruises on his
calf and the weal at the back of his knee and rolled along with a
stumping, determined gait that was both comical and heart-
breaking.

She had told Bobby that they were going to Gascoigne Street
and had expected eagerness and some mention of his friend
Jen. When they reached the corner, however, Bobby drew himself up and leaned his backside against the dusty woodwork to
rest. He tilted his head back, surveyed the overhanging eaves,
squinted along the plane of the window then folded his arms
and watched as Kirsty unlocked the gate padlock and set the
gate to one side. She unlocked the door next and pushed it
open. She was greeted by the faint, faint odour of wine, relic of
the days when John Vosper Vokes, Greenfield's famous mur-
derer, had traded here. She held out her hand. "Come on,
Bobby. In we go."

Bobby scowled, refused her hand but allowed himself to be
steered across the threshold into the gloom.

The big mechanical cashier still squatted upon the counter,
polished metal parts reflecting daylight from the doorway. It
had been Gordon's gift, a blessing on the store's success. Now it
seemed to commemorate better days, happier times, a period of
friendship and fellowship that Kirsty hadn't fully appreciated
while she was living through it. What, she wondered, was waiting
for her now?

Needing contact, she kept a hand firmly on Bobby's shoulder
as, still without light, she studied shelves and counter, the knobs,
bobs and odd-shaped objects that loomed out of the half-dark.
There was the worm of string and the twist of brown wrapping
paper just as she left them weeks and weeks ago. From the cave-
like recess behind the curtain at the rear of the shop she caught
the drip-drip-drip of the watertap, slow as time itself.

Bobby spoke. "Where's ma wee friend?"

Kirsty's throat closed and tears started into her eyes. She tried
to hold on to him but he wriggled from her grasp and darted
forward, dragging the caliper as if it had been applied simply to
restrain him.

"Jen, Jen, where are ye, Jen? I'm here t' see you," Bobby shouted. "Aye, I've gotta bad leg now. Come an' see."

Patience, not understanding, had stilled Bobby's tongue. He had not enquired after Jen before now because he had feared that he might be the cause of their parting; yet he'd been sure enough of her loyalty to believe that she would wait for him here, held fast and firm in a reality that would not change unless he willed it. He dragged open the old curtain and hobbled through into the back shop.

"JEN, HERE I AM. HERE I AM. I'VE COME BACK."

Into the silence of his waiting no sound fell except the drip-drip-drip of water drops tapping into the sink.

And Kirsty's stifled sobs.

*   *   *

"So, what did you tell him?" Craig said.

"I told him Jen had gone to heaven to stay with Jesus."

"Aye, I thought that might be your story."

"What else could I say?"

"You could've told him the truth."

"What truth?"

"That she's dead," Craig said.

"He's too young to understand what bein' dead means."

"Well, I'm dashed sure he didn't swallow all that holy guff about her bein' in heaven wi' Jesus," Craig said. "Did he cry when he discovered she wasn't there?"

"No, he was angry, more than anything."

"But has he grasped the fact that Jen isn't comin' back?"

"I think so."

"I'll talk to him about it."

"No," Kirsty said, "I'd rather you didn't."

"Why the hell not?"

"Just let it be, Craig. He'll come to terms with it in his own way. And then he'll forget."

"Huh, I wish it was that easy," Craig said.

"Look, if you're put out because I've gone back into retail then just say so," Kirsty told him.

"Was he there today?"

"Who?"

"This new manager you'll be splittin' the profits with?"

"Ernest, do you mean? No, he wasn't there today. And he isn't the manager. Lorna's the manager, at least for a while."

"What about Gordon?"

"Don't you ever listen? Gordon sold his share of our partnership to Frank Tubbs. Mr Marlowe's got signed papers so it's all legal and above board."

"Lawyers! I wouldn't trust a lawyer as far as I could throw one," Craig said.

"Who *do* you trust, Craig?"

He didn't answer. Instead he said, "Who are these folk that Lorna's got herself mixed up with? Where do they get their money?"

"Family funds," said Kirsty.

She did not elaborate. She had discovered by casual enquiry from Mr Marlowe that Frank Tubbs was a pillar of Glasgow's literary and artistic community, a member of the coterie that hung around the Art Club and the Atheneum. He was no Bohemian fly-by-night either but a through-and-through conservative who had edited, for a time, *The Scottish Pulpit* and who still wrote on Church history and similar droll subjects as well as authoring schoolbooks and works of fiction.

There was nothing sinister in the family's background and only Ernest's reticence about his family had made it seem as if there might be. She could not understand why Tubbs had kept mum about his unembarrassing relatives.

"You should have asked me first," Craig said.

"Asked you about what?"

"Whether you should do it."

"And what would you have advised?"

"Steer clear."

Kirsty said, "It's just as well I didn't ask you then."

"God," said Craig. "You can be so bloody smug at times. Mark my words, Kirsty, this partnership will just bring more trouble, more strife."

"Is that it, Craig? Is that your blessin'?"

"You'll see," Craig said. "An' don't come runnin' to me when things go wrong."

"As if I would," said Kirsty.

*   *   *

The acrimony between Kirsty and Craig Nicholson was mild compared to the howling row that broke out in the domicile of Mr Albert Adair after Lorna dropped her little five-word bombshell one evening after dinner.

"I am not going back."

Madge and Breezy had just settled in the big upstairs living room and hadn't been paying too much attention to Lorna or her words.

"Not goin' back where, dear?" said Madge.

"To Prosser's," said Lorna. "To college."

"Nonsense," said Madge.

"I've had enough education. I'm not goin' back — an' that's flat."

In fairness, Breezy had not been at all himself of late. The succession of scandals and disasters that he had weathered on behalf of his brothers and sisters had finally become too much for him and the tragic ending to Olive's affair with Tom Wells had all but broken his spirit. He'd married Madge Nicholson because he loved her, yes, but also because he believed that she would make a perfect companion for his declining years, that she would provide him with a rare excuse for pulling gradually out of involvement in business and commerce and letting go the strings of responsibility.

Now this: now Lorna.

Even Lorna, plated with Nicholson conceit and armoured by love for Ernest Tubbs, was initially humbled by the sudden terrible rage that her announcement induced in her stepfather. She watched agog as he stamped about the room, thumped his fist on the mantelshelf and kicked the stuffing out of a poor brocade footstool, shouting all the while, "I won't have it. I just won't have it. I've had enough. Quite enough from all of you. Enough. Enough, d'you hear." And then, breathing like a bull, stooped and wagged his forefinger right into her face. "You'll do as you're told, Lorna. You'll finish college an' like it."

She rose from the sofa like a harpy and flew right back at him. "You can't tell me what to do. I'm not your daughter."

"You sleep in my house, though. You eat my food — "

"Not another damned mouthful will cross my lips — "

"An' you're my responsibility — "

"Not for much longer."

" – until you come of age."

"I'm almost eighteen – "

"No, you're bloody not," Breezy yelled. "You're still a child an' you don't know what's good for you."

"Don't I? Don't I?"

"An' I say you're stayin' on at Prosser's until you complete your Certificate an' then you'll go to work for me until such times as – "

"No, I will not."

"Lorna, Lorna, what's got into you?" said Madge.

"I'll tell you what's got into her," Breezy ranted. "That bloody salesman's got into her."

Madge shot to her feet. "What? What are you sayin'?"

"I don't mean literally," said Breezy in a pained aside; then to Lorna again, "It is him, isn't it? He's put this daft idea into your head?"

"I'm goin' to work for our Kirsty, if you must know."

It was Madge's turn to raise her voice. "Oh, no, you are not, m'lady."

"I'm goin' to manage the shop."

"You! That's a laugh," said Breezy. "You couldn't manage a penny raffle."

Torn between conflicting loyalties, Madge stiffly informed Albert that her daughter was clever enough to do anything she liked; then, instantly, rounded on Lorna and informed her that Albert was right.

"It's all settled," said Lorna. "Kirsty's gone into partnership with Tubby an' I'm to be the manager. Didn't Gordon tell you he'd sold out his share?"

"Keep Gordon out of this," said Breezy. "It's got nothin' to do with Gordon. This salesman's just after your money."

"My money? I don't have any money."

"No, but I do."

Lorna was genuinely mystified. "What?"

"It's all a trick to ensure that they get their hands on my investments," Breezy said, nodding.

"Uh! Uh!"

"I think – I think Albert might have hit the nail on the head, dear."

"Uh! Uh!"

"I suppose marriage has been discussed?" said Madge.

"Ernest wouldn't – wouldn't just marry me for – "

"Some men have no scruples at all, lass," said Breezy, trying to soothe her.

"Aye, some men like you," Lorna cried. "You sold our Gordon to get that Adair girl wi'out a qualm. You traded him off just to get your paws on some of the Carruth fortune. Maybe you think I'm just a stupid wee lassie but even I could see through that one."

Stunned by the girl's passion, Breezy rocked on his heels and might have stumbled over the fire-irons if Madge had not clasped him by the arm. Lorna, however, was still on the attack. "As it so happens Ernest's not interested in your damned money. But even if he was, even if he wanted to marry me just for that reason, what would be the harm in it? It's how your precious sisters an' brothers made their pile. It's what you call 'enterprise' – except when it happens to you."

Madge hugged Albert to her bosom, as if he had been mortally wounded. "Lorna, that's enough! Apologise to your Father this very minute."

"Never," Lorna said. "I'll never apologise to him. I'm off. I'm gettin' out of this house for good." She rushed to the door, pulled it wide open then turned and gave back to her stepfather the gesture that he had given her, the wagging forefinger. "The biter bit, Daddy. The biter damned-well bit."

*   *   *

Gordon had just returned from Glasgow by hackney cab. He had opened the mansion's front door with his key and was on the point of closing it again when his sister called out to him from halfway down the staircase, "Leave it. Leave it. I'm goin'."

She wore a heavy cloak that billowed dramatically behind her, a long snaking scarf and had her newest hat stuck on the back of her head, unsecured by pins. She held it on with one hand, and lugged a case with the other, as she leapt down the stairs into the hall and headed straight for the open doorway.

"I've borrowed your big valise, Gordon," she said. "I'll bring it back. Some day."

"Lorna, for God's sake, what's happened?"

"Ask them. I'm gettin' out of here. For good."

Gordon followed her on to the step. "But – but where are you goin'?"

The valise had been stuffed too full, too hastily and the locks had not been secured. It was held only by the strap and threatened to burst open and spew its contents across the pavement as Lorna cut across the terrace. She headed for the gap in the privet hedge by which message boys gained access to Great Western Road.

"To Kirsty's?" Gordon shouted.

She did not answer in so many words, just raised her right hand and waved it in the air.

Gordon was not tempted to pursue her. He watched from the step, though, until she bundled herself into a hack. The hack ground away from the rank and turned right toward Hyndland Road, thus seeming to suggest that Greenfield was indeed her destination.

When he stepped back into the hall, he found his mother, in a great state of agitation, leaning over the rail at the top of the staircase. "Has she gone?"

"Bag an' baggage," Gordon said. "What happened?"

"Did she tell you where she was headed?"

"Gone to Kirsty's, I think."

"Come up here, son."

He did not take time to remove his topcoat. He tossed hat and gloves on to the hall table and climbed the grand staircase to join his mother on the landing.

She said, quietly now, "Daddy would like a word with you."

"Daddy?"

"Albert, I mean," Madge told him. "An' please behave yourself, Gordon. We've had enough trouble here for one afternoon."

Gordon had more than an inkling of what had happened and why Lorna had flown off in such high dudgeon. He had known for a week now what was in her mind and had expected some such outburst. He entered the living room to find Breezy seated on the sofa, brandy glass in hand, puffing away on a cigarette as if his life depended on it. The memory of their last little tête-à-tête was fresh in Gordon's mind and it diminished the concern he might otherwise have felt for his stepfather.

Breezy beckoned him towards the fire. "Come over here

where I can see you, son."

"Somethin' wrong?"

"Aye. Lorna's gone."

"So I gather," said Gordon.

"It seems Kirsty's openin' up the shop in Gascoigne Street again an' that Lorna's to be the manager. Manager! At her age!" Breezy tossed the cigarette into the fire and squinted at his stepson. "You knew about all this, didn't you?"

"I knew Kirsty had decided to go back to shopkeepin'," Gordon said. "In fact, I was offered a certain sum for my holdin' in the shop – an' I accepted."

"Why didn't you tell me?"

"I didn't think it was all that important."

"Have I not always taken an interest in what you do?"

"Absolutely," Gordon said. "But I thought it was time I learned to stand on my own feet."

"You didn't sell the property, did you?"

"No, I wouldn't do that," said Gordon. "You gave me the property in a gift, right enough, but it's only mine on trust."

"Is that the way you look at it, really?"

Gordon said, "The few quid I put into the business to get Kirsty started, that was my own; so I felt no compunction about recoupin' it – with interest."

"Do you need money?" Breezy said. "You're not in debt or anythin'?"

"'Course I'm not in debt. How would I be in debt?"

"I thought – well, a flutter on the horses."

"I can't help Kirsty now," said Gordon. "Come this summer I'll be married an' out of it. Tubbs can find her stock, keep an' eye on things."

"He's after Lorna, you know."

"Tubby's all right," said Gordon.

"He's after her money; my money."

For a moment Gordon wondered if his stepfather was making a joke, if this whole thing was some sort of music hall sketch with a big laugh at the end of it. He scrutinised Breezy carefully, saw no trace of the old, easy levity in the man's eyes.

"But," Gordon said, "the shop's got nothin' to do with you."

Breezy squinted, one lid screwed shut. He looked not only old at that instant, but ugly and sly. He tapped the side of his nose with his forefinger. "That's the cleverness of it."

"What?"

"Once they're in," Breezy said, "there'll be no keepin' them out."

"I think you've misjudged Tubbs," said Gordon.

"He's a salesman, isn't he?"

"Well – yes, but – "

"First he'll take over the shop, then he'll worm his way into Lorna's affections – "

"I think he has already."

" – an' then he'll expect me to finance him in some extravagant venture."

"Ah!" said Gordon, with sudden understanding.

"It's different wi' you," Breezy went on, turning the brandy glass round and round in his thin fingers. "You're a man, for one thing."

"Right," said Gordon, nodding.

"I'm goin' to let you into a secret, son." Breezy motioned him to come closer still and, peering at the door furtively, confided, "I'm on the verge o' makin' a killin'."

"I see," said Gordon.

"Guess how much?"

"Ten thousand?"

"Ninety thousand."

"What? Pounds?"

Breezy gave a cock of the head, grinned. "What do you think o' that then?"

"I'm – I'm flabbergasted."

"Out o' thin air too," said Breezy.

"Stock an' shares?"

Breezy tapped his nose with his forefinger again but the gesture, this time, had a different connotation. "Never you mind what or how, son. But that's the price. Aye, I'm not exactly a poor man but when this transaction is completed – "

"Does mother know?"

"God, no. Nobody knows," said Breezy. "But think of it, Gordon, ninety thousand pounds in one deal. Can you see why I'm worried about Lorna?"

For the life of him Gordon could not make an integral connection between his sister's act of rebellion and Breezy's sumptuous piece of business.

"Well – "

"I don't want anythin' to go wrong," said Breezy. "An' I don't want some tuppeny-ha'penny salesman tryin' to climb into my family by the back door, just to get his hands on a share of money that rightly belongs to you."

"An' to Lorna?"

"She's just a girl," said Breezy. "It's a fact of life that women don't count as much as men."

"I still don't see – "

"You will," Breezy said, "in time."

There was a term for the condition that had possessed Breezy Adair but Gordon could not think of it offhand. The name hardly mattered. It was sad to see it manifest in a man who had until recently been hearty and generous and who, under the influence of greed, was visibly changing not only his character but his very shape.

Curiously Gordon felt no excitement at all at the thought of inheriting the vast sum that Breezy had virtually promised him. He had been around the city long enough to realise what such a capital sum could be made to yield by diligent investment. In twenty years or thirty, certainly before he reached Breezy's present age, he would be not just well off but incredibly rich – even without marrying Amanda, without Carruth's Brewery to put in his pocket.

Breezy reached for Gordon's hand, gripped and held it.

"But, son," he said, "you've got to play fair by me."

"In what way?"

"All of you – you've got to play fair by me."

"Do as you say?"

"Exactly!"

Gordon did not withdraw his hand, though that was his immediate impulse. He smiled, but there was no warmth in it, no trace of the boyish charm that had once come so naturally. He was thinking how it was that every man had a weakness that might bring him down, that Breezy's weakness lay in the manner in which he had acquired power and the ease with which he'd used it until now. Power, money, sentimentality; even Gordon, young as he was, sensed what a dangerous compound that could be in a man who was slipping from grace.

He thought for a while then, choosing his words with care, said, "You can count on me, Albert."

"I know I can," said Breezy and, like some unctuous old jobber from the bourse, shook Gordon's hand in both his own.

Four

A Helping Hand

Marching fever had taken hold of Greenfield Constabulary with a vengeance. To the rank and file there seemed to be no particular reason for it, except that universal enthusiasm for matters military had shined up the image of the local volunteer corps, the Boys' Brigade and even the Band of Hope. All of them were marching, marching mad, and Chief Constable Organ certainly didn't want his fine body of men to be left behind in the smartness stakes.

The monthly shuffle round the drill yard behind Percy Street Headquarters had become a regular weekly parade led by Lieutenant Chittock, a pipsqueak martinet borrowed from Partick to instil discipline into the lesser burgh's Force. Mr Organ was, however, far too responsible a personage to squander time and money on teaching his squadrons a smart salute or a crisp *"Hab-hout Fice"*, just to give the public a show. There had to be more to it. It did not take long for intelligent constables, like Craig Nicholson, to work out that the new regime was not unconnected with outbreaks of violence that, in spite of the Second City's prosperity, indicated a growing unrest in certain sections of the industrial working class.

Mass meetings, Socialist rallies, Trade Union disputes and even strikes were becoming almost commonplace in the streets and squares of Glasgow. There had been some enormous demonstrations, with oceanic crowds voicing protest with such unremitting vehemence that at times it must have seemed that Ladysmith and Mafeking were not the only places in the world laid siege to by savages.

Recognition of the purpose behind the drills made them no easier to endure. Though night shift and back shift coppers were expected to sacrifice sleep to turn out, no extra payments were made for the duty. It became an exercise in stamina and patience to stand there after a night on the beat listening to ferret-faced Chittock squeaking commands and bearded Sergeant Byrne clipping your heels with a truncheon if you dared fall out of step. Only some of the old sweats, like John Boyle, actually enjoyed it. But one constable, one alone, had all his weaknesses exposed by the discipline of early morning turn-outs. If you couldn't walk a straight line an hour after daybreak you couldn't walk one at all and Andy McAlpine had only himself to blame.

How, in God's name, Andy managed to smuggle a half pint bottle of rotgut whisky on to the parade ground, let alone consume half its contents while actually on the march, was a dismal little mystery to which there was no solution.

"THAT MAN, STAND STILL."

"Oh-oh!" Ronnie murmured from the corner of his mouth. "He's at it again."

"Cooked his goose this time," Archie whispered.

"SILENCE, SILENCE IN THE RANKS."

"Sergeant Drummond, is that constable unwell?" Mr Organ spoke from the little wooden platform that served him as an observation post.

"I cannot be sure, sir."

"Well, I suggest you enquire, Sergeant."

"Yes, sir. I will do that immediately, Mr Organ."

There was nothing that Sergeant Drummond could do to protect Andy now. The Chief Constable was down off the po-dium and, hands behind his back, was sauntering towards the luckless Andy even as Drummond and Byrne converged. Andy, swaying from the ankles like Little Tich, seemed oblivious to the spotlight of attention.

"STAND STILL," yelled Lieutenant Chittock to hold the squadron in place while Mr Organ and the sergeants, almost simultaneously, reached the constable in question.

Mr Organ knew perfectly who McAlpine was of course, but he asked nonetheless, "What's your name, Constable?"

91

By way of reply Andy grinned and shook his head.

He'd been drunk when he'd rolled into barracks and it had been all Archie and the other lads could do to stop that fact being discovered. He'd been drunk again this morning before breakfast, and it was clear to anyone with half an eye that Andy McAlpine's career was hanging by the merest thread.

"Come away with you, McAlpine," Sergeant Drummond cajoled, "tell the Chief Constable who you are," while Mr Organ, stepping close to the aberrant copper, whispered angrily, "Damn it, McAlpine, tell me your name and tell me you're sick or something. Give me some excuse to save your damned neck."

Andy expressed himself by retching and, before the Chief Constable could retreat, was violently sick all over the senior officer's birdseye tweeds.

It was all too public, too extreme. Finally and irrevocably Andy was a goner. There wasn't a man on parade did not feel a certain relief when McAlpine was led off by the sergeants through the little back door of Headquarters never to be seen in a blue uniform again.

"Where's the wife?" said Ronnie Norbert, a half hour later as he, Archie and Craig left the precincts. "It's really all her bloody fault, you know."

"Blame the wife," said Archie. "Everybody always blames the wife. I mean, we all know he used to thump the poor woman, aye, an' brag about it later."

"He did worse than thump her," said Ronnie, darkly.

"What d'you mean?" said Archie."

"Shut it, Ronnie." Craig had also heard rumours about Andy McAlpine's proclivities but did not feel that such knowledge should be shared with an innocent like Archie.

"What's wrong wi' you?" said Ronnie, tired and prickly.

"Nothin'," said Craig. "I just don't think we should gloat over another man's misfortune."

"Bloody hell! When did you get so pernickety? I mean, it was your wife what started it."

It was like old times, those days when Ronnie had been a probationer under Constable Nicholson's wing. The hand suddenly clamped to the nape of his neck reminded Ronnie of hard lessons given but not received. He had sense enough not to struggle or retaliate for, though he was no coward, Ronnie knew only too well that he could not match Craig Nicholson's strength or aggression.

"Easy, Craig, easy," Archie, cast in the role of peacemaker, said. "Ronnie didna mean any harm."

"Right," Ronnie agreed. "No offence?"

"Andy hasn't been sober since I've known him," said Archie. "It has nothin' to do wi' Mrs Nicholson at all."

"Right," said Ronnie.

The vice-like fist released itself from the flesh between Ronnie's collar and helmet-rim. He waggled his head this way and that and tried not to show that it caused him pain.

"We've seen Andy at it," Craig said. "You an' me, Ronnie, we know who he palled up with. Bad company."

"I agree," said Ronnie. "She was right to leave him."

"I don't want to hear another word about McAlpine."

"But what if he comes back?" said Archie. "What if we find him drunk some night, lyin' in the gutter? What'll we do?"

Craig and Ronnie Norbert, in agreement at last, said in unison, "Arrest him."

*   *   *

Twenty minutes later Craig arrived in Canada Road and to his amazement and alarm found his mother hanging about the close mouth at No. 154. It had been weeks since last they'd met and then, as usual, they'd squabbled. On that occasion only concern for Bobby and Kirsty had obliged them to keep their Nicholson tempers in check. Now here she was, on a cold, dusty morning, looking just as haughty as ever but with an added touch of agitation that caused Craig to blurt out, "What's up? Has somethin' happened."

"There's nobody at home."

"Kirsty's probably gone round to the shop."

"What? Bobby too?"

"Aye, why not? He's long out o' danger an' the exercise does him good."

Madge sniffed disapprovingly. She had no servant with her today and her finery was very slightly dishevelled, as if she had dressed in haste.

"Well," she said, "what do you think of havin' your sister for a lodger."

"Eh?"

"I suppose she's gone round to that damned shop too."

"I don't know what you're bletherin' about, Mam."

"Last night – Lorna turned up uninvited last night, didn't she?"

"Not here she didn't," Craig said.

"God, then where is she?"

Almost as if he were effecting an arrest Craig put a hand on his mother's arm to steady her. "Come on, we'll toddle round to Gascoigne Street, see if she's there."

"Oh, God! What if she's not?"

"We'll cross that bridge when we come to it," Craig said.

By the time Craig and his mother had reached Gascoigne Street the woman had given him all the colourful details of Lorna's rebellious retreat from the bosom of her loving family but, curiously, blamed her daughter's behaviour not only on Tubbs but also on Albert Adair.

Lorna was indeed with Kirsty at No. 1 Gascoigne Street and, by an unfortunate coincidence, Mr Ernest Tubbs had just dropped in to cadge a cup of tea. It was hardly the time or place for a grand battle. The reopening of Nicholson's Domestic Emporium had attracted a certain amount of attention and the blazing row that flared up within seconds of Craig and his mother crossing the threshold soon drew quite a little crowd of eavesdroppers to the door. None of the housewives or messenger-boys who loitered outside would have dared to step indoors, though, for Nicholson's was clearly not open for business in any sense of that word. If the general public was entertained, however, there was no levity within. The family went at each other hammer-and-tongs, in voices so strident that they carried clear through the walls and relayed every word to interested parties in the street.

"What? You're sleepin' with him?" Madge shouted.

"I am nothin' of the kind," Lorna retorted. "I am merely residin' at Ernest's house in the meantime."

"With my mother's gracious per – " Ernest tried to say.

"Did you know about this arrangement, Kirsty?" Craig put in.

"No, but I see no harm in it, really."

"Christ, does nothin' offend you any more?"

"This dirty devil's ruined you, Lorna," Madge said.

"Here, steady on," said Ernest. "We're a perfectly respectable family. My mother an' brother would never stand for any hanky-panky, Mrs Nicholson."

"I've got my own room." Lorna stated.

"With a lock on the door," Ernest added.

"You've lured an innocent young girl away from her nearest an' dearest just to have your way wi' her," Madge ranted. "Craig, is there not a law against child-stealin'?"

"Well," Craig said, "Lorna's too old to be – "

"What did you want me to do, Mother?" Lorna chipped in. "Sleep on the damned pavement?"

"You might as well be walkin' the streets as livin' with him."

"Steady on, Mrs Nicholson," said Ernest again.

"Adair," Madge shouted. "The name's Adair."

"Was this your idea, Kirsty?" Craig said.

"Of course it wasn't."

"Right." Madge grabbed her daughter's arm. "I've had enough o' this nonsense. You're comin' home wi' me this instant, missy."

To his eternal credit Ernest braved Madge's wrath. He stepped nimbly between mother and daughter, arms folded across his chest.

"I don't think Lorna wants to go with you, Mrs Nicholson."

"ADAIR!"

"All right – Adair," said Ernest. "I assure you that Lorna's perfectly safe where she is. In fact, Lorna an' I are engaged to be married."

"Since when?"

"Since last night," said Lorna, smugly.

Madge wheeled to Craig then to Kirsty, screaming, "SEE!"

"Congratulations, Lorna," Kirsty said. "But you could've stayed with us, you know, rather than Ernest."

"He'd never have let me stay," Lorna pointed a finger at her brother. "He'd have marched me right back to mother."

"I'm bloody sure I would, an' all," Craig said.

"I do intend to marry Lorna, you know," said Ernest.

"Aye, now you've had your fun wi' her."

Lorna darted forward and gave her mother a shove with the heels of her hands. "How dare you say that. How dare you insult Ernest. He's always behaved like a perfect gentleman, I'll have you know."

"Huh!" Craig snorted.

"Don't be so sneery, Craig," Kirsty said. "Haven't you caused enough division in the family as it is?"

Bobby had been listening, fascinated, to the verbal warfare and decided at this juncture to throw in his lot with his mother. He slipped his fist into her hand and leaned his head against her thigh, scowling.

"Me!" Craig exploded. "God, if I'd been given my rightful place as the head o' the house in the first place none of this would have happened."

Madge now rounded on her eldest, her ally. "I hope you're not implyin' that Albert – "

"Albert didn't stop her from runnin' away, did he?" Craig hooked his thumbs into his belt and rocked on the balls of his feet. "Lorna will not be returnin' with you, Tubbs. She'll be goin' home with her mother."

"Says who?"

"Says me."

"Keep out of it, Craig," Kirsty warned. "Lorna's old enough to know her own mind."

"I am not goin' back to the terrace," said Lorna.

"Well, you can stay wi' us then," said Craig, magnanimously.

"I think Lorna's happy enough stayin' where she is," said Ernest Tubbs.

"Lorna, I forbid you to stay wi' this man," said Craig.

"You can't. You're not my father."

Madge said, "We'll just see what your father – "

"Albert Adair isn't my father either," Lorna declared. "My father's dead, in case you've all forgotten."

It was suddenly all too much for Madge who burst into a flood of tears and finding nobody willing, at first, to console her leaned her elbows on the counter and sobbed into her fur muff. Ernest was the only one present soft-hearted enough to offer the big woman comfort. Awkwardly, he patted her shoulder and muttered, "There, there, Mrs Nicholson."

"Adair," Lorna, uncontrite, said. "Remember that her name's Adair."

In the end nothing was settled and, with anger and energy pointlessly expended, Craig escorted his mother to the door.

"I'll see you about this later, Kirsty," he said.

"No doubt you will."

From the window Kirsty watched Craig lead his mother across Dumbarton Road to the cab stand at Peel Street and then, to her annoyance, saw him clamber into the cab too and ride off along the thoroughfare.

"Daddy gone away?" said Bobby.

"He's takin' Grandma home."

"Gramma's cryin'."

"Yes, she's got a sore tummy."

"Auntie Lorna got a sore tummy too?"

Lorna had retreated behind the curtain into the back shop where, weeping too, she clung to her traveller like an arboreal vine.

"I think so, son," said Kirsty.

She wondered why she felt no guilt at all at the part she'd played in encouraging the affair and resolved, there and then, to stand by her decision to offer Lorna a helping hand no matter what Craig decreed to the contrary.

*   *   *

Adair's wholesale warehouse in Partick East hadn't changed at all in the time that Gordon had been away from it. There was the same familiar muddle of packing materials, same familiar smell of straw and wood-shavings, and old Bert Ramsden was still whistling the same cheery tune as he cracked open boxes with the back of his hammer. It was all so different from the brewery and Gordon could not help but feel a twinge of wistful nostalgia as he hurried down the aisle towards the office at the rear. Bone china dinner services, painted vases, canteens of cutlery, rolls of carpet, gasoliers and enamel cold boxes cluttered the walkway, friendly junk that Gordon could have sold without breaking sweat. He returned the greetings of the porters with a wave, though conscious of the fact that he had no place here now, no status in the hurly-burly world of which John Whiteside was king.

Johnnie was the only son of Breezy's sister, Heather. He had been educated for the legal profession until Breezy had lured him, together with his cousin Eric, into commerce. Johnnie and Eric not only managed the warehouse but ran all sorts of shady errands for Breezy on the side and had been promised, in exchange, the lion's share of Breezy's fortune when the old boy eventually passed on to his maker. All that had changed, however, when Breezy had married a farmer's widow from Ayrshire and Gordon Nicholson had crept out of the hayricks to stake his claim. Gordon knocked on the pebble-glass door of the office and, without awaiting an invitation, opened it and entered. John Whiteside, at his desk, glanced up in surprise.

"Well, well, this is an honour." He was still the same supercilious and sarcastic beggar as he'd always been, the insolent smile on his handsome lips and the calculation in his eyes unchanged. "Buyin' stuff for the little love nest already, Gordie?"

"Nope. But if I was I wouldn't be after your discount rubbish," Gordon said. "Matter of fact, I just dropped in for a cup of coffee, since I was in the neighbourhood."

"Your wish is my command, old chum."

Johnnie furnished Gordon with a mug of strong black coffee from the Kaffé Kanne that steamed away on a gas ring on the floor behind the desk. He offered Gordon cigars from a box, cigarettes from a tin and, when the visitor had thus been graciously received, swung his feet on to the litter of invoices and bills on the desk, tilted back the swivel chair and studied the younger man from under half-lowered eyelids.

"How's your nephew? I heard that he was ill."

"Bobby's on the mend," Gordon said. "Thanks."

"And my dear Uncle Breezy? I haven't seen him for ages. Is he in good fettle?"

"Fightin' fit."

Johnnie paused to suck on his cigar before he said, "And Amanda?"

"Lovely as always," Gordon said.

Gordon sipped coffee and lit a fresh cigarette. He was not here to taunt. He had known for a long time that Johnnie's interest in his cousin was hardly pure and that a worm of envy nibbled at the edges of his cynicism. It was, however, he and not Whiteside who would eventually possess Amanda, he who had had the guts to take on Dolphus.

"Sellin' lots of froth for Uncle Dolphus, are we?" Johnnie said, at length.

"Lots an' lots," said Gordon.

It was a twig from the main branch of brewery business that had brought him here this morning. He was too shrewd, too well versed in the manners of the educated classes, to come directly to the point, however. He'd let Johnnie wonder for a while yet before he injected into casual conversation the questions that he'd come here to ask. It was only when Johnnie pushed the chair away from the desk and stooped to refill the coffee mugs that Gordon said, "Heard anythin' of Greta Taylor, John?"

Johnnie squinted round at him. "I'm the last person she'd keep in touch with. Why do you ask?"

"Curiosity."

Johnnie grinned. "Fancy a final fling with wee Greta before the bonds of matrimony are drawn tight?"

Gordon did his best to affect the knowing look that marked the Adair males from mere milksops. "Well – "

"You had your chance, once," Johnnie reminded him.

"Ah, yes, if only I'd known what I was missin'."

Johnnie hesitated. "Do you want an address?"

"Greta's address?"

"God, no. I don't know where she is," Johnnie said. "I meant the address of another fair damsel who, for a modest sum, would instruct you in the amorous arts."

"Damned decent of you, old son," said Gordon, "but I really don't require that sort of instruction."

Puff on the cigar: "Amanda will expect a certain, ah, worldly wisdom from her bridegroom, you know."

The lie was out before he could prevent it. "Amanda already knows what to expect."

He had the satisfaction of seeing Whiteside's face fall and of hearing a little stammer enter the implacable voice. "Wh – what d – do you mean?"

Gordon, borrowing one of Breezy's occasional gestures, tapped the side of his nose with a forefinger. "Enough said, I think."

"D – do you mean – "

"Oh, by the way," Gordon interrupted, "while we're on the subject of fair damsels, what can you tell me about Walter's eldest?"

"Josephine?"

"Yes, the reformer."

"Tight-buttocked bitch!" said Johnnie, nastily. "Why, what's your interest in that direction?"

"She's a leadin' light in the Temperance Association, I believe," Gordon said. "One of the odder wee jobs chaps like me have to do is to keep an eye on the opponents of strong drink."

"Oh, that one's into every joyless, interferin' cause you can name," Johnnie said. "Socialism, Radicalism, Suffragism, Temperance Reform – "

"Is she an Evangelist?"

"God, no. Nothin' churchy. She's the new breed of woman. She doesn't believe in meddlin' with God, only with the Rights of Man. You've met her – at Dolphus's garden party last summer an' at that little theatre supper Eric and I threw last year."

"Aye, I remember. Big girl, blonde."

"Built like a prize heifer," Johnnie Whiteside said.

There was two-fold pleasure for Gordon in fulfilling the latest task allotted him by Mr Friendship, an ongoing chore that Carruth's other travellers and clerks sought to avoid. Gordon congratulated himself on recalling that one of the Adair clan was a Temperance Reformer. What's more Josephine Adair was the only one of the younger generation who did not stand in awe of handsome Johnnie Whiteside.

"I'm surprised you haven't heard about Josephine before now," Johnnie went on, unsolicited. "She's quite a joke in family circles."

"Why's that?"

"Don't you know? Her father's a broker in whisky and wine. Tremendous irony, what! Old Walter selling the intoxicatin' while his darlin' daughter's out there supporting a platform that could ruin his business at the stroke of a parliamentary pen. Dolphus's business too, come to think of it."

"Where does she live?"

"Not sure," said Johnnie. "I hear she has lodgings in Glasgow. The family home is out of town, at Mosswell Bank in the wilds of north Ayrshire. Large house and a tidy parcel of land with it, all bought on the proceeds of the sale of liquor, of course. I wonder if the bitch would have been quite so Reformist in her views if she'd been raised without privilege?"

"Perhaps her father respects her opinions."

"Walter's certainly a retirin' soul," said Johnnie, "but I cannot believe that a born-and-bred Adair would put up with lip from a girl."

"Walter doesn't supply to Carruth's, does he?"

"He absolutely refuses to do business with the family," Johnnie said. "It's been his golden rule since he first went into whisky brokerage. He values his independence, apparently."

"Like Josephine," Gordon said.

"What? Oh, yes. Very droll," Johnnie stubbed out the remains of his cigar with a brusqueness that indicated he might be losing patience with his visitor.

Gordon got to his feet. "Thank you for the coffee, Johnnie, an' the information."

"Precious good it'll do you, old chum. Better men than you have tried to put a spoke in the Temperance wheel – and failed miserably," Johnnie said.

"All I have to do is attend a few meetin's an' submit a report on what's said an' done, what's mooted an' resolved."

"Josephine won't help you, you know."

"Well, I might chance my arm."

"Be careful she doesn't bite it off." Whiteside too got to his feet, offered his hand. "Incidentally, and strictly between ourselves, how was Amanda?"

"Delectable," said Gordon, with a wink.

"Does she ever ask about me?"

"No, can't honestly say she does."

"Well . . . Look, give her my fondest, will you?"

"Why, of course I will, old son," said Gordon.

He did not look back after he'd left the office, though he knew that Johnnie was still in the doorway, staring after him. He swaggered a little as he headed up the walkway and, just before he left the building, picked old Bert Ramsden's jaunty tune to whistle himself into the street.

*   *   *

In normal circumstances the wayward behaviour of a daughter would have drawn the Nicholsons into a council of war against whose unity and determination neither Tubby nor Kirsty would have stood a chance. Lorna would have been hauled back to the terrace with wailings and lamentation and would have had to settle for a more suitable beau than Mr Tubbs or remain forever a spinster. The Nicholsons, however, were not a family united and for that reason, among others, a strange paralysis stole over its various members in respect of Lorna's moral recalcitrance.

In Lorna's opinion, which she voiced often in the shelter of the shop, the calendar had conferred upon her, as on all young people, a certain right to be feckless and to discard, as a sacrifice to the twentieth century, the responses and repressions of their forefathers. Kirsty did not agree. Though only a few years older than her sister-in-law, she felt no magic in the air in the spring of the year 1900. There had been no thawing in the neighbours' attitude towards Kirsty – indeed, it had become even more chilly after Andy had been dismissed from the Force – and Craig was sulking again because she would not side with him against Lorna.

Days accumulated into weeks and nothing much changed or altered on the surface of things. Lorna continued to live with the Tubbs family and to travel down to the shop by tramcar every morning and Ernest, when he could, would pick her up in the evening and escort her home. From the Adairs of Great Western Terrace not another word was heard until the month was well and truly out.

Re-stocking the shop absorbed the best part of Kirsty's attention. Great packing cases from Mathieson, Mullard & Milroy's warehouse would arrive almost daily. To her consternation they would contain goods that she hadn't ordered and of which she had no knowledge whatsoever.

"Ernest, I wish you'd tell me what you're buyin'," she'd complain.

"But why?"

"Because I'm your partner an' should know what to expect."

"Expect the best, Mrs N, expect only the best."

"That's all very well but – "

"Do you want me to return the stuff?"

"No, but – "

The legion of commercial gentlemen who had once haunted the shop seemed to have melted away, as if they knew something that Kirsty did not. And there were no more penny oddments, gewgaws and trinkets in Mr Tubbs' consignments. Out came the heavy artillery; Lambent light fittings, Ready water heaters, posh, polished gas stoves, all goods that any housewife in Greenfield would love to possess but which she would never be able to afford on an average income of twenty-one bob a week.

"We'll never sell all this stuff, you know," Kirsty would complain.

"Tubby says we will," Lorna would retort.

"Tubby's not payin' for it."

"Oh, yes, he is," Lorna would remind her. "Half, anyway."

"Gordon never brought us anythin' like this. Where does Ernest find it all at these prices?"

"Connections."

"Warehouse connections?"

"And others," Lorna would say darkly, though she knew no more about Ernest's sources of supply than Kirsty did.

The hardware was ponderous, angular and difficult for the women to handle unaided, and there seemed to be so much of it. Bobby, however, was delighted by the packed shop. If he missed Jen and Greta he gave no sign of it. He would spend hours at the counter helping his Auntie Lorna by scrawling on scraps of paper and generally making a mess with the ink. He had also become fond of mountaineering and made perilous ascents of piles of boxes or, when Kirsty's back was turned, would embark on hair-raising traverses of the laden shelves, the caliper clinking behind him.

In spite of Kirsty's pessimism, one by one customers returned, schoolgirls and servant lassies in search of trinkets, and even one or two men, attracted by the ironware, would sidle in to inspect the gas appliances. The first lady from the illustrious heights of Dowanhill to grace the shop was old Mrs Briggs, a well-heeled widow who enjoyed spending money and whose house, so Kirsty had heard, was crammed with bric-à-brac. Mrs Briggs could not resist antique jardinières and kettles that hung like Aladdin's lamps from ornate copper stands. To the accompaniment of audible groans from her overworked maid, Mrs Briggs bought several convoluted metal objects and, as was her habit, paid cash for them there and then. She also gave Bobby, who was temporarily earthbound, a silver sixpence to 'help his leg mend' and, in case money was not enough, murmured a little prayer over him too, an act of kindness that brought a tear to Kirsty's eye and cheered her a bit as an omen for the future.

As the days passed, though, Kirsty became disturbed by the

lack of communication from her in-laws.

"Haven't you heard from your mother, Lorna?"

"No, thank God."

"What about Breezy? Hasn't he been in touch?"

"Not him."

"It's most unlike him," Kirsty said.

"I think he's frightened."

"What, of you?"

"I don't think Breezy knows what to do about me," Lorna said. "I mean, if he'd just let me marry Tubby, all our problems would be solved."

"If you married Tubby where would you stay?"

"With his mother, where we are now."

"What does Ernest's brother have to say about that?"

Lorna snapped, "Are you against us too?"

"No, of course not, but – "

"You're going to advise us to wait, aren't you? I don't want to wait, Kirsty. I want to marry Ernest as soon as possible."

"Are you engaged?"

"Unofficially, yes."

"How does Ernest's mother feel about it?"

"She's all for it," Lorna answered, just a shade too hastily.

"An' Frank?" said Kirsty again.

"Frank wouldn't stand in our way."

"What about Gordon?"

"Gordon?"

"Your brother," Kirsty reminded her.

"Oh, him! Gordon's all tied up with his own marriage and couldn't care less about me."

"But nothing from Madge? No word from Breezy?"

"Not a sausage."

Kirsty sighed. "I can't understand it."

Lorna paused and then, with a touch of sorrow in her voice, admitted, "Frankly, Kirsty, neither can I."

*   *   *

Dirt, vermin and low morals had no place within the precincts of the Claremont Model lodging-house. Standards had been set ten years ago by the Greenfield Burgh Improvement Trust and were maintained by regular inspections from the Sanitary

Officer. The appointment of Mr Black as Superintendent had been a stroke of good fortune for the burgh, though. Mr Black was a man of considerable character, tough yet fair. He had a genuine concern for the welfare of the men who called the Claremont 'home' and gave short shrift to those do-gooders who saw his modellers as mere creatures without souls.

The Claremont was registered to accommodate sixty-two males, forty residents in individual sleeping chambers and the remainder, all 'casuals', in iron cots in cubicles in the attic. The Claremont did not house women. Mr Black had nothing against the weaker sex. He treated his three cleaners and two female cooks with the greatest respect. Even so, he was relieved that his was an all-male establishment. Women in lodgings usually brought trouble and the Claremont had been remarkably trouble-free during his years of tenure – until, that is, Hog Moscrop arrived.

Widower Moscrop would never have convinced the members of the Management Committee that he was worthy of a permanent berth in the Claremont. Hog's son, however, had found work in Leicester and had expressed concern for his father's welfare and his ability to maintain the rented house in Benedict Street without supervision and occasional financial help. Hog's son had also agreed to remit, by a banker's draft, the sum of seven shillings each week for his father's keep, which was a small price to pay for being rid of the old devil. He also persuaded his father to relinquish tenancy of the council-owned property in Benedict Street. Hog was not entirely without means. He wasn't quite so old as he looked and still possessed a dock labourer's ticket which entitled him to seek casual work when he felt like it or needed money for booze. If Ottawa Street's constables had been consulted, Hog Moscrop would have had a character so black that the Union of Chimneysweeps wouldn't have taken him on, let alone the managers of the Claremont. Sonny Moscrop's pitch was convincing, however, Hog had no criminal record as such and, alas and alack for all concerned, there happened to be a vacant cubicle on the upper floor just begging to be filled.

Though he moaned and wailed something awful on the day of his departure from Benedict Street, Hog had a few bob in his pocket from the sale of his furniture and was secretly pleased to be shot of the responsibility of caring for his own welfare. In addition he cherished the arrogant notion that a man of his calibre would be welcome at the Claremont and would soon have the place running to suit himself. Hog had another think coming.

He made his first serious error about an hour after his arrival. Pecking order in the Claremont's canteen and communal room was well established and when, after supper, Hog lived up to his name by grabbing the best seat on the bench in front of the stove he was lifted, literally, by the scruff of the neck, swung away and dropped to the boards with a bump.

Hog's eyes turned red as smelting coals and his brown teeth showed in a snarl as he scrambled to his full height of five feet, four inches and swung round to confront his attacker.

"Somethin' wrong?" said Tinker Hulse.

"Eh – aw – naw. Nothin' at all," said Mr Moscrop meekly. "Your – your seat, was it but?"

"Aye," said Tinker Hulse.

"Eh – aw – where wid ye like me t' sit then?"

Tinker Hulse told Mr Moscrop where he would like him to sit and Mr Moscrop sat there, while the other occupants of the big, smoky room sniggered quietly.

The residents were, for the most part, quiet, likeable men, given to the practice of democratic principles. Fortunately for Hog Moscrop, Tinker Hulse was not a permanent resident but a casual who would drift in with the tide three or four times a year and would stay only a night or two before vanishing again. When he was around, though, Tinker Hulse was clearly the boss, and when you looked up at him you understood why. Tinker Hulse was six feet, seven inches tall and built like a Linthouse dredger.

Mr Moscrop remained seated on the coggle stool half a mile from the warmth of the stove for five long, long minutes, the smile riveted on to his face and then, when Mr Hulse's attention was diverted, slipped ignominiously away to seek solace, and smaller company, in Slattery's public house.

Few restrictions were placed on the movements of Claremont residents, except that an eleven o'clock curfew was imposed for those not on night work. Mr Moscrop had just enough sense left to leave Slattery's early and return to the model about ten minutes to the hour, full of Jamaica rum and Dutch courage and spoiling to avenge the insult to his honour. He walked past the Superintendent's cabin without a stagger, turned the corner into the half-tiled corridor, reeled forward and barged into the communal room with a terrific clatter.

"YOU!" he bellowed.

Tinker Hulse and the elderly Mr Thom were playing dominoes and drinking cocoa at a table by the stove. They looked up, surprised, as Hog did his war dance, shaking his fists, snarling, and challenging Mr Hulse to put up his bloody dukes and fight like a man.

"'Scuse me," said Tinker Hulse to his companion.

He rose. He crossed the room.

Hog Moscrop was spitting fire, stumpy arms flailing, boots shuffling in parody of the fancy footwork of Jimmy 'The Killer' Deans who had once, thirty years since, been his boxing hero.

"What dae ye want?" said Mr Hulse, politely.

"Puttim up, puttim up. Ah'm no' scared o' the likes o' ... *yoooooo ... oooooo ... oooooo ... oh!*"

The little man's challenge became a cry of astonishment that diminished into an echo as Tinker Hulse picked him up again, tucked him under his arm, carried him along the corridor, through the entrance hall, out of the door and deposited him unceremoniously on the pavement at the bottom of the Claremont's steps.

"Sober up," said Mr Hulse, admonishingly, and then went back inside to finish his cocoa and his game.

From his cabin just inside the door Mr Black peeped out at his newest lodger. If Hog Moscrop had not been so singularly unappealing and still bristling with unjustified conceit then the Superintendent might have gone out, offered a kind word and brought the wee man in. But Mr Black had by now identified Hog's type and knew only too well that if Hog Moscrop was offered friendship he would immediately demand admiration and then servility to follow it. Hog, therefore, sat alone and unloved upon the pavement. Head in hands, he sobbed drily, full of anger, self-pity and frustration. He was still there when Archie Flynn brought Sammy home from the Mission.

Sammy was in a right queer mood, indrawn and – for Sammy – almost sullen. Archie was worried about the lad, concerned lest he was sickening for influenza or the dreaded whooping cough. When questioned, though, Sammy declared himself to be fine and had scuffed along, hand-in-hand with the embarrassed constable.

"Who's 'at?"

Archie knew Hog, of course, but Sammy did not.

Sammy broke his grip from Archie's, put his hands on his hips and peered down at the strange little figure on the steps.

"Whit're ye cryin' for, mister?"

"*Sssh!*" Archie whispered.

"Is the mannie hurtit?"

"Naw, naw," said Archie softly. "He's been drinkin' too much, that's all."

Sammy would have none of this rational explanation. He knelt on the pavement. "Mister, are y' hurtit?"

"Eh?" Hog glared.

"If ye're hurtit Mr Black'll gi'e ye a plaister."

"I'm no needin' a plaister," Hog said, gruffly.

Something in Hog's small stature, large, tousled head and air of ferocity reminded Sammy of Mr Galletti, the hunchback who'd lived in the pig mews near the Madagascar and danced and played on the drums; such, at least, was the theory when the matter was discussed by sensible men at a later date. Whatever the reason, Sammy was not intimidated by Hog Moscrop and seemed drawn to him at once.

"Ah live here," said Sammy, confidingly.

"Aye, so da I."

"M'on then, mister. Since you're new, ah'll tak' ye in wi' me. Dinna be feart."

"For God's sake, Sammy," Archie said, "the mannie's no' feart. He doesn't want t' take your hand."

"Aye," said Hog Moscrop. "Aye, but ah do."

Hog gripped the boy's wrist and hauled himself to his feet. He put an arm about the boy's shoulders and let himself be led up the steps to the door.

"Hog," Archie called out.

The little man turned, glowering.

"Hog," Archie said, "you know, the lad's not quite right."

"He's right enough for me," Hog Moscrop snapped and, to prove the point, hugged Sammy tightly to him as they passed through the door and into the Claremont like long-lost, bosom chums.

* * *

Phyllis Tubbs did not consider herself or her family in any way unusual. She was most proud of Frank, of course, for he had manfully shouldered responsibility in the years following the untimely death at the age of forty-four of her husband Ronald. Frank, like his father, was serious-minded and industrious to a fault. Frank's busy pen had paid for his brothers' education and, year by year, had increased the level of domestic comfort. Now it was Frank's talent and labour that had brought Ernest what he most desired, a shop of his very own – or nearly so.

Phyllis had abundant mother love for all her sons, respect for her firstborn that knew no bounds, but it was Ernest whom she loved most of all.

Perhaps she best loved her youngest because he gaily insisted on ploughing his own furrow and had not bowed to that pressure of tradition which would have made him enter the teaching profession against his will. Now and then the thought strayed across her mind that the reason Ernest had such an amiable nature was because he hadn't been subjected for long to his father's scholarly influence and disciplined mind. She felt disloyal to Ronald's memory in permitting such a heresy to enter her thoughts but she could not prevent it.

Ernest reminded her of her own light-hearted girlhood, of a gaiety that had been subsumed by her love for Ronald Tubbs. Her father had been a saddler in the town of Nairn on the north-east coast, her mother the daughter of a tenant farmer. The snug little town and its surrounding fields had been her whole gay world until a new young dominie arrived fresh from Glasgow, promptly fell in love with her, flattered her by his gravity and learning, wooed her decorously for three years, and then married her. She had travelled to Glasgow with him, had supported him as he struggled to gain promotion as a teacher, had borne his sons, had endured his undramatic silences and long hours spent alone while he busied himself writing essays and reviews in the narrow back bedroom that he called his study. She had woven the threads of her life to the pattern of Ronald's moods and had never once doubted that he loved her. It had torn her heart in two when he had dropped down dead while walking out of the old Academy building at half-past five on a fine May afternoon.

Since then, since the dark, haunted year that followed the tragedy, she had found a curious liberation, felt lighter and more secure with Frank to look after her, Ernest to make her laugh and her other sons and grandchildren to visit at Easter and in summer. The truth, which she could not deny without guilt, was that it suited her to have the days patterned round her wishes and not to be dominated by the needs of one man.

She had not, however, been a schoolteacher's wife and mother to teachers for all these years without learning how to read character and to evaluate a person's worth. In Lorna Nicholson she saw a spiritedness that deserved to be cultivated, something novel and modern. But she had been just as impressed by Lorna's sister-in-law, Kirsty, who was calm and cautious and seemed mature beyond her years, a result perhaps of a hard and loveless childhood in an orphanage. Even so, Phyllis Tubbs did not much like having Lorna Nicholson as a guest in her house. Something in the arrangement offended her old-fashioned sense of propriety. She had no circle of friends to whisper about it and suggest that she was condoning immorality. If word fetched out to Frank's cronies in, say, the Art Club there would perhaps be a bit of sniffing and a lifting of eyebrows but it would do Frank's reputation no harm now that he was no longer a school teacher and at the beck and call of stiff-necked governors. Nonetheless, Phyllis did not feel comfortable, and her distress, though slight, was soon picked up by her eldest son, correctly interpreted and brought into the open.

"You're fretting over nothing, Mother," Frank assured her, as they sat together in the living room late one Friday night. "Lorna will soon tire of living here and will go back to her home."

"I think you underestimate her, Frank. It's my belief that she'll stay on here until such times as she marries Ernest."

"Don't you like her?"

"I like her fine."

"What is it, then? Surely, you don't suspect that Ernest has brought her to – "

"Certainly not," said Phyllis.

"Come on. Out with it, Mother."

"We're putting temptation in his way, aren't we?"

"Don't worry, I'm keeping an eye on him."

"The girl's very attractive, and very determined," Phyllis said. "I imagine that if she's set on capturing him, Ernest won't escape."

"You're making her sound like a Barbary pirate," Frank said. "She may be independently-minded but I really don't think she's a scheming minx. In fact, I wouldn't object in the least if Ernest married her and settled down."

"Here?"

"No, no – in a house of his own."

"How can he afford it?"

"He can't, not just yet. But when the shop – "

"Is that why you bought him a partnership, Frank?"

"Partly," Frank admitted.

"And the other part?"

"If anything happens to me," Frank shrugged, "Ernest will be in a position to take care of you."

"Oh, Frank!"

"One can't be too careful, Mother."

"Is it because of what happened to your poor father that you have this morbid belief that you'll die before your time?"

"Well, recent medical studies have shown that arterial weakness can be hereditary."

"Please, Frank, no more of this talk."

"No, I'm sorry."

"You work too hard, far too hard," Phyllis told him. "That's why you're so depressed."

"Depressed? I'm not in the least depressed," Frank said.

"What are we going to do about Lorna?" said Phyllis Tubbs to draw the conversation away from a subject that she found abhorrent. "Her family seem to be in no great rush to redeem her, do they?"

"Some families are very strange," Frank said.

"Well, son, what should we do about Lorna?"

"Not a thing, Mother," Frank told her. "Let's wait for the Nicholsons to make the next move."

"What if they don't?"

"They will," Frank said.

111

"But when?"

"When it suits them, I suppose," said Frank.

*   *   *

No prior public announcement was given of the Scottish Women's League of Socialism and Temperance's Saturday afternoon rally. Gordon only got wind of it through Gerald McDade. The SWLST was known to be a thrawn bunch which took a licking not only from the thirsty masses but from long-established sects within the international Temperance Movement itself. It was frowned on by clerics and templars alike for its affiliation to dangerously radical elements on the political fringe and for a propensity to model itself on rough, unfeminine, American female groups that had fought tooth and nail through the Whiskey Wars. Glasgow was not, however, the Wild West and this was no longer the good ol' nineteenth century. Action of the sort envisaged as effective by Socialist women, many of whom were self-declared atheists, cut no ice with their august Blue Ribbon brethren. It dismayed too the pulpit orators, in spite of the fact that several ministers' wives had kicked over the traces and met and marched defiantly with their sisters in social reform.

At first Gordon had been rueful about the sincerity of the women in the League and had trotted along to Kingdom Road that Saturday afternoon burdened by ill-informed male prejudice. He had, however, never shared the average Scotsman's belief that to be a man at all it was also necessary to be a near-drunkard, and his own distaste for cereal beverages had already set him apart from the bleary mob. He was, though, heir to a brewing fortune and an employee of Carruth's and therefore disguised himself with a hunting cap and big woolly muffler just in case he was recognised and ridiculed.

The League was composed mainly of middle-class women of practical bent and active disposition, grassroots do-gooders to whom drunkenness was inextricably linked to the greater blight of national poverty. Gordon found them both comical and, somehow, rather heroic. Let Tory barons shout the odds in Westminster and vicars petition education committees for formal abstinence instruction in schools; it took women of a certain distinct character to forsake the drawing-room for a picket line along pub-packed Kingdom Road at a quarter past five on a cold Saturday afternoon.

Gordon, a country boy, had never been comfortable with *homo industrialus* gathered in mass. Nightly surges from shipyard gates and factory yards still stirred in him an urge to run. Football crowds were the worst of the lot. Hundreds, thousands of supporters would appear out of the river mists, swarm up from the quays and ferry steps that linked Greenfield with match grounds across the Clyde and head like a pagan army for the nearest pubs where friends and enemies who had bussed it home from Partick and Whiteinch were already congregating.

In the nether end of Kingdom Road bars and public houses clustered four to a block and, around five or just after, you could hear boots clacking on cobbles and wild boys baying in the lanes that bristled about the Clyde, then a great dry-throated roar as the lamps of the Greenfield were sighted and a ramstam charge began. The women had elected not to spread themselves too thinly but to concentrate their little force on the Boar's Head which, mercifully, was not a house tied to Carruth's or one in which Breezy had a financial stake. In spite of the name the Boar's Head, Greenfield version, was no quaint old-English tavern but a grubby, ill-smelling howff famed for its mutton pies, pickled eggs and cheap brands of whisky. The League, it seemed, had gone about its summoning with considerable discretion and publicans and policemen had no early warning that trouble was about to erupt in the confines of the Kingdom Road.

Gordon had hidden himself in a close mouth, behind the female picket line, with the intention of watching the progress of events as dispassionately as possible. The women, thirty in number, presented no physical threat to the hordes of men that came stampeding up from the river. The mere presence of two ranks of middle-class ladies armed with banners and silly effigies of skeletal children – the sheer blinding audacity of it – gave the crowd pause, however.

"Jesus, wull ye look't them."

"Ne'er mind them. Lemme get past."

"It's the Teetotallers."

"Ah don't care if it's the bloody Scots Guards. Ah'm dyin' for a bloody pint, so ah'm are."

"You show them, Jimmy. You gi'e them whatfor."

"Ah wull an' all. Outta ma way, y' daft bitch."

Symbolically at least the Boar's Head was blocked off by two rows of determined, chin-up ladies. Even rash Jimmy was, for a moment, daunted and that was enough time for those lads who'd been heading happily for another howff to turn perversely aside and, assuming the grim, insulted scowls of the proud and the put-upon, to square up instead for a confrontation.

"Outta ma way," Jimmy said again.

"No, sir, indeed I will not make way for you. I will not permit you to squander your miserable pittance on the purchase of intoxicating liquor."

"Ma miserable *what*?"

The woman did not back down. She was small, about thirty-five years old, and wore a coat with a fox fur collar and long leather gloves, almost like gauntlets. "See," she said, and lowered a canvas banner upon which was painted a scene of suffering so horrible that even Jimmy could not quite bring himself to look at it for long. "Your wife, your child."

"Ah'm no' even marrit, missus," Jimmy said.

"Your mother then, and your sister."

Jimmy sidestepped – the woman matched his movement. He sidestepped again – she followed suit.

"C'mon, Jimmy. Ah'm dyin' o' thirst back here."

Angrily Jimmy swung round. "You c'mon. You get rid o' her."

"Oh, yes," the woman said. "You can get rid of me very easily but can you be so easily rid of the spectre of death that your addiction to alcohol carries in its wake."

Gordon found that he was tense, very tense. He also had a weird sense of the power that the women had already gained over the unruly mob. It was remarkable how the men had been halted by a single rank of women of a class they hated with all their hearts, a sex for which they expressed nothing but scorn.

"No, don't back away, please," the woman went on. "Listen to me, I beg you. Do you not realise the effect that whisky has on the human brain?"

"What brain, missus? Jimmy disna have a brain."

"Shut yer geggie, McDowell, or ah'll smash yer face in."

The woman tried to catch Jimmy's arm and simultaneously lower the canvas banner, and Jimmy as he turned caught her

114

with his elbow and sent her flying against the wall. He was taken aback. His mouth opened and then he decided to make the best of it, snapped his jaw shut, grinned and waved a fist at his silent supporters.

"That's it, lads. We're in," he shouted and was, at that moment, felled from behind.

Jimmy was no gorilla. He was, however, only twenty-six years old and in fair condition for a heavy drinker, yet he went down like a ton of bricks, knocked cold by the fist of a blonde-haired girl whose weight of punch Big Bob Fitzsimmons might have envied. Gordon groaned into his muffler and winced as Josephine Adair's knuckles struck the shipwright just above the ear, winced again when Jimmy struck the pavement – and then he was out of the close mouth and running like a hare a split second before fighting broke out.

Gordon couldn't blame the men. Women or not, you don't just stand there with your tongue hanging out and watch one of your own kind felled by a big, snooty lassie in a wine-red coat that like as not cost more than you earned from a week's hard graft. Besides, it was clear now that if you gave this bunch of lunatics an inch the next thing you knew all the bloody pubs would be shut and it would be a criminal offence to drink ginger pop never mind spirits or a pint of beer.

Gordon heard them shouting as he scraped along the wall by the low window of the Boar's Head and tried to find the big girl in the struggling throng. Josephine Adair's impetuosity had ruined the rally. Other women were being mauled and manhandled, and were fighting back. One elderly dame had raised her hands to the skies and appeared to be calling on the Lord to smite the enemy with His just hand, but while waiting for divine intervention most League members were content to do battle with fists, feet, umbrellas, banners and bags.

News of the happening spread like wildfire, of course. Urchins and wives came racing down from side streets just as another ferryload of football supporters rolled up in a wave from Clydeside and at the same moment two black vans galloped into view from the direction of Percy Street. Gordon didn't wait for the soon-to-be-famous line of march that enabled the burgh police to contain the riot and arrest the ringleaders. He ducked under Josephine's swinging left hook, shouted, "It's me. Your cousin," grabbed her by the waist and pulled her in through the door of the public house.

She did not have time to dig in her heels.

"Where – where are you taking me?" she cried.

At least she'd recognised him as an ally and hadn't tried to strike him down.

"Out of harm's way," Gordon told her.

"Oh! I see," she said and politely let him take her hand.

Gordon could not have predicted the fuss that would be caused by his arrival within the Boar's Head. Drinkers had deserted the bar for the windows and were watching the fun outside with smug amusement while a potboy struggled to secure the door and find the grids for the windows. When Gordon and Josephine burst in it was as if a smoking bomb had been tossed across the floor. Men dived for cover. The young potboy screamed and dropped a heavy wooden gate on to the toe of a senior barman who pushed it off so hastily that it smashed a table and rattled every bottle and glass in the place.

"Anarchists," somebody shouted, which increased the panic considerably.

Gordon had already pulled Josephine through the little gate at the left side of the bar and down the shoulder-wide passage that led to the lavatory outside. The night was pierced by police whistles, guttural cries and the inevitable canine chorus from tenements. Distantly some idiot was blasting out 'Cookhouse' on a battered bugle. Josephine's cheeks were glowing and fine blonde wisps of hair adhered to her brow. She was not in the least out of breath, however.

"Why are we running away?" she asked.

Gordon was already fiddling with the latch on the gate in the brick wall that backed the pub's yard. "You knocked one o' them down."

"I know. I meant to."

"That's assault an' battery."

"No, provoked assault is not the same thing at all," she said. "Can't you get that open?"

"Actually," Gordon said, "no."

"In that case we'll have to puddy-up."

"What?"

"Help each other over. You first." She flattened her palms

against the wall, braced her arms and bowed her back. "Come
along."

"Your coat'll be ruined."

"Do you, or do you not, want to rescue me?"

"Well – aye, of course."

"Then puddy," the girl told him.

Gordon clambered awkwardly on to the girl's back. He felt
foolish in the extreme, though she seemed well able to support
him.

"Now what?" he said.

"Hang on."

She raised herself with hardly a grunt until Gordon could
haul himself on to the top of the wall and straddle the brick
ridge there. "How will you – "

"I'll manage," Josephine said. "But I can't get over with you
sitting there. Dreep. You know how to dreep, don't you? All
boys know how to dreep."

"Right."

Gordon swung himself around, clasped the wall top with both
hands, draped his length and then let go. He landed badly in a
puddle of soft mud, his hunting cap cocked over one eye.

"Now you. I'll catch you," he called out.

"I think not," said Josephine.

"What?"

"You're safe now, aren't you?"

"Yes, but – Josephine, wait!"

"Thanks for the rescue," she said. "Good night."

He leapt up but could come nowhere near the wall top with
his fingertips. In any case he knew it was hopeless. Josephine
had gone back to the fray. As if in confirmation Gordon heard
the potboy scream again within the precinct of the public house.

He beat his fist softly against the brickwork.

"Damn, damn, damn an' blast." And then, deflated, he gave
up the notion of returning to Kingdom Road and set off, limping a little, for the quiet end of Banff Street from where he
might catch a tramcar home.

*   *   *

Breezy stubbed out his cigar with such force that leaf and cin-
ders floated up from the brass ashtray on the dressing table.

"Look, Madge," he said, "I can't take much more of this. What's more, the servants are beginnin' to talk."

"Let them," Madge said. "Servants will always talk."

She spoke as if her experience of the domestic class had been gained from her present lofty position and not, as was really the case, from years of drudgery in Bankhead's laundry rooms and dairy. She was propped up haughtily on frilly bolsters and wore a ribboned bed-jacket that, in Breezy's eyes, made her appear as desirable as a young bride. Folded arms and furrowed brow indicated all too clearly, however, that Madge was not about to relent and allow him to share her bed that night. He tightened the knot of his dressing-gown cord.

"Madge, it isn't my fault," he said, trying not to whine. "I can't just barge into Tubbs' house an' bring Lorna back by force."

"You mean you won't."

"No. No, I won't," Breezy said. "She's made her bed, let her lie on it."

"Aye, but who's she lyin' on it with?" Madge said.

"That's havers," Breezy said. "Lorna's not in that sort o' danger. It's not as if Tubbs has put her up in an establishment."

"A what?"

"A love nest."

"God!"

Breezy said, "If Lorna comes back of her own free will an' apologises for her behaviour then, of course, I'll take her in an' say not another word about it."

"You say that only because you know she hasn't any intention o' comin' back," Madge fumed. "She's got everythin' her own sweet way right now so why should she come back?"

"But it isn't my fault."

"It was you started it all off when you gave Gordon that dashed shop," Madge said.

Breezy sighed. "I did it for the best, Madge."

"You did it because you wanted to be liked, because you thought you needed a family. Now you've got one, you don't much like it, do you, Albert?"

Breezy knotted the dressing-gown cord once more and pulled it tighter still about him as if to contain the anger that swelled in his belly. In fact there was some truth in Madge's accusation. Lorna's wilfulness had knocked the feet from him. He was supposed to be a jolly good fellow, a generous old buffer, to love Gordon and Lorna like a father, but nobody had told him what that sort of loving involved.

He cleared his throat. "If, just supposin', I let Lorna marry this chap, would that do the trick?"

"Trick? It's not a trick," Madge said. "It's my child's life an' her future."

"All right, all right. Tell me what you think I should do. Tell me, for God's sake."

Madge slid her arms over her bosom, and tilted her head as if the weight of it had become too much to bear. "I don't know. I don't know," she said, and began to cry.

Breezy's anger evaporated immediately. He went to the bed, seated himself by her and put an arm about her shoulders.

"There," he said. "There, there."

"Get away from me, Albert Adair."

"Och, Madge. I just want to give you a hug an' a cuddle. It'll make us both feel better."

"No, it will not. Nothin' will made me feel better. I wish – I wish I'd never set eyes on you sometimes."

Breezy got up. He turned, shoulders square and rigid, and walked stiffly to the door.

"Albert?"

He hesitated but did not turn to face her. He didn't want her to see how much she had wounded him, that the famous Breezy Adair, terror of the Exchange, had been reduced almost to tears by the flightiness of a woman.

"You can't just walk away, Albert," Madge said. "You *will* have to do somethin'."

"What?"

"Go an' see Lorna, apologise, bring her back."

"Apologise for what, though?"

"That's up to you," Madge said. "An' your conscience."

He wiped his moustache with his forefinger and brushed his cheeks surreptitiously with his knuckle, glanced over his shoulder at his wife in the bed.

"I have no conscience, Madge, remember?" he said.

"Won't you do it for me?"

"No, Madge," Breezy said flatly and, without further discussion, left the master bedroom for his cot down the hall.

119

*   *   *

Lorna's stormy romance with Ernest Tubbs and her selfishness in quitting her family to be with him impressed Kirsty more than she cared to admit and introduced a trace of envy into the swing and sway of her feelings towards the younger girl.

Ernest was nothing like David, yet watching how tenderly he behaved towards Lorna awakened in Kirsty emotions that had been dormant for many months. She had had no response from David to her last letters and, though sense told her that he may not have received them at all, she could not help but feel that he had finally abandoned her and that silence was the kindest reply.

In quiet hours in the shop Kirsty would try to imagine what it would be like if David returned from Fanshi, no longer committed to his duty or his calling, no longer willing to settle for anything in life except life with her. What would she do? What would she be willing to give up to be with him? All – or nothing? What distressed her was the realisation that it might well be nothing. She was no Nicholson. She lacked Lorna's fine, sharp edge of improvident self-possession, her assurance that, through love, all would work out for the best.

For a young woman who had mastered typewriting, shorthand and the mysteries of bookkeeping, though, Lorna could be incredibly naive at times.

"What I can't understand," Lorna said, taking up an all-too familiar theme, "is why my stepfather hasn't been round, breathin' fire an' smoke."

"Do you want him to?"

"No, but – " Lorna shrugged. "I wonder what they'd do if I just popped off an' got married."

"They'd be terribly hurt."

"I don't need their approval, you know."

"That isn't the point, Lorna."

"I can't think why they hate Ernest so much."

Kirsty said, "They're frightened of him."

"Frightened of Tubby! That's ridiculous!"

"He wants to take you away from them," Kirsty said, "an' Breezy can't fathom why there's no price attached."

"God, yes! I never thought of that," said Lorna. "What does

Craig have to say about all this?"

"Craig doesn't have much to say about anythin' these days."

"I suppose my dear big brother still feels a bit guilty about runnin' off with you."

"I doubt it," Kirsty said.

Lorna was polishing the pendulum of a small, standing clock. She was dexterous and surprisingly patient in executing such work. The clock, one of Gordon's acquisitions, had been in stock for a full year now and Kirsty doubted if it would ever sell. In fact she rather hoped it wouldn't.

Lorna said, "I haven't done anythin' wicked, you know."

"I didn't think you had."

"I want to, though."

"Aye," Kirsty said, cagily. "That's quite natural."

"Is it? I wondered if it was," Lorna said. "I mean, accordin' to what you hear in kirk you're damned forever to the fiery pit if you even so much as think about – you know – that."

"We all think about it," Kirsty said.

"Really? Did you? I mean, before – "

"I suppose I did. I can't remember," Kirsty said.

"Men are different, though, aren't they?"

"Well, I'm glad you've noticed," Kirsty said.

"One of the girls in my French class at Prosser's got pregnant." Lorna concentrated on polishing the pendulum. "Her father had been dead set against her chap for a year or more and then, suddenly, it was 'welcome in' and 'when's the wedding day'?"

"That isn't what I thought you meant about men bein' different," Kirsty said.

"What did he think of it?"

"Who?"

"That minister you knew – David – the one who went off to China," Lorna said. "He was nice."

"Yes, he was."

"Wonder what he thought of it."

"Of what?"

"You know – out of wedlock."

"It – it wasn't somethin' we ever discussed," Kirsty said. "Bein' a minister I don't suppose he'd have approved."

Lorna worked the cloth up to the pendulum's slender shaft and did not meet her sister-in-law's eye. "My mother thought you were sweet on him."

"I liked him, of course."

"I suppose it was natural you'd like him after he saved your life an' delivered Bobby."

"I liked him before that."

Lorna said, "Did you ever think you'd like to – you know – with him instead of Craig?"

"Lorna, that's enough, quite enough."

"Go on, you can tell me," Lorna said. "You must have fancied him, at least a wee bit."

"It hardly matters now, does it?"

"You did. I knew it. You fancied him."

Kirsty got up suddenly from the stool behind the counter and moved towards the back shop where Bobby lay curled in blankets on an old armchair.

"He's fast asleep," Lorna said. "You just don't want to talk about David Lockhart, do you?"

"No."

Lorna went on with her polishing then, after a while, said, "Perhaps I should get myself 'with child'."

"Don't you dare," Kirsty snapped. "Apart from anythin' else just think how Ernest's family would feel if that happened."

"Oh, I doubt if they'd mind too much."

"They'd see it as a betrayal of trust," Kirsty said, sternly. "What's more, your mother would assume I'd encouraged you, an' there would be another family row to contend with."

"Hmmm."

"Lorna, are you listenin' to me?"

"Yes," Lorna said. "But it's all right for you, Kirsty; you're married."

Kirsty was too practised to blurt out the truth, to inform Lorna that she was not, under law, married to Craig at all.

"Lorna – "

"No, no, no. You're quite right. It was just a passing thought, that's all," Lorna said. "Be rather nice to have a baby, though."

"After you're married," Kirsty said, "not before."

"I hate bein' sensible," Lorna said. "I hate havin' to wait for good things to happen."

"In this case, you'll just have to."

"Yes," Lorna sighed. "Provided it doesn't take too long."

"Besides, it takes two people to make a baby an' Ernest would never – "

"Don't be too sure," said Lorna.

*   *   *

Breezy had been awake for hours. He'd tossed and turned in the single bed in the guest room, punched the pillow and longed for a nice hot cup of tea to settle his indigestion and perhaps melt the knot of fear and worry that pinched below his breastbone. He hadn't the temerity to get up and go down to the kitchen to boil a kettle and brew tea for himself. Though it was his house, his domain, servants had some rights and deserved some privacy below stairs. More to the point, he did not want to give them more food for gossip. He willed himself to stay where he was until he heard sounds of activity in the corridor then, and only then, he rose and headed down the staircase to the lower dining room in search of relief from his tormenting doubts and grumbling stomach.

Gordon, dressed for the day, was already well through breakfast. If Gordon was aware that his stepfather had been banished from the matrimonial bed he was tactful enough to make no comment on the matter. In dressing gown, pyjamas and slippers, Breezy seated himself at the table, reached for the toast rack with one hand and the coffee pot with the other, then paused.

"What's that, son?"

"Came with the early post," Gordon answered, casually forking poached haddock into his mouth.

"For you?"

"Aye."

"What is it?"

"What it looks like – a tea caddy."

Intrigued, Breezy set down the coffee pot, reached over the table, lifted the stout little tin and gave it a shake.

"Full, too."

Gordon nodded. "One pound of best Darjeeling."

"Send away for it, did you?"

"Hell, no."

Breezy put the caddy back into its nest of brown wrapping paper then reached for the white card that Gordon had propped against the salt cellar.

Gordon lightly rapped his stepfather's knuckles with the handle of his knife. "Naughty!"

"Well, it's none o' my business, right enough," Breezy said, "but who is it from?"

Gordon dabbed his mouth with a napkin, rose and gathered the paper and the caddy into the crook of his arm. Deliberately he plucked up the white card and slipped it into his vest pocket.

"If you must know," Gordon said, "it's a gift from an admirer."

"Some gift!" said Breezy.

"Some admirer!" said Gordon, and thereupon left Breezy alone at the table to ponder on that little mystery too.

The Biter Bit

The brothers had never been easy in each other's company and, through the years, it had only been Breezy's equanimity that had kept Dolphus from flying off the handle. Breezy, however, seemed at last to have lost patience and was blustery and snappish during the course of the luncheon that Dolphus had arranged.

The Ceres was Dolphus's one and only club, a gloomy little mausoleum off Ingram Street in Glasgow's centre which was never very busy, even at the dinner hour. Professional disharmony did not affect the Adairs' appetites and they loaded their plates at the carvery before taking seats at a table in an isolated corner to fork and sup and play games with the condiments before getting down to picking at the bones of the deal that lay between them.

"The question is, Dolphus, do you still want to buy the properties?" Breezy began.

"The question is, hah, will you let me have them at a decent price?"

"Stop beatin' around the bush," said Breezy. "You know the price. I'm in no mood for negotiation. Is it on or off?"

"Why are you suddenly so prickly?" Dolphus said. "I told you I'd take them off your hands."

"Off my hands! Hell's bells, Dolphus, you're gettin' a rare bargain — an' you know it."

"I'm not so sure," said Dolphus. "Things have changed."

"Damn it! Nothing's changed on my side of the fence."

125

"You're very touchy today, Albert."

"I'm not in the least touchy," Breezy snapped. "I just want you to confirm our agreement. You're not havin' second thoughts – because of Olive?"

"Olive? Olive has nothing to do with it."

"Last time we spoke," Breezy said, "Olive had everythin' to do with it. It wasn't my idea to sell off my pubs."

"No, but you jumped at the chance, didn't you, hah?"

"I make no bones about that," said Breezy. "I want to liquify my assets an' retire."

"Seven public houses, each with a licence – "

"Yes."

" – an' an asking price of eighty-nine thousand pounds?"

"Yes."

"How many of these properties are within the jurisdiction of Greenfield burgh?" Dolphus asked.

"You know as well as I do – four."

Dolphus picked a fleck of gristle from his teeth with a fingernail. "Legislation?"

"What legislation?"

"Prohibition."

"For God's sake, Dolphus! We're a million miles from the imposition of prohibition on spirit sales in Scotland. The public would never stand for it."

"What if I take purchase of your public houses only to discover that the new licensing authority won't grant me renewals."

"Why shouldn't they?" Breezy said. "There's never any problem with renewals. You know as well as I do that the monopoly value of licences has gone sky high in the past three or four years."

"But why, hah?"

Breezy was caught in a trap of his own setting. He pushed away his plate, drank from the glass of German beer, wiped his moustache and tried to phrase an answer that would not play straight into his brother's hands.

Dolphus said, "Isn't it because the magistrates have got sticky about granting new certificates?"

"All the more reason," Breezy said, "to apply for transfer of certificates soon. The monopoly value of the licences are of enormous value now, Dolphus. If you want Carruth's – "

"What if the community decides to repossess them?"

"Why should it?" Breezy said. "My houses are well-ordered, clean. I've never so much as had a police penalty against any one of them. The authority will just nod through a transfer of certificate, and you'll have your licences for ever more."

"How did you obtain the licences in the first place?"

"Through the usual channels."

"Greased a few palms to make passage smooth, did you?"

"'Course I bloody didn't," Breezy said, frowning. "I know what that would mean. Some wee clerk gets caught shakin' pennies from a publican's tree and bang goes the publican's licences for ever."

"So you didn't bribe McAlmond?"

"What the hell is this, Dolphus? Bribe McAlmond? What would I want to bribe the Burgh Provost for?"

"He had the loudest voice on the licensing committee for years – and he was on the take," said Dolphus. "Didn't you know that ex-Provost Bob McAlmond was on the griddle?"

"On the griddle; what d'you mean?"

"Under investigation."

"Well, McAlmond took no grease from me," Breezy said. "Where did you come by this wild story, anyway?"

Dolphus winked. "Little bird told me."

"Does the little bird have a name?"

The brewer sat back and gave his brother a smile that was almost sleek. "No matter. Since you've never had shady dealin's with McAlmond you've nothin' to fear, hah?"

"I don't even know McAlmond."

"Excellent," said Dolphus. "Excellent."

"I take it this doesn't affect our agreement?"

"Why should it?"

"So it's still on?"

"Yes," said Dolphus. "But – "

"But?"

"I think it might be prudent to wait a little while before putting our names on the same piece of paper."

"What? Why?"

"Well – just in case," said Dolphus.

"In case?"

"In case the bottom drops out of the market."

"Don't be bloody – "

"Or Bob McAlmond goes to jail."

"Dolphus, I told you – "

"You're innocent, hah?"

"Yes, damn it," Breezy shouted, loudly enough to suggest that perhaps he was not so sure.

*   *   *

Late at night and in the early hours of the morning Lorna experienced in her breast little shivers of unease. She was intelligent enough to realise that she had imposed upon Phyllis Tubbs and that it was no small thing to defy convention and take into the house a son's young sweetheart.

Frank Tubbs also disconcerted her. She did not know what to make of him. He was by no means surly or unfriendly but he did tend to keep himself to himself and she could hear the sounds of his industry emanating from the study bedroom from the moment she wakened in the morning until she fell asleep at night. The *teck-tick-tick-teck-tack* of the gigantic new-model Remington typewriting machine was so constant that she sometimes wondered if Frank had found a means of making it work in his absence, endowed with a life of its own.

"Ah, brother Frank's money machine is runnin' well tonight," Ernest would say; and Phyllis Tubbs would grumble, "Yes, but he works far too hard, that boy."

Lorna had been in Frank's study only once, when he had invited her in to inspect the typewriter of which he was justly proud. The air about the desk smelled, not unpleasantly, of tobacco, machine oil and dusty books. Dozens of volumes were piled on the desk top and on a side table, many neatly tabulated with spills of paper, and hundreds of other books lined the room, shelved between a plain mahogany wardrobe, a dressing table and, in a corner, an iron bedstead with a thin woollen coverlet upon it.

He drew out the piano stool that served him as a chair, then rolled a single sheet of foolscap into the Remington.

"See what you think of it, Lorna."

She seated herself and stared down at the keyboard. She had put in hundreds of hours at similar boards at Prosser's but this machine was so new and modern that it daunted her. She was also acutely aware of Frank's scrutiny.

"Go on. Don't be afraid of it."

She arched her wrists and tapped out the only exercise that she could recall: *Once upon a time there were three bears.*

The keys whisked up and fell back and the patten clicked with a certain reproachful quality, as if sensing that a stranger was at the helm. She stopped.

"Don't you like it?" Frank said.

"Yes, it's – it's very nice. Thank you."

He nodded, stripped the foolscap from the roller and crumpled it into a ball which he dropped into the wicker basket below the desk. Lorna did not know what to do or say next.

She looked ostentatiously around, pointed at the shelves and asked, "Were any of these books written by you?"

"No," Frank said, and politely ushered her from the room.

It was from Ernest that Lorna acquired the information that she later passed on to Kirsty.

"He writes under other names, that's why we haven't heard of him," Lorna said.

"What other names?" said Kirsty, trying to disguise her interest with a casualness that did not fool Lorna for a moment.

"Grant McKenzie."

"Frank Tubbs is Grant McKenzie?"

"*And* Charles James McIntosh."

"He writes stories for the *Journal*. I've read them all," said Kirsty. "*A Flower of the Forest*; I remember that one very well. It made me cry."

"Don't tell him that," said Lorna. "He hates to talk about his stories."

"Because they're romances?"

Lorna shrugged. "I think he's just modest. He made a lot of money from a book on history, written for the classroom. It's all over the place. But he doesn't like it, apparently. And then he turned to writing stories. He's had stories in *Chambers'* an' in *Blackwood's* too an' he's been an editor of a religious weekly called *The Scottish Pulpit*."

"David used to read it," Kirsty said.

"Ernest says Frank's not really religious. It's just that he's good at history," Lorna said. "Won't it be excitin' to have a famous author for a brother-in-law?"

It was much later that night before Kirsty admitted to herself that she shared Lorna's stimulation over their acquaintance with Frank Tubbs. When Craig had gone out and Bobby was asleep, she raked among the newspapers that were stored in the bottom of the kitchen cupboard and found there several issues of *Home Journal* which contained episodes of fiction written by Grant McKenzie. She did not know why it should, but just holding the browning issues, looking at the name – not even Frank's name – and knowing that the words there had come out of the imagination of somebody she could identify made her feel oddly warm and, for a little while, as close to her new partner as if he had shared secrets with her.

She arranged the odd copies of the *Journal* in sequence and, with her feet on the hob and a cushion at her back settled down to read again of the poor Highland girl and the soldierman who loved her more than life itself, until, because it was late, she fell asleep where she lay, with Frank Tubbs' stirring fiction fallen softly against her face.

*   *   *

It was Johnnie Whiteside's custom to nip out of the warehouse and around the corner to the Beehive for a slice of hot beef and a pint of beer in lieu of a more elaborate lunch. As a rule he was accompanied by his cousin Eric and the pint might become two or even three and a little nap in the office chair be called for afterwards to restore equilibrium. On that particular day, however, Eric had been detained at a carpet manufactory in Uddingston, and Johnnie had been quick into and out of the Beehive. Consequently he had all his wits about him when Uncle Breezy rushed in in a great old state of alarm over some cock-and-bull story Dolphus had told him.

It was immediately obvious to Johnnie what Dolphus was up to and he was astounded that his mentor, Breezy, had fallen for it. Breezy, though, did not seem at all himself in all sorts of other ways. Johnnie's manner became outwardly more soothing, placatory and respectful but his concentration was as hard and penetrating as a steel bit.

"I didn't pay McAlmond money, did I?" Breezy cried, for the third or fourth time.

"Now, Uncle, calm yourself."

"Did I?"

"No, not – "

"See! That lyin' beggar, that Dolphus. I'll have his guts, so I will."

" – not exactly."

Breezy shut his mouth with an audible snap and stared at his nephew for almost half a minute, wordlessly.

"I'm afraid," said Johnnie, "that Bob McAlmond *did* receive the odd shillin' or two from our coffers."

"Oh, Jesus! You paid him for the certificates?"

"Not them all," said Johnnie.

"How many?"

"Four."

"Damn it, we only applied for four in Greenfield burgh. Are you sayin' we greased McAlmond for all of them?"

"I – I did ask for your approval," Johnnie said.

Breezy shook his head, not in denial but, it seemed, to clear his head. He kneaded his fingertips against his brow.

Johnnie said, "Don't you remember, Uncle?"

"No, I can't – "

"When the first one came up, when we applied for a certificate for licence in the spring of ninety-six – "

"The Windsor Road Vaults?"

"Yes, that's the one. Ah, so you do remember?"

"No," Breezy said. "What did I say?"

"You told me – and I recall it very clearly – you told me to do what was necessary to ensure that the certificate came through without a hitch. I remember it distinctly because you were set on puttin' in Jack Peters and you were afraid he would go to Ruthven instead. You must remember. We spoke about it right here, at this very desk." Johnnie had leaned gradually forward during the course of his speech and his voice had become a sympathetic blur, emulating the tone one would use to an invalid.

"An' the others?" said Breezy.

"Well, I didn't ask you about those. McAlmond's hand was still out, so I just assumed – you know," John Whiteside said. "Look, I'm really terribly sorry, Uncle, if something's gone amiss but you *did* tell me – "

Breezy slapped himself on the brow. "I – I didn't even know

McAlmond was on the take."

"Oh, you did. You must have. Everyone knew that Provost Bob was featherin' his nest hand over fist. Can't you recall?"

"No. No, I can't."

Johnnie sighed, reached under the desk and brought out a bottle of brandy and a single small glass. He uncorked the bottle with his teeth and poured a fingertip of the liquor into the glass while Breezy, hand to jaw like a man with toothache, watched as if entranced. Johnnie pushed the glass to his uncle who, without changing position, downed the brandy in a swallow.

"I don't think I even knew that Bob McAlmond was on the joint committee at that time," said Breezy, plaintively.

"We were buyin' up so many things about that time," said Johnnie, leaning again so that he could purr into his uncle's ear. "Greenfield isn't Glasgow. It's a parliamentary burgh."

"Aye, I know that much."

"Greenfield has only two magistrates. At that time Ritchie and Gould held the positions on the four-man joint committee."

"Temperance men."

"Yes, good show. It's coming back to you now. As serving Provost, Bob McAlmond had a casting vote if the committee was divided on whether or not to grant a certificate for licence."

"I – aye, I remember somethin' about it." Breezy clamped both hands to his jaws now. "Oh, God! You bribed a Provost under the noses of two magistrates."

"But Uncle, you told me to do it."

"An' it's my name on the certificates. Did I appear before the committee to support the final hearin'?"

"Of course you did, on each separate occasion."

"Two minutes, an' a nod through," Breezy said. "God, I didn't even realise we'd soaped the slipway." He looked up. "The Northern Lights?"

"'Fraid so," said Johnnie Whiteside, then innocently asked, "Why are you so upset about it? It was years ago now an' McAlmond's retired."

"He's – he's under police scrutiny."

Johnnie sucked in breath and stroked his chin. "Well, yes, actually I did hear *something* to that effect, but I assumed it was just wishful thinkin' on the part of some of his enemies, and there's quite an army of those, I believe."

"What did you hear, John?" Breezy grabbed his nephew's sleeve. "Tell me what you've heard."

"Oh, just a vague whisper, that's all."

"Tell me the worst, son, for God's sake. Don't keep anythin' back."

Never had Johnnie Whiteside seen his mentor so distraught, not in all the ten years he had worked for him. In that time Johnnie had acted for the Adair interests in several transactions that wouldn't have stood examination in the light of common day, but bribing a serving Provost had not been one of them. McAlmond had been tyrant enough to beat down opposition from two teetotal magistrates and had always believed that the more pubs Greenfield could boast the better for all. To the best of Johnnie's knowledge there had never been any need to bribe McAlmond; Breezy had had his licences at no cost at all. But Johnnie Whiteside was too much the opportunist to let his uncle slip off the hook. He had, after all, learned at the feet of a master, Uncle Breezy himself, and had an innate sense of how power was gained, inch by little inch.

"If Dolphus told you," Johnnie said, cautiously, "then there must be more than a grain of truth in it."

"If McAlmond's arrested and put on trial," Breezy said, "there's no sayin' what he might tell the police."

"Nor do we know what sort of records of his illicit transactions he may have kept for his own satisfaction," said Johnnie. "Still, no real need to fret, Uncle. The worst that would happen to you under Scots law is that you'd be fined."

"And lose the licences."

"Well, yes, that goes without sayin'."

Breezy gripped his nephew's hand as if it were a buoy that might keep him afloat. "John, see what you can find out, about McAlmond, I mean."

Johnnie nodded, "I'll certainly do my best."

"But listen, not a word to a soul about this, understand?"

"Not even Eric?"

"No, not even Eric," Breezy said.

*   *   *

"And then what did he say?" Eric Adair asked.

"Not much more," Johnnie Whiteside answered. "I gave him

another snifter of brandy and sent him on his way."

"Do you believe that guff about Bob McAlmond?"

"Lord, no!"

"But Breezy does?"

"Oh, yes," said Johnnie. "He's swallowed this ridiculous story that Dolphus has told him hook, line and sinker."

"I didn't think dear Uncle Dolphus had it in him."

"Ah, Uncle Dolphus isn't so daft as all that. He smells weakness and, being an Adair, he's ready to exploit it."

"I can't understand why Breezy doesn't see through it."

"That," Johnnie said, "is the real mystery."

"What will you do, old son? About Breezy, I mean?"

Johnnie said, "Keep him guessin' for as long as possible."

"What can we get out of it?"

"I'm not sure, just yet." Johnnie filled two small glasses from the brandy bottle and passed one to his cousin. "It ain't our fault that poor Uncle Breezy's going a little soft in the head. Let's drink to senility, shall we?"

"Premature, or otherwise," said Eric, and touched glasses across the littered desk.

"And to the lovely Amanda," Johnnie said.

"Amanda?" said Eric. "I thought you'd given up on her?"

"On the contrary, old chum," said Johnnie Whiteside, with a strange little smile. "I haven't even started yet."

*　　*　　*

In February the garrison town of Ladysmith, in distant South Africa, had been relieved of its torment but the grim siege of Mafeking immediately took its place as a focus of national concern. Newspapers and journals were filled with the stuff of war and seemed, thanks to the Boers, to have developed a consciousness of the value of foreign news, particularly if it involved suffering and slaughter. Kirsty was less interested in South Africa than in the deteriorating situation in China, and she was short of news now that the Boxers' gory rituals had, as it were, been given second billing to the Boers.

Lorna had attended church with the Tubbs family on Sunday and, on Monday, told Kirsty that the Reverend Robert McKinnon, who had been in Peking until three years ago, had prayed for the safety of God's people in China and had even

134

mentioned a few missionary colleagues by name.

"Not the Lockharts, though," said Lorna. "I listened extra special careful for David's name."

"He isn't in Peking. He's hundreds of miles to the north."

"Are you worried about him?"

"Aye, of course."

Lorna nodded. "I'd be worried too if my man was in China."

"David Lockhart isn't 'my man', Lorna."

"Friend, I meant," Lorna said. "Have you had a letter from him?"

"Not for months."

"Too busy to write, I expect," said Lorna. "Reverend McKinnon told us that some missionaries are fortifyin' their missions while others are tryin' to get back to Peking while they can. You could ask Frank Tubbs about it."

"Frank Tubbs? But why?"

"He's very well informed about history and geography. He's also acquainted with lots of ministers," Lorna said. "And he knows David Lockhart."

"Did – did he say so?"

"I heard him discussin' it with his mother."

"I hope you didn't tell him that I – "

"You what?"

"Nothin'," said Kirsty.

It wasn't Kruger or the Dowager Empress of China who provided the good folk of Greenfield with stable conversation, of course, but incidents and events that occurred not round the globe but around the corner. 'Kipperfeet', a madcap dancer, had the neighbourhood agog, and respectable wives, who would not normally be caught dead in a midden like the Gem, ganged up to buy tickets just to see if the boneless mannie really could stretch his leg over his shoulder and scratch his nose with it.

Nicholson's Emporium was ideally situated for viewing another new phenomenon, the motor car. The blacksmith at the bottom of Gascoigne Street had set himself up as an expert in fuelled vehicles and pioneers from far and wide would bring their machines to him for modification and repair. The sight of one of the noisy, smoke-breathing beasts would send small boys and grown men into paroxysms of amazement and delight, and the police had been issued printed instructions on how to control this latest hazard to safety and health. Automobiles and contortionists paled as conversational topics when compared with the reletting of McAlpine's house at No. 154. All kinds of speculation was rife about the kind of family that might move in. The reality was mildly disappointing; no copper but another fireman, Mr Clark, his plain-spoken wife, Martha, and their seven children. The wife seemed an amenable, neighbourly sort of woman and Jess Walker soon had her under her sway and versed in the rules of communal living. She even introduced her, somewhat stiffly, to Kirsty who, unfortunately, was rushing out at the time and did not have an opportunity to be as welcoming as she might have been.

Business at the shop had become exceptionally brisk. The carriage trade from the heights of Hillhead, where new and expensive houses were under construction, seemed to have found its way across Dumbarton Road. Advertisements in the *Partick Star* and *Citizen* might have had something to do with it; another of Ernest's devices for changing the tone of the Emporium and increasing its turnover. The back shop was jammed with packing cases containing the sort of large items that a new householder might require; lighting and heating fitments, electric, gas and oil-fuelled paraphernalia, cooking pots, saucepans and whole dinner services too. It did not take Kirsty long to accept that Ernest was a vastly more experienced businessman than Gordon, and to realise that there was nothing sharp or shifty in Mr Tubbs' plans for expansion of trade.

For several weeks the increase in custom, the settling of bills, invoicing and general sale and dispatch of stock kept Kirsty and Lorna fully occupied and, in spite of her best intentions, Kirsty found herself a little neglectful of Craig. He made no overt complaint, however, and fitted himself into the regime as best he could. Bobby too was demanding of Kirsty's attention. He was full of beans and, now that he had come to terms with the caliper, was as active as a colt. Just hanging on to him as they walked from Canada Road to Gascoigne Street was wearing, and by the time she arrived at the shop of a morning Kirsty was almost worn out by controlling her son's mischievous energy. On that particular Wednesday she arrived late. She expected to find gate and shutters down and already stowed away for, as a rule, Lorna was very punctual. There was, however, no sign of the girl and, at first, Kirsty was more annoyed than concerned.

Three early customers occupied her attention; in particular a new-married lady from Ockram Crescent who purchased an entire white china tea service which had to be carefully packed in straw before it could be taken away. Bobby skiddled about Kirsty's feet and showed off infuriatingly to the lady and it was ten o'clock before Kirsty had a moment to herself and leisure to worry about Lorna and wonder why the girl hadn't turned up for work. She made tea to calm herself, subdued Bobby with a cup of milk and a currant bun, then peered out of the window to watch the tramcars come and go along Dumbarton Road.

She was still watching out for Lorna when the shop bell rang and, turning, she found Frank Tubbs in the doorway. He was smartly dressed in a long overcoat, kidskin gloves and a felt hat with a broad silk brim. He was no dandy like his young brother but, at this hour of a weekday morning, he seemed every inch a gentleman.

"It's Lorna, I'm afraid," he said.

"Oh, God! What's happened to her?"

"Its nothing to get upset about, Mrs Nicholson," he said, sensing her alarm. "She has a heavy, shivery cold. Perhaps even a touch of 'flu. To be on the safe side my mother thought it best if she stayed warm in bed today."

"Yes, yes, of course."

"Ernest had a very early call to make and he was out of the house this morning before we realised that Lorna was not up to the mark."

Frank spoke with a soft but clear enunciation, every word distinct, perhaps a legacy of his days in the classroom. In grey morning light he looked a shade older than Kirsty had remembered him. She had met him only once before yet she nursed a feeling of security in his presence and, in spite of the unwelcome news he'd brought, she was pleased to see him. To keep him in her company a little longer she offered him tea. He glanced at his pocket watch then took off his hat.

"Tea would be very welcome, Mrs Nicholson, thank you."

"It's the least I can do. It was kind of you to sacrifice your own work to come down here on Lorna's account."

"Most folk imagine that I do no work at all," Frank said. "They seem to believe that a Muse descends on downy wings every so often and, hey presto!, a story appears on the page."

"Lorna's told me how hard you work."

"Not as hard as you do, I expect," Frank said, then, noticing Bobby, stooped to address the little boy. "Hello, young man, and what might your name be?"

"Boab."

"Oh, Bobby, not that voice again," Kirsty said. "Answer Mr Tubbs properly."

"Baw-bee Nick-awl-son."

"Well, if you're Bobby Nicholson, I've a present for you," Frank said. "It's from your Auntie Lorna." From his pocket he produced a fat chocolate cigar wrapped in silver paper. "Do you know what to do with it?"

"Aye," said Bobby enthusiastically.

After receiving permission from his mother Bobby took the cigar, clambered up on the counter, rested his elbow on the mechanical register, unpeeled the paper and sucked on the chocolate, noisily.

Chatting with Frank Tubbs soon allayed Kirsty's lingering suspicions that there was anything sinister about the Tubbs family's desire to enter the retail trade. It was, after all, just a generous investment made on Ernest's behalf, a means of making the best possible use of the money that Frank had earned. Time passed quickly and Kirsty was aware of a growing rapport with Frank Tubbs, an affinity that was both casual and at the same time deep. She could not explain it and did not seek to try. She was surprised, however, when without warning he said, "You knew David Lockhart, I believe."

She had no reason to be ashamed of admitting the fact of the friendship. Indeed, she wanted to talk of David, to allow this man to guess what David had meant to her.

"Yes, I knew him very well," Kirsty said.

"I met him on several occasions," Frank Tubbs said. "I even heard him preach one Christmas in Edinburgh."

"He lodged in Walbrook Street when I worked there," Kirsty said. "His aunt was my first friend in Glasgow, my first real friend anywhere, come to think of it."

"Nessie Frew?"

"Oh, you knew her too?"

"Everyone knew Nessie. The boarding house was quite

famous in its day. I expect it was beginning to run down a bit before you arrived there, Kirsty, but in its day – " Frank smiled. "I can't count the number of times I've dined there when I was editor of *Scottish Pulpit*."

"You're not ordained, or anythin'?"

"God, no! In fact there was a strong body of opinion in certain kirk circles that I was in league with the devil."

"You don't look very demonic to me," Kirsty said.

Frank grinned. "Ah, but you don't know me very well. I was always being accused of having a dangerously enquiring mind." He glanced at his watch again. "Kirsty, I really must go now."

"Wait just a moment more," Kirsty said. "I would like to ask you a question."

"Sounds intriguing," Frank said. "What is it?"

"Perhaps you can tell me why David went back to China?"

"He had no choice."

"He could have stayed in Scotland, found a charge here."

"I don't think you knew David Lockhart all that well."

"I think I did," Kirsty said.

The question, though it came without warning, did not seem impetuous or impertinent. "Were you in love with him?"

She lifted her head and tossed her hair, a ridiculous gesture of unrepentance but all that a woman in her position had to fall back on in the circumstances.

"Yes, for a little while."

Frank Tubbs seemed neither surprised nor offended.

"And was Mr Lockhart in love with you?" he asked.

"He said he was," Kirsty answered.

"Well, he can't be blamed for that," Frank said. "Has he written to you?"

"A couple of letters. I haven't heard from him in months."

"Hmmm!" Frank nodded. "The situation in China's dreadfully uncertain, Kirsty. I wouldn't worry unduly about a lapse in your correspondence."

"It isn't that," Kirsty said.

"Are you concerned that it was you who drove him to return to China?" Frank said. "Is that it?"

"I suppose that's at the back of it," Kirsty said. "Is it very conceited of me to think I might be responsible?"

"He'd have gone back to China in any case," Frank told her.

"You probably just made it a trifle more difficult for him."

"No, I think I might have chased him away."

"Because you had a husband?"

"I still have a husband," Kirsty said.

Frank gave no appearance of being embarrassed by this turn in the conversation, by the sudden intimacy into which she had drawn him. Kirsty wondered if it was maturity or vocation that made him so easy to talk to, so understanding.

"What do you want me to tell you, Kirsty?" Frank said. "Do you want me to say that if trouble boils up in China then David Lockhart will come back to you?"

"Perhaps that's it."

"He won't."

"How can you be so sure?"

"Believe me, he won't."

"Because," said Kirsty, "they won't let him go?"

"Not 'they'," Frank Tubbs said. "I think I know the type of man that David Lockhart is, Kirsty. It wouldn't be guilt that drove him back to China, or God, for that matter. It's not faith, not his family, not duty to the North China Mission that'll hold him there."

"What then?" said Kirsty.

"David's debt is to himself. He's a good man, and the motives of good men are very difficult to understand."

"Do *you* understand?"

"I wish I did. I wish I could."

"But – "

"I haven't the will for that sort of goodness," Frank said. "I'm not well enough made."

"Are any of us?" Kirsty said.

"Damned few," Frank told her.

It was quiet in the shop, quiet in the street too. Even Bobby seemed to sense it and kept himself still in the neuk under the counter where he had gone to finish his chocolate bar in peace. Kirsty said, "Will I see you again soon?"

"Come for tea on Sunday," Frank said. "Can you?"

"Yes," Kirsty said, without hesitation. "Meanwhile, tell Lorna I hope she keeps better."

"I'm sure she'll be fine," said Frank and a moment later was gone out of the shop, leaving it strangely empty and Kirsty's mood, for a while, quite forlorn.

*   *   *

Tucked out of sight in a close mouth, a bottle of dark rum held down by his side like a club, he waited. Now and then he'd peep out, furtive as a footpad in search of a victim. Hog's victim wasn't long in coming. Before long Sammy came shooting round the corner from Scutter Street, wooden rifle slung over his shoulder and a knitted balaclava covering half his face. Stepping forth, Hog raised a hand.

"Whoa!" he shouted.

Sammy grinning, ground to a halt. "Here, ah was jist lookin' for you, Mr Hog."

"Found me now. So what are y' gonna do about it?"

Sammy shouldered the wooden weapon, slapped the butt, yelled, "Re-sent *hams*. Hoff-sar hon par-ay-ay– *ed* ," and snapped off such a sharp salute that it almost took Hog's nose off.

"Here, stop that bloody nonsense," Hog said. "What are y' doin' wi' that thing anyway?"

"Goin' t' be a copper."

"Aye, that'll be the bloody day."

"Ah'm ur, ah'm ur."

"Right, right. Keep your shirt on."

Hog glanced towards the corner to make sure that Nicholson or one of the other nosey-parkers from Ottawa Street hadn't trailed Sammy from the mission. No sign of a blue uniform. Over the past couple of weeks Hog had successfully trained Sammy to sneak away early, so that the bloody nursemaids never knew quite where the lad had got to.

"Here, never heed yer gun," Hog said. "Tak' a taste o' this good stuff instead." Hog exchanged rifle for bottle and watched the boy tilt his head and let the liquid trickle, burning, down his gullet. "Hey, that's enough."

Sammy had his eyes squeezed shut in suffering ecstasy and would have sucked the bottle dry if Hog hadn't grabbed it away and hid it behind his back. Sammy wiped his mouth with his hand, licked his fingers and stared down at Hog, pleadingly.

"Costs money, rum does," Hog said.

"Got money, see," Sammy said.

"How much?"

"This much."

Sammy dug into his pocket and produced a handful of coppers and one silver sixpence.

"Where did ye get it from?" Hog asked.

"The box in the hall, like y' told me."

"Did nobody see ye?"

"Naw."

"Was there a lotta money in the box?"

"Aye."

"How much?"

"A lot."

Hog was not unaware that sooner or later Sammy's dip into the People's Mission charity box would be discovered but he was determined to make the most of the opportunity while it lasted. He supposed, vaguely, that he would be able to talk himself out of any bother that might accrue from his part in the pilfering, and that Daft Sammy would take the biggest share of the blame. One shilling and one penny; it wasn't a fortune but it was the second 'contribution' that he'd received from Sammy that week and the fifth in all. Anyway, the bloody money was supposed to be for the care of the poor and needy – and who was poorer and needier than he was these days?

"Gi'es another sook, eh?" Sammy said.

Hog gave the boy the bottle, let him swallow twice, then swiftly retrieved it. It was nearing eleven; curfew time. Old Black had a nose like a bloodhound and would turn you out if you smelled too strong of drink. He would never turn Sammy out, though, and Sammy was now his, Hog's, best pal.

"More," Sammy demanded.

"Naw, naw. Once we're safe inside, ah'll gi'e ye another sup," Hog said and, handing Sam back the rifle, grabbed him by the arm and set off at a fast shuffle for the Claremont.

*   *   *

Ernest had been in the sickroom since half past four but it was not until close to midnight, when Lorna's fever intensified, that he panicked. He was alone with Lorna at the time for Frank had gone off to complete an episode of a new serial story which was due for delivery the following day and his mother had gone to the kitchen to make a jug of cocoa to keep her sons sustained in their separate vigils.

"Mama, Mama, come quickly. She's stopped breathing."

Frank and Phyllis Tubbs reached the bedroom door simultaneously but Frank, neglectful of good manners, rushed in ahead of the woman. He found Ernest on his knees by the bedside, right hand clasped to his head, left arm raised in a gesture of supplication. He was crying out in a voice that Frank had never heard him use before, "Oh, God, God, please don't take her from me."

Phyllis Tubbs would have none of that. Sternly she told her son to pull himself together while Frank turned up the gas light and, without touching her, carefully examined the girl in the bed. Clearly Lorna's fever had risen. Globules of sweat stuck out from her brow, the collar of her gown was soaked, and straggles of hair clung to her cheeks. Mercifully she hadn't stopped breathing as Ernest, in his fright, had indicated. There was, however, a stentorian note to the laboured inhalations that instantly caused Frank to turn away and announce, "We must fetch her parents at once."

"She's dyin', isn't she?" Ernest wept. "And it's all my fault. Oh, Lorna, Lorna, don't leave me."

Phyllis Tubbs gave her son a firm, painful smack across his left ear and told him to fetch a grip on his emotions and his common sense. "Frank, should we send for the doctor again?"

Frank shook his head. "No. But we'll have to get her out of here."

"What! No, you can't take her away from me," said Ernest, aghast at the prospect and its implications.

"Can she be moved without risk?" said Phyllis.

"Well, it isn't entirely safe, Mama. But what if the situation becomes worse – what then?"

"Let her stay, Mama, please."

"Ernest, enough! Yes, Frank, we must return her to her parents' house immediately."

"You can't move her, not in this state," said Ernest.

"Yes, we can," Frank said. "And that's exactly what we're going to do. You, Ernest, dash down to the rank and find me a cab. Don't come back without one. Mother, would you be good enough to undress Lorna, sponge her and dry her, put on a fresh gown and stockings, a shawl about her head and shoulders and wrap the rest of her in my big, woollen dressing robe."

"We'll need blankets too, son."

"Yes, and a couple of hot water bottles."

Ernest caught desperately at his brother's arm. "Frank, please don't do this to me."

At this moment Frank lost his temper. Out of consideration for the patient he kept his voice to a seething hiss. "Are you going to help her, Ernest, or am I going to have to do it all myself?"

"I'll never forgive you for this, Frank."

"Of course you will," Frank said. "Now jump into your overcoat and boots and cut off down to the all-nighter. Take money."

Ernest hesitated and then as if a soft, whimpering groan from the girl in the bed had been a command, spun round and rushed out into the corridor. Frank blew out his cheeks in an audible sigh of relief.

"*Is* she in mortal danger, Frank?" Phyllis asked.

"No, but I think she may be nursing a pneumonia."

"Would it not be more prudent to fetch her mother here?"

"Lorna should never have been here in the first place, Mother," Frank answered. "If her condition deteriorates we simply cannot bear the responsibility."

"Are you sure she'll survive a journey in the cold night air?"

"Yes." Frank patted his mother's arm reassuringly. "I'll take best care of her, never fear."

"He'll want to go with you, you know."

"Oh, let him," Frank said.

*   *   *

Madge had not been sleeping well these past weeks. The sedative drops that Dr Wilkinson had prescribed seemed to have no effect at all. On that particular night she had taken a little extra and had lain on the rock-hard bed, dozing and waking, waking and dozing, until her mind had become filled full of woes and dark forebodings. She missed the comfort of Albert's arms, his flanks warm against her back, the purl of his breathing, masculine and reassuring. Only her stubborn streak had prevented her from allowing him back where he belonged, by her side in the wide double bed.

The clip-clop of hoofs, the crackle of wheels seemed to float in her head, imaginary sounds, linked to voices, the jangle of the doorbell and the pounding of fists on the front door. She kept her eyes tightly closed, afraid to open them now. Everything bad that had happened had started up at her from the empty hallway at the bottom of the staircase, had blown in from the world outside Albert's house like leaves on the wind. The pounding continued unabated; and tonight there was no wind at all. Madge opened her eyes wide. The house had that hideous unsealed feeling to it. She sat bolt upright and, just as the door opened, shouted out for Albert.

As if by magic her husband appeared at her side.

"It's all right, chookie. It's all right."

"Who – who is it?"

"Lorna. She's come home."

"What time is – "

"Late," Albert said. "Lorna's been taken ill, Madge, an' those people have brought her home."

Madge, senses gathered, was out of bed immediately. She tore off the lace nightcap, pulled on her dressing gown and stepped into her slippers while Albert told her that he'd sent one of the servants to fetch Dr Wilkinson and another to make Lorna's bed ready.

"No, put her here, in mine," Madge said, and hurried out of the bedroom and along the corridor to the stairs.

The street door stood wide open. She could see men outlined and threatening against it and the cab at the terrace pavement as it rolled away. One of the men, a total stranger, was obscured by the bundle in his arms but he responded without hesitation when Madge called down to him.

"Bring Lorna up here."

He was no stripling, Madge saw, but a man not so very much younger than she was. Even so, he carried Lorna seemingly without effort and, following Madge's instruction, moved on into the master bedroom and laid Lorna gently down upon the bed.

When he began to unfold the swaddle of blankets, however, Albert yanked him back. "Get away from my daughter."

"No, Albert," Madge said. "No, they – "

Lorna struggled to sit up. Her eyes were glassy and she did not seem quite to know what had become of her.

"You're home now, dearest," Madge soothed her. "You're with Mammy. She'll take care of you now."

"Where – where's Ernest?" Lorna gasped.

"Och, he's not far away," Madge said.

She positioned herself on the bed, blocking out Lorna's sight of the door where Frank Tubbs and Albert were poised in bitter argument.

"No, your brother can't stay here until the doctor comes," Madge heard Albert shout. "Haven't you done enough harm as it bloody is?"

"Our family doctor tells me it's influenza."

"Well, we'll see about that when my doctor arrives. Now, sir, I'll thank you t' leave my house."

"Mr Adair, my brother's extremely anxious to stay."

"Out of my house, the pair o' you, before I send for the police."

"Albert," Madge snapped, "let them wait downstairs, if they want to."

"Damned if I will."

She heard the bedroom door open and close, voices, arguing still, upon the stairs then, a minute later, the slam of the front door. Albert had imposed his will; he had thrown the men out.

"Mammy?"

"Aye, dear, I'm here."

"Where's – where's Ernest, Mammy? I want Ernest."

"Tomorrow, love, tomorrow," Madge told her. "When you're feelin' better."

For a fleeting moment Madge had an image in her mind of the tall, tall young man who had been in the hallway, all tragic and tear-stained, and felt very sorry for him and for herself too, for the fact that no man had ever wept for love of her, not even when she was young.

*   *   *

Olive Adair's continuing depression was discreetly referred to, in and out of The Knowe, as an 'indisposition'. It was more than that, of course, but Amanda had been conditioned to regard her mother's most selfish moods as tinted with romance and, in private discussion with her sister Phoebe even referred to the current decline as a 'natural melancholy'. Phoebe Adair was much more hard-headed than her elder sister. Though she buttered up to Amanda and seemed to offer sympathy to her repining mother, she had begun to swing away from allegiance to female – no, feminine – ideals and drawing-room principles. She had become disenchanted with the notion that a woman was only as good as the men who admired her and that the object of a woman's life was to capture first a husband and then a handsome lover.

Phoebe had begun to despise her mother and sister and to realise that perhaps her father, fool though he could be at times, was as much a victim of family tensions as their originator. Marriage, Phoebe had decided, would not be the first option in her curriculum but a last desperate resort. When her casual education in Glasgow was completed in July it was her intention to ask her father to put her to a scientific training in Edinburgh and pay for her to lodge in one of the new women's Unions until such time as she could earn her own keep and be free and independent. Phoebe would have discussed her plan with Amanda and Olive, but she had recently learned discretion. Cunning, in fact, kept her mouth shut about her ultimate intentions as she played sweetly along with the desultory preparations for Amanda's wedding day.

Olive, apparently, could rouse little or no interest in nuptial arrangements but did not object when the aunts, Polly and Heather, offered to put Amanda up in town for a day or two and undertake on Olive's behalf necessary first approaches to dressmakers and milliners. Not even Phoebe, for all her newly-minted cynicism, however, could have guessed that the person behind the invitation was her cousin Johnnie Whiteside who had reasons of his own for wanting the bride-to-be loose in Glasgow and lodged, for a night or two, in a bedroom next to his own.

Initially Amanda had hoped that she would see Gordon, might persuade him to take her to dinner and to a theatre, anything to reintroduce a touch of intimacy to an engagement that had become so sober that at times it seemed almost sour. In the past months her fiancé's character had changed so, the gaiety gone out of him and with it that strain of desire that had first attracted her to Breezy's boy.

Amanda had been bred to believe that her beauty was utterly irresistible. It did not dawn on her that Gordon did not love her

any more. Even so, she was curiously relieved to learn that
Gordon would be out of town during the days and nights of her
visit to the city. Apparently he had been sent off with Mr
McDade to assess the commercial potential of some remote hotel
at the tip of the Mull of Kintyre and would be absent for the best
part of a week.

How Johnnie had discovered that Gordon would not be
around was a mystery, but many things that Johnnie knew and
did had a mysterious quality. He went about the process of
seduction with a subtlety and skill born of much experience with
women. To entertain Amanda he organised a theatre evening
for a party of cousins, a box at the Queen's to see the latest
Gilbert and Sullivan operetta and then, singing, back to French's
supper rooms for a bite to eat before cabs were summoned to
transport them all, slightly tiddled, back to their respective
homes.

During the evening Johnnie had watched Amanda closely
and, to his gratification, saw her thaw, saw worry and fatigue
slough away under the influence of music, wine and laughter.
He assumed that she had been dunned down by the enthusiasm
of her aunts' endless chatter about muslin and silk, bruised by
dressmakers' tapes and the fuss of first fittings. Amanda chose
not to disillusion him. She had more awareness of what Johnnie
was up to than the man would have found comfortable. Johnnie
had always been attracted to her and, as the evening progressed,
she allowed herself to flirt with her handsome cousin and to
think disparagingly that it was no more than Gordon deserved
after his recent displays of indifference. She was, of course,
parched for attention and thirsty for the compliments that
Johnnie whispered in her ear in the box at the Queen's and,
later, in the booth at French's. The cab had barely left the stoup
outside the supper rooms before Johnnie paid the driver to
extinguish the lamps and, without invitation, pulled Amanda
into his arms.

She was not quite prepared for the passion of his kisses, the
effect of the pressure of his lips upon her own or the brushing of
his fingers upon her throat and shoulders.

"Amanda, you're so beautiful. I can't resist you for a moment
longer. Yes, darlin', I know you're promised to another and will
soon belong to him body and soul. But don't deny me, I beg you,

the lingerin' memory of your kisses and of this one night together."

Lips close against her ear, Johnnie's declarations seemed urgent and delicious. She was not frightened of his ardour. There had always been something between them. Indeed, if he had not worked for Uncle Breezy then Johnnie might have been Daddy's choice of a husband for her.

"Johnnie, that's very naughty."

"If you were mine, dearest, I wouldn't desert you. I wouldn't leave you alone for a single moment. I would want to be with you every hour of every day. And every night."

"John! John– *nie!*"

"To hold you as I hold you now."

"I think – think you've gone – far enough."

"To clasp you in my arms, kiss your breast, make you mine in every way that a man can pay homage to a woman. Do you understand what I'm saying?"

"But – Gordon?"

"Damn Gordon! Tonight, Amanda, you're mine."

Without conviction she tried to extricate herself but somehow his hand had already found its way through frills and ribbons, strings and hooks. When he shifted his weight she found herself pinned against the corner of the seat and all protest squeezed out of her. She could see the rump of the horse, muscular and glossy, the cab's tarry black hood before Johnnie's face, huge and sleek, blotted everything out. She was engulfed in waves of sumptuous excitement that swept forcefully through her, made her gasp and then cry out.

"Hush, hush," Johnnie hissed. "Hush, and hold still."

Her lips parted to let each word come but the utterance was soft, like invitation not rebuff.

"Oh, John, please, no, don't, please, don't. No."

Johnnie ignored her protests. He smothered them. After a while she lay quite still in the cab's dark corner, gasping and crying, while her cousin's hands and mouth told her how much he loved her and prepared her for what would come later in the wee, small hours when the rest of the Whiteside household had fallen asleep.

*　　*　　*

149

"Look," said Madge from the window, "it's started to rain again." Breezy did not respond to this piece of information from his wife. He slumped deep into the chintz-covered armchair, puffed on his umpteenth cigar and scowled as if unflagging surliness might scare away not only the idiot who waited under the trees but all the other problems that had come to roost in and about the house of Adair. "Aw, look. He's gettin' soaked."

"That's his fault, not mine," Breezy growled.

"He wants to see her."

"He's been informed she's not in mortal danger," Breezy said. "An' I've told him – an' you – that he's not setting foot inside my house again."

"But, Albert, he's been there for two days."

"Aye, well, by God, if he's still there tomorrow I'll send for the polis."

"Lorna's been askin' for him, you know."

"Oh, I've heard her." Breezy struggled into a sitting position and glowered at his wife. "She doesn't know he's out there, does she? You haven't told her?"

"Albert, what harm could it do to – "

"Damn it, Madge, no."

Breezy thrust himself out of the chair, flung his cigar into the fire and stalked to the window. He brushed Madge to one side, plucked up the net curtain and squinted down at the figure on the grass of the terrace. Ernest Tubbs had turned up the collar of his long black overcoat and hunched his shoulders almost to the brim of his hat. When he tilted his head to meet Breezy's jaundiced eye a little trickle of water ran down each cheek. He looked ridiculously mawkish, like one of the cheap steel engravings Breezy used to sell when he was first making his way in the world.

"GO AWAY," Breezy shouted and waved his arms.

Tubby didn't move a muscle.

"What have you got against him?" Madge said.

"He's a bloody opportunist."

"No, he's not. He's in love with our Lorna, that's all."

"He's only out for what he can get."

"You didn't used to be like this, Albert," Madge said. "I can't think what's come over you."

"Nothin's come over me," Breezy snapped. "It's the rest o' you that seem hellbent on destroyin' – "

Madge interrupted him. "See, here's Gordon."

Through the rain-speckled glass Madge and Breezy watched a station hack draw up at the kerbstone below. Gordon, carrying a leather valise, climbed out, paid the cabby and immediately crossed the terrace's flat cobbles to meet and talk with Ernest Tubbs. Conversation between the young men was brief but intense. During it Gordon pivoted and glared up at the window, causing Breezy to shift uneasily behind the curtain. An envelope was transferred from Mr Tubbs to Gordon.

"That's supposed to be for Lorna, no doubt," Breezy said. "By God, he's got gall, I'll say that for him."

The couple shook hands and Tubby resigned himself to his forlorn vigil under the leafless tree while Gordon marched up the steps and rang the front doorbell.

Breezy hurried out of the upstairs drawing-room and Madge followed. She reached the top of the stairs just as the little servant girl opened the front door and Gordon entered. With the speed and agility of a dancing footman Breezy descended the stairs and, before Gordon even had time to set down his valise, greeted his stepson with hand outstretched.

"I'll take that," Breezy said.

"Take what?"

"The letter that chap gave you."

"It's not for you."

"I know who it's for," Breezy said. "Give it to me, Gordon."

"I certainly will not. It is for my sister an' I intend to see that she gets it."

"Don't you cause any trouble," Breezy said. "You've no idea what we've been through while you've been away."

Gordon divested himself of hat and overcoat but visibly retained his grip on the letter that Tubby had given him. He ignored Breezy now and addressed himself instead to Madge.

"Where is she, Mam?"

"In her own room now."

"Is she all right?"

"She's recoverin'," Madge told him as he raced upstairs with Breezy in hot pursuit. "We thought it might be pneumonia but it wasn't quite so serious."

"You're not goin' in there, Gordon," Breezy shouted.

"Try an' stop me," Gordon said.

He opened the door of Lorna's bedroom, slipped inside the room and closed the door firmly behind him while Breezy tried to find a way around his wife who had determinedly blocked the landing with her body.

"Get out of my way, woman," Breezy raged.

"No, I won't. That's my bairns in that room, Albert, an' you're goin' to leave them be," Madge shouted. "Why are you behavin' like this? Tell me the truth."

Breezy suddenly capitulated. He sank against the wallpaper and, as she approached, put his hands on her waist and his head down against her chest.

"Madge, I'm scared."

"You – scared?"

"Aye," Breezy admitted. "I'm scared o' everythin'."

Her anger dampened in bewilderment, Madge asked, "But why, Albert, why?"

He shook his head. "What if I was to lose everythin'?"

"Albert, what are you sayin'?"

"What if it all just slid away!"

"Is this somethin' that's goin' to happen?"

"No," he said. "But I want Gordon to be happy, Lorna settled with a man who can look after her properly. It takes money, doesn't it? I mean, that's how I got you."

"Is that what you think?" Madge said. "Do you really think I just married you for your money?"

"I don't know what to think these days. I'm so – so damnably confused, Madge."

Patting his broad back she strove to hide her own hurt and to comfort him with all the sincerity she could muster. She remembered her own recent fears and irrational terrors of the night. It seemed heretical to think that the famous Mr Albert Adair shared the fears of the multitude, anxiety about growing old and concern about the fate of his children. How could it be that a man as strong as Albert could be shaken by fatherhood and marriage?

"I wish things would stop hurryin' on," Breezy said. "Oh, God! How I wish it could be like it was when we first came to this house, new-married, and the children both young and biddable."

152

"What are we goin' to do about Lorna?" Madge said, unable, just at present, to grapple with larger issues.

"Och, Lorna's a good girl. I know she's done nothin' to make either of us ashamed. I'm just afraid she'll make a terrible mistake because she's so young."

"Albert, none of us can stand in the way o' the future."

"No, but how was I to know it would all go to pigs an' whistles?"

"You should have thought."

"About what?" Breezy said.

"Consequences."

To Madge's surprise he nodded agreement. "You're right, chookie. I took too many chances. Now I'm goin' to be made to pay for them."

At that moment the door of Lorna's bedroom opened and Gordon helped his sister out into the corridor. Lorna had lost a great deal of weight in the short span of her illness. She was pale and weak and clung shakily to her brother for support. She wore bedsocks and a quilted dressing-gown and had tried, without success, to arrange her hair into some semblance of neatness. She looked every inch an invalid, except for the little sparkle of determination in her eyes, a light, Madge knew, that had not been there an hour ago.

"Don't try to stop me," Lorna's voice was so small that her warning seemed less defiant than pathetic. "I'm not going to be stopped, not this time."

"You're not goin' out like that?" Madge said.

"Nope," Gordon said. "We're just takin' a wee walk into the front room, aren't we, sweetheart?"

Madge and Breezy stood prudently to one side as Gordon steered his sister along the corridor and into the drawing-room.

"Oh, God! What is it now?" Breezy muttered.

Madge could only shrug, though she had a motherly inkling that something momentous was about to take place. She sought her husband's hand and held it tightly as they entered the drawing-room and, hanging back, watched Gordon gently lead Lorna to the window that overlooked the terrace.

"She's not goin' to – " Breezy whispered.

"Yes, dear, I think she is."

Madge had noticed the letter in her daughter's hand and the

glimpse of it had made her heart thump as if it had been addressed to her and not to her youngest. Gordon settled Lorna on the velvet tub chair while he heaved up the window in a flutter of damp net curtain, then he gave her a wink and helped her to her feet once more.

"Is he still there?" Lorna asked.

"'Course he is. See for yourself."

Rain drifted into the room on the breeze, a newspaper by Breezy's chair rustled, the antimacassars stirred and the leaves of the castor oil plant nodded. On the terrace the cobbles were glazed with rain and the tall trees in the gardens receded into its soft trailing veils. Snatching his hands from his pockets, Ernest came out from under the boughs.

"Tubby?"

"I'm here, my love."

Lorna rested her forearms against the window frame and leaned out into the soft rain.

"Did you get my letter, Lorna?"

"Gordon gave it to me."

"What do you say to it?" Tubby called.

Lorna shook straggles of hair from her face and drew in a deep breath. "I say *Yes* to it, Ernest."

"You *will* marry me?"

"*Yes, Ernest, I will.*"

Madge heard the young man's whoop of joy and sagged into Breezy's arms.

"Now," Gordon said, "may I let Tubby in?"

"I suppose you'd better," said Breezy, grudgingly.

*　　*　　*

It fell to Gordon to carry the glad tidings to his brother and sister-in-law. He found them both at home the following evening, Friday. Kirsty was anxious for news. She had been told by hand-delivered letter that Lorna was ill and would be absent from work for three or four weeks and, in consequence, had been chained to the shop counter for a dozen hours a day. Only Craig's indulgence had saved her from going batty with worry and overwork. Craig had generously sacrificed sleep to collect Bobby and take him out into the park each afternoon and had even prepared supper now and then. He was not, however, well pleased to learn that his sister had become engaged to Kirsty's business partner and slid rapidly into one of his dour, sarcastic moods.

It would be a long engagement, a year at least. In the meantime, for the sake of harmony and decorum, Lorna would continue to reside at Great Western Terrace. Mr Tubbs would no longer be treated like a leper and would be free to woo her openly and above board.

"Big pow-wow on Sunday afternoon," Gordon said, "to which you are both cordially invited."

"Huh!" Craig said. "I've more to do wi' my time than sip tea with a bunch of chin-waggers an' chancers."

"For God's sake, Craig, when are you goin' to accept the fact that Mam married into money?" Gordon said.

"Dirty money."

"Nothin' of the kind."

"No?" Craig said. "I suppose you'll be tellin' me that Breezy never had any dealin's wi' Bob McAlmond."

"Who?"

"He used to be the Burgh Provost."

"Oh, that McAlmond. I thought he retired from the council last year," Gordon said.

Craig had just finished washing at the sink and he put on a clean shirt that Kirsty had laid out for him and dressed without embarrassment in front of his brother, while Kirsty went into the front room to tuck her son into bed.

"Aye, he did," Craig said. "In the nick o' time too, or so the old bugger thought."

"What's this got to do with comin' to the terrace for tea on Sunday?" Gordon asked.

"McAlmond's had his hand out for years. Now his affairs are under scrutiny. He might even be arrested." Craig buttoned his uniform. "An' some o' the bigwigs that greased his greedy palm over the years might be in for a fright an' all."

"I still don't see what this has to do with Breezy?"

Craig grinned, shrugged. "Ask him."

"I will," Gordon said. "I take it this is your excuse for not joinin' the family on Sunday afternoon?"

"Kirsty can go. She loves hob-nobbin' with the high an' mighty."

"I'd hardly call Ernest Tubbs high, or mighty."

"She knows him. She can go," Craig said then, as Kirsty reentered the kitchen. "You just love all that kind o' thing, don't you, dearest?"

"If it's just to be close family, I don't want to – "

"You're family," Gordon reminded her. "Close family. Anyway, they're your partners now, the Tubbses, so it wouldn't look right if you were missin'."

Kirsty nodded then moved around the table where Gordon, still in his overcoat, was drinking tea and smoking. She put her hands on Craig's shoulders and moved him into the pool of gas light by the hearth and then picked lint from his tunic, adjusted his collar and the line of his belt.

Gordon watched the ritual and wondered how many such little intimacies it took to shore up a marriage that seemed to him to be sagging like an old gable-end. He had never understood why Kirsty endured his brother's sullen, bad-tempered moods or why she showed him such attention when he had treated her so badly. He had in mind some model for his own marriage, though its circumstances would be vastly different. There was no intimacy in The Knowe's gloomy chambers. Any closeness between Amanda and him would have to be manufactured since it wouldn't happen naturally because of a shared sink and inescapable lack of privacy.

Craig's chin was up and his eyelids hooded as he waited for Kirsty to close the metal hooks that held his collar in place.

He said, "I'll look after Bobby."

"I can easily take him with me," Kirsty said.

"No, I'll look after him."

"If you like," said Kirsty.

"I like."

"What time's the gatherin', Gordon?" Kirsty asked.

"Three for half-past."

"In that case – "

"She'll be there," said Craig.

*   *   *

In a lull between the disappearance of the soup and the serving of strips of boiled cod that would pass as the fish course, Gordon said, "My sister's gettin' married."

"Oh, to whom?" said Phoebe.

"Ernest Tubbs is his name."

"What does he do, hah?" Dolphus asked.

"He's a salesman with Mathieson, Mullard and Milroy."

"A salesman!" Amanda said, with just a hint of scorn.

"Johnnie's a salesman," Phoebe said. "If marriage is what you fancy then I suppose a salesman's as good a catch as any."

Gordon said, "He also has a partnership in my sister-in-law's business, so his prospects are fair."

From the head of the table Dolphus uttered another little 'hah' to indicate that he had fielded the information but he didn't wish to dwell on it.

Both the old man and Amanda seemed vague and distracted tonight. They'd hardly said a word to Gordon since his arrival and his polite enquiry about Olive had been turned aside with a single sharp word from Dolphus – "Indisposed" – which might mean anything from alcoholic stupor to a first brush with catalepsy. More than likely, though, it simply indicated that Olive couldn't stomach another dreary dinner in her husband's company.

It wasn't Dolphus's truculence that tweaked Gordon's curiosity so much as changes in the behaviour and appearance of his fiancée; the loose setting of her hair, the dark-red velvet dress that was too mature and heavy in its styling, the deep, bruised circles under her eyes.

He went on, "Lorna doesn't plan to marry immediately so there will be no confusion with our weddin' plans."

"Confusion?" said Phoebe. "What an odd word to use."

"In arrangements, I mean," Gordon said. "Which leads me to enquire if anythin' has been decided yet as to where the wedding will be held?"

Dolphus gave himself a little shake. "Here, of course."

"Oh, good," said Gordon. "And the list of guests?"

"Soon," said Dolphus.

In the old, innocent days of sisterly rapport, Amanda would have guessed what Phoebe was about to say and would have dissuaded her, but Amanda was fiddling with her silver fish knife and seemed distanced from the limping conversation.

Phoebe said, "Amanda was up in town this week, bein' arrayed for the jolly old bridals. Didn't you know, Gordon?"

"No," Gordon said. "No, I didn't."

"Mother didn't feel up to it, so Aunt Polly and Aunt Heather Whiteside did the honours," Phoebe said.

"I see," said Gordon. "Did you stay over?"

"Amanda." Phoebe leaned across the table and snapped her fingers softly. "Amanda, Gordon's talking to you."

It was like watching a patient emerge from a mesmeric trance. Amanda started, lifted her shoulders and tucked a hand down into her lap as if she'd suffered a stab of hysterical pain.

"No," she said.

"What?" said Gordon.

Dolphus's attention had been caught too and he watched, frowning, as Amanda struggled and stammered out an account of her first fittings for bridal clothes and the evening she had spent in her aunt's company.

"Aunt Polly?" Gordon asked.

Amanda did not respond to this simple question and it was left to Phoebe to answer for her: "Aunt Heather."

"Did you see Cousin John then?" said Gordon.

"Yes."

"How nice," said Gordon.

"Went to the theatre, didn't you?" said Phoebe.

"Really!" said Dolphus. "I don't think I heard that."

"No, Daddy," said Phoebe. "There's a lot you didn't hear."

"Hah?"

Gordon said, "How very nice."

In a flurry of words, Amanda blurted out, "You weren't at home. You were away. If you'd been at home – if only you'd been there – " She finished lamely, "You'd have been invited too."

"'Course he would," said Dolphus.

"Stands to reason," said Phoebe. "Cousin Johnnie wouldn't have left Gordon out. Cousin Johnnie's far too civilised to leave Gordon out."

Amanda raised the silver knife and pointed it at her sister, wagging it with more menace than mischief. "Phoebe, I warn you – "

"Ah!" said Dolphus, who was not inexperienced in averting spats between his daughters. "The fish."

A middle-aged maid, yet another new face from the servants'

hall, shuffled in with a big silver serving dish, dumped it clumsily on the tablecloth directly before the master and, without pause, immediately began to slap out ragged cuts in puddles of maritime gravy.

"Cod?" Dolphus asked.

To which Gordon answered, "For sure."

Six

Family Fortunes

Kirsty took the best part of Sunday morning to prepare herself for the formal ceremony of afternoon tea. Craig, who'd risen earlier than usual, was scathing about her thoroughness, teasing rather than malicious, though. He watched, amused, as she washed and dried her hair and set about an elaborate ritual with American curling tongs. When that was eventually done, though not to her satisfaction, Kirsty tackled last-minute alterations to a dress she'd bought in the autumn and had not had an opportunity to wear until now; a visiting gown of brown voile trimmed with lace and edged with narrow velvet and chiffon. The skirt fitted snugly at the hips and the front-fitting bodice was mounted over a tight lining. Considering the weight she'd lost recently, she was pleased enough with the result and, with a spanking new hat perched on top, she looked and felt quite the ticket. Craig gave her a chirp and whistle before he kissed her goodbye though she was less pleased when husband and son leaned out of the front room window and rendered a chorus of some rude music-hall song as she hurried towards Dumbarton Road to find a cab.

New gowns, new hat, travel by cab; it was a far cry from the struggling days when every penny counted. Kirsty was, however, no longer intimidated by money or made guilty by her possession of it. As the cab jogged up the Byres Road she glanced at the handsome tenements that had been erected recently and speculated on what it would cost to buy one, if only she could persuade Craig to leave burgh employ and exchange the tied house in Canada Road for the illustrious heights of Hillhead. Craig was so resentful of their upward progression towards respectability, the direction in which circumstances had thrust them. Even when they weren't quarrelling, there was no real harmony between them. She tried to put her discontent to one side as the cab approached Great Western Terrace.

Breezy was in the hall to greet her and Ernest, grinning like mad, leaned on the rail of the balcony above.

"Kirsty, m'love, I'm delighted you could come," Breezy said as he hugged her.

"Couldn't keep away, could she?" Ernest said and, when Kirsty reached the landing, lifted her from her feet and planted a smacker on her cheek. "What do you think of our news, then?"

"Well, I think it's dreadful."

"What?"

"It's bad enough havin' you pop into the shop every now an' then but takin' you on as a relative – I suppose I'll just have to learn to put up with it," Kirsty said. "How did you do it, Tubby? How did you persuade a nice, sensible lass like Lorna to marry a skinamalink like you?"

"I got her at a weak moment," Tubby said.

"How is the invalid?"

"She's up today and dressed for the occasion," Breezy said. "But we mustn't make a night of it and tire her out."

"In other words," said Kirsty, "there's a curfew."

"Five o'clock," Breezy said and ushered Kirsty into the long drawing-room where the others had already gathered.

Dressed in a warm wool dress, with a Paisley shawl tucked about her knees, Lorna had place of honour by the fire. She was as white as chalk and clearly not yet fully recovered from her illness. Kirsty put all thought of trying to persuade her to return soon to the shop out of her mind immediately.

After kisses and congratulations had been bestowed, Madge rang for tea to be served. As a rule Breezy was an admirable host but today, Kirsty thought, he was more subdued than usual and seemed willing to let Madge conduct the tea-party while he took a back seat.

Kirsty chatted with Madge and Phyllis Tubbs for a while and then, carrying a tea-cup, drifted to a seat by the window where Frank Tubbs had positioned himself. He welcomed her with a

161

smile and a little nod, almost as if he had been poised for a moment of exchange since she'd first entered the room.

"I was hoping you'd come," he said, quietly.

"It wouldn't have been polite to stay away," Kirsty said. "Apart from that, I wanted to congratulate the happy couple."

"Is your husband on duty?"

"Craig doesn't much care for tea-parties." Kirsty glanced over her shoulder at the group by the fire who, at that instant, were being entertained by repartee between Gordon and Tubby. "To tell you the truth, Frank, my husband has no time for the Adairs."

"Is he jealous of them?"

"Yes, that's it," said Kirsty. "You've put your finger on it straightaway, an' you haven't even met Craig yet."

Frank shrugged softly. "I expect he wants you to stay at home, where he can be sure you're safe from harm."

"That's an odd way of puttin' it."

"From the attentions of – other men."

"I don't think it's even occurred to Craig that other men might find me attractive."

"Oh, yes, it has," Frank said. "Besides, it would take a very special sort of chap to adapt to the steep rise in your family fortunes, especially if he felt, rightly or wrongly, that he was somehow being left behind."

Kirsty was a little embarrassed by Frank Tubbs' directness and by his understanding of her domestic situation. She had voiced her doubts to nobody except Gordon and he wasn't the type to betray confidences.

"Are all authors so perceptive?" she said.

They were close, a little tense with the effort of balancing cups and saucers. Kirsty glanced down modestly, as the knee of Frank's trousers brushed against her skirt, but she did not pull away. There was no flirtatiousness in his manner yet by focusing his attention upon her so completely he seemed to draw her to him and to exclude the others in the room.

"Lord, no," Frank said. "It's just that I've seen more of life than you have, Kirsty."

"What a right old chestnut that is."

"Don't you think it's true?"

"I'm not a wide-eyed country girl, you know. I've seen my fair share of 'life' since I came to Glasgow, believe me."

"Ernest tells me you were raised in the Baird Home in Ayrshire and that you worked as a farm servant until your marriage."

"Aye, that's the way of it," Kirsty said. "But it wasn't at all like it's depicted in storybooks, feedin' duckies and milkin' cows in a floral dress and nice poke bonnet."

"I know it wasn't."

"How would a man like you, a teacher, know that?"

"Long ago, before you were born," Frank said, "I worked out my summers on the Biggins o' Kilsyth. Dirty, monotonous, backbreaking labour it was too. I detested every minute of it."

"Why did you put up with it?"

"I needed the wage, and farm work was all I could find."

"Oh, I thought – "

"No, a clean collar doesn't always indicate a fat purse, Kirsty."

To hide her confusion she ate the slice of bread and butter from her plate and sipped tea daintily. Frank Tubbs, she noticed, did not push conversation along like a street sweeper with a broom. He seemed content to say nothing, to observe her, a habit she might have found disconcerting except that Frank somehow made it seem courteous, even protective.

At length he said, "I take it you're short-handed in the shop right now."

"Yes, an' I thought my troubles would be over when I took on a partner an' a manager."

"Ernest will resign from Mathieson's in four or five months and apply himself fully to organising the shop."

"Well, it was nice of him to tell me."

"Won't it suit?" Frank said.

"Yes, it suits just fine. But in the meantime – "

"I'll come down and lend a hand, if you like."

"I suppose you've worked as a shop-keeper's assistant too," Kirsty said, "long before I was born?"

Frank laughed. "No, can't honestly say that I have. But there can't be much to it, can there? If a pretty, young farm lassie can master the retail trade in a matter of weeks surely a wise old goat like me can pick it up in half a day."

"You're not *that* old," said Kirsty.

"I'm not that wise, either," Frank said, "or I might never have made the offer. What do you say?"

"What about your own work?"

"I'm pretty well up to the mark with my commissions, and the rest can wait," Frank said. "Shall we say about ten o'clock tomorrow morning, Mrs Nicholson?"

"Shall we say prompt at half-past eight, Mr Tubbs," Kirsty said and then, because she did not know him well enough to take his kindness for granted, she touched his sleeve and told him, "Thanks."

*　*　*

Craig was less embarrassed at being seen in the streets with Bobby now that the boy was crippled. The iron brace, the obvious limp made him exempt from the unwritten law that stated that childminding was woman's business. Unconsciously, Bobby co-operated in this masculine demonstration by hopping as energetically as a sparrow, in a manner that seemed to the casual onlooker to be more brave than childish.

On Sunday afternoon Craig took him up to the police gymnasium where fitness fanatics grunted and groaned with weights, hung on wallbars and leapfrogged over the leather vaulting horse. The coppers were friendly towards the little boy and encouraged him to see-saw on the vaulting board and clamber about on the horse.

"Aye, we'll make a champion out o' him yet, Craig," Sergeant McRory declared, then, noticing the caliper for the first time, blushed beetroot red and didn't know where to put himself.

After the visit to the gymnasium Craig took Bobby to Benito's café, bought him a bun and an ice-cream drink while he had a coffee, and then, with his son by the hand, began to stroll back home towards Canada Road.

It was around half past four when Craig and Bobby turned into Scutter Street and ran into a very public altercation on the steps of the Peoples' Mission. No constable was involved. Perhaps just as well since Mrs Lamb, Superintendent of the Senior Bible Class, might have risked arrest for disturbing the peace on the Sabbath. Mrs Lamb was a small, stout, pretty woman of about forty. Normally placid, this afternoon her character had been changed by anger and outrage. She wagged a finger into the face of Mr Roper, Chairman of the Bible Class Committee, and gave Caretaker Dugdale billy-o, nagging them in a high, febrile voice that echoed among the tenements like a tribal chant.

"I've never been so humiliated in all my born days," Mrs Lamb shrilled. "Even on the street corner, never mind in a house o' the Lord, I have never heard such lewd, foul an' disgustin' language."

"It's not my fault, not my fault." Mr Roper, younger, leaner and taller than the woman, was agitated too, strung between contrition and retaliation. "What could I possibly have done about it?"

"Broken down the door. Got him out of there by force."

Several of Mrs Lamb's flock had gathered in the doorway to observe the fun but they had sense enough not to take sides and listened, smirking mutely.

"The door's got bolts on it, Mrs Lamb." Mr Dugdale immediately regretted his intervention.

The woman swung from the hips and shouted. "Could you not have broken a window then?"

"No windows in the boiler room, Mrs Lamb."

"Who gave him the drink in the first place, that's what I'd like to know." Mrs Lamb's dander was rising by the minute. "I suspect it was you, Mr Dugdale."

Mr Roper jumped in. "Madam, that's totally uncalled for, a slander on the good name of our caretaker. I can't stand back an' see Mr Dugdale thus maligned."

"Somebody gave him drink, you can't deny."

"I don't deny it, but – "

"Tell me, Mr Roper, what sort o' impression do you think words of that nature make on my innocent charges? Scarred, they'll be, morally scarred for life."

The charges endeavoured to appear both as innocent and as morally scarred as possible, though a couple of pimply lads at the back nudged each other and mouthed the offensive phrases just in case they should forget them.

"I do not think we should discuss this matter in the street, Mrs Lamb," said Mr Roper, through clenched teeth.

"We'll discuss it right here an' now," Mrs Lamb insisted. "If it had been your class occupyin' the big hall when it happened you'd have done somethin' positive about it, instead of just dashin' about like – like a chicken wi' its head chopped off."

Craig, and Bobby too, had been engrossed in the argument but Craig decided that it was now time to intervene. Though not garbed in the authority of his uniform, he nonetheless posed a constable's standard question, "Now then, what's all this?"

Mr Roper spun round, his face lit with relief.

"Ah, now here's a timely arrival if ever there was one," he said. "I reckon Providence has sent us a responsible person, right in the nick o' time."

Craig addressed himself to Mr Dugdale, calmest of the trio, and from the caretaker elicited the whole sorry story which he absorbed with customary inscrutability in spite of an urge to laugh out loud at several points in the narrative.

Early in the afternoon, it seemed, Sammy Reynolds had quietly hidden himself in the boiler room, perhaps to take a nap. When the harmonium in the Bible Class hall had disturbed him, however, he had cheerfully joined in the singing. By a curious acoustic phenomenon the building's steam heating pipes had amplified Sammy's voice and conducted it clearly into the ground-floor hall. Now this would have been fine if Sam had been filled by the spirit of the Lord. But Sammy was filled with spirits of another kind and had chosen to render not a dour old Scottish hymn but umpteen choruses and verses concerning the sexual exploits of a roistering laird whose stamina and invention were legendary. For the next half hour Sammy had thus serenaded the Bible Class. "Without repeatin' himself," Mr Dugdale told Craig in awe. "Without repeatin' himself once."

Attempts to persuade Sammy to come out of the boiler room had failed. Mrs Lamb had persevered with the Class as long as possible until a gradual sea-swell among her charges had indicated that they were enjoying daft Sammy's operatic performance and were not at all shocked by the Laird of Ardentinny's obscene adventures.

"I always thought Sammy Reynolds was a decent lad," said Mrs Lamb. "Where did he learn such a revoltin' song?"

"He could have picked it up anywhere," Craig said. "Sam's always been able to parrot things that caught his fancy."

Craig had no doubt that Sam had heard the lewd saga in the basement of the Claremont and wondered what other tidbits he had picked up since Hog Moscrop had become a resident there.

"See if you can persuade him to come out, Mr Nicholson," Mr Roper said. "He's always been influenced by members of the constabulary, has he not?"

"I'll talk to him," Craig agreed.

Carrying Bobby, he made his way into the halls and down to the boiler room at the back of the building. The passageway was as narrow as a tunnel. On entering, it became apparent where a majority of Mrs Lamb's Bible Class students had found refuge. A dozen or more boys and several girls were piled in the passage and Craig, as he approached, could hear them egging Sammy on. Sammy, who never could resist an audience, had just embarked on verse forty-seven or thereabouts, his voice loud and ragged but still tuneful.

"God, it's the polis!"

Craig drew Bobby aside as the audience scarpered, ducking past him and heading at the gallop for the three shallow steps at the passageway's end.

"You, McCluskey. I know your mother!" Mr Roper shouted.

"Why, Vera Wishart, I'm surprised at you," Mrs Lamb yapped.

Craig put Bobby down, took his hand and moved on towards the door of the boiler room which, as indicated, was securely bolted from within. Sammy was oblivious to the loss of his audience. He was beating out the tempo on an improvised drum and went on with his singing, woozy and joyful – and the Laird of Ardentinny piled conquest on conquest.

"Sammy, it's me, Constable Nicholson. Come out o' there this minute." Sammy's row ceased abruptly. "Come on, Sam, draw the bolts."

"*Nah!*"

"Mrs Lamb's got tea an' an iced bun for you."

"*Nah!*"

"He's drunk as a lord," whispered Mr Dugdale from behind Craig's shoulder. "He'll not listen."

Craig paused then said, cajolingly, "Well, if you won't come out, Sammy, how about singin' the song again? Just for me. Sing it nice an' I'll give you a packet o' ciggies."

"*Aye,*" Sammy shouted unsuspectingly, and returned to the opening verse with enthusiasm.

"What did ye do that for?" asked Mr Dugdale.

"I'm goin' to have to go in an' get him," Craig said.

"But how?"

"Down the coal-shute," Craig said.

"Hell's bells! I never thought o' that."

Several minutes later Craig was on his knees in the lane that flanked the Mission, unlocking the padlock that secured the double trap-door of the coal cellar. He had left Bobby with Mr Dugdale and now that he was alone he could allow himself the luxury of anger. He wasn't mad at Sammy's mischief but at himself. He should not have ignored the rumours about Hog Moscrop's friendship with the daft boy. As he eased himself quietly down the wooden chute he vowed that if he discovered that Hog was behind all this then he would seek revenge.

It was dark in the cellar but Craig moved quickly to the boiler room where his protégé, whiskery, spike-haired and grubby, was seated on a bucket by the furnace. He was beating time with a poker on the furnace barrel, rather listlessly now, pausing now and then to lick the neck of the empty bottle that was clutched in his left hand. Craig stifled the sudden surge of fury that rose within him and said quietly, "Time to come out now, Sam."

Sammy did not seem at all surprised by Craig's sudden appearance behind him. Perhaps, unlike the caretaker, Sammy had not forgotten about the coal-chute and had expected to be pounced on long before now.

"Good, eh?" Sammy said.

"Great," Craig said. "Here, I brought your ciggies."

Sammy had no interest in tobacco at that moment, however. Now that he had lost the impetus of the song, all strength seemed to drain out of him in an instant. Without warning, he slumped forward and fell to the stone floor, the bottle ringing as it slipped from his grasp. Craig knelt and turned him on to his back.

"Ach, Sammy, Sammy," he murmured. "What the hell have we done t' you?"

The acne on the boy's face stood purple against flesh sapped of all colour and his big, round, ogling eyes were reduced to insensible slits. He groaned faintly as Craig lifted him, slung him over a shoulder and headed for the door.

He paused only to stoop, grunting, and retrieve the empty rum bottle that would be all the evidence he'd need to prove a case against Moscrop and find the wee man guilty without redress.

*   *   *

Quite worn out by the events of the week Ernest had toddled off early to bed. When she had gone into his room to tuck the quilt about his shoulders and kiss his brow, she'd discovered that he was still smiling, even in sleep. Ernest had always been a smiler. Frank, on the other hand, was prone to frown and to carry all the woes and worries of the day to bed with him, to lie scowling at the ceiling in the dark.

It had been a strange day, Phyllis thought, not entirely pleasant. She had not taken to Albert Adair, of whom she had heard so much for and against. She had thought his ebullience brittle and forced and had judged him, perhaps wrongly, to be a shallow fellow. His wife, however, had turned out to be a surprise. Phyllis had quite taken to the woman. Madge Adair reminded her of several gruff Highlanders she'd known as a girl, rough diamonds, unyielding but not unforgiving. She saw the quiet, brooding brother, Gordon, and the effervescent girl who would eventually become her daughter-in-law for what they were – children half-grown. She could excuse them anything because of their youth for, like Ernest, they were at one and the same time naive and sophisticated and quite unafraid of the twentieth century and what it might hold. She envied them their optimism and their ability to see the future bathed in a welcome light.

She would be dead soon, too soon. She didn't stem from a long-lived family and no matter how much Frank pampered her he could not strengthen a heart that had already begun to show signs of defectiveness and that would probably wear out completely in four or five years time. She did not fear the passing hour for her own sake. But Frank worried her. His loneliness and underlying sadness, the sacrifices he'd had to make to make gains for the rest of the family were apparent to her as to no other. More than anything now she wanted Frank to find a measure of happiness, to see him settled before she left this earth.

Wrapped in these melancholy thoughts, Phyllis didn't notice that the typewriting machine had ceased its pecking rhythm, that the fire in the living-room grate was almost out or that the lined shawl that Frank had put about her shoulders when he'd brought her tea an hour ago had slipped to the floor. She did not even hear him enter the room.

"Mother?"

She wasn't startled, for he spoke softly.

"Yes, dear," she said, stirring.

"Look, the fire's all but out. Aren't you cold?"

"No, I'm fine."

"It's late. You should be in bed."

"Aye," she said; an inflexion reacquired from Madge Adair, perhaps. "Aye, I am fair wearied."

Frank lifted the shawl, folded it and draped it over the back of her chair. "Are you feeling well enough?"

"Perfectly fine."

"Here, let me help you."

"Frank, don't fuss so. I'm not an invalid."

"Sorry," he said, but gave her his arm to lean on, nonetheless. She rested her weight against him. He was so large, had such solidity, more than his father had ever possessed.

"Haven't you work to finish?" she asked.

"No, it's done."

"Get to bed. Have a good night's sleep, for once."

"I shall." He paused. "I've an early start tomorrow morning." He paused again. "At the shop."

"Shop?"

"Yes, I'm taking a turn behind the counter, just for a change."

They were in the long, long hallway, lit by two small night-lights, one at each end. Phyllis had sufficient presence of mind not to falter, to keep her tone as casual as she possibly could.

"Did she ask you; Mrs Nicholson, I mean?"

"No, I volunteered."

"Isn't it possible for Ernest to help out?"

"He has a full book of appointments until Thursday."

"What about your own work, your commissions?"

"They'll get done, never fear."

"Well," Phyllis Tubbs patted his hand, "I expect it'll do you good to get away from the desk for a bit."

"Yes," Frank said. "I'm actually quite looking forward to it."

She was moved to warn him, tell him to be careful, but she

checked herself and offered no advice and no further comment. She inclined her head to receive his good night kiss and went into her room not, however, to sleep but to fret for hours with worry that her dear son Frank was about to be hurt, again.

*   *   *

"You won't hurt him, will you?" whispered Mr Black as he admitted Craig to the Claremont an hour after midnight.

"Nope."

"I really shouldn't be doin' this at all, y'know."

"You'll only have to do it once," Craig said. "I promise you there'll be no more trouble in that direction."

"Here." Mr Black held out a thin wooden shingle from which dangled the key to cubicle No. 37. "It's on the first floor, left at the top of the stairs."

"Where's Sammy?"

"Same floor, but the other end," Mr Black said. "He won't hear you, though. He's still out for the count. He'll be in a sorry state in the mornin', I'll bet."

"Might teach him a valuable lesson," Craig said. "If he's really sick will you let him stay in bed tomorrow?"

"Of course."

Craig was in uniform and on duty and Scutter Street was not on his beat. If he was found here he would be reprimanded and fined again. But he would not be the first copper to mete out rough justice in the wee small hours and he would not be the last. Mr Black, however, locked the street door then hid himself in the cabin to the side of the hall, thus removing himself from involvement, ethical or moral, in what would occur upstairs.

Day room and canteen, common kitchens and the long half-basement lay south of the stairs. Out of the Stygian darkness came groans and sighs, whimpers and wheezes as if the men in residence were as restless and tormented in dreams as in daylight. Craig trod lightly on the creaking, hardshell linoleum that protected the stairs. Faint blue-glass light gave shape but no definition to banister and walls. He could smell poverty all round, held in suspension with gas and foul breath, boiled cabbage, white beans and carbolic disinfectant. When he reached the first floor's rank of box-like cubicles, the smell became a stench, almost overpowering in its corporeality.

Cubicles filled the interior of the broad vaulted loft like so many upright coffins. Each door had a padlock to secure it during the day. Within was a box-shaped bed with a locker beneath it, a shelf in lieu of a table, and not much else. No window or aperture, no light save that which filtered through the heavy metal-mesh netting that roofed each two-berth box.

Here poor Sammy lived, to this prison Craig had condemned him. What shook Craig most of all was the realisation that there were worse places than the Claremont; the slum where Sam had been reared, for instance, and the lunacy ward where he might yet end his days, and places in the city worse even than those. Craig shuddered, hesitated then, gathering himself again, he unlocked the door of Hog Moscrop's cubicle and stepped quickly and quietly inside.

Hog had brought with him into exile a few appurtenances of former independence, genteel touches that seemed comical in the Model's barren landscape. A grubby, silk-tasselled nightcap clung to his hair, and a clock balanced on three little claws on the shelf above his head, though how the timepiece had escaped the pawnbroker's clutches Craig could not imagine. Sentimental attachments seemed out of character for the ugly wee man who lay on his back in the oblong bed and stirred the nightcap's tassels with his boozy breath.

Carefully Craig seated himself on the edge of the mattress. Hog was a heavy sleeper. He did not stir. In striped nightshirt and cap he resembled some minor Biblical character to whom Craig could not put a name. For fully a minute Craig listened to his snores then, saying nothing yet, slid a hand under Hog's head and gingerly extracted the pillow. There was something cruel in his calculation. Perhaps it was that element that excited him. He placed the pillow over Hog's mouth and pressed downward with both hands. Hog's eyes flashed open. He kicked out frantically and grabbed Craig's wrists with fingers like steel claws. Craig bore remorselessly down upon the flock pillow, smothering the sounds that flooded from the wee man's throat.

"Recognise me?" Craig whispered.

The berth next door was separated by only a partition of thin board and Craig did not doubt that Hog's stifled outcry had wakened its occupant. He was sure enough of the character of the lower orders to be certain that nobody would rush to Hog's aid. "Know why I'm here?"

Even in semi-darkness Craig could see signs of Moscrop's distress grow by the second. His brow was knotted, his cheeks the colour of Oloroso, his eyes enormous bloodshot orbs that threatened to pop out of his skull through fear and oxygen starvation.

Craig whispered, "Give the boy one more drink, Hog, one more damned drop, an' I'll come back some night an' finish you off. Do you understand?" He plucked the pillow an inch from Hog's face and heard, with grim satisfaction, the long raucous grab for breath. He shoved the pillow down again. "Next time you won't know what hit you. You'll just waken up in hellfire, Hog, burnin' like a bit o' dry tinder. Do you understand what I'm sayin'?"

Hog was still, no longer struggling. His eyes, glazed with hatred, were fixed on Craig's. He managed a nod of sorts and Craig let him breathe again. Hog jerked up his arms to protect his head, tucked knees to belly and, like a foetus, cowered away with his face to the wall, gasping.

Craig no longer had the heart to insist on an answer. He dropped the pillow and, without wasting another word, let himself out of the box and walked quietly between the listening cubicles to the head of the stairs. He paused, looking down the floor, in the attic where Sammy Reynolds slept, not innocently now but stunned by rum and all the other irrational desires that a boy had to cope with to make him into a man. He had delivered Hog a warning and could do no more for Sammy. He experienced no sense of power. The thrill of intimidation swiftly waned as he lingered on the Model's upper floor. All he felt now was sadness, sadness and pity not just for daft Sam Reynolds but for old Hog Moscrop too.

*   *   *

The Temperance Movement was international and long-established. In all corners of the civilised world opponents of alcohol harangued the populace of nations in a hundred different languages and a thousand different dialects. The control of the sale of drink was no longer just a platform for preachers and killjoys but had become a prime political issue which no parliamentarian worth his salt could afford to ignore. In Scotland

173

vested interest and vulgar opinion were stumbling blocks to more rigorous legislation. The kirk had had its fling by having the pubs closed on Sundays. Now it was up to the new breed, those who came armed not with texts and catechisms, pledges, medallions and free tea-caddies but with a rational, integrated rhetoric backed by more facts and figures than it would take to wrap the Wallace Monument for parcel post.

Gordon felt a reluctant affinity with the social reformers. He found their literature stimulating and was quite stirred by speeches that propounded a universal Utopian ideal. In spite of the weather he went along without reluctance to the Wedderburn Hall in Glasgow's Anderston ward that Monday night to attend a general meeting of the Scottish Women's League of Socialism and Temperance.

Rain cascaded on to the roof and flayed the north-facing windows and the attendance was very sparse, only twenty-five or thirty folk having braved the elements. There were no hymns and no prayers but a straight plunge into statistics and an outlining of programmes of state control and municipal responsibility which had been effective in foreign lands. The audience was thinly scattered in the Wedderburn's vast auditorium. The majority seemed to be converts to the cause already, except for the mandatory wee drunkard who had staggered in out of the rain and, Gordon noted ruefully, was summarily 'bounced' before he could express an opinion on the policies promulgated on his behalf.

Josephine Adair was the fourth speaker of the evening. Whatever Johnnie and Eric might think to the contrary, their cousin was a highly intelligent young woman with a commanding air of authority and a fine gift of the gab. She addressed the little multitude with head held high, blonde hair shining, her ungloved hand stabbing this way and that as she hammered home her points: "Gambling may reduce a family to starvation. Commercial speculation may lead to ruin. Capitalism may bring sickness in its wake and drive honest women to shame. But the relation between cause and effect in such cases is not nearly so obvious and immediate as the connection between drink and misery, between drink and poverty, drink and crime, drink and lunacy, disease and death."

Impressed by the messenger as much as the message, perhaps,

one elderly gentleman called out a fruity, "He-ah, he-ah!"

He was rewarded with a tiny, cold smile before Josephine continued: "The degradation that drink drags after it cannot be hidden or disguised. Its evils obtrude upon us at every turn. Public houses spew their disgustin' contents on to the public pavements and the reelin' brutalised victims of drink dunt against us at every street corner in every city, town and village in our fair land. The slums of Glasgow stink with the foul odour of alcohol and our newspapers are chock-a-block with accounts of debaucheries, outrages, assaults and murders done while under its pernicious influence."

Rain stotted off the roof. Wind whistled through the hall's lofty beams. Gordon gave an involuntary shiver and dug his hands deeper into his overcoat pockets. He was suddenly very conscious of being a cog in the great wheel of social evil. Apprenticed to a brewer and engaged to a brewer's daughter, he could not help but feel prickles of guilt. He tried to remind himself that public houses were also warm and welcoming refuges for decent working men and that not all publicans were deep-dyed villains. In the blast of Josephine's rhetoric, however, the voice of self-justification seemed pale and hollow. He knew only too well that public houses existed for just one purpose; to make as much pelf as possible for brewers, publicans, distillers and all their avaricious kin.

"What is the answer to this problem?" Josephine cried. "Legislative restraint is the only answer that will ever work."

"Aye, lass but *will* it?"

The question came from a humble artisan who was seated near to the rear exit as if he feared that he might be set upon for his temerity and have to beat a hasty retreat. Josephine was not offended and certainly not daunted.

"Well," she answered, "I grant you that it can't be proposed as a substitute for moral self-control. In the last resort every man's character must remain in his own hands. But there are aids and legislative control over the manufacture and distribution of strong drink is surely one of them."

With a shake of his head the humble artisan said, "Aye, but an Act o' Parliament canna make a man stay sober if he has a mind set on drink."

"Yes, that's right," Josephine agreed. "But our present

175

licensing system makes it far too bloomin' easy for a man *not* to stay sober." She took a breath, stabbed her hand. "Do you, sir, believe that everybody should be allowed to sell drink everywhere, at any hour of the night or day, to any person at all, whether he or she be old or young, sober or already drunk?"

"Naw, but – "

"Would you repeal the present laws?"

The humble artisan was harried but, being a true Glaswegian, would not admit defeat. He grinned, raised his hand in the air and unfolded a spotless white handkerchief in signal of surrender. "Hey, missus," he cried. "You're preachin' t' the wrong bloke. I've already signed the Pledge."

"I'm delighted to hear it," said Josephine. "Now, if I might press on."

"Aye, do," said the artisan, sweetly.

Josephine fell into her stride again immediately: "Let me interject a word or two about monopoly capital and the value in cash terms of obtaining a drink licence. Now, you may wonder what a young female person might be expected to know of such exalted matters. Let me confess that I was suckled and weaned on the proceeds of just such extortion."

Gordon raised his eyebrows in surprise that such personal revelations would be acceptable in this gathering.

Josephine continued, unabashed: "My father was, and still is, a spirit broker and my uncles were, and still are, brewers and publicans. So, you see, I've seen how this invidious trade in human misery is actually conducted. I've seen how young men, *like that young man there* – " She pointed straight at Gordon. " – are inducted into its devilish legions to provide for its future."

"Oh, Jeeeze!" Gordon muttered and, as several reproving faces turned in his direction, sank down and down until nothing much remained to goggle at but a pair of furiously unrepentant ears glowing red above the seat-back and a neck that blushed like a rose.

*   *   *

"You didn't really mind, did you?" Josephine Adair said.

"Of course I really minded!" Gordon told her.

"I've absolutely no scruples when it comes to making a point."

"So I've begun to realise."

They were standing together by a trestle table at the back of the hall, sipping stewed tea from chipped cups. Josephine's cheeks radiated heat from the exertion of her speech, Gordon's from enduring embarrassment.

"What are you actually up to, Gordon Nicholson?"

"I'm not up to anythin'."

"Why, then, are you following me about?"

"Don't flatter yourself, Miss Adair. It's the Temperance Movement I'm interested in, not you specifically."

"Oh, rubbish!" Josephine said, with just a hint of annoyance. "By the way, how did you like the tea?"

"This stuff? It's awful."

"Do not, pray, be churlish."

"All right," Gordon said. "Yes, the tea was quite delicious, and I thank you for it."

"It was the least I could do," Josephine said. "It isn't every day that a young woman finds herself being rescued by a gallant gentleman."

"Some rescue! You didn't need rescuing at all, did you?"

"It's the thought that counts," said Josephine. "However, you're evading my original question; what are you up to, following me about?"

She was a good four inches taller than he was, broad-shouldered, full bosomed. She had candid, irreverent eyes of a peculiar green colour that reminded Gordon, inappropriately, of a famous French liqueur.

"I'm interested in monopoly capital," Gordon said.

"Pull my other leg."

"No, it's true, I swear."

"You've been sent to spy on me, haven't you?"

"Spy?"

"I honestly don't mind," Josephine said. "It's just the sort of thing I'd expect from Uncle Dolphus. Half the men in the audience tonight were here only to report back to their masters in breweries or distilleries. We're always glad to see them. It means that the blackguards take us seriously and regard us as a threat."

"Oh, you're a threat all right," Gordon said. "The League, I mean, not you personally. If ever you do manage to nudge the government into shavin' the openin' hours dear old Dolphus will

177

feel the pinch where it hurts, right in his pocket."

"He will not, I assure you, be alone," said Josephine. "However, that still doesn't answer my question."

They were interrupted by the arrival of a cheerful, chubby woman toting a tray of pink buns. It seemed to Gordon that she was angling to be introduced to him but she received short shrift from Josephine who pointedly directed her to peddle her wares elsewhere.

Josephine took up the conversation again, but on quite a different tack: "You are to marry my cousin, are you not?"

"Hmmm – in June."

"Will I be invited to the wedding?"

"Of course."

"She's very pretty, my cousin."

"Hmmm!" said Gordon.

"I must say, in all honesty, that I'm surprised she took you on. I always imagined that Amanda would wind up spliced to Johnnie Whiteside."

"I think," said Gordon, "that I'm what they call 'new blood'."

"Dear God!" Josephine exclaimed. "Are we still deludin' ourselves that the Adairs are next best thing to a royal dynasty? The way my kinfolk prattle on you'd think we sprang from the aristocracy. Did Breezy – "

Gordon interrupted. "Breezy's not like that."

"Nonsense! Uncle Albert's quite the worst of the lot."

"Cannot agree!"

"Why? Because he married your mother?"

"Leave my mother out o' this, please."

Josephine's sudden gesture of abashment took Gordon by surprise. Shame seemed to peel away the years and for a fleeting moment he glimpsed the child that she had once been, wide-eyed, uncertain, frightened of her own intelligence.

"I'm sorry, so sorry." She put down her cup and quickly took both his hands in hers. "I didn't intend – I didn't mean – I'm not a snob really, you know."

Gordon nodded, then smiled. "One can't be a Socialist and a snob at the same time; not even you."

Though she was relieved to have been forgiven her gaffe, she was back on the attack at once. "Not even me? Why do you say that? What makes me so singular?"

"Fishing!" Gordon wagged a finger. "You're fishing."

"I am not."

"What makes you so singular, if you must know, is that you are odd, very odd, Miss Adair."

"Did Johnnie Whiteside tell you that?"

"He didn't have to," Gordon said.

She mulled over his reply for ten or fifteen seconds then gave him a smile. "If we're going to be friends I think you'd better call me Josephine, don't you?"

"All right."

"And walk me home?"

"What?" said Gordon in alarm. "To Mosswell Bank?"

"No. Heavens, I haven't lived in the ancestral home for several years," Josephine told him. "I have rooms of my own."

"Really! Where?"

"Park Gardens. Ten minutes from here."

"In that case – I'll walk you home with pleasure, Josephine."

"In exchange, I'll tell you all you want to know."

"About what?"

"Monopoly capital," she said and, ignoring the stares of her Temperance colleagues, took a firm grip on Gordon's arm and led him, without further ado, towards the door.

* * *

The orthopaedic examination rooms were tucked away at the rear of Glasgow's Hospital for Sick Children and Kirsty could not approach the building, let alone enter its corridors, without a clammy nausea stealing over her in remembrance of what she had suffered here on behalf of her child. She would have preferred a private consultation with Dr Anderson at his home in Cheadle Court but, it seemed, the doctor required a range of medical equipment that only the hospital could provide. Perhaps he also required the expert advice of Dr Kettleby, an older physician and quite the hairiest man that Kirsty had ever seen. Kettleby had a chest-length beard the colour and texture of coconut matting and a thick down of similar hue on the backs of his hands and knuckles. Fortunately, he also had warm, brown eyes and a gentle manner that swiftly reduced Bobby's initial howls of terror to mere uncertain sobs.

Nurses frightened Bobby more than doctors did. He

associated milkmaid bonnets and starched cuffs with the memory of pain and isolation and, when one of the women would appear, would hide behind Kirsty's skirts or plead to be taken into her arms. Though he had learned to ignore the undeveloped limb and its iron brace at home, within the hospital's antiseptic atmosphere he seemed to shrink in stature and become prey to all a young child's fears. He was even afraid of Dr Anderson's spotless linen jacket, brilliantined hair and sleek black moustache as if he sensed, perhaps, that for all his charm the man was more interested in the wasted leg than in the child who was attached to it.

The examination room was remote from the public dispensary and quarantine ward. Even so, Kirsty felt depressed by their proximity and recollection of the hours she'd spent at the window of the Parents' Room made her shudder. She was obliged to appear calm, however, to wait motionless and unprotesting in a corner of the examination room while doctors stretched her son out upon a long leather-padded table, twisted and manipulated his leg and finally fitted his feet into the stirrups of a fiendish-looking metal frame from which hung ropes and pulleys and wedge-shaped weights. After his initial outbursts Bobby was more composed than his mother. He obeyed every instruction from the doctors with the purse-lipped scowl that Kirsty had come to know so well these past months, with a rim of tears in his eyes but a proud and stubborn determination not to let these men get the better of him and make him cry again. At length he was lifted down and returned to her. She picked his clothes from the wicker basket at her feet and dressed him while the doctors conferred over their pencilled notes.

The shuddering feeling had gone into her stomach and she was tense as a watch spring as she waited for their pronouncements.

Dr Kettleby grunted, nodded, turned and with a wave to Bobby, bid Kirsty a good day. He hurried out of the room, leaving the younger man to break the news, good or bad as it might be. Dr Anderson leaned against the examination table and appeared to read from the papers in his hand. "Bobby's perfectly sound, Mrs Nicholson. Remarkably, he does not seem to have been much set back by the illness."

Kirsty bit her lip and waited for the physician to deliver

judgement. There was more to come, she knew, and her stomach churned at the prospect of what it might be.

"As to the leg itself," Anderson went on, "well, that hasn't healed quite as thoroughly as we'd hoped it might. I feel that muscular damage, though not excessive, will be permanent."

"What *exactly* does that mean?" Kirsty demanded.

"Certain groups of muscle in the lower part of the limb will not bulk and develop as Bobby grows."

"Would you explain, please?"

"Some degree of wastage, a shortening of the limb in relation to the other, is inevitable, I'm afraid."

"You mean he'll be crippled for life?"

"He will have a slight limp, yes."

"An' the brace – what about the brace?"

"It will have to be replaced every so often, as he grows."

"For how long?"

Anderson shook his head. "That I cannot say."

"Don't you know?"

"No, Mrs Nicholson, I can't even make a guess."

"It'll be on him forever, won't it?" Kirsty said. "The doctors can't cure him."

"He is 'cured', Mrs Nicholson." The doctor's tone became almost haughty. "I'd ask you to bear in mind that infantile paralysis is a very rare disease in this part of the world and our clinical knowledge of it is far from complete."

"What are you tellin' me?"

"Your son's been lucky, Mrs Nicholson. Yes, very lucky. Damage to his central nervous system has been minimal. If the infection had been severe, he would not have survived at all." Anderson held up a hand to quieten Kirsty's protest. "The wasted muscles will shorten with the passage of time. A prolonged period of treatment, specifically of exercise, will be of benefit in this respect. I will arrange to have it carried out."

"Where?"

"Here."

"It is not good enough," Kirsty said. "It is just not good enough."

"It will have to be. It's all that can be done. I'm sorry."

The doctor had no need to apologise. Kirsty was well aware that it was only Anderson's early diagnosis that had saved her son's life. Even so, she could not help but feel cheated by the fact that this rare, random disease had marked her child and changed the pattern of his life before it had properly begun. She gathered Bobby into her arms, forced herself to thank the doctor for his ministrations then turned her back on the ropes and pulleys and yanked open the door.

"Mrs Nicholson?" Kirsty checked her headlong flight and spun round to face the physician, who said, "You will have to bring him back, you know."

The pain in her stomach turned liquid. The guilt and frustrations of the past month mounted in her. She felt control slipping. She could barely contain herself, barely squeeze out the words, "I know."

"Shall I send you a letter of appointment?"

"Please do," said Kirsty thickly, then, with Bobby pressed against her body, hurried out of the room and out of the hospital before she burst into tears.

*   *   *

Nobody seemed to like the big girl. Gordon's casual enquiries among family members uncovered an unsubstantiated disgust with Walter's child and evidence of a whole basket of unsuspected prejudices. Josephine's size, her strength of character, her independent style of life seemed to mitigate against her more than her political eccentricities. Several of the Adairs referred to her as 'unfeminine', an adjective that seemed to Gordon to be entirely inappropriate. The truth was that the Adairs knew little about Josephine and even less of what she represented.

Amanda, like Dolphus, was scathing and dismissive. She declared that the only reason Josephine Adair had become a leading light in the Socialist Temperance Movement was because she was too ugly to attract men and trap a husband. Gordon did not bother to enlighten his fiancée on that score but when he met Josephine the following Monday for a quick bite of lunch in central Glasgow, passed on the information for what it was worth.

Josephine laughed; he'd known she would.

"Oh, yes, they'll be telling you next that I have a predilection for members of my own sex," Josephine said. "I think that's

Aunt Heather's favourite slander."

"Your own sex?" A slice of Grosvenor pie hung poised on Gordon's fork.

"Oh, Mr Nicholson, do not be obtuse. I thought you were a man of the world."

"You don't mean – ?"

"Yes, I do mean."

"It's not – ?"

"Of course it's not. I may share accommodation with other women," Josephine said, "but I have no inclination to share my bed with them."

Gordon choked on a fragment of pork and reached hastily for the water glass.

"It's a convenient sort of thing for my relatives to believe," Josephine continued, "something they can comfortably grasp without straining their intelligence. Since they are, for the most part, driven only by a need to be admired and desired they assume that all women are equally shallow. And if they are not, then they must be perverted. Aren't you eating your coleslaw?"

"No."

"Give it here then. No sense in it going to waste."

Gordon transferred the cabbage to Josephine's plate, watched her spread most of it on to a second slice of pie and devour the lot in two mouthfuls.

There was something admirable in Josephine's appetite, a heartiness that matched her scale. He had to admit, however, that he had been brought up a bit by her directness.

"I'm preaching," Josephine said. "I shouldn't preach. It's a dreadful habit. My substitute for flirting, perhaps."

"I think," Gordon said, "that under the circumstances I prefer preachin'."

"What circumstances?"

"I'm practically a married man, Josephine."

"Oh, I'm not trying to steal you away from Amanda. She's quite welcome to you."

"Thanks so much," Gordon said.

Her jacket *was* rather mannish, open upon the bodice, with a vest of gathered white silk. French canvas epaulettes made her shoulders seem broad and imposing. It was a practical sort of suit, Gordon supposed, ideal for her work as an office

183

supervisor in Alfred Dundee's Wholesale Tea Importers. He could imagine how she must terrify the juniors. She had found the position through her connections with Temperance, for Alfred and Norman Dundee were, naturally, both staunch supporters of the Prohibition lobby. It paid something more than a living wage, but not much. It was only because Josephine had inherited a tidy sum from a great-aunt – also a lady of independent spirit – that she had been able to leave home and set up in comfort on her own.

Gordon was more intrigued by Josephine Adair than attracted to her – or so he told himself. He saw no harm in fostering a friendship with a woman who was, albeit distantly, related to him and in whose company he found stimulation, purely of the intellectual variety, of course.

"You're drinking water?" Josephine said.

"Yes."

"Miss Romola's isn't dry, you know. Do you prefer water?"

"I have to work this afternoon," Gordon said.

"Clear heads think best," Josephine said. "They do a lively rice pudding here, if you're interested."

"I've had enough, thanks," Gordon said. "But do tuck in, Josephine. I'm not in that much of a hurry to be off."

She hesitated, scanned a pudding as it passed on a serving-girl's tray, shook her head at her own lack of will, and ordered a rice and raisin soufflé.

"What about tomorrow?" she said, looking away across the dark brown acres of the basement towards the kitchen doors. "Are you in Glasgow tomorrow?"

"Not far away," Gordon said.

"I take lunch here almost every day," Josephine said. "At a quarter past twelve, precisely. Creature of habit, you see."

"If I dropped in – "

"I'd be here."

"Preachin'?" Gordon asked.

She glanced at him quickly, slightly startled perhaps to find that he had not immediately taken flight.

Gordon grinned.

She smiled back at him, gave a little shrug of the French canvas epaulettes. She had, however, no time to invent an evasive reply before the rice pudding arrived and no inclination, then or later, to tell him an outright lie.

*   *   *

Kirsty did not return at once to the shop. She had no thought at all for how Frank might be faring there. She needed to go home, to be with Craig and seek his comfort in the face of the depressing news that Dr Anderson had imparted.

Once clear of the hospital Bobby immediately put the unpleasant experience behind him. He swiftly recovered his exuberance when treated to a ride on one of the new electric tramcars, with its clanging bell, chattering wheels and fizzing overparts. He shared his excitement not with his mother but with two of the lead tribesmen that Tubby had given him. He had a young child's instinct for a parent's mood and respected, at least for a while, his mother's gravity. He did not try to involve her in his playful fantasies but was content to converse with the tiny painted men, lame and braced like himself.

It was just after noon when Kirsty and Bobby reached home. To Kirsty's surprise Craig was up and dressed. He had even made and consumed a breakfast of sorts and was seated at the kitchen table with a second cup of tea. A cigarette clung to his lips and a newspaper was propped against the milk jug. Collarless, unshaven and dishevelled, he looked unwholesomely like one of the petty criminals that languished overnight in Ottawa Street's holding cells. The grunt he gave her by way of welcome had, to Kirsty's ears, something of a snarl in it and her desire to have his arms about her evaporated there and then. She caught Bobby just as he started around the table towards his father, settled her son on her knee and began to unbutton his overcoat.

"T'amcar. We all wented on a t'amcar."

Bobby was keen to regale his father with the tale of the morning's adventure but Craig ignored him.

"Well, what did Anderson say?" Craig asked after a full minute of silence. "Or is that another secret I'm expected to drag out of you?"

"The damage is permanent," Kirsty stated. "He's not goin' to get any better."

"Aye," Craig said, after a pause, "I could have told you that without a doctor's opinion."

"I suppose you're a medical expert too, now?"

185

"No, but anybody with half an eye could see the leg wasn't recoverin' its strength. He'll just have to learn to live with it, I suppose."

"Didn't you even *hope* that the doctors might be able to repair it?" Kirsty said.

"I don't believe in miracles."

He removed the newspaper from the table, tossed it on to the armchair, poured black tea from the pot and lit another cigarette. Bobby, meanwhile, had settled himself on his mother's lap and had put the two lead figures on the table where, by leaning forward, he could whisper to them. Now and then he would peep up at his father, head cocked quizzically, but he had evidently decided that it would not be prudent to fuss for attention just yet.

Kirsty nodded towards the teapot. "Will I make fresh?"

Craig shook his head. "This'll do me."

Kirsty said, "I'm surprised you're up. Is there a parade this afternoon?"

"Nope."

"Still night shift?"

"Aye."

She rose, put Bobby down by her side but continued to hold on to his hand. "Well, I'll have to get round to the shop. I'll take him with me."

"Who's there, at the shop?"

"Ernest Tubb's brother. That's why – "

Craig leaned and twisted his hips so that he could look around the table at his son. "Do you want to go with Mammy?"

Having been offered no alternative as yet, Bobby scowled but did not answer.

Craig said, "Or stay here wi' me?"

"Aye," Bobby said.

"Aye, what?"

"Stay."

"It's not necessary," Kirsty said. "He wasn't given exercises this mornin' at the hospital so he doesn't need to rest."

"No' go to the shop today," Bobby said in a tone that could in an instant deepen into a stubborn sulk. "Stay wi' Daddy instead."

"He needs his dinner," Kirsty said.

"I'll see to that," Craig said. "We'll be fine, him an' me. Won't we, son?"

"Aye."

Kirsty smoothed the folds of her coat and adjusted her hat. She did not want to leave Bobby, did not want him out of her sight. But she had committed herself. Her son galloped round the table and threw himself against his father's knees, the painted tribesmen abandoned on the table top.

"All right," she said.

Bobby had turned outward and reclined against his father's strong thighs, calipered leg jutting stiffly before him, all the rest of him relaxed and indolent. Kirsty stooped to kiss his mouth but Bobby tilted his head, chin up, and presented his cheek instead.

Unsmiling, Craig looked up at her, waiting for her to leave.

"I won't be late," Kirsty said and then, with no response from Craig, went out and left the pair of them together at the table by the fire.

* * *

Craig heard the house door close and the click of the mortise lock that he had recently installed. He sat quite still, the boy's weight against him, listening to the sound of Kirsty's heels vanishing down the stone stairs. He drew in a deep, discreet breath – and then another.

Bobby glanced round and up at him, said, "We wented on a new t'amcar."

Craig stroked the boy's hair, brushing up the cowslick that had recently begun to show itself above the left eyebrow.

"Ah could take you on a new t'amcar," Bobby suggested.

"We'll see," Craig said. "At the hospital, did the doctors hurt you?"

Bobby gave a snort and, clambering up his father's body, scornfully answered, "Nah!"

Craig lifted him, the iron brace dangling. He wrapped his arms tightly about the child's body, clasping him as if for a moment he were a baby again. He patted his son's back gently, took in another deep, unsteady breath – and another still.

Face up close to his father's ear, Bobby whispered a sympathetic question. "Daddy gotta cold?"

"Aye, son," Craig murmured, thickly. "Daddy's got a cold."

187

*   *   *

Perhaps, Frank thought, he had missed his true vocation, should have been a butler not an author. The image reflected in the shop's shiny surfaces was that of a pompous, slightly portly man in narrow striped waistcoat, shirtsleeves secured by wire garters and with a large yellow dusting cloth in his hand. He had prepared himself to play the salesman, to turn on the charm and part well-to-do ladies from oodles of cash but the shop had been dead as a tomb all morning long. Out of boredom he had decided to polish a canteen of cutlery that had become tarnished during its sojourn in the window.

Leaning over the fitted shelves at the back of the window, he felt very self-conscious. While balanced on tip-toe and stretched to secure a grip on both sides of the polished box he was observed by two shawled women who laughed at his acrobatics and gave him a thumbs-up sign of approval before he tugged the little green curtain shut to hide his blushes. It took several minutes for the irony to sink in. For all his education, all his talent he, Albion Francis Tubbs, B.A., had become no more than a passing diversion, a peepshow for Greenfield's raggedy wives. It was a long, long time since he had felt so out of place. The experience, he told himself, would do him no harm. But to restore feelings of competence he found a tin of Sefton's Best Silver Paste and a duster in the backshop, unrolled a length of baize cloth along the top of the counter, and set to on the ornate forks.

Three forks into the dozen it occurred to Frank that the cutlery lacked a hallmark. The queer greeny-bronze colour that was showing on handles and tines was not quite what one expected from sterling silver. He put the three forks in a row on the baize and, fishing his spectacles from his pocket, inspected them critically. He glanced from the implements to the duster which, for some reason, was speckled with something that might have been stardust – except that it wasn't.

Frowning, Frank toddled to the high shelves along the shop's inner wall, reached up and extracted from stock an identical canteen. He held it along his left arm, opened the lid and looked down at the printed card that glared up at him from the top of the cutlery:

Finest Plated Birmingham Queen Anne Pattern
Wash in Soap & Water Only: Polish with Soft Cloth
WARNING: DO NOT USE PROPRIETARY PASTES
OR SOLUTIONS

"Oh!" Frank said.

He had his jacket on again and his hands washed clean and was just tying a knot in the string on the parcel when Kirsty entered. He had not expected her quite so soon. He slid the heavy parcel deftly below the counter, bridged his fingers on the counter top and said, without a smile, "Yes, Madam. And what may I do for you?"

There was, however, no response from the young woman. Frank regretted his juvenile attempt at a joke. He did not know where she had been or why she had asked him to take charge of the shop that morning. He had assumed that there would be some mundane domestic reason for her absence. Now, he was less sure. The dainty hat, the Sunday-best coat, the heeled shoes, plus the fact that Bobby was not with her, indicated something serious enough to cancel out his concern with three spoiled forks.

It was her smile that he had first fallen in love with. It had come rarely to her lips on the occasion of their first meeting, a surprise, something unexpected, like a blink of sunlight in a November sky. She had a wide, attractive mouth and when she smiled the bridge of freckles that dusted her nose seemed to become a shade more prominent. There was no trace of a smile that afternoon, however, and Frank had sense enough to say nothing. He folded his arms and leaned upon the counter, watching her, waiting to cope with whatever burden she'd brought him.

She said, "What's been happenin'?"

"Nothing. No sales. No customers at all."

"There's a guinea ticket on the register."

"Yes, I bought one of the Queen Anne canteens for myself," Frank said. "The cash is in the drawer. Here's the receipt."

She nodded, uncaring. She seemed almost at a loss to know what to do with herself, as if she had stumbled into the shop without intention or purpose. For one brief moment he imagined that she had hurried here to see him and had become disconcerted by emotions that were joyous but unwelcome. He stood up and moved to the end of the counter.

"Kirsty, what's wrong?"

"I've been to the hospital."

"What, are you ill?"

She shook her head. Her lips were compressed against tears – or confession. He had a longing to put his arm about her, to show kindness. He did not yield to the impulse. Bitter experiences in the past had taught him how such impromptu gestures were open to misinterpretation.

"With Bobby," she said.

"God, I thought he was well again?"

"An examination. He'll have the limp forever."

She gave a wave of the hand as if to indicate that she was indifferent to medical opinion or that the loss of power in a limb was nothing compared to the loss of a little life. The dismissive gesture was all bravado, though. Frank was not deceived by the mannerisms of courage.

"Where is he; the boy I mean?"

"At home. With my husband."

"Shouldn't you be with him?"

"No. I'm not needed."

"I can stay for the whole day, you know."

"It won't mend. It won't heal an' get better," Kirsty said. "I'll have to take him to that dreadful place, again and again, watch him suffer. I wouldn't mind if it would make him well, but it won't."

"Going there – did it bring it all back?"

"Yes."

"I wish I could do something to help," Frank said.

Again she shook her head. "You can't. Nobody can."

"Have you been crying, Kirsty?"

"No," she snapped.

"Why not?" he asked.

"Cryin' doesn't do any good."

Frank dipped into his jacket pocket and produced a folded, perfectly clean handkerchief which he shook out and held towards Kirsty.

"Oh, yes, it does," he said.

She broke down and wept then. She allowed him to put his arms about her and hold her, her head against his shoulder, her soft breasts touching his chest. It was not the first time that he had held a tearful woman in his arms, nor the first time he had offered sympathy as a substitute for desire. On each of the three previous occasions he had put honour before satisfaction and had broken off the affair before it could properly begin. He'd refused to admit that he might be low enough to steal the affections of another man's wife. This time he was not so sure.

He was strongly aroused by Kirsty Nicholson. He wanted her so badly that it drained his considerable resources of will to resist. Thankfully, in her distress, she seemed unaware of his needs. When she had cried herself out, she separated herself from him, relieved by but a little ashamed of her tears, and full of needless apologies.

Five minutes later, with hat and coat off and face washed in cold tap water, she was drinking the tea that Frank had made and chattering nineteen to the dozen about her son, her fears for her son's future and her feelings of helplessness in the face of life's vicissitudes.

Frank listened attentively but was careful to say nothing that might betray his intentions before the time was ripe and he was ready, one way or another, to make his move.

*   *   *

The little blue devil that gnawed at Breezy's conscience did not seem to have a deleterious effect upon his physique. In fact, since brooding was such a solitary and sedentary occupation, Breezy had lost his lean, whippet-like appearance and, as spring advanced towards summer, thickened in the face as well as about the middle. An increase in girth did not restore his jollity, however. New fat folds beneath his eyes and around his moustache soon sagged with the collective weight of his woes and gave him the droopy mien of a basset who has forgotten where the bones are buried. Madge was worried in case her husband was still fretting about Lorna's future, but Breezy kept his own counsel about what was really getting him down.

Morning routines had gone by the board. He did not rise and shine, breakfast, dress, shave and depart on a casual round of his money-making enterprises. He did not stroll down to the

Northern Lights or the Glenmore Bar or cab it into the Exchange to crack with his cronies and crow when his shares climbed on the board. Naturally, he did not dare venture near Adair's warehouse to confront his nephews face to face. He did, however, communicate with Johnnie by a recently-installed telephone system. One heavy, trembling hand cupped over the speaking-piece, eyes darting furtively this way and that he would ask the same question every day, "Any news?", and with shoulders sagging hear the same pessimistic reply, "None that's good, Uncle, none that's good." What Breezy failed to realise, because it was foreign to his nature, was that the budding generation had managed to confuse ambition with cupidity and malice with power, that it had become second nature for Johnnie and Eric to kick a man who, if not quite down, was certainly on his knees.

There was more to Breezy's depression, however, than anxiety over what Bob McAlmond might reveal to police investigators. Unsuspected layers of guilt had been disturbed in him and dust from the distant past fogged his reason, clouded his judgement and caused him to stumble into a mire of indecision. By the month's end, he had become so unsure of himself that he hardly dared leave the house. He frittered away his days slumped in a chair in the downstairs parlour surrounded by a strew of newspapers, or upright at the window, hands dug into cardigan pockets, gazing out at the pale sunlit terrace as if he expected a squad of constables to arrive at any moment bearing manacles and leg irons and a warrant for his arrest. Yet there was still a spark, a tiny spark of the old driving, conniving, down-to-earth Breezy within him. He was rational enough – just – to realise that he had to do something, trust someone before his nervous system collapsed and he was carried off babbling to the nut-hatch at Gartnavel.

Screwing up his courage he decided to confide in Gordon, tell the boy the squalid truth and at least share his misery. He was gratified when his stepson listened to his admission in silence as if sensitive to the effort it cost to own up to the fact that he, Albert Adair, had been scared by a slanderous rumour. When Breezy finished his tally of woes, however, Gordon snorted and shook his head.

"What's wrong?" Breezy asked. "Don't you believe me?"

"Oh, I believe you all right," Gordon answered. "In fact it's a relief it isn't more serious. We all thought you were sickenin' with a fatal disease or somethin'."

"It may not seem serious to you but it's damned serious to me."

"Who told you this tale in the first place?"

"Dolphus. But Johnnie confirmed it. We did pay bribe money to ex-Provost McAlmond."

Gordon snorted again. "What do you want *me* to do about it?"

"Ask your brother, ask Craig if it's true, if McAlmond *is* bein' investigated by the police."

"What if he is?" Gordon said. "That won't prove anythin' against you. From what I've heard of Bob McAlmond he's a slippery customer. Besides, even if he does get caught he won't remember who paid him what by way of pifflin' sums."

"Records. He might have kept records."

"I thought you were in cahoots with bigwig coppers. Can't you have a quiet word in the Chief Constable's ear?"

"An' alert Organ to my involvement in a crime?" Breezy said. "No, son, you're the only one I can trust. Will you not do it for me?"

Gordon hesitated. "Already have."

"Have what?"

"Spoken to Craig about this matter," Gordon said.

"How did you know I was in trouble?"

"I didn't," Gordon said. "Craig raised the issue, not me. I thought he was just being daft, that's why I didn't mention it to you before now. It was *me* didn't take it seriously."

"Well, come on, out with it; what did Craig say?"

"He mumbled on about 'dirty money' an' asked if you'd ever had dealings with Bob McAlmond."

Some of the nervous anxiety had already gone out of Breezy's expression. His hands were no longer clasped together at the level of his navel but rested squarely on his thighs and his mouth had lost its droop. "So McAlmond is under police scrutiny?"

"Seems like it."

"Do you think it was Craig's intention to warn me?"

"Nothin' so charitable," Gordon said.

Breezy sat back in the armchair, crossed his knees, folded his arms. "What to do?" he said, peering up at the curtain rail as if for inspiration. "What to do?"

Gordon said, "Take action."

"How?"

"Only one person can tell you how much trouble you're in."

"Who?"

"McAlmond himself," Gordon said. "Pay him a visit."

"But I don't know the man. I mean, we met casually once or twice, but that's all. I never had much to do with burgh politics and I certainly never made any contribution to McAlmond's welfare."

"This isn't like you," Gordon said, "mopin' about the house, cowed by a scaremonger's rumour. You only have Whiteside's word for it that the Provost's palm was greased on your behalf."

"You know, son, I think you're right."

"Square up to it. Go an' see McAlmond."

"By God, Gordon, I think I will."

"I'll come with you."

"What for?"

"Moral support," said Gordon.

*   *   *

The house that Provost Robert McAlmond had purchased early in his second term of office was a plain, two-storey mansion constructed about the year of 1820. Some said that the burgh had grown around it and McAlmond himself was quick to foster this claim, though the truth was that it had been built by a wealthy Glasgow merchant to appease a voluble and mercenary mistress. It had a flying staircase, a simple but impressive Doric doorpiece and a great many shrubs packed densely into gardens fore and after. It was as far removed as possible from the boiling-pans, cesspools and resinous tanks of the McAlmond Oil Works on Clydeside. McAlmond's fortune ostensibly derived from sale of the products of lard-crushing, tallow-melting and the manufacture of lamp black. But there were five brothers all drawing from the business and none of the other four seemed to have grown as fat on the profits as Provost Bob.

Reputation and a strength of character that added up to tyranny had been Bob McAlmond's hallmarks for the thirty years he had served, in one capacity or another, on Greenfield's burgh council. His most famous achievement had been the expansion and reorganisation of the Cleansing Department and the building on a Wolfe Road site of a forced blast screening plant for the reduction of refuse, whose roars and groans kept bairns awake and troubled the dreams of light sleepers all through Greenfield north. The *Partick Star* even printed a caricature of Provost McAlmond with vents in place of ears and a mouth like an open furnace, and the base-line 'Owd Bob Sings a Lullaby', after which the plant was nicknamed 'Owd Bob' and the Provost 'The Destructor'.

Proud days for a proud man, a man so marinated in conceit, that his abrupt resignation from the council office in January had shocked his few friends and his many enemies. It was not to protect McAlmond that councillors kept mum about the reasons behind their colleague's departure but only to salvage the reputation of the burgh. When, however, investigation of paperwork related to McAlmond's terms was undertaken by an accountant appointed by Chief Constable Organ, and a Percy Street detective began to interview clerks and councillors, the rumours could no longer be suppressed.

Some thought that McAlmond would brazen it out, others that he would make a run for it, seek refuge with his son in Canada. Nobody realised that Mr Organ and Mr McAlmond had had a very private conversation in which the Chief Constable had made it pikestaff plain what would happen if the ex-Provost tried to escape justice and explained that it was only a matter of time before a case was prepared and criminal charges brought against him. If Breezy's brooding had been bad then McAlmond's was ten times worse. The ex-Provost knew exactly what lay in store for him and had no doubt at all that the might of the law would see him not just fined and humiliated but stripped to the bare bone and shipped off to rot in jail.

Very little of his situation was known to Breezy when, somewhat revived in spirits if not exactly jaunty, he presented himself with Gordon at the door of McAlmond's residence about half-past six o'clock on a mellow evening in April and asked the female servant if he might have a word with the master of the house. What was surprising was that McAlmond, who had been lurking under the staircase within, recognised the voice of Mr Albert Adair and for some reason known only to himself, some final inexplicable whim, admitted him without warmth but without hostility.

The great Robert McAlmond was one of those small-statured, broad-shouldered men with a head that seemed too large for his body. He had once been famous for exotic waistcoats and cravats, for bristling eyebrows and a corona of sandy-red hair that seemed to symbolise a crackling energy and personal magnetism. There was nothing exotic or magnetic about him now, however. McAlmond was clad in shabby corduroy trousers, collarless shirt and a baggy, brown, knitted cardigan. His canvas house slippers whispered wearily on the bare linoleum as he shuffled away from the door and, without a word, ushered Breezy and Gordon into a small breakfast room so devoid of furniture as to be almost barren.

The house was queerly silent. No sound or sign of the wife or two dependent daughters, no clish-clash of dinner preparations, no warm odour of cooking from the kitchen. Only the stringy female servant and a room stripped down to a solitary old ladderback chair which stood to attention under a pendant gas fitting from which the glass globes had been removed.

"Well? Out with it. I'm in a hurry," McAlmond said.

He had one of the harshest voices that Gordon had ever heard, a grating rasp made unique by the manner in which he disguised his common origins. The affectation made him sound drunk, which he was not. He folded his arms over his chest, elbows stuck out like one of the bare-knuckle boxers that Gordon had seen in sporting prints. His eyes were as red as cornelians, though faded.

"Allow me to introduce myself . . . " Breezy began.

"I know who you are, Mr Adair. What's more I think I can conjecture your purpose here," McAlmond said. "You're not the first 'honest citizen' to come bangin' at my door, I can tell ye. I don't suppose you've come to offer to stand by me either, uh?"

Breezy was struck dumb by McAlmond's directness. Though he had dealt with hundreds of men forged by ambition and conceit Gordon suspected that his stepfather had seldom encountered a pride so raw.

McAlmond said, "Not so glib now, Mr Adair?"

Breezy bit his lip. "I do not know what I can do for you, Mr McAlmond."

"Nothing," McAlmond shook his head. "It's too late in the day

196

for help from any quarter."

Breezy took a deep breath. "It is not my intention to cast aspersions upon your integrity, sir, but nonetheless I must ask you an impertinent question in the hope that, in confidence, you'll give me an honest answer."

"Ask it."

"In years past did you accept money from my nephew, John Whiteside?" Breezy said. "Payment for the favour of grantin' publican's certificates."

"Are you implyin', Mr Adair, that I would pervert the duties of my office in the burgh for personal gain?"

"I do not know what I am implyin', Mr McAlmond," Breezy said, with unusual formality. "I am simply askin' a straight question in the hope that you will be equally straight with me. Did you, or did you not, take money from my agent, Johnnie Whiteside?"

Arms still folded and chin thrust out, Bob McAlmond exuded such an air of pugnacious defiance that, for a second, Gordon supposed that he intended to deny all knowledge of corruption; then he said, "No, Mr Adair, I did not take money from you or your agent."

"Do you know who I mean: John Whiteside?"

"Aye, I know the lad well enough," McAlmond said. "He must be about the only businessman with premises in the Greenfield from whom I haven't extracted money."

"What?" said Breezy.

"If you are askin', delicately, if I took bribes at all, the answer is that I did. Every fly-by-night, every upstart who thought he could squeeze a shillin' or two from Greenfield folk had first to pay me for the privilege. Aye, I took money from everybody. But not, Mr Adair, from you or from your nephew."

Breezy let out breath.

Gordon said, "Whiteside says that you did."

"Then he's lyin'."

"It's not you that's lyin', by any chance?" Gordon said.

"Enough, son," Breezy muttered.

"He's right to ask," said McAlmond. "Is he your boy?"

"He is," said Breezy.

"I'll answer him then. I have nothin' to gain by deceivin' either of you. The game's up with me, as you've no doubt heard. I'd rather have a last word with a man of my own kidney than with some glum priest. Take my word on it, Breezy Adair, the police have nothin' against you on this score, not in deed or letter. There! Is that what you want?"

"It is, Provost," Breezy said. "I thank you for your honesty."

For a second it seemed that Bob McAlmond was about to say more, to exercise the gift for long-winded oratory that had served and pleasured him so often in the past. Instead he shut his mouth with an audible little snap, thrust out his hand and shook Breezy's hand, and Gordon's. His fingers were strong and firm but the forearm trembled and he did not retain contact for long.

Breaking quickly away, he shouted, "Sadie, show them out."

*   *   *

Sundown above the river reach filled the April sky with mackerel clouds set against an infinity of translucent blue from which tenements and mansions, steeples and bridges seemed snipped off with pinking shears. It was all silk above and sailcloth below as Kirsty and Frank turned into Riverside Road to admire the view that swept away from the Greenfield shore. They had come out of their way for the purpose and, saying nothing, moved across the cobbled road to the railings that bounded the back of the lading docks. From there they looked down the long slot between warehouses to waters that rippled and glistened and reflected the heavens impatiently as they ebbed, rushing, towards the sea.

Slung across Frank's shoulder, Bobby was asleep. One arm dangled limply, face tucked into the man's collar. Calipered leg knocking painlessly against the man's hip they strolled along Riverside towards the bottom of the Kingdom Road. Tomorrow Lorna would return to her place behind the counter, Frank would imprison himself in his study to catch up on all the words he had sacrificed to keep himself close to Kirsty.

There was nothing to say, nothing he dared say. He held the minutes of sunset dearly, aware of what they might mean to him in years to come. All that was required to make it perfect was the freedom to put his arm about her waist or rest it protectively upon her shoulder or, better still, to have Kirsty link her arm in his so that they might walk united like the other couples who had been tempted out to watch the April evening cool into gloaming. Women leaned on the ledges of tenement windows and men gathered about the close mouths, faces ruddy in the soft slanting light. Even the gangs of children seemed subdued, pacified by spring twilight, oddly quiet at their play.

Bobby stirred and resettled his weight and Kirsty, quite involuntarily, put a hand on Frank's arm to hold herself in balance while she peeped up at her son.

"Isn't he too heavy for you?" she asked.

"No, he's no great weight."

"I'll take him in a bit," Kirsty said. "When you're tired."

"I'm fine with him, really."

"I'll miss you tomorrow, Frank."

"Will you?" he said.

She looked so pretty, so fresh and unsophisticated that he almost broke his resolve and kissed her. He was seriously in love with her and knew it, knew too that he did not dare express his feelings in case he lost her friendship and sent her away, demeaned or dismayed. He had hoped that by getting to know her better, by working with her every day, he would find flaws behind the pretty face, would discover pettiness and selfishness, perhaps a tartar's temper. But in Kirsty Nicholson he had found none of these common failings.

"Of course I will," Kirsty said. "It's been fun havin' somebody different to talk to every day. I've learned a lot."

"What, for instance?"

"Oh, about – I don't know – you're not so gruff as you pretend to be."

"I'm not gruff, am I?"

"At first I thought you were. I thought you disapproved of me somethin' awful."

"Oh, no," he said, taken aback. "I can't imagine how you got that impression. I've liked you – I've approved of you from the first, Kirsty."

"I'm glad."

"I'm just sorry that you're – "

He saw wariness in her eyes and she drew away from him, stepping back into her place at his side. Hastily he said, "Kirsty, I didn't mean – "

"We'd better be gettin' along," she said. "Will I take Bobby now?"

Frank shook his head. He was angry with himself for misjudging her acuity. He shook his head again, then followed after her as she quickened her step and cut diagonally across the cobbles away from the river towards the protection of the tenements.

It was as well that he had done nothing, given no obvious offence. He had no means of knowing, without asking, how long the man had been following them, observing what passed between them. As soon as he saw the chap he knew who he was. He did not need Kirsty's surprised little cry of "Craig!" to tell him that the lean, dark young man was her husband and that her abrupt change of direction had caught him out.

Craig Nicholson, Frank thought, looked cheap and shabby. In an unbrushed suit and collarless shirt he was unworthy of Kirsty's smartness. But Craig Nicholson had the advantage of being young, with a dour, unlearned arrogance that only time and experience would diminish. Frank strove to feel superior to Nicholson but handsome, unsmiling features and physical poise deflated him. He felt old in their presence, heavy and dull as sacking.

"What are you doin' here?" Craig asked Kirsty.

"We came down to look at the sunset."

"Uh?"

"Over the river," Kirsty said. "It's gone now."

Still ignoring Frank's presence, Craig nodded at Bobby. "He should be in his bed."

"We'll be home in a minute," Kirsty said. "Have you not had your supper?"

Craig did not answer. He met Frank's eye at last. "I'll take him."

"By all means," Frank said.

He waited for Craig Nicholson to jerk the child roughly from his arms but the young man transferred the boy to his shoulder with surprising tenderness. Bobby opened a sleepy eye, saw that he was being borne by Daddy now, and smiled. Frank felt suddenly excluded and stepped back a pace or two.

To her husband Kirsty said, "Lorna's back tomorrow."

"Not before bloody time."

"I don't think you've met Frank before."

Frank said, "I'm Ernest's brother. I've been – "

"I know who you are," Craig said. "Come on, Kirsty, I haven't got all night to blether in the streets."

Kirsty hesitated. For an instant she seemed torn. She was embarrassed by her husband's boorish behaviour but had just enough guilt in her to obey him without argument. As Craig turned away, however, she paused long enough to touch Frank's arm and murmur, "Thank you."

Frank tipped his hat and gave her a bow, gentlemanly gestures that did not adequately substitute for his desire to kiss her full upon the mouth, husband or no husband. He glanced past her at Craig who waited with glowering impatience at the pavement's edge.

"I'll see you soon, Kirsty," Frank told her.

"I hope so," she said then turned and hurried off to follow her husband and son on the homeward march.

*   *   *

It had been a quiet afternoon and the evening promised to be no more lively, thank God. The winter months had left a legacy in Sergeant Hector Drummond's bones, a rheumatic ache that it would take more than a blink of April sunshine to shift. Painful stiffness in his back, knees and fingers made him irritable and he'd had to struggle manfully these past few weeks to maintain the patience for which he was famous and of which he was justly proud. There was, however, nothing in the Sergeants' Log that required his immediate attention, nobody bawling for attention from the holding cells. All in all, Ottawa Street police station was as quiet as the burgh morgue in the last hours of the weekday back shift.

Constable Peter Stewart, nursing a verruca on his left heel, was sharing station duty. He had just brought Sergeant Drummond a fresh mug of tea when the street door creaked open and a tall, gaunt woman tentatively stuck her head round it. "Is this the police office then?" she asked.

Drummond slipped the tea mug under the lid of the desk and, with some effort, answered in a calm, reassuring tone.

"Indeed it is, Madam."

"Ottawa Street police office?"

"Aye, that is correct. Is there something we can be doing for you?" The Highland accent was as evident as it had been thirty

201

years ago when he'd first come down on the boat from Skye. "Will you not be coming inside?"

She was a domestic servant. Drummond could tell by the plain, neat clothing and by something deferential in her manner. She was no kitchen drudge, though, not this one. More like to be a housekeeper to one of the new middle-class families on the hill. Peter Stewart had hobbled out of the clerks' room and stood by the glass door watching the woman approach the desk. She brushed her coat skirts, adjusted her hat, straightened her spine, sniffed and only then placed the letter on the blotter under the sergeant's nose.

"What is this?" Drummond said.

"I have to deliver it."

"Who is it for?"

"To . . . t' who it may concern."

The letter was contained in a long cream-inlaid envelope of the sort that the better-class lawyers might use for court documents. It did not seem fat enough for a document, however, and the handwriting was not legal copperplate but a jagged, self-taught scrawl: *To Whom it May Concern.*

A wisp of steam from the tea mug drifted faintly from under the lid of the desk. Sergeant Drummond sucked his teeth thoughtfully and contemplated the missive with a passivity that was, as a rule, foreign to his nature.

"Had y' not better open it, Sergeant?" Peter Stewart said from somewhere behind him.

"All in good time, Constable."

The woman had been weeping. Her eyes were pink and swimmy and the flanges of her nose had the raw look that comes with too much wiping.

Sergeant Drummond said, "Who gave you this letter?"

"My master, Mr McAlmond."

"Robert McAlmond?"

"Aye, he's – " She twitched a balled handkerchief to her mouth as if to smother an opinion that might be construed as incriminating. "Open it, I beg you."

The little ivory ruler had a cutting edge with which Hector Drummond slit the end of the envelope. Still using the tool he fished within and extracted a single sheet of good quality notepaper blackened with inky script. He opened the note carefully

202

and read it and then, still holding the paper between finger and thumb, he lifted his head and stared at the woman again.

"When were you given this?"

"Twenty minutes since."

"Why did you not take it to Percy Street?"

"I was told – he told me to bring it here."

"Is he at home?"

"Aye."

"Is he alone in the house?"

"Aye, he sent his wife an' daughters awa' yesterday."

"Sent them where?" Sergeant Drummond said.

"To stay wi' his brother in Dundee."

"Did they take much luggage?"

"Everythin' they could carry," the woman said.

"What is it, Sergeant?" Peter Stewart said.

Hector Drummond gave the young man no answer. He turned and, still carrying the letter, strode to the new wooden cubicle on the rear wall where, only weeks ago, electrical experts from Glasgow had installed a telephone that connected Ottawa Street with Headquarters and a handful of other exchanges in the burgh. Uncertainly Drummond unhooked down the hearing piece, put his mouth an inch from the speaker and clicked down the lever which bore the paper label *H.Q.* upon it. He glanced round at the woman, frowning, then back to the instrument as a voice crackled in his ear.

Speaking very loud, Drummond said, "I want to talk to the Chief Constable. Is he there?" He paused. "Ottawa Street. Sergeant Drummond." He paused again then shouted. "Well, find him, damn it, find him wherever he is and fetch him down here right away." He released the lever, swiped the hearing piece at the hook, once, twice and then again, as if the new-fangled device had angered him and not the import of the letter, the last letter that Robert McAlmond wrote before he hanged himself from the gaselier in the breakfast room of his plain, two-storey mansion on the hill.

*   *   *

Breezy had had his first untroubled night's sleep in weeks. He had lain in his wife's arms, secure and soundly snoring, had not wakened when Madge had risen but had turned over and

203

snuggled down for an extra couple of hours. By ten o'clock, however, he was up and about. He felt remarkably chipper and quite his old self again now that the weight of worry had been removed from his mind. He planned the business of the day while he bathed and towelled himself. And the business of the day included, as a starter, a visit to Adairs' warehouse and a little quiet conversation with his treacherous nephew, Johnnie.

Anticipation of revenge put a glint of malice in the eyes that looked back at Breezy from the big mirror over the bathroom sink as he lathered cheeks and chin and lifted the elegant cut-throat to shave off the night's stubble. Razor poised, Breezy practised his smile, suave and unrevealing and, he thought, more dangerous around the edges. He tried it with a little more teeth, shook his head and, before the lather dried and became sticky, touched the whetted edge of the razor to his cheekbone. A sudden rapping on the door almost cost him a piece of his nose or, worse, half his moustache. He cursed, set the razor down on the marble and reached swiftly for a hand towel to stanch the floret of blood that stained the soap on his face.

The rapping continued, loudly.

"Who the hell is that?" Breezy shouted.

"Me. Gordon. Let me in."

"I thought you'd gone," Breezy shouted, twisting his head to catch the light from the window as he nursed the nasty little nick on his flesh. "I'm shavin'. Use the one downstairs."

The door handle rattled violently. Finally Breezy, in pyjama bottoms, robe and slippers, stepped to the door and unlatched it, tutting in annoyance at his stepson's impatience.

"What – "

Gordon, clad in neat tweeds, thrust a newspaper into Breezy's face. "Look, look at this!"

"What? I can't read it without my glasses."

Gordon pushed the man before him and closed the bathroom door behind him. He glanced round as he did to make sure that Madge had been excluded from the narrow, wood-panelled room.

"It's Bob McAlmond. He's dead."

"*What!*"

"It's here on the front page of the noon edition of the *Citizen*. Black and white. Plain as day. McAlmond's dead."

204

Breezy wiped lather from his cheeks with the back of his hand and, in the same motion, grabbed the newspaper from his stepson. He wrestled with it and then held it out at arm's length, squinting. Now that he had shared the news and discharged his excitement, Gordon seemed deflated and slumped on to the lavatory seat.

"But we – we saw him only last night," Breezy said.

"Did himself in. Hanged himself. It's all there."

Breezy peered and squinted at the blocks of tiny print below the column headline.

Gordon said, "Know what they say in the paper? Poor health. Strain of his responsibility as Burgh Provost takin' a belated toll. What utter balderdash! He bloody did himself in before the coppers could catch him an' send him to jail."

Breezy had turned white, whiter than the webs of foam that still adhered to his moustache. He staggered, put out a hand to steady himself then sank slowly down to seat himself upon the rim of the bath, the newspaper between his knees. "I – I – I can't believe it."

"It's there. It's true. What's more, he did it – hanged himself – yesterday evening. Right after we saw him, I reckon."

Shocked and trembling, Breezy turned to the young man for advice. "Gordon, what should we do?"

"Us?" Gordon pushed himself to his feet. "Not a thing."

"Did we give him reason to – "

"Of course we bloody didn't. He was all set up to do the deed before we arrived. All we did was interrupt him."

Breezy drew up the newspaper and stared at it, at the blurred print and discernible headline: *Provost McAlmond Found Dead.* He shook his head, dazed by the tragedy, by the implications that spread out from it like rings in a broad pool. "Killed himself. Took his own life. The Destructor, old Bob McAlmond," he murmured. "To do that, rather than face public exposure and humiliation."

"Yeah, I can't understand it," Gordon said.

"I can," Breezy told him. "Oh, Jesus, son, I can."

Seven

What Friends Are For

The spell of warm weather extended into May and brought with it a general change towards benevolence in all but the most embittered citizens or in those too old or too sick to experience summer's quickening.

There were none of that ilk in the City & Burgh Police Swimming Club, however. When the afternoon sun slipped between Cranstounhill's tenement roofs and found the windows of the long sandstone building, you could almost believe that the shimmer on the surface of the swimming pond meant that the water temperature had got above freezing, and even the less hardy constables ran exultantly from their boxes, hopped the rail, slithered and plunged, with manly whoops, into the rippling pool. Mistake, dreadful mistake! However tropical the light above the pond might be, fiends from the corporation department responsible for filtration, aeration and control of steam injection nozzles made dead certain that, unless you happened to be a polar bear, sudden carefree immersion would end in numbing shock, popping eyes and shrivelled tiny parts.

Archie's yodel of abandonment changed, after the splash, to a strangulated cry, a splutter of obscenities and a desperate dash for the steps. Peter Stewart, who had cautiously paused to brace himself before effecting an odd little bunny-hop into the water, came up like something scalded, and swarmed back over the edge of the catwalk so quick that his bathing suit hardly got wet. Only big, old blubbery sergeants and diehards from the River Police seemed comfortable in the silky green substance. They

206

trudged up and down, up and down, surging and dipping, squirting tiny jets of water from their mouths like strange aquatic mammals captured in the Baltic or off Cape Cod.

Bobby watched the antics of his Daddy's friends and eyed the dogged swimmers with gravity but no sign of apprehension as Craig carried him down the stairs from the upper tier of changing cubicles and walked him along to the steps at the shallow end. Bobby wore a brand new costume, exactly like Daddy's except that it didn't have letters stitched to the bodice. He had a rough towel, with letters on it, draped across his shoulders. He did not look up at the high arched roof for it worried him, somehow, more than the sheet of trembling green water or the funny men that moved about in it. Daddy had taken the iron from his leg. That, combined with the snug smooth wool of the costume, made him feel both liberated and secure at one and the same time. In Daddy's arms he was not afraid. He did not even flinch when Archie, nose and lips all blue, grinned and flicked water on him from his hair.

"How is it, Archie?" Daddy asked.

"G-g-g-gr . . . great!" Archie answered.

Peter had come up too. He held his arms across his chest and was making a noise with his teeth.

"Ve-ve-very ref-f-f-freshin'," Peter said.

Daddy laughed.

They had gone through a gap in the railing. Bobby could see men in a room, swaying and holding their arms over their heads, mist about them and a river of soapsuds creeping down from the room and into a hole in the floor.

"You're not just p-puttin' him in, Craig?" Peter said.

"God, no. I'll tak him in wi' me."

"Hold him tight," Archie said. "He's no' very big."

"Stop fussin'," Daddy said.

"Here, I'll h-hold his towel," Archie said.

"Get down in there an' show him how easy it is," Daddy said.

"Awww!"

"I'll d-do it," Peter said.

With his arms stuck out from his sides Peter went down the steps into the water and waded away from the side until the water was up to his tummy. He put his hands down and scooped water over his chest and shoulders, then smiled, nodded and

207

beckoned to Bobby. "It's fine when you get used to it," he said. "Come on, Craig, bring the wee lad in."

Daddy had gone down two steps. Bobby could see Daddy's legs below the water. They looked as thin and wobbly as his own bad leg, bending this way and that as the water lapped about Daddy's knees. He was not dismayed by that. On the contrary; he felt that somehow the green water might cure him, not by making him better but by making everybody else the same as he was. "Put your arms round my neck, son, an' hang on," Daddy was saying. "Don't be scared. I'll not let you go."

"No' scared," Bobby growled.

He did not turn away, did not hide his face in his father's neck. He sat out on Daddy's arm, craned out and watched as the water came up and touched him. It was cold on his feet, colder on his ankles, very cold on his legs. He gripped tight, the fingers closing on Daddy's hair.

"Easy now, easy," Archie said. "Take it easy, Craig."

Archie was seated at the side with his feet dangling in the water, watching. Daddy said, "Archie, will you shut up."

Bobby said, "It's cold."

"Is it too cold?" said Archie.

Bobby said gruffly, "Naw."

It was too cold. But it was something else as well. It felt light, slippery as soap; not the water, him.

The water snaked up around his thighs, into his costume, gripped his skin. They were off the steps now and away from Archie. He clung tight to Daddy. The water seemed to want to take him, to draw him out flat on to his tummy. His bad leg hurt suddenly and he reached down and slapped the water above it to make it stop hurting and spoiling things.

"I think he likes it," Peter said. "Do you like it, Bobby, d' you want t' splash?"

Peter came closer and Daddy said, "Hang on," again then slowly bent his knees. The water came up higher and higher. He would have been scared if Daddy hadn't been there to hold him, yet he wanted to be let go, too. He could smell the water, taste it. It was all sort of one thing and being cold was just part of it.

"Jeeze!" Archie said, and pushed himself off the side and down into the water too.

There were Daddy's friends, Daddy and him, all together in

the water. Bobby heard himself laughing.

"Now, just hold my hands, Bobby," Daddy said. "An' let yourself go. Let yourself float, son."

"We'll no' let you drown," said Archie.

"Shut up, Archie," Peter said.

He felt like soap in the water. He knew what float meant. It meant letting go, letting the water take his legs away. He could feel his father's hands on his arms, the rubbery touch of Peter's tummy against his elbow, the big swirl of water Archie made right beside him. He wanted to float. He wanted to do everything except look up at the roof and nobody expected him to do that anyway.

"That's it. That's it," Daddy was saying. "Look at that, lads, will you?"

"Aye, it's great," said Archie.

"Born to it, I'd say."

It wasn't Daddy that seemed to be holding him now, but something else, something cold but fizzy like lemonade out of a jug. He felt himself come and go, as if his arms were stretching and shortening, stretching again.

"Kick, Bobby. Kick your feet."

He kicked, kicked, kicked. He heard the roar the water made, glanced round and saw the splashes, kicked, while Daddy held him and Peter, blowing water, stood beside him and laughed.

"By God, Nicholson," said a huge man with a tummy like a coal sack under his costume and a big, wet beard. "Is he yours?"

"Aye, Sergeant Byrne," Daddy said. "He's mine all right."

The man stuck a towel in his ear and turned it round with his finger. "You've got the makin's o' a champion there."

"Maybe I have," Daddy said. "Maybe I have at that."

Bobby, sensing his father's pride and expectations, thrashed his feet harder, lips pursed against the cold.

"He loves it," Peter said.

"Do you love it, Bobby?" Archie said.

And Bobby, spitting, answered, "Aye."

*   *   *

As closing time drew near Lorna became agitated. It was not uncommon for her to fall into this condition. Love and influenza had taken their toll and left her thinner and more nervous than she had been before. Now that she no longer lived under the same roof as her intended, she had come to doubt the quality of his passion and the depth of his fondness for her. She was afraid that Tubby was 'cooling off', though the only sign that the poor chap gave of any such thing was an occasional tardiness in reaching Gascoigne Street before the shutters were secured. Not once had he failed to present himself before the key turned in the padlock, though he was often hot, breathless and bothered by a mad rush in from the railway station or down from the tramcar depot. It did not seem relevant to Lorna that Ernest was still employed by Mathieson, Mullard & Milroy and did, now and then, have to put business before pleasure.

"Where is he today?" Kirsty would ask.

"Gourock, I think."

"There you are then."

"He should be here, though. He should."

"Perhaps something's happened to him," Kirsty would say, casually.

"What! Oh, God, an accident!"

"No, no, Lorna – a delay to the train, that's all."

Late customers did not receive the best of attention from the Emporium's young manageress and, as a rule, Kirsty tried to be on hand for the closing hour of the day. On that particular afternoon she had left Bobby at home with Craig who had volunteered to take him to the park. The spell of sunny weather had increased her reluctance to make Bobby a prisoner of the shop. Even so she had not adjusted yet to Craig's sudden rush of paternalism, the fact that he seemed willing to put himself out to accommodate her needs. She missed Bobby. She felt strangely dispossessed and anxious when he was out of her sight for long.

Lorna had reached the stage of hand-wringing. She could not tear herself from the window behind the counter, not even to assist Kirsty in dragging out the shutters. She had her nose pressed to the glass when, without warning, Ernest appeared. He capered across the frame, straw hat in hand and a grin on his face in emulation of the stagey entrance of a pierrot or minstrel.

"*Tubby!*" Lorna cried. She rushed to the door to embrace him as if he had just returned from the war in South Africa and not a day trip to Gourock. She flung open the door, flung herself against him, flung her arms about his neck, received his kisses as thankfully as a parched flower might receive rain.

Kirsty leaned on the heavy, iron-rimmed shutter.

"Do you mind?" she said.

"What? Hmmm?" Ernest, flushed, squinted over his beloved's shoulder. "Oh, yes, sorry."

Five minutes later, after a final flurry of energy and activity, the shop was shut fast and the young couple were gone. They crossed Dumbarton Road, linked arm in arm like trotting ponies, Ernest's sample case swinging featherlight in his hand and Lorna's face, wreathed in smiles, turned up towards him as he recounted the story of his day's adventures.

Kirsty sighed as she watched the lovers vanish into Peel Street. She had no idea where they were going, where they would eat supper, if they would eat supper at all, or at what ungodly hour they would go through the painful ritual of parting until the morrow. She had never really experienced love like that. It had been different with David. Guilt had been there from the first, guilt and a sense of inappropriateness which had made true love seem doomed. Wistfully, though, she recalled the evening of the April sunset when she'd walked with Frank Tubbs by the riverside. She wondered, not for the first time, why it was that she had felt cheated when Craig had appeared. She wished that Frank was with her now as she walked home through Greenfield's dusty streets with a scuffed canvas shopping bag weighted with comestibles for her husband's supper.

When Kirsty reached No. 154, however, a surprise awaited her. The supper table was already laid. Stew bubbled in one pot and potatoes knocked against the lid of another. She put down the shopping bag and glanced around at the tidy kitchen. She'd arrived just a bit too early. Craig was caught at the sink, naked above the waist, in the throes of shaving.

"Ach, you're early," he said.

"I thought you were on night shift?"

"I am."

"Where's Bobby?"

"Fast asleep."

Craig dipped his face into the basin, rinsed off soap, rose and, dabbing himself with a towel, came to her and kissed her. He said, "Don't look so worried, Kirsty. He's been fed an' watered, an' he's absolutely fine. He was just tired, that's all."

Something in Craig's manner disturbed her. Smugness, arrogance were much in evidence but when he put his bare arm about her and kissed her again, on the mouth this time, she did not resist. She sniffed, then raised her eyes to the rope of the drying pulley, hoisted high towards the kitchen ceiling. "What's that?" she asked.

"My bathin' costume."

"That?"

"Bobby's bathin' costume."

"What did you say?"

"Look at the size o' it." Craig pretended to ignore her outraged tone. "Pathetic, isn't it? I bought it in Langford's before we went – "

"You did what?"

"It was the best one they had, love."

"You let him into the pond in the park?"

"Hell, no, I'm not that bloody stupid," Craig said. "I took him to the swimmin' club proper, at Cranstounhill."

"Oh, God!"

"What's wrong wi' you? He had a rare time. Peter an' Archie were there too. Jeeze, you should have seen him, Kirsty, splashin' an' kickin' like a wee puddock."

"His – his leg?"

"Nothin' wrong with his leg."

"He could – could have drowned."

"Away an' don't be bloody daft," Craig said. "I took the caliper off before we went near the water."

"Is he sick? Is that why he's in bed? Has he got the cold?"

"Kirsty, will you stop it. He's tired, that's all. We were havin' fun for nearly an hour. Bobby along wi' the rest of us. Do you think I'd let him come to any harm? Sergeant Byrne says – "

"I don't care what Sergeant Byrne says," Kirsty snapped. "Sergeant Byrne doesn't have – a delicate child."

"Delicate? God, there's nothin' 'delicate' about our lad, Kirsty, I can tell you. It's you that imagines he's delicate. It's you that seems to want him delicate."

"How dare you say – "

Craig slung the little floral hand-towel over his shoulder and it somehow emphasised his muscular strength. In spite of the faint medical odour of the swimming pool, he looked scrubbed, and so strong that she quailed a little before him. Had she been goading him? Had she been hoping that she might spoil that pride he'd taken in Bobby's performance in the pool by making him lose his temper? If so she had failed.

"He's not a Mama's boy," Craig said, evenly. "He's a Nicholson through an' through. Aye, bad leg an' all."

She opened her mouth, then thought better of it. She took off her jacket and draped it carefully over a chairback then went through the hall into the bedroom.

Curtains were drawn and the room was warm, sleepy with muffled sounds from the street outside. Bobby lay on his side. One soft fist was tucked under his chin but he did not have his thumb in his mouth nor did he lie hunched up, all tightly drawn. He was relaxed, totally relaxed. His skin had the same smooth, clean, pale appearance as his father's. The iron brace hung from its strap on the bedpost and clinked slightly when Kirsty leaned to kiss him. His dark lashes fluttered. He stirred, but only a little, smiled and shifted his left hand which lay outside the bedclothes and clasped the coarse, damp towel with its beading of faded red letters – C & B PSWC – the police swimming club, a man's world from which she would be forever excluded.

Craig had seated himself on one of the kitchen chairs, pulled out at an angle from the table. The kitchen was filled with motes of light as a corner of the westering sun found a slot between the tenements. The wholesome aroma of the stewpot and steam from the boiling potatoes floated in the air too.

"Well?" Craig said.

"He's – all right."

"Did you think I'd deliberately do harm to him, Kirsty?"

"I know you wouldn't."

"Or to you?"

She paused. "No."

He had not dressed yet. Tunic and boots were laid out in the front room but Craig showed no sign of his usual obsessive urgency to be fed, clad and ready an hour before his scheduled time of departure. She sensed his desire of her. In the cramped, hot kitchen his newly-washed skin was sleek with perspiration. She found him attractive and repellent at one and the same time. But to her surprise she wanted him as she had not wanted him for months.

Craig watched as she crossed the kitchen, turned down the gas pressure under the pots on the stove, flicked the long curtain across the window and then, with her hands behind her neck, unhooked the collar of her blouse and let it slide from her body.

"What's this?" Craig said, thickly, pretending that he'd had no such thing in mind. "I'm out tonight. I'm on duty."

"But not yet," Kirsty said.

She put her hands on his shoulders and leaned over him, let her breasts press against his flesh, gently cocked his head so that she might kiss him on the mouth. She felt his hand touch her, cup her as he drew her round before him, drew her between his knees. She braced herself stiffly against him, tense not with distaste but with reciprocal need. Craig fumbled with the strings and buttons of her skirt and underclothing.

"Wait," she said.

"What?" he said.

"Wait."

She disengaged herself, went to the hole-in-the-wall bed, seated herself upon it and, as he watched, kicked off her shoes and unfurled her long stockings. He got to his feet, unbuttoned his trousers, stepped out of them, kicked them away.

Kirsty lay back across the bed. She let the curtain close over her. She could see flecks of coppery light on the wall of the alcove and a feather from the bolster floating in the slit of light that penetrated the bed-curtain. She was taut, breathless and perspiring even before Craig parted the curtain and moved against her. He checked, then came down, easing the weight of his body on to her. She gave a cry, tilted her hips and clasped him to her. She cried his name softly, "Craig, Craig, Craig," and, as his dark head blotted out the evening light, for a time there was nothing in her world but him.

*   *   *

Brewers were, quite naturally, delighted at the spell of warm weather so early in the season. After hasty consultation with salesmen production of light ales and shining lager beers was increased to meet the sudden upsweep in demand for liquids that would quench a thirst. There was also quite a clamour in the ranks of victuallers and publicans for bottled stock; everybody knew that certain processes could not be hurried and that nature, in the form of fermentation, had her own sweet, sluggish pace, and that the sun would not shine forever.

Carruth's was more fortunate than its larger competitors. It had gone early into the brewing of a brand of new Germanic lager which had not taken off in the autumn months and lay now, both in the wood and bottled, in dusty vaults behind the bottlers in Milton Street. Phoebe Adair, of all people, had been responsible for giving the new light beer its name, had tossed it off in a casual aside to her father who, before other matters claimed him, had been brooding about it at the dinner table.

"Valhalla," she'd said.

"Hah?"

"Paradise of the brave," Phoebe'd said. "Feast hall of the gods."

Dolphus had appeared not to be listening but the name had stuck in his memory and, in course of discussion with brewhouse pundits some days later, out it had popped.

"Is that a German word?" somebody had asked.

"'Course it is," Dolphus had said. "It means 'Food of the Gods'."

Gaudy labels with an orange sunburst inset with a horned helmet had been duly drawn, approved and printed, brands of similar design wrought by St Rollox smiths. But the gentlemen of the west were not initially attracted by something as fancy and ethereal as a brew with a foreign monicker and the stuff, fortunately a genuine 'keeping beer', languished in store while Mr McCabe tried desperately to open a market for it through Carruth's agents on Tyneside.

Gordon knew only a little of the inside story of this failed venture until the advent of the warm spell in the May month of 1900. *Valhalla* – sixty-four crates of it to be precise – was, nevertheless, to be the instrument of his fall from grace.

The landlords of cottage pubs and rural inns scattered in and around Milngavie were, for the most part, uninterested in exotica. With the failure of Ushers to deliver enough juice on time, however, Gordon had pushed *Valhalla* on to desperate publicans. Carts had rolled up from Milton Street in profusion, making the long haul under a hot summer sun ungrudgingly. It was at the very end of his persuasive stint in outlying districts that Gordon found himself with time on his hands and elected to

215

walk out as far as The Knowe and cast an eye on his fiancée.

The wedding was now only seven weeks away and Gordon assumed that there would be a fever of activity among the women in Dolphus's domain. He had heard very little about it, though, and had waited patiently for somebody to tell him what to do and what exactly his role in the ritual would be. In fact he had spent a great deal more time in the company of Josephine Adair than with Amanda. And Josephine was emphatically not the sort of female to get excited about bridal gowns and bridesmaids' bouquets. Though Josephine was full of advice and opinions on all sorts of subjects she seldom mentioned matrimony or Amanda. She seemed to wish to pretend, as Gordon did, that the horizon was unblemished by the fulfilment of his promise to wed another and that there was calculation behind the arrangement.

It was a highly pleasant sort of day, with light cloud to temper the heat of the sun and the May trees all heavy with blossom when Gordon completed his business at Milngavie's Black Bull and set off on foot along the road to Blanefield and Dolphus Adair's estate. Early-planted crops had begun to show green in the fields and the spring drop of lambs had grown sturdy, though the new calves still had that stunned look as if the big wide world was too much for them and the teat their only consolation. The trees that massed behind The Knowe were still and heat shimmered not only on the gravel drive but even on the lawns. The house, for once, looked dignified and grand in its painted passivity. There was no sign of life about the place, however, save for a single unaccompanied figure on the lawn. The lonely figure occupied an encampment composed of fringed garden sunshade, a slatted lounging chair scattered with silks and Oriental cushions and a rug the size of a ballroom carpet. On the carpet, in the chair, under the sunshade lay Olive Carruth Adair.

Gordon was hot and perspiring. He had taken off his jacket and carrried it across his shoulder. He had unloosed the knot of his tie, though not his collar-stud, and had furled his shirtsleeves to the elbows. From a distance, perhaps, he looked like some farm labourer strayed into the lady's private garden. Olive did not stir, did not lift herself languidly from the cushions or show her face from beneath the fringe of the shade. Motionless as a lizard on a rock, she watched Gordon approach.

At first he wondered if she was asleep. Beside her, half hidden by the chair was a tray upon which reposed an ice bucket stuck with three bottles, three glasses and a small, sticky, green-glass jar about which a brace of flies droned dopily.

In Olive's hands, in her lap, was a broad-leaved straw fan and, under the band of shadow formed by the sunshade he glimpsed the rim of a broad, corn-yellow straw hat that laid another plane of shadow upon her face. She wore a thin, pale dress of green silk, trimmed with cream lace but she had removed the chiffon filling from the neck and unhooked the patent fasteners at the top of the bodice to let what breeze there was find her flesh. She appeared cool enough to Gordon, leaning back on the cushions, not, as he had first thought, like an invalid but more like a sentinel. Only the moist glint of her eyes told him that she was aware that he had come and who he was.

Gordon stood before her, shoes on the edge of the heavy carpet and said nothing, waited brazenly for acknowledgement if not welcome.

"What do you want here?" Olive said, at length.

"I've come to see Amanda. Is she at home?"

"Oh, yes, she's very much at home."

"Where is she then?"

Olive's hands were the hands of an old woman, spotted and veined, and she tapped the handle of the fan with a forefinger as brittle as a stick before she spoke again.

"Why did you choose today?"

"I had business in Milngavie."

"Business!" Coolness turned to scorn. "Selling beer to drunken rustics – business!"

"Carruth's beer," Gordon reminded her.

"Do you rub your hands when you rise to find the sun shining?" Olive said. "My father always did. He had a glass gauge to measure the temperature. It hung just outside the door and every warm morning he would bend to study it and rub his hands as if he could feel the sovereigns sticking to his palms."

Gordon did not know how to answer, and said nothing.

Olive went on, "Perhaps it's something you will learn to do too. Perhaps my husband will instruct you. Why are you here? We do not store beer here, you know."

"I told you. I came to see Amanda."

"She's over there," Olive said. "In the summerhouse."

"Will you send a servant to fetch her, please?"

"Fetch her yourself," said Olive.

Gordon glanced towards the glasshouses that hid themselves behind a long brick wall that flanked the kitchen gardens and separated the lawns from the east wing of the house.

"All right," Gordon said.

"Do you know the way?"

"Yes."

She lifted herself on one elbow and showed him her face. She smiled and held a forefinger to her lips.

"Go quietly," Olive said.

Gordon headed away from the carpet and the chair, diagonally across the quilted green lawn towards the gate in the wall. He paused when he reached it and looked over his shoulder. The woman was leaning out of the chair, watching him, straw hat tilted back from her brow, a glass in her hand. He went through the gate and down the flagged path that led to an unpainted door in the glittering, glinting, ramshackle summerhouse. Softly he turned the brass handle, softly stepped into the humid, salt-tasting interior, into a dense, secretive community of half-tended palms and tropical ferns. For an instant he was tempted to stop there, to call out Amanda's name. Better still, to retreat, to close the door, pretend he had never been there at all, had never heard the little sounds, faster, softer, more feathery than any Greta had ever made yet instantly recognisable for what they were if not – not yet – for what they signified.

Drawn by curiosity however, Gordon went on around the path until, laid out like pointers on the flagstones, he saw first a ribboned hat, then a lacy dress and finally a man's linen jacket and waistcoat. He paused. Brushing aside a great canoe-shaped leaf, he looked into the shadowy green interior and saw them together, upright against the smooth grey sweeping slope of a palm tree trunk. There was nothing pretty or romantic in the sight. The couple were dishevelled, sweating and grunting, totally involved in the act that engaged them.

Gordon held the waxy leaf up with the back of his wrist and watched without excitement, without anger or bitterness. What he felt was disappointment – and a faint supercilious relief that it was John Whiteside there and not himself.

The tail of Whiteside's shirt covered him but Amanda's up-lifted chemise, lacy suspenders and sprung corselet revealed that her calfs and thighs were pale and smooth but thin, not even slender – thin. That fact somehow eased Gordon's hurt and, letting the leaf nod back into place, he slipped out of the summerhouse as quickly and quietly as he had come.

Olive Adair had gone in under the shade of the big tasselled parasol again. She did not raise herself when Gordon ap-proached. She remained languid, seemingly indifferent to his presence. She had a cordial glass in her hand and sipped a greenish liquid from it. She made no other movement except to waft a fingertip at a fly that had followed the sticky substance to her lips.

From the carpet's edge Gordon gave her a courteous nod, almost a bow. "Thank you," he said. He turned and set off across the lawn.

"Nicholson."

He hesitated, looked round. She was leaning forward, squint-ing in the glare of sunlight, hat tipped raffishly back from her brow. She raised a forefinger to her lips and, grinning, said, "Not a word now, Nicholson, not a word."

Gordon turned and headed for the gate and when she called his name again felt no gentlemanly obligation to respond.

"Sod off!" he murmured under his breath and walked away forever from Olive, Amanda, marriage and The Knowe.

*   *   *

Dinner was served a little late, without Lorna. His sister's ab-sence dismayed Gordon not at all. To his surprise, he found himself calmly putting away all that was set before him, oxtail soup, roast forequarter of lamb and a Nelson pudding, as if everything were normal and no Damoclean sword hung over him and the peace of the household. He waited until his mother and stepfather had retired to the upstairs drawing room to take coffee before he broke the news.

They took it well, much better than he had anticipated. His mother seemed almost relieved. Even Breezy, with whom he had been on good terms of late, was not nearly so fiery or enquiring as Gordon expected him to be.

"The weddin's off, just like that." Breezy snapped his fingers. "You're not in love with her, is that it?"

"No, Amanda isn't the right girl for me."

"Have you told her yet?" Madge said.

"I thought I'd tell you first."

"There is such a thing as breach of promise," Breezy reminded him. His stepfather had sunk into the big armchair and had steepled his fingers in front of his face, lightly brushing the ends of his moustache with the balls of his thumbs. It was a pose that usually signified concentration rather than bristling rage.

Gordon said, "I don't think it'll come to that. In fact, I'm certain it won't."

"Amanda – ?"

"Amanda will understand," Gordon said.

Madge said, "Is she not very keen either, is that it?"

"Yes," Gordon said. "That's it."

"When did you make this decision?" said Breezy.

"I – I've been thinkin' about it for a long while."

"Hmmm," Breezy muttered. "Dolphus will be furious. I wouldn't be surprised if he dismissed you from the firm."

"He won't have the chance," Gordon said. "I've resigned."

"Oh, Gordon! Is that wise?" said Madge.

"It's the only decent thing to do," Gordon said. "I must say, I'm surprised you're both takin' it so well."

Madge glanced at Breezy who pursed his lips, stroked his moustache and shrugged. Madge said, "We – we expected it."

Gordon said, "I'm sorry to let you down, Breezy. I mean, about the transaction an' – you know."

"Those are my problems, not yours, son," Breezy said. "But I can't take you back into the warehouse. It wouldn't be fair on Johnnie."

"No," Gordon said. "Not fair on Johnnie at all."

"I'm not goin' to keep you, Gordon," Breezy said. "I don't believe in supportin' idlers."

"Albert!" Madge said, with a trace of reproach.

"I have some money set aside," Gordon said. "Enough for the summer. I'll take my time, I think. Look for a good opportunity. Not rush it, if that's all right with you?"

Breezy said, "Is there somebody else?"

"What?"

"Have you found another bunty?"

"Me? Hell, no!"

"Take the summer," Breezy said.

"You sure you don't mind?"

"I won't stand in your way, son, but do let it go on the record that I think you're a fool."

Gordon got up, not in a temper. "Aye, that may be," he agreed. "But at least I'll be my own fool, nobody else's."

"Where are you goin' at this hour?" Madge said.

"Out for a walk," Gordon said.

"Second thoughts, son?" Breezy asked.

"No second thoughts," said Gordon.

*   *   *

The hall was panelled in varnished wood and had along its length a series of pretty, ebony-framed watercolours depicting, for the most part, young girls in floral landscapes. Beyond, in Josephine's living room, Gordon could see a haze of cigarette smoke and hear the odd, hovering silence that indicated that the folk there were listening with more curiosity than diplomacy.

"Oh, you've got friends in," Gordon said. "I didn't mean to intrude. I'll – I'll come back another time."

"Don't be silly. It's only the girls." Josephine held the door wide open and said in a very loud voice. "And they're just leaving anyway."

There were three of them. They departed, without umbrage. As they brushed past Gordon in the hall they gave him the glad eye, cheerfully shook hands with the hostess and murmured words of advice and admonition while she handed out scarves and hats from the tiny cloakroom that lurked behind the door. Two were girls of about Josephine's age, the third somewhat older. She was small and dark and roguish and reminded him faintly of Greta. He stood awkwardly in the hall, hat in hand, and watched them depart out of the corner of his eye. Josephine closed the door at last, turned and leaned against the woodwork. "*Phew!* Thank God you came Gordon, otherwise they'd have been here all night."

"I shan't stay long, Josephine. I just – "

She put a hand on his shoulder and steered him firmly

221

towards the living room. "Nonsense. Stay as long as you like. You look as if you'd seen a ghost. Come along, tell Jo your troubles."

It was a winter room, really, all stuffed armchairs and draped blankets, with an aspidistra in a Japanese bowl on a table in front of the window, and a cottage fireplace. Its studious cosiness did not adapt to summer, became just a touch stuffy and musty, unlike the girl herself. In a light Grecian dress, her blonde hair in fluffy curls at the sides and braided at the back, Josephine seemed to shine in the shadowy room.

On a long table before the fireplace were stacks of pamphlets of various kinds, all to do with Temperance, of course, two brass ashtrays still purling smoke like ritual incense, and four tall glasses which appeared to contain whisky.

"Russian tea," said Josephine, catching the direction of Gordon's glance. "Lemon and brown sugar. Like some?"

Gordon shook his head. He let her take his hat, then seated himself in the hollow of a deep moquette armchair, knees together, elbows tucked in. He felt uncomfortable and wished that he had never come. But where else would he find a friend, a confidante, someone sympathetic with whom he could share his confusion?

Josephine had vanished. He looked around, heard her moving in the narrow kitchen – 'the galley', she called it – across the junction of the hall. She was gone but a moment and returned with a glass held out between finger and thumb.

"What's that?" Gordon asked.

"Brandy and water. Medicinal purposes only. For gentlemen in states of shock. Take it," she said. "Drink it."

Obediently he did.

"Now, what's up?"

Gordon took a deep breath. "It's all off. I'm not goin' to marry Amanda Adair."

"What happened?"

"She – she has another man, a lover."

"John Whiteside."

Gordon finished the brandy at a gulp, nodded. "Right first time."

"But how did you discover – how can you be sure?"

"I saw them."

"What?" Josephine said. "Together?"

"Yep."

"What? Doing it?"

"Yes."

"Poor boy. Poor lad," Josephine said. "How absolutely hideous for you."

"Oddly enough," Gordon said, "it wasn't hideous at all. It seemed sort of – fitting, sort of justified."

"Aren't you cut to the quick?"

"Not to the quick, no."

"And you don't object to talking about it?"

"On the contrary."

"In that case," Josephine said, draping her long limbs comfortably on the sofa, "tell me all."

*   *   *

For days now Ernest had seen little or nothing of his brother. In spite of the fine weather Frank had hardly left the bed-study. The typewriting machine had been clacking when Ernest left home in the morning and clacking when he'd returned at night, however late the hour. According to mother the only respite came in the afternoon when, for an hour after lunch, Frank rested on top of his bed with a copy of the *Glasgow Herald*, unread, folded over his face to keep out the sunlight. For the rest though it was work, work at a most frantic and furious pace as Frank drove himself to catch up with commissions that had been put aside for Kirsty Nicholson's benefit and to aid the business into which Ernest and he had bought.

Ernest had more notion of the toll that fast writing extracted from brain and body than Frank imagined. He had seen the dead, bloodshot look of his big brother's eyes, the drained-white complexion, stiffened muscles and paralysed joints that excessive creative effort induced. He worried for Frank and about Frank. He felt, as Mother did, a degree of guilt as if it were family needs that drove the old chap to the grindstone hour after hour, day upon day, and not some inner compulsion to shoulder more responsibility than a man could reasonably be expected to bear.

It was very, very late, after midnight, when Ernest took his courage in both hands, knocked and then entered his brother's sanctum.

Frank was crouched in one of the positions that seemed to favour writerly flow, legs twisted around the foreleg of the piano stool and head sunk low over the keys of the machine. He wore a collarless shirt, stained flannel trousers and had kicked off his shoes. Spread around him on the carpet, in and out of the pool of light from the lamp, were scraps of paper and sheets of half-typed foolscap. Books, calf and cloth bound, were stacked precariously on the edges of the desk and, on the table to his right hand, were teacups, water glasses and a tin ashtray mounded with cigar butts. The air in the room was foul. Ernest coughed. The typewriting machine chattered, seemed to go on even after Frank plucked his fingers from the keys and shot round, eyes glazed and staring, and quite wild.

"What? What? What?"

"Sorry. I didn't mean to interrupt you."

"What?" Frank blinked and rubbed his reddened eyes with his fingertips. "Am I disturbin' Mother, is that it?"

"No, no, no, no," said Ernest soothingly. "I'm just off to bed now. I wondered if I could fetch you somethin' before I toddled. Tea, perhaps? Some bread and butter?"

Frank shook his head. Ernest could hear the little bones at the top of his spine crack.

"Sure?"

Frank slumped, peered down and cautiously detached his ankles and shins from the stool's leg. He stretched and groaned.

"Oh, God!" he said. "Oh, God!"

"You're overdoing it, Frank."

"No, I'm not. I'll be finished in a couple of days."

"Your serial story?"

"Yes."

Frank pressed his hands to his lumbar region, eased himself off the piano stool and slowly straightened his upper body.

"What's it called?" said Ernest. "The story?"

Frank paused. Even with his brother he was faintly embarrassed by his endeavours, by their existence as much as their nature. "*The Fallen Woman*," he said, gruffly.

"Ah. Now that sounds mighty interestin'," said Ernest. "Just my cup of tea. Talkin' of which – "

"No, really, Ernest, I'm awash with tea."

"You should go to bed, Frank."

"I will."

"When?"

"Soon."

Ernest said, "I can take a hint. I'll leave you to it."

"Wait," Frank said. "I have something for you. Been meanin' to give it to you for weeks. Now you're here – "

"What is it?"

"Nothing much, just a little gift."

Ernest watched curiously as Frank fumbled in a drawer at the base of the table and produced an oblong box of veneered wood. Ernest knew at once what the box contained. God knows, he'd peddled enough of them in his time. He kept his face poker-straight, however, and accepted the gift solemnly.

"To mark your engagement," Frank said.

Ernest opened the canteen and looked down at the cutlery.

"How wonderful!" he said. "Useful, too. Lorna will be thrilled." He ran a fingertip along the knives, then lifted the box and slanted it to the light, picked out a fork, held it up critically and laughed. "You devil!"

"Yes, well – "

"What did you use on them? Sefton's paste?"

"'Fraid so," Frank said, sheepishly.

"How many did you ruin?"

"Only three. I felt obliged to buy the lot, though."

"Rather than confess to Kirsty," Ernest grinned. "Of course. Soap an' water, Frank, plain soap an' water for anythin' that comes from the 'three Ems' in a varnished box. Remember that in future. I hope you claimed discount."

"Oh, yes," Frank said. "But I couldn't think what to do with the damned thing, that's why I gave it – Lord, that really is miserable of me, isn't it?"

"Not at all," Ernest clicked the lid and clasped the canteen to his chest. "We'll treasure it forever, Lorna an' me. We won't use it – but we will treasure it."

Frank seated himself on the piano stool once more as if to indicate that he was ready to begin work again. He did not turn his back on his brother, however, for, even with his family, he could not bring himself to be impolite.

Ernest said, "Frank, I'll always be grateful to you for what you've done for us."

"Nonsense. It's no more than any brother would do."

"Ah, but it is," said Ernest. "You've not only set me up in business but you've enabled me to marry someone whom I love very deeply."

"Yes, I know you do."

"Why, Frank, do you not find a wife?"

"I'm not the marrying kind," Frank said.

"Is there nobody that you like, who likes you?"

Frank did not reply. It was not a genuine question; Ernest needed no answer. He was sensitive enough to the situation to have divined the answer to it in advance.

Ernest said, "Would you not wed a woman like, say, Kirsty Nicholson?"

"She's too young for me." Frank did now turn away. He swung round on the stool to face the desk and the window. "Besides, she's already married."

"Not happily."

"That has nothing to do with it," Frank said.

"She asks after you, you know."

Frank looked round. "Really?"

"Really an' truly. Every time she sees me, near enough, she enquires after your health an' welfare. I think she's puzzled that you haven't been to call."

"How can I?" Frank said, "I can't pay court to a girl, a married – "

"You did with Ellen Holman," Ernest reminded him.

"Yes, damn it, and look where it got me."

"Do you regret it?"

"Of course I regret it. After what happened, how can I not regret it?"

"But you loved her, didn't you?" Ernest persisted.

Angry and embarrassed, Frank swung himself this way and that. "I wish you'd go now, Ernest, and leave me to my work."

Ernest said, "Bachelorhood is an unnatural state. You *should* be married. You *need* to be married."

"Please, Ernest, enough."

"All right. I'm sorry. It's none of my affair, I suppose." Ernest put a fraternal hand on his brother's shoulder. The stale smell clung to Frank too and the slope of his shoulders was steep, like that of an old man. "We worry about you, you know."

"Well, don't."

Frank kept his eyes upon the metallic keys but, being Frank, reached up and patted his brother's hand affectionately. "Good night, old son," he said.

For several minutes after he'd left the room Ernest lingered in the hallway. He heard nothing, no sound except the scrape of a match, and a hesitant *teck-tack* from the typewriting machine. He wondered which girl Frank was thinking about – Ellen Holman whom he had loved and lost or Kirsty Nicholson, who, but for the encumbrance of a husband, would make his brother a perfect wife.

*   *   *

However much he'd detested working for Carruth's Gordon found time hanging heavy on his hands after he'd resigned. He was not by nature a layabout and, within a week or so, was bored and out of sorts. Indeed, if Dolphus had tried to persuade him to return to Carruth's Gordon might have been tempted, to swallow his pride, in that respect only, simply to have something to give shape to the days. But Dolphus did not try to persuade him to return. In fact, Dolphus did not respond at all to the letter of resignation that Gordon had so carefully composed. The silence from The Knowe was nothing short of resounding. Guilt or guile on Olive's part had obviously communicated itself to Dolphus. For all Gordon knew, he had been painted as some kind of villainous ingrate unworthy of being incorporated into the family. And he did not give a damn. So far, he had held his tongue about the real reason for breaking off his engagement. He had revealed the truth only to Josephine and he trusted her implicitly not to pass it on.

Josephine was a law unto herself. Her beliefs and philosophies had separated her from the ensnaring circle of the Adairs, had liberated her from dependency upon collective family approval. She had a job of her own, rooms of her own, a life of her own, and no particular desire to exchange her freedom for anything more conventional, like marriage. Of all of the subjects upon which Josephine waxed lyrical, and there were many, marriage and the subjection of women were the ones that raised her to heights of eloquence. Gordon would listen raptly, too intimidated to disagree with anything she said, even the most outrageous slanders against the male sex.

"You agree?"

"What? Yes, yes."

"You're not supposed to agree."

"What am I supposed to do?"

"Argue."

"I don't know how to argue, Josephine, particularly when you have such a grasp of these things."

"What you mean is you can't get a word in edgeways."

"More or less, aye," Gordon would say.

She would look at him, head cocked, and give him a wry grin that inevitably brought a dimple to her cheek and made her look like some gigantic and exuberant schoolgirl.

"You are a 'wronged man'," she would tell him. "Defend yourself, defend your sex. Cast a few aspersions. Rail against the fickleness of womankind. Don't just sit there like a tailor's dummy."

"I'm not just sittin' here like a dummy."

"What are you doing then?"

"Eatin' your share of the pudding."

"Good God, so you are," Josephine would say and, reaching hastily for her spoon, would temporarily bring her diatribe to an end.

It was at Josephine's request that Gordon turned up on the platform of the railway station at Partick West shortly after noon on the first Sunday in June. It was at this station, not so long ago, that he'd boarded the early train for Bree Lodge, and his first thought was that Josephine's 'mystery excursion' was leading him in that direction.

"Bree Lodge? Where the Smiths have stables?" Josephine said, in response to his question. "What on earth would we go there for?"

"Where are we goin' then?"

"You'll see soon enough."

She wore a summery dress of tender blue and a large hat but, Gordon noticed, had spoiled the pretty effect by donning a pair of heavy, low-heeled leather shoes. She carried a straw basket within which chuckled picnic things. Even after they disembarked at Bearsden station and set off westward, Gordon had no notion of their destination. Josephine enjoyed his bewilderment and teased him with his ignorance of geography as they emerged from the edge of the village into an area of heat-bathed woodland and pasture.

The day was very fine and Gordon was contented enough to be out and about, walking with the young woman on one arm and the picnic basket on the other. He listened to Josephine's lecture about Antoninus Pius who, in 140 A.D., it seemed, had built a great wall near here to keep the ferocious Picts at bay, and forts and garrisons to protect the Roman legions who were stationed on it. He found the history interesting, Jo's voice relaxing, the solidity of her arm most comforting. The square, rolling fields tucked between the moors and the valley of the Clyde reminded him, a little, of Ayrshire, of home. They came at length to a crossroads, unmarked by any sign, and Josephine stopped there.

"Last chance to guess where I'm taking you," she said.

"I really have no idea where we are," Gordon said, "let alone where you're takin' me."

"Old Garscadden Mains."

"Ah!" He understood now.

"To meet my grandparents," Josephine said.

Clasping his hand instead of his arm she led him eagerly up a cart track that climbed in a gentle curve to a ridge of rock and heather below which lay the farm.

"I doubt if you'll take to them. They're very old now and not at all friendly," Josephine explained. "But I thought it was time you saw where we came from, we Adairs, and what it is that put my whole family to flight in the first place, what they are all running from."

"Breezy never talks about them."

"He's ashamed of them," Josephine said. "They all are. Aunt Polly used to visit now and then but even she has given up."

"But you haven't?"

"No," Josephine said, "nor will I."

Gordon could smell Old Garscadden, the sour, static odour of cow manure and splashed milk, long before its roofs and sheddings came into view. He noted the thick, yellow weeds in the grazings, untended hedges, gates that might have been put up in Roman times, and scrawny, dung-caked cattle held in a haze of black flies. Rusted iron roofs sagged underneath the weight of rotted ropes and wind-stones, and the dry stone walls that partitioned the yard were tumbled in places, old bedsprings, paraffin drums and churns flung in haphazardly to stop the gaps. The ramp to the byre was foul with slime and the manure pit had overflowed.

Josephine led him down to the yard, picking her way fastidiously between the moulting hens that pecked desperately about the verges and rushed towards them, on warped feet, as if in hope of salvation. She said nothing now. She had anticipated Gordon's disapproval and offered no excuse for the degraded state of her grandparents' dwelling place. Gordon felt only dismay and anger. He had expected something gnarled and neglected but the filth and squalor of Old Garscadden sickened him.

The windows of the cottage that backed the yard had not seen water since the last rain. Draped with frayed sacks, they peered gaunt and haggard from under weed-choked eaves. On the grey, unpainted wall a narrow door opened, suspiciously, a half inch on the hinge. Josephine let go of Gordon's hand and, reaching across him, took possession of the picnic basket.

"Grandpa," she said, in a soft, cajoling voice, as if to wheedle a timid animal from its hole. "Grandpa, it's Josephine. May we come in?"

The man was as thin and sapless as a bean straw. His head, like the heads of starved cattle, seemed far too large for his body and the weight of it dragged his chin down on to his chest. His hands too, protruding from the chafed cuffs of a tweed jacket, were massive and knuckly. He wore no shirt, only an unwashed vest that showed frosty chest hair, and trousers hitched up with string. The only thing that was remotely fresh about him was a smart blue felt trilby crammed on his tousled grey hair. He held the door ajar with one arm that, though crooked, formed an efficient barrier to entry. "Wha' dae *you* waaant?"

"Grandpa, it's Josephine."

"Who?"

"Your — your granddaughter, Josephine."

"Naebuddy here b' that daft-like name."

"Look, I brought you a basket. Food. Tea, sugar, and a sultana cake. You like sultana cake, don't you? Sultana cake in a tin?"

Gordon could hardly bear to watch Josephine's eagerness curdle into disappointment. There was no edge to her patience, however, no pretence. This visit, like all the others perhaps, was rooted not in duty but devotion.

"Tak' it. Tak' it," said a shrill little voice and, like a hedge bird crying a warning, swiftly repeated, "tak' it, tak' it, tak' it."

At first Gordon could hardly make out the woman in the gloom of the kitchen behind the man, then he thought that she must be kneeling, then he realised that she was not. She was as small as a dwarf, shrivelled inside a man's woollen overcoat that had been shorn and seamed to her size. It covered all of her, except her face, and her head was topped by what appeared to be a frizz of brown hair, a knitted brown-wool balaclava with the flaps down. Grandma Adair stood beneath her husband's arm, hardly reaching the level of his ribs, and peered unblinking up at them.

The old couple displayed no curiosity at all about who had come to call, about Gordon. Both pairs of eyes were fixed on the basket which Josephine extended at arm's length and let the man snatch away.

"Grandma, won't you let us in?"

The man lowered the basket and the woman took it from him, hugged it against her breast. For an instant things seemed to hang in the balance, as if decisions were being made by some process that involved neither word nor gesture.

Josephine took a step forward. "Grandma, this is Gordon, Albert's – " The door closed, not slammed, but fanned shut, and the brown, reeking gloom of the old farm kitchen once more became the couple's refuge against intrusion.

Josephine did not persist. Gordon watched her straighten her shoulders and inhale. Under her dress, above the line of her half-corset he could see the muscles of her back fill out and stiffen. "Well," she said, "they are being bad today."

"Aren't they always like this?"

"No, just lately."

"Perhaps if I waited out of sight – ?"

Josephine shook her head. She seemed, temporarily, at a loss. "We've nothing to eat now. I should have kept back some of the fruit. Sorry."

Gordon touched her shoulder sympathetically. Raised by

stitched bone the little swell of flesh was slippery under muslin. She glanced round and down at him.

He shrugged. "I've seen old farmers before. I know how thrawn they can be."

"Never like this. Never so bad."

"Come on," Gordon said. "Take me for a walk. Show me the ancestral estate."

"Aren't you hungry?"

"Nope. Are you?"

She thought about it. "No."

Gordon took her hand and let her lead him round the back of the byre and over a stile. With the farm buildings behind him and his eye to the hills he felt better. It was not the rudeness of the elder Adairs that had offended him so much as their mean-spiritedness. No matter how Josephine might defend them, excuse them by reason of age, Gordon knew that they had always been close-fisted, ignorant and ignoble. For fifty years and more they had worked the sixty or seventy acres, tending thirteen or fourteen cows at a time, and raised children on the proceeds of milk sold, which could never have amounted to more than an annual yield of three hundred gallons or so, even in years when the hay was good. What the couple did now, how they managed was a mystery. Perhaps they just went on as they had always done, fighting aches in the bones, weariness, the tide of the seasons. There would still be early and late milkings, the byre to muck out, churns to fill and transport to the dairy in Dalmuir or Bearsden or wherever it was that the seller had his market. Pickings would hardly be enough to keep them alive. Breezy, Gordon suspected, had given them some kind of financial help, otherwise they would have starved, along with the cattle, long since.

Josephine took him down a straggling track to the low end of the acreage where a stream meandered out of a Roman wood. There was little enough to see, except massy trees, shallow brown water and smooth stones at the drinking place. But the weeds were in flower and there was colour and heat and, away up in the afternoon sky, a buzzard circling on the currents of warm air, crying distantly.

Josephine seated herself on the grass by the burn bank, arms about her knees, then lay back, hand covering her face. She did not seem to care about her pretty dress. "Isn't it sad?" she said.

"What?"

"They were young once," she said, "but soon they'll be gone. And there won't be any of us like them left to do what they did."

"Hmmm!" Gordon murmured.

She raised herself and frowned at him. "You don't agree?"

"Josephine, for God's sake, why must everythin' come down to a discussion?" Gordon said, without heat. "All right, put it this way – would you want to live as they have? I've seen it. I've done it. Believe me, it's a mean, hard, bitter life. It eats you up an ounce at a time. Nah, nah. You'll never persuade me to pine for the old-style life. We're better by far as we are."

She rolled on to her tummy. Her shoe heels had rims of fresh dung on them, he noticed, and he waved at the black flies that hovered about. She fiddled with a broad leaf of grass, put it to her lips, nibbled it. She looked even stronger in this position, her back curved, bottom raised, the shape of thighs and calves contoured by the dress. She would have made a perfect wife for a farmer, Gordon thought.

"Perhaps we should be gettin' back now," he said.

"Why? It's so peaceful here," Josephine said. "Do I make you uncomfortable, Gordon?"

"No, of course not."

"I'm not going to pet. I'm not like Amanda."

"You're certainly not like Amanda, thank God."

She rolled on to her elbow and sat up, put out one arm and pulled him to her, kissed him firmly on the lips. She smelled of meadow grass, and was not heavy at all.

"There!" She gave him a playful push and settled back on her knees before him.

Gordon kneeled too. He put a hand behind her head and brought her face against his, returned her kiss, only more gently, then released her and got to his feet.

She said, "Have you ever had a sweetheart, Gordon?"

"Yes," he said.

"I don't mean Amanda."

"I don't mean Amanda either."

She gave him her hand and he hoisted her to her feet. She brushed at the grass stains on her dress, unconcernedly.

"What was her name?"

"Greta Taylor."

"Were you in love with her?"

"Aye, that's the trouble," Gordon said. "I think I still am."

She offered him her hand, thrusting it out.

"Poor lad," she said. "Come along, let's go home."

"Home?"

"To my place."

"What for?" Gordon said.

"Afternoon tea," said Josephine.

* * *

The weather had taken a turn for the worse with the ending of the May month. Three days of rain had given way to drifting blue-black clouds that carried torrential showers across the city. Shop owners, concerned with the safety of their awnings and the durability of their window displays, popped in and out brandishing brass-hooked lances or wooden stepladders to wrestle with the canvases, cursing under their breath as heavy rain came and went and the sun blazed as it should in June.

Leaden skies and raindrops on the panes had given the ward in the Sick Children's Hospital a depressing aspect for the half hour that Bobby had been there. Kirsty, as usual, had hated the whole experience. Seated meekly on a hard wooden chair in a corner she had been obliged to watch her son endure the handling of a very grim nurse and a doctor who seemed bored by the whole proceeding as if he had no faith in the restorative power of the weighted devices with which Bobby's leg was stretched and flexed. Bobby was a brave soul. He endured humiliation, discomfort and even little flickers of pain with a pouting stoicism and stubborn Nicholson pride and simply refused to show how close he was to tears. Bribery had not been necessary to keep her son quiet. Nontheless he had his reward in the shape of a dish of ice-cream laced with raspberry syrup as soon as his ordeal was over and Kirsty had led him away at a near trot over the hill from the proximity of West Graham Street to a little café at Charing Cross. She had calmed herself with tea and a toasted bun and had watched the grey clouds slide apart to break into hot and confident sunshine.

Lorna was manning the counter in Gascoigne Street and Ernest had promised to try to free himself to help her some time after two o'clock. Kirsty had no particular desire to return to the confines of the shop and with the sunshine her spirits lifted and she contemplated an hour or two of freedom in the town.

She wiped Bobby's sticky face and fingers with a handkerchief, set him down by the café table and studied him critically. "Does your leg hurt?"

"Nah."

"Is the strap too tight?"

"Nah."

"Will we walk down Sauchiehall Street an' look at the shops an' then get a train home?"

"Aye."

Sauchiehall Street was strong-smelling in steamy heat. The tall, handsome sandstone mansions and galleries that cut away over the hill into the heart of the city had lost a little of their classical aloofness. The awnings did that, the gleam of sunlight on the shops' mullioned windows and, further down, on acres of plate glass in new department stores. Kirsty's depression changed into a cheerful, glad-to-be-alive sort of mood. She had time at her disposal, money in her purse, Bobby, stimulated by the town's bustle, hanging securely on to her hand.

The street seemed to have bloomed after the last black, spattering shower. Flower sellers and fruit peddlers, hawkers of gewgaws and trinkets had set up their stalls again and the last of the businessmen were stepping out of luncheon-rooms and clubs to join clerks, messenger lads and shop girls on the pavements. Where money was, however, beggars were too. Some were discreetly impoverished and feigned shame at their fallen state, stood, heads bowed, and hats out. If they were old, though, they seated themselves on boxes with a tray of pins or matches at their feet and fixed faded eyes and faint pleading smiles on the faces of the passers-by. It was as if they were offering a contract in charity, shares in the satisfaction of generosity. This inner life of the city always took Kirsty by surprise, the knowledge that it went on thus day after day, week in and out, that only the complexions of the indigents changed with the seasons, not their needs.

The man was on his feet, swaying. He wore a ragged, greasy jacket and dark blue trousers frayed at the hems and stiff with mud and urine. He was no contractor of charity but a bully who if he'd had sense left and energy would have buttonholed pedestrians with an aggression that would have come close to assault. He had been rendered quiet, though, by the passage of two mounted policemen who had swung in the saddles of their stallions to give him a hard eye. The cap in his fist was empty. He may or may not have been scrounging for handouts. If he was then he was doomed to disappointment, for no honest citizen would deign to dole him out a farthing. He seemed blind to everything and yet he had spotted Kirsty many yards away and was ready, as she passed, to pounce.

"Haw, you. It's you, is it?" the man growled as he lunged forward and grabbed at Kirsty's arm. "Mrs bloody, stuck-up Nicholson."

"Mammy," Bobby shouted and tugged his mother away in the nick of time. The man's hand brushed her sleeve. Kirsty's shock at the sudden attack turned to horror then instantly to revulsion as she recognised the features under matted stubble, and the whisky-thickened voice. She stopped, frozen, by the pavement's edge, with Bobby clinging to her skirts.

"Oh, God! Andy! Andy McAlpine!"

"Aye, it's me all right." He shook the cap at her. "Gotta spare penny for an old frien', then?"

"Yes, I – " She made the error of fumbling for her purse.

"Penny or a pound, all the same to you, Kirsty, eh? Just money, money t' spare, money t' throw away, eh?" He reached out. She jerked away. "Buy me a good drink, what you've got in there."

She fumbled still, saying, "Don't touch me. Don't you dare touch me. I'll give you something, if you just wait."

"WAIT? ME, WAIT?"

"Come on, Bobby. Quick."

She tucked the bag under her arm, grasped her son's elbow and set off along the pavement's edge.

"WAIT FOR WHAT? HAVE YE NO' DONE ENOUGH TO ME ALREADY?"

Bobby was ahead of her, pulling her along, stooped, the braced leg swinging. He glanced over his shoulder at the gaunt and raging wraith who staggered, ranting, after them. "Hurry, Mammy, hurry."

Pedestrians split before them, paused, stared after them, did not intervene. Andy was less drunk than he had appeared to be, or perhaps rage had restored some of his senses. He strode after the woman and child, one arm raised, shouting hoarsely. "SEE HER, SHE DONE IT, SHE DONE IT, THE INTERFERIN' BITCH, BUTTER WOULDN'T MELT, EH, I CAN TELL YE DIFFERENT."

Forcing herself not to panic Kirsty crossed the thoroughfare. Carefully guiding Bobby between carts and horse-drawn omnibuses, she tried to give the impression that the man was not following her, that his remarks were aimed at someone else. She found the pavement, stooped and swung Bobby into her arms. In the hope of finding that Andy had given up the chase or that the commotion had attracted the attention of a constable she glanced behind her.

"STOLE MY WIFE, RUINT ME, DROVE ME T' THE DRINK, HER 'N' HER MONEY . . . " Luck was not with Kirsty. Andy remained in lurching pursuit and there was not a blue uniform in sight.

" . . . HER 'N' HER FANCY IDEAS, DROVE ME T' THE BOTTLE SO SHE DID, NOBODY ELSE T' BLAME."

Andy was travelling fast. His appearance of decay was deceptive for he had learned to live, if not to thrive, on alcohol. Bottles clinked in his pockets and he held one arm about his middle to protect his store of drink as he chased her along Sauchiehall Street, bawling insults. Scarlet with embarrassment, Kirsty sought refuge in the nearest shop, a little haberdashery that slotted itself between a print gallery and an auction room. She entered, under the tinkling bell, an atmosphere that was warm and serene. Trays of cuffs and collars, cases of ribbon, tape and coloured spools of thread, together with polished wood and brass gave an impression of sanctuary, the sort of shop where never a voice was raised. The mistress of the establishment, Miss Threave, was patience and kindness personified. A doll of a woman, about sixty, she was dressed in smooth gingham and old lace. Her smile of welcome faded, though, when Kirsty backed to the counter and, almost at the same instant, Andy struck the window glass with fist and shoulder and shouted, "Y' CAN'T GET AWAY FROM ME, KIRSTY NICHOLSON, YE'LL NEVER GET AWAY FROM ME, I KNOW YOU'RE HIDIN'."

Miss Threave sized Kirsty up with little pearl-like eyes then slipped through the gate in the counter's end.

"Husband?"

"No," Kirsty said. "No, no."

"Who is he?"

"Used to be a neighbour. I – I hardly know him. He accosted me in the street."

"Huh!"

Little Miss Threave glided to the door just as Andy flung himself against it again. She tripped the bottom bolt with a dainty toe and, stretching as tall as she could, shot the upper bolt too. Andy rattled the door handle, kicked the wooden panel in vain. They could see him plainly, a fierce, unshaven visage pressed against glass that became hazed with spittle as he shouted his imprecations. "Y' CAN'T HIDE FOREVER, KIRSTY NICHOLSON. I'LL BE HERE, I'LL BE WAITIN'. WHERE IS SHE, WHERE'S MY JOYCE THEN? THAT'S WHAT I WANT T' KNOW, Y' BITCH."

Miss Threave was not intimidated by Andy's half-drunken state, or by his ferocity. She stood close to the door, squared up to him, waved her hand and told him to go away. But Andy, thwarted again, would not. He pounded upon the glass with both fists, kicked at the door with the petulance of a child and then danced and pranced in insensate fury before the vertical window, his eyes fixed on Kirsty all the while.

"Is he mad?" said Miss Threave.

"I think he's – he's a drunkard," Kirsty said. "I'm sorry to have – "

"Think nothing of it," said little Miss Threave. "The constabulary will turn up shortly and put an end to his nonsense."

Bobby struggled in Kirsty's arms. He was duly set down upon the counter. He was not distressed by the apparition at the window, though he did not seem to identify the man with Mr McAlpine. He rested among the boxes of new white cuffs and stiff collars and watched Andy's mad dance with a faint, almost derisive smile.

Miss Threave's prediction was correct. Within thirty seconds the police had arrived. But there was a twist to it that neither the shopkeeper nor Kirsty could have foreseen. Accompanying the two burly constables and directing them to the scene was Frank Tubbs.

"Mr Tubbs, Mr Tubbs," Bobby said, pointing.

"Ah – rescue!" Miss Threave shifted her position to get a better view of the proceedings.

Frank peered through the glass. He raised his hat to Kirsty and gave Bobby a wink. It was strange to see him there, the shock of it was increased by Kirsty's embarrassment. She felt responsible for the disturbance and out of her depth among the city-dwellers.

The constables were large men, like most City of Glasgow officers, and they had dealt with types like Andy McAlpine a thousand times before. One loitered at Andy's back and the other spoke with him, tried – though not for long – to reason with the wrong-doer. Common sense had been boiled out of Andy McAlpine, however. He stamped his foot, gesticulated, shouted, sprayed the big copper with spittle and then, like the fool he had always been, swung a roundhouse right at the officer's head. He was armlocked and pinned within seconds and, doubled over between the constables, was frogmarched out of sight without more ado.

"Daddy?" Bobby said.

"No, not Daddy. They're Glasgow policemen," Kirsty said.

"The other gentleman," Miss Threave said, "is he a friend?"

"Oh, yes," said Kirsty.

"I'll open up then," the woman said.

Kirsty heard bolts clink and saw Miss Threave draw open the shop door again. Suddenly she felt dazed and shaky, her knees weak as Frank entered. Politely he took off his hat.

"I was passing," he said, "with some chums from the Art Club. I thought it was you. I hope I wasn't out of order in summoning the might of the law?"

"Frank," Kirsty said. "Oh, Frank."

Near to tears, she threw herself into his arms, and clung to him in relief. She hung on to him even after he disengaged himself and, on Kirsty's behalf, thanked Miss Threave profusely for her brave assistance then led Kirsty and Bobby out into the brilliant, bustling sunshine. There was no sign of Andy McAlpine or of the two tall policemen now. The crowd had swallowed them up.

Frank glanced at his watch. "You've had a fright, Kirsty," he said. "My recommendation would be a good strong cup of tea to

239

steady your nerves. What do you say?"

"But – but your friends – ?"

"Hang my friends," Frank said. "Bobby, take my hand," and he led them off, together, towards the Lyric tearooms.

*   *   *

The letter from Dolphus was delivered to Great Western Terrace by hand. Hardly more than a note, cryptic in the extreme, it gave nothing away. Breezy did not reply. He simply turned up at the Ceres Club at noon on Friday, ready for battle of one sort or another. He had been angered by Dolphus's long silence, by the fact that Gordon had been allowed to break an engagement without a word of explanation or redress, had been 'let go' like some hireling whose term had expired. In vinegary mood, he was shown into the small bar that hid behind the Ceres Club's so-called grand staircase and found Dolphus waiting at a corner table there. With some satisfaction Breezy noted that his brother looked pale and nervous, an indication that Dolphus had not been entirely unaffected by recent events and that his silence had been timid not doughty in the least.

Within minutes of their meeting it became clear that Dolphus was also puzzled by the breakdown of matrimonial intentions between his daughter and Breezy's stepson. He professed – and Breezy believed him – to have no inkling as to why Gordon had terminated the engagement. When pressed, he admitted that Amanda had been terribly upset by Gordon's letter and that only her mother's influence had prevented her rushing there and then into Glasgow to try to patch things up.

"Is that why you're here today, Dolphus?" said Breezy thinly. "To patch things up?"

Dolphus did not answer directly. He swirled the dregs of bitter in the glass before him and considered before he spoke. "Young things," he said, "who knows what gets into them, hah? Be that as it may, I'll take Gordon back into my employ as soon as he wishes it."

"Gordon doesn't wish it," Breezy said.

"Should he not be allowed to speak for himself?"

"I don't think Gordon wants to speak to you, Dolphus," Breezy answered. "You take it from me, Gordon felt nothin' but relief to be out of the brewery trade."

"Not suitable, I see," Dolphus said. "Is that the final word, hah?"

"On that score, yes."

"And *our* little bit of business?" Dolphus asked.

"Do you still want to buy my pubs?"

"If the price is right," said Dolphus.

"Now that poor old Bob McAlmond is no longer a threat," said Breezy, "I assume that we must begin negotiations again?"

"Yes, you were fortunate that McAlmond did what he did," said Dolphus. "It could have been very nasty for you if a police investigation had opened that Pandora's box."

"I saw him, you know."

"Pardon?"

"McAlmond: shortly before he – before his demise."

"Ah!"

"He was very frank, very honest. He had nothin' to gain, or to lose for that matter, by being absolutely truthful."

"Ah!"

"There never was a threat to me, Dolphus. McAlmond never took a penny of my money in exchange for licences."

"I must have picked up the wrong – "

"Listened to the wrong little bird," Breezy said. "Yes, I'm afraid that our dear nephew wasn't singin' in tune."

"Nephew? What nephew?"

Breezy said, "That's also water under the bridge, old man. It's no sale."

"Ah?"

"My licensed properties are no longer on the market."

"But we had an agreement, Albert. You can't go back on your word."

"What can you possibly want with the properties now, Dolphus? You've got Olive in the palm of your hand now her lover's gone off to fight in the war."

"For God's sake – "

"There's no marriage contract, no damned 'dowry'," Breezy said. "There's nothin' you can offer me, Dolphus. Except money. God knows, I've enough of that to see me through."

"I thought I was doin' you a favour," Dolphus tried, unsuccessfully, to appear hurt. "I really thought you wanted rid of responsibility, that you were anxious to retire an' enjoy your old

241

age."

"Aye, well, I've decided I'm not *that* old," Breezy said.

"Let me put together a – a revised offer."

"You never give up, Dolphus, do you?" Breezy said. "Nope, no more offers, deals, transactions. I'm hangin' on to what's mine. I'd advise you to do the same. If it's not too late."

"I don't know what you mean."

"Oh, yes, you do," Breezy said. "An' here's another wee thing for you to think about: Mammy an' Daddy."

"Who?"

"Our parents."

"What about them?" Dolphus said. "I was under the impression that you had taken care of – well, of that side of it."

"They're old, old an' ailin'," Breezy said. "The farm is runnin' to absolute seed because they can't look after it any more."

"Hire a hand, hire a manager."

"For seventy acres? Don't be bloody daft, man."

"Why are you telling me this? Do you want a contribution, is that it, hah?"

"I want to know who's goin' to take them in?"

Dolphus sat back. Nothing that his brother had poured upon him in the course of the last quarter of an hour had had such a startling effect. He blinked his pouchy eyes, swallowed several times, then blustered, "I – I can't. Can't possibly. Not in my situation. You see that, Albert, don't you? Polly will take them in."

"I doubt if she will."

"The farm can't be as run down as you say or the Duke would have flung them off by now. They're only the Duke's tenants, after all."

"No, they're not," Breezy said. "Daddy owns Old Garscadden. Has done for twenty years."

Dolphus blinked again then leaned forward, hand hovering over his mouth as if the conversation suddenly required a degree of secrecy.

He said, "I didn't know that. Why wasn't I told, hah?"

"Would it have made any difference, Dolphus?"

"No, I suppose not. It will now, though."

"What do you mean?"

"The land must be worth something, let alone the stock."

"God Almighty!"

"If they — if they depart, shall we say, won't the land be sold and the profit divided among the survivin' children? Isn't that the way of it?"

Breezy put his hands on the table and pushed himself to his feet. "Aye, Dolphus, that's the way of it. After he dies we'll all get our pick of Daddy's scraggy wee bone."

"Better than nothing, hah!" Dolphus said.

He reared back in surprise as his brother spun on his heel and headed for the exit.

"What about lunch, old man?" Dolphus called.

"Stuff lunch!" Breezy snapped and rattled off, stiff-armed, through the bar room's swinging doors.

* * *

Affairs in China had been squeezed off the front pages of newspapers by the nation's fascination with its 'own war' in South Africa. Reuter's telegrams, however, had begun to appear more frequently in the *Glasgow Herald* and their terseness added a sense of danger and drama to the unfolding events on the other side of the globe. *"500 Boxers fought equal number of Imperial troops between Hohan and Shantung, close to Yellow River. Total effacement of Christian Religion is purpose"*, Kirsty would read. *"Missionaries cut off at Paotingfu. Fengtai being burned. Belgian families fighting for their lives."* At first she was only slightly concerned about David's safety. She imagined that she had learned something of China, how great were the distances between its provinces. She picked up key words, place-names and nationalities and convinced herself that Fanshi was far from the troubles, that the North China Mission field could not possibly be under attack. In any case, American cruisers and French war vessels were hurrying to the scene and, she felt sure, rebellion would very soon be quashed. Her optimism was encouraged by Frank who told her that he had heard nothing on the mission grapevines to indicate any of the NCM stations were threatened. The fact that there had been no letters from David for months signified nothing. Communications in the hinterland were never reliable at the best of times.

"A chartered Japanese steamer has left for Tang-Chai-Kau to rescue American and British missionaries stranded west of Shantung and

Hohan." Stranded: the word suggested disturbance not destruction.

Kirsty had so many other things on her mind in that June month that the curt little items of news in the Glasgow daily stimulated rather than dismayed her. She was sure that the Lockharts, inland and north in distant hill country, would be far away from the agitations that surrounded Peking. They would surely be protected by their converts and, failing that, by God.

*   *   *

The year's longest day had been fair, muted with a pinkish haze that absorbed and tinted the rolling smoke of Glasgow and the Clyde and gradually dispersed it, as the long, long evening waned, in trails of colour no denser than the petals of a rose. Gascoigne Street had been stifling in the forenoon but, as shadows gathered in the lane, found the whisper of a breeze that brought the odours of the river and the park into the little corner shop.

Trade had been so slack that Lorna had taken Bobby out in the afternoon to ride a tramcar's open deck and eat ice-cream in a cool shop off Kelvin Way, and Kirsty had frittered away the day by reading a penny novel instead of rearranging stock. It was close enough to closing time for Lorna to be anxious and Bobby to be fractious when, instead of Ernest, Frank Tubbs passed by the window and, a moment later, entered under the chiming bell.

"Oh, it's you," Lorna said, from her place at the counter. "Where's Tubby? Is somethin' wrong with — ?"

Kirsty peeped out of the backshop. She had been washing cups and, to relieve his fatigue, had permitted Bobby to roll up his sleeves and splash water from the cotton mop about the floor. It would only take her a minute to dry up the mess and they would be shuttered, locked and gone in a quarter of an hour. It was not that she longed particularly to get home tonight but simply to be out in the air, to feel the summer night coolness on her skin and smell the fragrances that the evening had distilled.

"Frank!" She felt a skip in her heart even as her rational mind told her that she would now have to choose between walking home along the riverside and being escorted by the companionable Mr Tubbs. Though Craig was on night shift she could not be sure that he was not skulking in the street near the shop and watching. Dumbarton Road was a safe route, innocent and acceptable. She might be accompanied along the main thoroughfare with impunity, provided that she did not take Frank's arm and left him casually before the corner. Craig could say nothing about that.

"Shan't be a minute," Kirsty said.

Ernest would arrive shortly. Tonight she would watch Ernest and Lorna without envy for she would have Frank at her side. As soon as she emerged from the backshop, however, she sensed that something was wrong, seriously wrong.

Lorna and Frank were whispering together; no smiles, no welcomes, no jocularity. Kirsty nudged Bobby before her, her stomach tense with apprehension. Frank and Lorna started, almost guiltily, and the whispering ceased.

"What's wrong?" Kirsty asked.

Stooping, Lorna beckoned Bobby to her and when he approached lifted him into her arms and, oddly, turned away from Kirsty to face the window.

Frank said, "Why don't we go for a walk, Kirsty? In the park, perhaps?"

"What? Now? I can't, Frank. I must put up the – "

"I'll do all that," said Lorna. "Ernest'll be here any minute. He can help me with the shutters and then we'll take Bobby home."

"No," Kirsty said, "not until you tell me what's wrong?"

"I've had news from China," Frank Tubbs said. "Bad news."

Kirsty put out a hand and found the counter's edge, steadied herself. "I'll get my hat," she said.

She appreciated his method of breaking the news to her. She knew why he wanted her outdoors. He could not be sure how she would react and felt, perhaps, that he could better cope with her tears amid the green acres of the Forrester Park than within the confines of the shop. He offered privacy, an opportunity to share her grief with him, to keep it, for the most part, hidden from her husband. Without a word she handed Lorna the keys to No. 154 and went out with Frank into the dusty air. She took his arm as they turned left down Gascoigne Street along the Windsor Road and, by the riverside, to the park. She said nothing, put no question to him, until the trees were in sight.

She could hear the merriment of children at play, the inevitable dog barking and distant music of a street organ.

"You may tell me now, Frank."

"Twelve or fourteen days ago," Frank said, "the North China Mission station at Fanshi was attacked by a horde of Boxers. It was razed to the ground. Jack Lockhart, his mother, and a Miss Fraser escaped by the river."

"But not David?"

"David and his father stayed with the sick and to defend the mission hospital."

"He's dead, isn't he?"

"Yes."

She was glad Frank had brought her out, brought her here. She did not need to go into the park. It was enough to stand at the broad corner within sight of the trees.

"Is there no doubt?" she said.

"None, I'm afraid."

"How – how was he killed?"

"Kirsty, it's best if – "

"Tell me, Frank, tell me the truth."

"Beheaded."

She closed her eyes.

She could smell grass, trees, the earthy odour of the river, hear children's laughter still, and still the distant strains of the barrel organ rising from the Govan shore. For a split second she rejected the truth, believed with all her heart that David was not dead, not gone, that he was waiting on the bench in the grove in the Forrester Park, that Frank had been appointed to bring her to him. But the image of the axe tore that from her. She stood stock still, eyes closed, imagining the blood, the body bent, the head . . . He caught her in his arms and held her close against him.

He said, "The North China Mission had news by telegram this morning. Fanshi has been relieved by a contingent of International troups, Germans, I think, and the Boxers put to flight into the hills." He kept talking, talking, kept holding her tightly to him. "They were both executed, father and son. By the little account I have from the London offices, they died swiftly and courageously on the steps of the hospital."

"Where is he now?" Kirsty opened her eyes to search Frank's

face for an answer. "Do you know? Can you tell me?"
He shook his head. "No."
"Where will he be buried?"
"In Fanshi, I expect."
"Where he belongs," said Kirsty and, putting her cheek against Frank's shoulder, let herself weep for David and all that she had lost.

*   *   *

"What's wrong, old son? Can't you sleep?" Ernest Tubbs said.
"No," Frank answered. "Can't work either, alas."
"What's that you're drinkin'?"
Frank swung his feet from the desk and twisted the bottle towards him. "Gin, I think."
"I'll take a spot, if I may."
"Help yourself. There's a glass on the dressing-table."
Clad only in undershorts and bathrobe, Ernest padded to the dressing-table, poured colourless liquid from bottle into glass and, sipping from it, seated himself on a chair by the window. The house in Lindenhall Gardens had not cooled with the coming of night. Soon, very soon, the sky would redden and it would be dawn, unnaturally early and unsettling.
"What are you thinking about? Her?" Ernest said.
"No – him. I can't get him out of my mind."
"Beheaded. God!" Ernest said. "I never met him."
"I saw him once or twice. Heard him preach."
"What was he like?"
"A boy, just a boy."
"He didn't die like a boy, though, did he?"
"Oh, no," said Frank. "That he did not."
"How did you come by the news so quickly?"
"I've been keeping in touch with the NCM's London office." Frank swung his feet to the carpet and leaned his elbows on the desk, the little glass still in his hand. "Harry Ballater's down there now. General secretary. Do you remember Harry?"
"Nope."
"No, he's older than you. We went to the Academy together."
"An' you've kept in touch?"
"Vaguely," Frank said. "I wrote to him, asked him for news of the Lockharts."

"To pass on to Kirsty."

"Just out of interest."

"Did she really love him, do you think?" Ernest said.

"He really loved her, of that I've no doubt."

"Yet he left her?"

Frank finished the gin, pushed the glass away and got to his feet. He came to the window and looked out at the gardens, passive and still, and at the houses opposite, all still too and dark. "She has an enormous capacity for love," he said. "Lockhart realised it, discovered it. How I know not."

"Are you tellin' me he ran away from it?"

"She needs someone, Ernest, someone loving."

"She has Nicholson."

"More's the pity."

Ernest shifted his weight, crossed one long knee over another and balanced the glass on the window ledge. "Are you in love with her, Frank?"

"If she wasn't married I'd – "

"You'd what? Steal her away?"

Frank lifted his shoulders, gave a soft grunt. "The point's moot in any case. She's wedded to Nicholson and that's all about it. I do not steal other men's wives."

"What if she wasn't Nicholson's wife?"

Frank glanced at his brother. "She is, though."

"Perhaps she isn't – not under law, not legally."

"What?"

"Lorna doesn't think they're married at all."

"But the child – "

It was Ernest's turn to shrug. "Baptised at St Anne's. Kirsty was well-favoured at St Anne's, remember, when Lockhart was Assistant there."

"Does Lorna know this for a fact?"

"I doubt it," Ernest said. "It's no more than inspired guesswork, really, based on certain things that Craig's let slip over the years. Lorna's very quick, you know."

Frank placed both hands on the window frame and leaned his weight into his arms.

"Not married," he murmured. "Not married. Damn me!"

"In the eyes of the world," Ernest reminded him, "she's still Nicholson's wife."

"But not under law," Frank said.

"Perhaps, perhaps not," Ernest said, frowning. "Does that make such a difference, Frank?"

"To me it does," Frank answered and gave the window frame an exultant little slap with the flat of his right hand.

*   *   *

Craig had been at home when Lorna had brought the boy upstairs. It had been weeks since he'd seen his sister and he'd been startled by her appearance on his doorstep, angry and concerned when he'd learned the reason for it. He'd had sense enough to keep his mouth shut, however, and, as if to demonstrate his sympathetic nature as well as his competence, he'd heated and served Bobby's supper, washed his son and got him off to bed in not much more than half an hour.

"Where's your man?" he'd asked.

"Waitin' downstairs."

"What's he doin' down there?"

"He wasn't sure if he'd be welcome."

"Better fetch him, Lorna. God knows how long she'll be."

But Kirsty had returned before Lorna could pop down to the close to bring Ernest up to the house and was, in fact, accompanied by both brothers.

Craig saw at once that Kirsty had been weeping. Her eyes were pink, her nose red and the freckles on her cheeks stood out vividly. It was obvious that she'd had a shock but had cried it out and had regained complete control of herself before she stepped into the kitchen. Whatever comfort she'd required had been delivered by the stranger, Frank Tubbs.

They'd sat about the table drinking tea and eating scones and talking in hushed voices about China and David Lockhart, things Craig knew little or nothing about. Even on that solemn occasion there was an ease between the four, Kirsty included, which somehow fenced him out. He was not like them, could never be like them no matter how he tried. Even Lorna, it seemed, had grown away from him. Gradually, Craig's sadness had turned inward, became a sense of isolation, of separateness. He'd longed for the bustle of the police station, the comradeship of the muster, the peace of the night time streets.

They hadn't stayed long. Lorna had offered to spend the

night with Kirsty but Kirsty would have none of it. She'd assured them that she had quite recovered now, that it was just the sudden shock that had affected her. She would be fine now, she'd said. Craig had known better. He suspected that she'd wanted rid of them, rid of him too, so that she might dwell undisturbed on Lockhart, moon over the handsome, educated, well-to-do young man and weep into her pillow for what might have been, and never was.

Before he'd left for shift he'd put an arm about her. She hadn't resisted but had let her head fall back against his shoulder and had voluntarily turned her cheek to be kissed. He'd held her a moment longer than he'd intended to, as she'd stood with her arms half raised, hands wet from dishwater in the basin at the sink.

"I'm – I'm sorry about Lockhart too, y' know," he'd said.

"I know you are, Craig," she'd said.

"When'll it be in the papers?"

"Days, weeks. Frank will let me see any reports he gets before then."

"He seems concerned about you."

"Frank? Aye, he's very kind."

Thirty-five minutes later Craig was walking down Ottawa Street towards the 'change'. He had a single-duty beat that fortnight and was damned glad of it. He did not want some prattling idiot like Norbert or Archie to disturb the fine soft summer night. Besides, he had some very serious thinking to do and required a calm frame of mind.

Craig had recognised, as Kirsty had not, that Frank Tubbs was a rival in a manner that Lockhart had never been. Though fearing that he might lose Kirsty and with her his son, he was no longer sure that he had the stomach for a fight. That contest might have been lost already, squandered by his own indifference somewhere along the line.

"Craig, is that you?" Peter Stewart winked his torch from the peach-blossom shadow of a close where he'd been indulging in a crafty puff on a cigarette.

"Who the hell else would it be?" Craig said. "What's happenin' tonight?"

"Not a blessed thing," said Peter. "It's quiet as the grave out there."

"Just the way I like it," Craig said and, with a parting nod to his chum, set off on the first leg of a circuit that would take him all night to complete.

Eight

The Welcome Light

Gordon was, he realised, more than a little in thrall to Josephine Adair. With no work to do he had time to follow her energetic quest for causes to support. The Temperance Movement provided a foundation for other social and political interests and she skipped from meeting to meeting with a fervour that Gordon could not emulate but only admire. It was assumed by the more conventional of Josephine's female friends that Gordon had become Josephine's 'sweetheart' and that the relationship would inevitably end in wedding bells. Those of more independent bent, however, guessed the truth, that Josephine had taken a lover, a personable and articulate young man who would not be daft enough to spoil a good thing with a marriage proposal.

It was July before Josephine suggested a second visit to Old Garscadden. Though the prospect did not delight Gordon he did not resist and, on a grey, lowering Sunday travelled with the woman to the broken-down farm.

The weather was tuning itself up for the Glasgow Trades Fair holiday. Chill winds strayed over the moor and cloud hung low on the Kilpatrick hills. Hedgerows dripped with pearly dew and the track to the farm was slabbered with black mud. Even Josephine, too practical to be fastidious, wrinkled her nose a bit and permitted Gordon to guide her over the glaur. As they approached the farmstead certain signs impinged upon Gordon and raised in him a mixture of anger and concern. No smoke came from the house chimney and in the dip to the yard cows

252

ran loose. Milk-bags swollen, udders ruddy, they bellowed in discomfort. In the paddock, calves hooted in response and rubbed their budding horns sorely against fencing and stone dykes. There was the cart without a horse. On it, all flung about, was a clatter of empty churns and the big round trays in which milk was cooled and separated. Sour milk stained the oily clabber of the yard. The byre doors creaked in the damp wind, jammed against the body of a beast that had fallen, could not rise again and lay, pitifully waiting to die. "Have you ever seen it this bad before?" Gordon said.

"No. Never like this."

"Somethin's up," Gordon said.

"I agree," said Josephine. "We'll try the house."

The farmstead door was closed but unlocked. Josephine pushed it open, entered and called out, "Grandpa? Grandma?" She received no response at all. She reached behind her, found Gordon's hand and drew him nervously after her into the kitchen-cum-living-room.

The old woman was seated on a wooden chair by the fire. Six or eight pots, filled with stale food had been placed on the flagstones about her feet. Two leery cats who had been feeding on the contents hissed and shot away, tails stiff and ears held back, as if they had been surprised in shameful misdeed and feared punishment. Ashes coated the grate and spilled on to the threadbare rug. Shovelfuls of coal had been scattered upon the dead embers and a basketful of brown eggs had been hurled at the wall and in breaking, had woven a tapestry too gay for this dun-coloured cell.

"Grandma?" Josephine bent to the old woman. Hesitantly she touched the hand that rested on the chair-arm. She instantly recoiled and stepped back.

"I think she's dead, Josephine," Gordon said.

The old woman's eyes were wide open. Wrinkled lids were fixed and unfluttering. The little mouth had opened slightly. Two tiny brown teeth were visible like prongs in a mousetrap. The body had been propped into a sitting position by old bolsters and empty meal sacks but at Josephine's touch it sagged and the head slipped slackly to one side.

Josephine drew in a huge, shuddering breath.

"I – I agree, Gordon. My Grandma's dead, yes."

"I think," Gordon said, quietly, "that your Grandpa did this. Set out food for her to cook, had a stab at lighting the fire, and then got mad because she hadn't put away the eggs. It must have happened last night or early this mornin'."

"But where is he?"

"Look in the bedroom," Gordon said. "I'll try the byre."

"Wait. Don't leave me alone here, please."

Adair was not in the cramped ground floor bedroom, the parlour, nor either of the upstairs rooms. Gordon discovered him in a stall at the far end of the byre. He squatted in gelid gloom against a cliff of decayed straw. He was barefoot, bare-chested, wore only long woollen combinations that hung wrinkled from his shanks like shedding snakeskin. And, like his wife's, his eyes were fixed wide open. The cow at the door scraped and lowed, gored at its flank with the stump of its horn, and the door creaked and creaked and creaked.

"Oh, Gordon, is he — ?"

Gordon squeezed the young woman's hand.

"No," he said, "I'm afraid he's still with us."

"Grandpa?"

"Margaret?" the old man said. "Margaret? Margaret? Margaret! MARGARET! MARGARET!"

"Was that his wife's name?"

"No," Josephine said. "It's me. It's your granddaughter, Josephine."

Suddenly the old man rose and advanced upon Josephine as if entranced, but when he opened his mouth what spewed forth was a stream of foul invective directed against his wife. Josephine, it seemed, had undergone not one but two transformations in the course of ten seconds. She had become first a forgotten sweetheart out of the past, next the wife who had abandoned him by dying. Loving arms changed to fists and he would have pummelled at these figments of his imagination, at Josephine, if Gordon had not yanked the girl back and pushed her, without ceremony, through the cowshed's small door. Gordon closed the door behind them, leaned his shoulder upon it while Josephine found a slat of wood to wedge it shut. Pounding fists beat helplessly upon the door and the old man babbled in mourning and wrath.

"Gordon?" There were great fat tears in Josephine's eyes and she sniffed and rubbed at her nose with her cuff like a child. "Oh, Gordon, what's happened to my Grandpa?"

"Well – he's gone mad," Gordon said. "That much is obvious. We'll need to report your grandmother's death and find a doctor to deal with the old fellow. Somebody'll have to tend the cattle too. Where's the big house, the Duke's place?"

"Over behind the woods."

"Is it nearer than the railway station?"

"Much."

"Right," Gordon said. "Go over there. Explain what's happened. Somebody will know where the local doctor lives and might also send over a byreman to help out here. Listen, Jo, if there's a telephone at the house, put through a call to Breezy." He fished in his pocket, and extracted a visiting card. "Ring up that number. He should be at home. Breezy, I mean. Tell him what's happened. Tell him to get up here as quickly as possible."

"But Aunt Polly – "

"Not Aunt Polly; Breezy," Gordon said. "Breezy will know exactly what to do."

She sniffed again, dabbed her eyes. Stretching, Gordon kissed her on the brow. "Go on, Josephine, fast as you can."

She managed a faint, watery smile, then turned and ran for the stile.

* * *

By the end of July it had become clear that things could not go on as they were. Correspondence between the brothers had all but petered out and with customary guile Donnie, Edward, Dolphus and Walter had managed to evade their share of responsibility. Breezy had been first on the scene. Breezy had attended to the sordid details of death certificates and burial arrangements. Breezy had taken the old man home with him. What was it to do with them? What could they do that Breezy had not done already?

They had said as much at the funeral, standing under black umbrellas at the gate of the rural burial ground by Hackerson kirk on a Tuesday afternoon, while their carriages waited down the road apiece. These four sons of Donald Albert Adair and the not-much-lamented Jeanne made small talk about the farm and expressed surprise and embarrassment that Breezy had been rendered almost speechless by grief. It was left to the cousins Russell and Sinclair Smith to help Gordon get Breezy to the big hooded carriage and ride back to Glasgow with him, all silent amid the reek of tobacco smoke and the smell of damp overcoats.

Russell and Sinclair Smith, together with Aunt Evelyn Mungall and Uncle Willy Todd, asked permission to visit Great Western Terrace and offer condolences, as best they could, to the bereaved, and later expressed shock at the old man's state of derangement and admiration for Breezy's 'big heart' in taking his father to live with him. Nothing at all was seen of the brothers. Some mild interest was expressed by letter as to the exact state of affairs in respect of the farm, who owned what and what might be put into the melting pot and what – in this matter – they might do individually or collectively to assist in sorting out business affairs.

Polly came round often, Heather from time to time. The girls, however, found it difficult to deal with the mad old man, to conceal their relief that they had not been landed with him and to link their lives with his distorted visions and wild waking nightmares. Only Breezy had served a long enough term in the hulks of time past to bear remembrance of it, to share with the raving, mumbling old man some crumbs of reality.

For instance, only Breezy recalled who Margaret had been; stout, black-haired daughter of the Reverend Logie, minister of Hackerson kirk in the years when his father had been young. How Breezy had scratched that fact from the gravel as a hen will a seed, he had no notion, but that *was* the Margaret who had dwelled in his father's head in a lustful fantasy that only now had been revealed. Memory, however, was fickle and cruel. Hundreds of names floated in the old man's mind but not that of his son. Albert remained a nameless stranger. Only a trace, a vestige remained, some mumbled words about 'the lad', the hint of an episode, a trivial incident that Breezy too recalled. Breezy would sit forward eagerly and offer the soup spoon or the fork and say, "That was me, do you not recall?" and the old man would give him a suspicious, glowering stare and snap in his food without acknowledgement. Soon, it seemed, he had forgotten everything, except how to eat and how to fill his little burnt-clay pipe with shreds of black tobacco and fire it and puff, and spit.

The spitting drove Madge to distraction. She strewed newspapers on the carpet in the old man's room and lifted them herself with firetongs twice a day, burned them in the grate in the drawing room. She was too ashamed of what Breezy had brought home to ask the servants to attend him. Besides, they were afraid of the ranting apparition in the first floor bedroom at the back.

Doctors gave no hope of a recovery and prescribed heavy sedatives to give Mr Adair, and his keepers, rest. Breezy fed him. Breezy sat with him when he was still. Breezy unbuttoned him in the lavatory. Breezy sponged his dirty, desiccated flesh and dabbed him dry. Breezy tied the soft, silk cuffs that strapped him to the bed in the half-dark to keep him from plunging through the window or flailing about the room and breaking his old bones on the spartan furniture. Breezy fought with him, listened to him, sat in the quiet times, knee to knee, dozing in the sunlight, sharing, it seemed, his father's last decrepitude.

"It can't go on," Madge repeated beneath her breath to Heather, Lorna, Polly and even to Gordon. "The old devil could live for twenty years yet."

One month was enough.

Breezy came through to the drawing room one early afternoon to find his wife and elder sister seated, side by side, on the sofa, backs to the window, spines straight. Though they wore light summer dresses, they had the corseted look of females armoured in righteousness.

Breezy sighed.

"Albert," Polly said, snappily. "You look dreadful."

"I'm all right. Have you seen my cigars?"

"No, and don't run away," Polly said. "I want a serious word with you."

"I can't leave him for long," Breezy said.

"Sit."

"Listen to Polly, Albert," Madge said.

"I know what you're goin' to tell me, the pair of you," Breezy said. "I am lookin' for the right sort o' person."

"No, no, a nurse isn't the answer," Polly said. "And well you know it."

"He has to stay somewhere. Will you take him?"

"Don't be damned ridiculous, Breezy," Polly answered. "He has to be *put* somewhere – somewhere professional."

"Good God! He's our Daddy. You can't just toss him into a lunatic ward."

"It'll make no difference to him. He has no idea where he is," Polly said.

"I can look after him fine," Breezy said.

"No, you cannot," Madge said. "Another month of this, Albert, an' you'll be a candidate for the loony bin yourself."

"You don't want him here, do you?" Breezy said.

"'Course I don't. Besides, he doesn't know where he is or who any of us are. He doesn't even know who *you* are."

"Aye, he does. He may not show it but he knows me."

"Doctor Erskine says – "

"Aye," Breezy said, sighing again. "Erskine's spoken to me about it too."

"Where do you think you're goin'?" Madge said.

"I can hear him. He's callin' out for me."

"Nothing of the kind," Polly said. "He's just creating a fuss. What sort of life is this for him, a prisoner in your back room? He'd be better off in Gartnavel where at least he'd have company."

"Some company!" Breezy muttered.

Nonetheless, he seated himself wearily in the library chair by the fire. It was a fine, bright day outside. He could see the green of trees reflected in the big windows, hear horse traffic on the boulevard, the sparrow chatter of girls from a school nearby. None of this impinged on the old man in the back room; not the sunshine, the greenery, the lively sounds. If he was taken back to Old Garscadden what would be there for him? What connections would he make with the realities of the world about him? None, Breezy realised. None at all. What Polly said was true. He would never be able to hack through the weedy tangle of the past, impress his father with the elegance of his big city mansion, the comfort that money could buy. His father was already gone from him, lost forever. Yes, Polly was right. Donald Adair would be better cared for in another place.

"I'll talk to Erskine," Breezy said.

Polly and Madge glanced at each other, nodded with the smug air of women who have, by team work, triumphed over an irrational male.

"And the rest of it?" Polly said.

"The rest of what?" said Breezy.

"The farm, the stock, that sort of thing?"

"Ah, God!" Breezy exclaimed. "All right, Polly. I'll arrange a family council, give you all a chance to air your views."

"When?" said Polly.

"As soon as father's been taken care of."

"Won't your brothers want a say about that too?" Madge asked.

"Not them," Polly answered.

And Breezy grunted, "Huh!"

*   *   *

Frank kept Kirsty abreast of what little news came in from China. From acquaintances in missionary circles he gleaned information that did not appear in the press and was generous enough to share it with her. It did not encourage Kirsty to believe that there was any hope at all that initial reports were mistaken, that David would be miraculously restored to life and returned to her. Down, down deep within her, however, under the sorrow, beneath the layer of emptiness, was a thin and strangely selfish seam of relief, a broken edge of gratitude; relief that David's story was complete, gratitude for the fact that she had known him at all.

Based on a Reuter's telegraph, routed through Paris, the headline appeared on the second page of the *Herald* towards the end of August: *Reported Great Battle in Pekin, Allies Lose 1800 Men.* Beneath the cryptic text was a sub-heading that made Kirsty's heart pound in her chest, her throat turn dry; *News of Missionaries.* Only at that moment did the event in Fanshi become irrefutable fact. It was as if Frank's spoken words had been too insubstantial to carry weight and she had irrationally suspected him of exaggeration or of lying. *Dr M. Robertson, arrived in Hankow. Miss Whitechurch, Miss Searle, 9th ultimo. Mr & Mrs G. O'Connell & son, Miss A. King, Miss E. Barton, 12th ultimo – murdered. Mr & Mrs Sutty and Civil Workers – no information received. Dr D. Lockhart & Mr D.M. Lockhart, 2nd ultimo – murdered. Dr J. Lockhart, Mrs D. M. Lockhart & Miss J. Fraser arrived here safely, all well.* The printed statement stamped David's death as authentic and she sat alone with the *Herald* and scanned it in her lap for a quarter of an hour or so staring out at dusk gathering in the backcourts behind No. 154 Canada Road.

The newspaper had been waiting for her, neatly folded, on the table in the kitchen when she had returned from the shop. Craig had obviously put it there. Craig was on a thirty-six hour relief and had said that he would take Bobby to the swimming baths and then, Kirsty vaguely recalled, on to an early-evening Magic Lantern show somewhere in Glasgow. All day long the newspaper had been spread on the table, waiting for her. As a rule she purchased a copy of the *Herald* and scanned it in the shop or Lorna would bring an issue down from Great Western Terrace. Today, of all days, neither Lorna nor Ernest had seen the newspaper. And Frank – why hadn't Frank brought her the report? Why hadn't Frank been there to offer her sympathy and a shoulder to cry on?

It was almost nine o'clock before Craig and Bobby returned. The boy's hair was still slicked down with water and he had the medical smell of the swimming pond upon him again. It was the Magic Lantern show that had really tickled his fancy though, and he was full of prattle about dancing elephants and other wonders of Africa and India that he had seen as images flickering unsteadily on a cloth screen.

Kirsty managed to serve supper, to feign interest in her son's chatterings, to persuade him at last to go to bed. Strung between melancholy and guilt, she grew more tense as she performed the round-up of the evening's chores and approached that moment when she would be unoccupied and Craig would stir, glance at her, challenge her.

Craig had been still since supper time. He was sprawled in the chair by the fire, smoking and browsing through not the *Herald* but the *Partick Star*, content with snippets of trivial local news. He looked dark and brooding, older than his years, and every movement that he made was deliberately casual. At last, well after eleven, Kirsty had nothing more to do and, with a last swipe at the rim of the sink, wrung out the wash-cloth and hung it on its little brass hook. She rubbed her hands on her apron and, reaching behind her, untied it and hung it in its appointed place.

Craig said, "I take it you read the *Herald*?"

"Yes," Kirsty said. "Yes, I did. Thank you for leavin' it out for me."

"Old David Lockhart. Dead an' gone. Officially."

"Yes."

She went out of the kitchen and down to the water closet on the stairs and sat there in the semi-darkness for ten minutes in the hope that Craig would go to bed before she returned.

He was waiting for her, however, the newspaper discarded, his position hardly changed.

"Havin' another wee weep, Kirsty?" he said, quite softly.

"No," she said. "I've done my weepin' for David."

Craig said, "I thought your new boyfriend might've been down at the double to show you the news."

"What new boyfriend?"

"Tubbs – the pansy."

"The what?"

"Pansy – you heard," Craig said. "You seem to have a fair passion for pansified men, Kirsty. First a minister an' now this bloody author – or whatever he is."

"Frank isn't my boyfriend. An' he isn't a – a pansy."

"Talks 'awfelley' proper, though, doesn't he? Is that what you like, Kirsty, fancy manners an' fancy words?" Kirsty did not respond and Craig, after a pause, went on. "D'you think you'd be happier with a chappie like that?"

"David Lockhart was a fine man. I'll thank you to keep your slanderous remarks to yourself," Kirsty said. "It's wicked to miscall him now he's dead."

"What about the one that isn't dead?"

"If you mean Frank – "

"Frenk, oh, aye, Frenk."

"He's a partner in business."

"An' what else, eh?" Craig said. "Bloody hell, Kirsty, do you think I'm blind, or somethin'? I know fine well you fancied Lockhart. God, you've been traipsin' around with a face like a fiddle ever since you heard he wasn't comin' back."

"He's dead, Craig. *Dead!*"

"Still, it didn't take you long to find another 'friend', did it, after Lockhart ran off t' China?"

"What are you drivin' at, Craig Nicholson?" Kirsty cried. "Do you think I'm sleepin' with Frank, is that it? If it is, come right out an' say so."

"I don't know *what* you're doin' with Frank Tubbs but, by Jeeze, I know what he'd like to do to you."

She tried to find a reply but her tongue seemed stuck to the roof of her mouth. All the tension that had mounted in her during the last hours accumulated in her stomach and chest. She uttered a series of astonished little cries.

Craig rose, tossed his cigarette into the grate, said, "I suppose you'll be tellin' me next that you never managed to get the breeks off the minister."

Kirsty lost control completely. She struck him with the flat of her hands, first the right and then the left, and went on slapping and slapping at his face and head until he covered himself with his forearms and ducked out of her reach. She followed him, hands still flailing. Tears streamed down her cheeks and her complexion was livid with anger and humiliation.

It was not her attack upon his person that chastened Craig so much as the realisation that she had, after all, found something in Lockhart, something that he had been unable to give her. He no longer tried to defend himself. He permitted her to beat at his unprotected head, flinching with each blow, turning his face again towards her until her assault upon him weakened and finally ceased. They stood by the hearth, face to face. Kirsty was breathless and panting. Craig held his hands behind him, fingers locked together, chin tilted as if to demonstrate his willingness to take whatever she had strength to mete out.

She looked down at her hands, sore and reddened, then she went to the sink and ran them under the cold water tap. She dried them carefully and at length, then she walked past him with never a glance and seated herself on the bed in the corner. She sank in through the curtain and drew it about her, so that all Craig could see were her feet, shins and knees, very prim and proper in a silky brown skirt, shoes in line.

"Kirsty, I – I shouldn't have said what I did."

"It's too late for apologies."

The fact that she spoke at all caught him off guard. He had not expected her voice to be other than moist and remorseful or perhaps to have anger trembling in it. She sounded stern and controlled, however. He longed to have the heart to pull aside the curtain and look at her, to see for himself what she was really like at that moment. He could not bring himself to do it, though. Instead, he said, "I'm sorry, Kirsty. I'm really sorry."

"I don't care," she said.

"Do you want me to – ?"

"Do what you like," she said.

He hesitated. He felt lost, uncertain, then habit took over and he yielded to it, gave a disparaging grunt and left her where she was, to sulk or snivel or do whatever she chose. He went into the dark, warm, summer-musty bedroom at the front of the house, seated himself on the bed facing the uncurtained window and waited for her to come to him, though he knew that she would not.

After three or four minutes he stirred, fumbled for his cigarettes and matches, took out a Gold Flake and put it in his mouth. His face, ears and neck smarted now, throbbed at the slapping she had given him but he endured the discomfort stoically. He struck a match and held up the flame. It weaved and bobbed before him, and he realised with astonishment that his hand was trembling violently. He blew out the match flame and let the burnt stump fall to the floor.

He was filled with dismay at what he had said and done, with dread at the thought that he might lose her or, worse, had lost her long ago to a man who was better than he was. Even now he was too proud and stubborn to admit his need of her, not to Kirsty or to himself. He braced himself, struck another match and, gripping right wrist with left hand, held the flame to his cigarette, unflickering and, apparently, as steady as it had ever been.

* * *

August was not the best time to hold a family gathering. Several Adairs had taken off on annual vacations, heading for sea or hills or, in Walter's case, for the region of the Loire. Edward did not deign to reply to Breezy's letter of invitation but apologised via Heather's husband, Robert Whiteside, who came in the company of his wife. Both Whitesides were brown as Lascars after a fortnight's sailing in unusually fine weather on the Sound of Mull, and Edward – whose yacht it was – had elected to extend his absence from his soft goods manufactory by another week. Donnie too had opted out, though he was in town and could concoct only the feeblest of excuses for not being present. Hurt and disappointed, Breezy had to make do with the Whitesides, Polly and Dolphus at dinner table on that oppressively hot and thundery Friday in August.

As it happened there was no decision to be taken regarding the welfare of father Adair. After hasty consultation with Polly and Heather, Breezy had obtained the two medical certificates necessary for a Sheriff's order to commit the old man to the Royal Mental Hospital, and a day later had driven with his father along Great Western Road to Gartnavel and had gently handed him into custodial care.

The building, a suburban landmark for half a century, was substantial and dignified. It crowned the ridge of a well-wooded estate hardly more than a mile from Breezy's mansion and the proximity of his father's final abode gave Breezy some comfort. Less comforting were the rods on the doors, grilled windows and the sight of so many senile and organic dements lost in chronic delusion, though the appointments of the West House were very luxurious, as so they should be at £160 per annum.

There wasn't much jollity among the hatful of Adairs who eventually sat down to dinner. Dolphus in particular seemed glum to the point of tears. He uttered hardly a word during the course of the meal, ate with eyes cast down as if Breezy's account of Gartnavel filled him with foreboding about his own eventual demise.

It was left to brother-in-law Robert Whiteside, with his plummy, lawyer's voice, to quiz Breezy about the farm at Old Garscadden. Breezy informed him, and the company, that Old Garscadden would not be sold while their father remained alive. Whiteside was too familiar with the power of sentiment to challenge his relative's reasons for hanging on to such a white elephant but drew from Breezy the admission that the Old Garscadden lands did belong to the family, that he, Albert, had purchased them from the Duke and assigned them to his father many years ago. A retired cowman had been hired to attend the stock and generally manage the place but the farmhouse would remain unoccupied until such time as it could be renovated prior to an eventual sale.

To all of this, and more, Dolphus listened in stony silence, wrapped, it seemed, in solitary and contemplative thoughts of his own.

Dishes were cleared, a fresh bottle of wine was brought into the room and two great round flans of grape and greengage put upon the servery. Outside, the terrace and gardens were scratched in charcoal and from the distance came the sound of a dray rumbling over tramlines. They were all looking at Dolphus now, all except Whiteside. He had moved on to the matter of just who was legally entitled to the profits from Old Garscadden. He remained insensible to the fact that he had lost his audience until, at last, even he became aware of the queer wee noises emanating from his brother-in-law, swung in annoyance and snapped, "Dolphus, what *is* wrong with you, man?"

Dolphus answered with a sob and, with a delicacy too extreme for such a large individual, draped his napkin over his forefinger and wiped away his tears.

Unfortunately Heather was first to respond to her brother's grief. She rose and glided towards him, saying soothingly, "There, there now. Daddy will be all right."

She reached from behind Dolphus's chair to put a soothing arm upon his shoulder but Dolphus batted her away and cried savagely, "Don't *touch* me, you – you *viper*."

"I say, old man," Bob Whiteside advised, "steady on there!"

Napkin now clenched in his fist, brow scarlet as a strawberry stain, Dolphus shouted, "*Shut – your – damned – mouth*." In the hiatus that ensued he pitched the napkin at Whiteside, reared up and shot his chair back against the servery.

Stunned by the outburst the Adairs gaped at their brother. Only Madge chose not to look. Fat, bare forearm draped over her chairback she stared over her shoulder at the view from the long window as if she wished that she were there in the gardens and not here at all.

Puce-cheeked and snorting Dolphus blurted out the truth: "Amanda, my daughter Amanda is expectin' a child."

"Gordon!" muttered Heather. "Oh, God!" She addressed herself to Madge, "I'm so awfully, awfully sorry."

"Not Gordon," Dolphus said. "Not *his* son. *Your* son."

"Our son?" Whiteside scratched his eyebrow reflectively, as if giving weight to an unsubstantiated rumour. "Certainly not. Johnnie would never – "

"Johnnie *did*," Dolphus shouted.

"Who told you this monstrous lie?"

"Amanda."

Heather seated herself on the edge of her chair, hands on her lap. She seemed to have aged five years in five seconds. Her husband, however, was icy calm. He placed his knuckles against his hip and cocked his elbow, as if to hold back a lawyer's gown. "We are not compelled to take her word on it. Is it not a plain fact that young girls are prone to distort the truth when it suits them? When did this alleged – "

Breezy wrapped his fingers around the stem of a wine glass. He began to tap the base of the glass against the tablecloth, tapped and tapped until Bob Whiteside's harangue ceased, tapped until the glass shattered and fine fragments rained upon his hand.

"Where is Amanda now?" Breezy asked of Dolphus.

"Edinburgh."

"And Olive?"

"Gone with her, all of them, to stay with Jane Carruth at Duddingston until I decide what to do."

"What do you mean? What to do?" said Robert Whiteside.

Breezy held up his hand to quiet the man. A tiny trickle of blood ran down the base of his thumb on to the linen cloth. He licked the invisible wound with the tip of his tongue for a moment before he spoke again. "It's not up to you, Dolphus. It's up to Johnnie to decide what to do. What has Johnnie got to say about it?"

"Johnnie doesn't know," Dolphus said.

"Ah," said Breezy.

"He'd have told *us* if he'd known," said Robert Whiteside. "Do you suppose we'd have had the audacity to present ourselves here tonight if we'd known."

"Why didn't you tell Johnnie?" Breezy asked Dolphus.

"Amanda is mine, my daughter."

"Are you sure she is pregnant?" Polly put in. "I mean, young girls can have such fancies about these things."

Breezy, Dolphus too, ignored the question as being too naive to warrant an answer. Amanda was daughter to Olive Carruth Adair and if anyone could be depended upon to confirm the signs and symptoms of an unwanted pregnancy it was she. She also would terminate it or, worse, see it through to the point where the new little life was lost, not to existence but to the Adairs, put away as inconvenient, with tears but without compunction.

"Olive took her away, didn't she?" Breezy said. "And she's not comin' back, is she? You've got what you thought you wanted, Dolphus, am I right?"

The sisters, Madge too, watched intently. They had but scant sense of the true history of the conflict between Dolphus and Breezy, what lay not only behind it but ahead.

"What Olive and I decide to do is none of your business, Breezy. My private affairs do not concern you," said Dolphus loftily.

"But if – if John is the father – " Heather began.

"I will not see my daughter's future impeached through the callous actions of a filthy young scoundrel," Dolphus said. "Your son will be under no obligation to marry her, be assured of that."

"Jesus Christ!" Breezy snapped and got, at last, to his feet.

At the same moment Robert Whiteside flung down his napkin and stood too, crying, "Just one moment, sir."

Dolphus had no stomach for debate. He had attended Breezy's dinner party only to discharge himself of the truth. Now that he had done so he turned and hurried to the door, tugged it open and went out into the hall.

Heather wept; "Oh, dear! Oh, dear! Our Johnnie, our little Johnnie," and Whiteside shook an accusing finger at Breezy and shouted, "It's all your fault. If you'd allowed my son to go into the legal profession none of this would have happened. He would have been *respectable*. Do you hear me, Adair! *Respectable!*"

"Where is Johnnie?" Breezy said. "Heather, answer me."

Heather shook her head.

Without another word, Breezy left the dining room, buttoning his dinner jacket as he went and, a minute later, hurried from the mansion, hard on Dolphus's heels.

*   *   *

The Albion Sporting Club hid itself away in one of the long, plain streets that ran west from St George's Road. The building itself, in nicely weathered sandstone, had a classical portico, a stained-glass transom and tall, discreetly-curtained windows.

The management committee were careful to vet all

prospective members and few of the frayed-cuff gents who frequented other gaming clubs in the region of Charing Cross ever crossed the Albion's threshold. No thugs, extortioners or confidence tricksters were to be found at its card tables or at its long bar. All in all it was the sort of place where a man could go to hell dourly and without fuss, in true Presbyterian fashion.

Pure luck and good guesswork took Breezy there as his third port of call after he had been to French's and an iniquitous den in Monkton Street where the favours of foreign girls were bought and sold. Nephew Eric, on holiday, was shooting in Ireland; Johnnie was on the loose and the Albion was just the ticket for a quiet evening on the town.

Johnnie's quiet evening ended suddenly however, when Breezy stalked into the long bar about half past ten o'clock and without ceremony called his employee out, not just into the foyer or one of the side-rooms but right outside into the dusty street. For once Johnnie did not protest at the interruption to his night's entertainment. He followed his uncle meekly through the doors and down on to the pavement. He expected to find a cab waiting to whisk him away to some private place. At the back of Johnnie's mind was a suspicion that Breezy had at last found out about the little jape he'd played in respect of the licences and the late lamented McAlmond. He had rehearsed his lies, polished and perfected them and, being used to avuncular indulgence and the benefit of the doubt, was ninety percent sure he could weasel his way, yet again, out of blame and punishment.

It did not occur to him that his uncle's appearance at the Albion had nothing to do with money but with betrayal of a more intimate kind.

The street lamp's hazy glow enclosed him. He could taste old Glasgow's horsey dust, peppery on the tongue, hear thunder lying off like some great iron ship groaning on the Clyde. Even before Breezy spoke, greasy beads of sweat had formed along Johnnie's hairline where the brilliantine brush had left a scented smear.

"Congratulations, John," Breezy said in a tone that contained no trace of ire but rather of irony.

"Wha – what am I bein' congratulated for, if I may ask?"

"Your impendin' marriage," Breezy said.

"Ma – marriage? To whom?"

"Your cousin Amanda."

"Whatever that little bitch has told you," Johnnie said, abruptly, "is a damned lie. I had nothing to do with what happened between her and Gordon. It was doomed long before I appeared on the scene. What *has* she told you? When did *you* see her?"

"You'll have to go to Edinburgh – Duddingston to be precise – to bend the knee, Johnnie. Tomorrow mornin' will be soon enough," Breezy said.

Breezy's dinner suit, dark and heavy-lined, seemed far too formal for a public street. Towards Woodlands Road two women loitered by a close. Beyond them Johnnie thought he saw a constable hovering between the lamp-posts. It all seemed very vivid and significant, as such moments do.

"Gordon wouldn't do it," Johnnie said, "so I must?"

"She's expecting," Breezy said.

"Expecting what?"

"She's pregnant."

"So?"

"It's yours, Johnnie. You're the father."

"How can that be proved? Amanda, for your information, is no model of maidenly virtue." Johnnie leaned against the lamp-post and folded his arms. "It may well be Gordon's bastard, not mine."

"Did he know? Did Amanda tell him about you?"

"I don't know what you're talkin' about, old man."

"How many times?"

"Oh, don't be so bloody prurient," Johnnie said. "In any case, Olive will know what to do about it. A sojourn in the country and – " he snapped his fingers " – the problem is removed. For Amanda and, of course, for me too. Olive's done it before."

"Don't you feel any compassion for Amanda, one iota of tenderness or sympathy?"

"She was perfectly willin', *ergo*, she must share the consequences."

"Well, here's a consequence," Breezy said. "You no longer work for me. You are, from this minute, unemployed."

"You can't pull that one."

"Aye, but I can. The warehouse is still mine."

"We, Eric and I, have your promise that – "

"Show me a document."

"Blackmail, Uncle? Two can play at that game, you know," Johnnie said. "I've done a great many things for you that won't bear scrutiny in the light of day."

"True," Breezy said. "But when you're charged with embezzlement it'll be very hard to make the stories stick."

"Embezzlement?"

"Cooked books."

"I never cooked – "

"No, but I did," Breezy said. "No use hurryin' round to the warehouse, I've got the ledgers in my possession. All of them. Now here's the situation, Johnnie – you're out of employment, come what may. If you try to make trouble – aye, you can, I admit – then I'll charge you with embezzlement."

"My father . . . "

"I know what he's like better than you do," Breezy said. "He won't stand by you, John. He might blame me for corruptin' you – he already has, earlier tonight – but he won't lift a finger when it comes to it. He's ashamed, ashamed on your behalf."

"So they know, do they?"

"Tomorrow you visit Dolphus at St Rollox. Tell him that your intentions are honourable an' that you want Amanda's hand in marriage. Offer yourself to him as a suitable son-in-law."

"He won't take me, you know."

"Aye, he will," Breezy said. "He'll take you because he's got no choice. He *needs* a son-in-law. You're the only candidate, Johnnie. Carruth's brewery can use a man of your calibre."

"I'm not Gordon Nicholson," Johnnie said. "I refuse to be traded like a damned commodity."

"To put it bluntly, John," Breezy said, "you either marry Amanda and secure your future or you clear out of Glasgow an' take your chances without the protection of the family."

The young man's capitulation appeared to be swift but, from the instant that Breezy had uttered Amanda's name, Johnnie had been weighing loss against gain, unprecedented doubts. Breezy appeared confident that common sense and mendacity would prevail, that he had the upper hand. Johnnie was forced to agree with him. He would not however, go down humbly. He leaned back and arrogantly folded his arms again.

"All right, Uncle," he said. "Have it your way. Since you're so insistent I will marry the little cow."

For an old man in a heavy dinner suit Breezy moved with astonishing speed and agility. All the anger that had been bottled within him was syphoned into the blow. Johnnie did not see it coming. The first he knew of it was a sudden, violent burst of red pain across the middle of his face. Tears squirted from his eyes and, even as he sat back in mid-air and dumped on to the pavement, blood began to pour from his nose and lip. Dazed, dazzled, he sat there like a broken puppet, arms and legs flung out. Breezy bent over him, thrust a white linen handkerchief against his snout to stanch the blood and, when it had stuck, straightened and stepped back.

"Wha'd you do dat for?" Johnnie asked.

"I hope some day you'll find out," Breezy answered and, his work done meanwhile, turned and walked wearily away to pick up a cab on St George's Road.

*   *   *

The great autumn rally of the British Temperance Movement was held in September in Edinburgh, a city suitably divided by natural elevations and Georgian terraces to keep rich and poor apart. Up in the wynds of High Street and down in the vennels of the Cowgate life sprawled on with hardly a whiff of the hot air that tainted the stench of brewers' wash. Perhaps there was just a wee taste more edge to the perennial thirst of the old town's honest citizens as they drank toast upon toast to the two thousand ranting killjoys who marched along Princes' Street to spout their heresies within the vaulted splendour of St Magnus hall.

Friday was given over to meeting and greeting pilgrims from the South, to the Free Speech of Free Thinkers, the preaching of Bunyanesque idealists who would have had the nation – nay, the world – exist on plain brown bread and well water. On Saturday, after prayers, the morning was spent in listening to reports delivered by all sort and manner of men and women, representatives of social, moral and spiritual sects and unions, Grand Lodge Good Templars, Rechabites, Danielites, Band of Hopers and a hundred and one Temperance leaguers, right down to a 'speaker' from the Deaf and Dumb Order. Whiskers fair bristled in this long session, chests were beaten and facts and figures flung about with reckless abandon.

At Gordon's suggestion, Josephine and he slipped away for an early lunch, to save their stamina for the afternoon's political debates. Gordon had done his best. He was not uninterested in the social implications of the unrestricted sale of strong drink or in strategies for combating it, but he found crusading energy thus channelled very tiring and, in the middle of a long speech by a tiny, bearded Welshman on the subject of Sunday closing in pit villages in the Rhondda valley, he fell asleep.

"And snored," said Josephine.

"God, did I really?" Gordon said. "I hope nobody thought I was drunk."

"You'll have to learn to do what I do."

"Which is?" said Gordon.

"Sleep with your eyes open."

"I thought you were fascinated. Don't tell me you were nappin' too?"

"Here an' there. Now and again," said Josephine.

"Savin' your strength, were you?"

"Absolutely," Josephine said and with a little rolling motion curled her long left leg across his thighs, and let her breast rest against his bare shoulder. "How many have we left?"

"One each," Gordon answered, peeping into the brown paper bag that rested on top of the bedclothes. "How many have you had?"

"Two," said Josephine.

"God, what a pig!" Gordon said. "Still, you can have mine if you're really hungry."

"Now that offer," Josephine licked her fingers, "I would regard as being the mark of a true-blue gentleman. To give away one's last cream bun to a girl in need deserves a reward."

"Finish your snack first," Gordon said.

Josephine drew away from him, took one of the pale brown confections between finger and thumb and, in case the gent changed his mind, ate it in two bites.

Thick, fresh, clotted cream clung to the corners of her lips. "Do you think this is depraved?"

"Sittin' in bed in Edinburgh's grandest hotel, eatin' bought buns out of a paper bag, Jo, would be depraved even if we weren't in the state of Adam an' Eve." Gordon leaned a little and kissed the clotted cream from her mouth, licking it away with the tip of his tongue from the fine, golden hairs that downed her upper lip. He sat back and studied her. "There! That's better! You look almost respectable now."

They had taken single rooms in the recently completed McNab's Bridge Hotel. It was an expensive indulgence, but the splendid two-hundred room hotel, with electrical lighting and elevators to every floor, provided a rare kind of privacy and got them away from the ruck of Temperance buddies and chums of Josephine's who had travelled through from Glasgow for the rally. McNab's was strictly not T.T., and the flitting of a woman along the third-floor corridor in the middle of the evening had gone entirely undetected.

They had made love at once, as if the long day in the St Magnus hall had been but a strange, prolonged act of wooing. They would make love again and, later, again.

Josephine's 'modern' lack of inhibition both amused and excited Gordon. It had been at Josephine's suggestion that they had called in at Scott's bakehouse, purchased cream buns and smuggled them through the elegant, palm-fronded lobby. It was at Josephine's insistence that they had eaten them in the broad, hard bed, lying naked side-by-side.

His suit and underclothes were folded neatly on the wooden valet, Josephine's dress and underthings scattered in a trail from door to bed, her boots discarded as if she had leapt out of them. The intimacy of sharing a room, a bed, increased and enhanced his desire but the sight of lace-frilled petticoats and French drawers brought back a faint, unwanted echo of Greta's kitchen with its racks of new-washed undergarments.

Josephine smacked her lips, licked her fingers, took the paper bag from his hand, crumpled it into a ball and lobbed it across the room towards the basket by the dressing-table. She patted the mound of her knees beneath the clothes and glanced at him sidelong.

"When's dinner?" she said.

"Last serving's ten o'clock."

"Oh, good!" Josephine said and, with a large, enthusiastic surge, spread her body half over his.

"Temperance," Gordon said, "I love it."

"There won't be much more of this, will there?" Josephine said, her face close to his. "Days off, I mean."

"Not when I take over Adair's warehouse, there won't."

"It's what you want, isn't it?" she said. "I think you were born to be a salesman."

"Perhaps."

Josephine's playfulness had been altered by his contemplative mood. Though she continued to lie upon him, she did not move now but looked down into his eyes with unusual gravity. "Do you regret not having Amanda?"

"Depends what you mean by – "

"No – the truth, Gordon."

"I don't regret not marryin' her, if that's what you mean."

"Do you think about her?"

"Often."

"Oh!" She pulled from him just a little, her skin sticky on his. "Really?"

"I often think what a lucky escape I had."

Jo chuckled. He could feel her tummy throb against his ribs and the quiver of her breasts against his chest.

"Will she make him happy, though?"

"Johnnie?" Gordon said. "I expect she already has."

"Shall we go to the wedding?" Josephine said. "Thee and me, Mr Nicholson. Shall we put our moral disapproval to one side to gloat over poor John's plight?"

"I hear there's to be no celebration, no reception, just a service."

"And half the family will *not* be there. Sniff-sniff and tut-tut, that sort of thing. The hypocrites. Shall we accept an invitation to the kirk?"

"Do you want to?"

"I don't see why not." said Josephine.

"If we turn up together," said Gordon, "folk will talk. They'll assume that sooner or later we'll be toddlin' up the aisle to the altar too."

"But we never will, Gordon," Josephine said, adding, after the briefest pause, "will we?"

He shifted position slightly, caught her hips between his knees, held her pinioned against him. "Why spoil a perfect friendship, Jo?"

"Why indeed," said Josephine sadly.

* * *

It came as the most almighty shock to see him here in Edinburgh. She had been thinking of other things, of nothing at all, really. Her mind had been devoid of purposeful thought since the day she'd slipped out of Glasgow with nothing but her basket and the clothes she stood up in. Even now, going on a year later, she felt like a spectre, a shadowy, insubstantial shape that drifted about the streets of the friendless town, too small and insignificant to be seen at all, much less recognised.

So adjusted had Greta Taylor become to her phantom state that she did not try to slink away or hide herself. She stood, quite alone, on the narrow strip of cobbles that knit High Street to the Royal Mile and gaped at Gordon and his lady.

She watched as they separated themselves from the dribble of latecomers that hastened towards the great west door of St Giles out of which came the solemn, swelling sound of an opening Paraphrase, and, with a sprightliness frowned upon in Sabbatarian Edinburgh, they ran hand-in-hand across her bows towards the cathedral.

The shock was physical, like cramp in her loins. She crouched and hugged her arms to her middle with an old woman's stoop. She felt sick, sick at the sight of him, for he, and perhaps Kirsty, were the only ones she could have looked at without the anger which steeled her against guilt. Not for one instant, though, did she suppose that Gordon had come for her, that somehow he had found out where she had gone and where she could be found. Only Johnnie Whiteside knew that and Whiteside would never tell.

So low had Greta become that hopes of redemption, dreams that had once sustained her, had also become part of the unimaginable past. If there had been dreams, fond, feeble yearnings for a fairytale prince and a future bright, they would have been snuffed out by the sight of the big, blonde woman who clung to Gordon's hand and the loving glance she gave him when they paused to compose themselves before entering the kirk for worship. Greta did not know the girl, whether she came from here or Glasgow, whether she was Gordon's lover or his wife, or what possible point there was to his being in Edinburgh on a Sabbath morning in September. All of that knowledge was lost to her. Gordon was as depthless, suddenly, as a stranger.

The weight of the months that had elapsed since last they'd

met came abruptly upon her. She staggered and might have fallen if she had not from somewhere found a grain of the old stubborn pride to keep her upright and, shortly, to help her move on.

*   *   *

An unseasonably early frost had turned the moorland bracken brown and brought leaves in profusion from the oaks that protected the gates of Merryburn kirk. The rustic church, austere as a hermitage, perched on a ridge between sheep pasture and grouse moor. It was picturesque in fine weather but on that misty Saturday, with a faint, cold haze of rain in the air it was no place for a bride to find joy as she was given away in wedlock.

Arrayed in fine old ivory lace and carrying a bouquet of wildflowers and followed by her sister-maids, Amanda was pretty enough. Dainty, tiny and cowed, she performed her part well and her lack of exuberance was put down to shyness and an awareness of the solemnity of her vows. Johnnie made up for it. He had leapt briskly from the carriage, chin up and smiling, and had exchanged muttered witticisms with Eric, his best man, as the pair loitered by the vestry door awaiting a signal that the bride's party had arrived from The Knowe. The forty seats in the body of the church were but half filled, however, and the narrow balcony empty. There was to be no reception afterwards, no free feed or even a glass of wine to toast the happy couple. Many invited guests pretended to take umbrage at this miserly breach of etiquette but were secretly relieved to have been given an excuse for staying away. Edward did not attend, nor Walter, nor the Smiths. Uncle Willie Todd and Aunt Evelyn Mungall, though they waited in hope, received no invitation at all and had to make do with crumbs of gossip that Polly scattered before and after the event.

Whether the Reverend Hamish Brodie was aware of the true state of affairs was a matter much discussed among those relatives who did observe the service. It was impossible to tell from Brodie's manner. He was a renegade from Free Church circles and still had the mien of a man who disapproved of everything. He certainly made his prejudices plain in his 'few words' to the new husband and his spouse at the conclusion of the marriage ceremony.

All over at last, and out to umbrellas, furtive cigars and a bleak view of autumn mists thickening over the fells. Dolphus and Robert Whiteside did their bit by shaking hands with all those who wished it. But Olive and her girls, and Heather, dived at once for the protection of the carriages; and bride and groom were gone in a skit of silk ribbons and country mud before anyone had a chance to bless their union with a handshake or a kiss or a scatter of white rice.

"Bit of a dud, what?" whispered Josephine, holding on to Gordon's arm as they dawdled down the gravel drive towards the waiting transportation. "Or are you deeply moved?"

"Not deeply, no."

"Church weddings are so depressing at the best of times. Simply legal acknowledgement of a bond of union before a registrar would seem more suited to the essentially proprietorial nature of marriage." Josephine paused. "Don't you wish you were ridin' off on honeymoon in old Johnnie's stead?"

"Josephine, stop it, please."

"Apologies," the young woman said, hugging his arm. "Too cynical by half, that's my trouble."

"Son?"

Gordon turned and Josephine, with a little start, released her hold upon him. Breezy came towards them, moving with his old bustling efficiency but without a smile.

"This won't do at all, son," he said. "Waste of a perfectly good Saturday. If you can bear it an' have nothin' better to do, come back to the Terrace with us an' we'll all go out for a damned good dinner later on. My treat."

"I have – "

"Josephine too, of course."

Madge joined her husband and the couple waited, with a faint air of eagerness that came close to pleading, for Gordon's reply. He looked at his mother's expression, at her simper, and realised with horror that he had slipped off one hook only to slip on to another.

"Oh, aye, Josephine too," Madge said.

Gordon glanced enquiringly at the young woman who, shedding all trace of cynicism on the instant, answered not him but his mother, "Why, Aunt Madge, I'd be delighted."

"Are you sure now?"

"Absolutely," said Josephine. "It's high time we got to know each other, don't you think?"

*　　*　　*

It did not take long for Eric Adair to follow his cousin Johnnie into oblivion. At his father's insistence he pulled out of the warehouse business and went into a big Glasgow brokerage firm where his indolent habits and insolent manner would soon be ground out of him. Within days of Eric's departure Breezy installed his stepson as manager of Adair's warehouse in Partick East. Sisters and brothers who had financial stakes in the concern did not dare complain about the nepotistic manoeuvre lest Breezy find some devious way to cut them down to size too.

Breezy, these days, was in no mood to be trifled with. He hadn't, however, lost his cutting edge as a businessman and, to Gordon's relief, did not throw the lad in at the deep end but personally took up the reins of enterprise. He was there on the spot for part of each working day to show Gordon the ropes and break him gently into responsibility. In imparting commercial wisdom to his stepson and heir, Breezy rediscovered a pleasure in and an enthusiasm for trade that he had supposed, like youth, to be lost and gone forever.

"I'm not so old, chookie, am I?" Breezy would enquire of his wife as they lay in bed of a night. "While to go before they wheel me away, right?"

"A long while, dear," Madge would assure him and draw him against her breasts as if he needed mothering still, which might very well have been the case.

Madge was not at all put out by the changes that fate had meted out during the course of the first long summer of the twentieth century. She did not grudge the time that Breezy spent with Gordon or the exclusive rapport that her husband had developed with her son. In the calm, cold autumnal days, with winter not far hence, she felt more settled than she had done for years. She regretted only that no reconciliation had been effected with her eldest, that Craig would not be drawn into the comfortable ambience that she, through Breezy, could provide. She was still too proud to make overtures to Craig. She remained daunted by her son's obdurate refusal to compromise, a stubborn bullheaded streak that Madge chose to believe he had inherited from his father and not from her. What news she had of Craig, Kirsty and her grandchild came through Lorna. Chit-chat, shop gossip, all the trivial nonsense of which other folks' lives seem to be composed had much less substance for Madge than quarrels with cook over menus, visits to the milliner's or the taking of tea with Polly Beadle two or three times a month. She assumed, wrongly, that all was well with Craig and his wife down in the tenement in Canada Road.

Lorna, however, was not so blinded by love and selfishness that she had not noticed the effect that David Lockhart's death had had on her sister-in-law; nor was she oblivious to Kirsty's hardening attitude towards Craig. Although she was more efficient than ever in her management of the shop Kirsty had grown increasingly lax about her domestic responsibilities. Two or three mornings in the week she would leave Bobby in Lorna's charge and go up into Glasgow on unspecified 'business'. Though Lorna fished and wheedled, Kirsty remained vague about the purpose of these trips to town. Lorna did not fail to notice that they usually coincided with the luncheon hour and that her sister-in-law invariably returned softened and in good humour.

New tailored outfits began to appear on hangers in the back-shop in Gascoigne Street, shoes and smart hats too. While Kirsty made no secret of their purchase and would put them on and show them off to Lorna, Lorna noticed that they were seldom taken home to Canada Road. It was as if extravagance had become a secret vice, a vanity linked to an ambition to rise above the dusty streets of Greenfield burgh and climb the hill that soared beyond Dumbarton Road. Estate agents' broadsheets and factors' drafts would now and then appear on the counter. Kirsty would pore over them when she had time to spare from shop work and, once, a young man called to take her off to look at apartments in a brand new tenement block that was being constructed west of Crow Road.

"You're not thinkin' of movin', Kirsty, are you?" Lorna would ask.

And Kirsty would answer enigmatically, "How can I when I'm stuck with Craig?"

In mid-October, rather to Lorna's surprise, Kirsty proposed inviting Lorna and Ernest, Gordon and his latest conquest,

Josephine Adair, to Sunday tea.

"At Canada Road?" Lorna said.

"Well, I'm not boilin' a kettle in the Forrester Park," Kirsty answered. "Of course, at Canada Road."

"Will Frank be invited too?"

"Not this time, no," Kirsty said.

"Is Craig on duty, then?"

"I've really no idea."

"He – he won't like it, Kirsty."

"Then he can lump it," said Kirsty.

* * *

It was clear from the first that Craig was an unwilling party to the ritual of Sunday high-tea. Smoked fish casserole, plates of bread and butter, trays of scones and cakes and a general steamy atmosphere of plenty did nothing to thaw him out. He sullenly refused to be drawn or cajoled into the general jollification. It was significant, Gordon thought, that his brother had chosen to wear not his best suit but his blessed uniform. He sat there in state at the head of the cramped kitchen table with collar buttoned and belt drawn tight, less like the host of the feast than a dour and reproachful navy-blue ghost.

At first it had been damned awkward. But Tubby was used to Craig's ill manners and Josephine had been well warned as to what sort of reception she might receive. Being shrewd, too shrewd, perhaps, she had elected to ignore Craig's aloofness and soon fell to baiting him, teasing with just enough subtlety to make sure that she did not cause outright offence. She laughed a lot. When Josephine let loose with her unladylike guffaw it was difficult to remain unaffected. By the time the casserole had been emptied to the last delicious drop of gravy and the big teapot was going the rounds for the third or fourth time, they had all been infected by the spirit of wit and were laughing at absolutely everything that was said or done.

Even Bobby was having a grand old time of it. He bounced up and down on his cushioned stool, giggling fit to burst, while Tubby and Josephine did their Dolphus and Olive impersonation as a sort of variety-hall double act while arguing about the number of seeds in a dish of raspberry jam.

In the breathless lull that followed the latest gale of merriment, Lorna dug her brother in the ribs and said, "Go on, Craigie, give's a wee smile."

He pushed her elbow away.

"Why the hell should I?"

"'Cause it's funny," Lorna said.

"Well, I don't see anythin' funny in it."

Gordon and Kirsty were watching him now, stiff and tense, all the laughter drained out of them by the expression on Craig's face, that patronising half-sneer which they both knew could presage trouble.

Josephine held up her hand, palm out. "Nope, Craig's absolutely right. We should not mock poor Uncle Dolphus and Aunt Olive who cannot, after all, help their afflictions."

"I suppose you'll all be stayin' late so that you can make fun of *me* after I've gone?" Craig said.

"Jeeze!" Gordon murmured while Tubby, shocked, protested, "No, no, old chap. Nothin' to mock about you, nothin' at all."

Craig got to his feet. He hitched the broad leather belt at his waist and cinched the buckle into a tighter notch, looking down at it as he did so. He had their attention now. All of them, even Bobby, were watching to see what he would do next.

"Aye, well, I'll save you the bother o' waitin'," Craig said, with a strange little nasal grunt. "I'll be on my way right now an' leave you free to say what y'like."

Lorna and Tubby glanced towards Kirsty who, with the gigantic china teapot in her hands, stood impassively by the stove, shielded in part by the cupboard door. She gave no sign that she was upset by Craig's announcement and after only a slight hesitation came to the table and, cradling the big pot, leaned forward and said pleasantly, "More tea, Josephine?"

"Why, thank you," Josephine answered. "I do believe I will."

Craig left immediately.

For several seconds there was silence in the kitchen.

"Milk?" Kirsty said.

"Please," said Josephine.

"I – I trust it wasn't somethin' we said that offended him," Ernest said.

Lorna patted her fiancé's hand to assure him that he was both blameless and innocent while Gordon, who had swung round in his chair to stare at the door, got to his feet.

"You can't just let him go like that," he said.

"Why can't we?" Kirsty said. "If Craig chooses to be rude, then it's up to him. I don't intend to let him spoil our party. Eat up, please."

Gordon, however, was not to be appeased and with a nod of apology, left the kitchen too. Helmet and gloves were gone from their place on top of the coal bunker in the hall. Gordon wasted no time but hurried out of the house and downstairs, trailing the clatter of his brother's boots out of the close and into Canada Road. He looked this way and that, spotted Craig some fifty yards away and, running, caught up with him.

"What the hell's wrong with you?" Gordon demanded, putting a hand on Craig's arm to restrain him.

Craig shook him off. "Some of us have work t' do."

"Come bloody off it, Craig. You're not due at muster for another four hours yet. Come on, come back."

"To get laughed at?" Craig said.

Uniform or not he had lighted a cigarette. He smoked in the quick furtive manner that all coppers acquire, Gold Flake cupped in his hand, hand down by his trouser leg. He kept walking, unchecked, down the quiet mid-evening street towards the riverside.

"I don't understand," Gordon said. "We were all havin' such a good time, man, an' you had to spoil it. What *is* wrong with you?"

"Ach, it's all very well for you. You've got your big blonde to keep you happy. Lorna's got her pansy-faced traveller – "

"God, Craig, you're surely not jealous?" Gordon said.

" – an' she's got her Frank."

"Who has?" Gordon said. "Surely you don't mean Kirsty?"

"Who else would I mean?" Craig said. "First it was Lockhart, now it's another one out of the same drawer, another o' those fancy-talkin', educated *nyaffs* she seems t' find so bloody irresistible."

"You're awa' wi' the fairies," Gordon said. "Kirsty would never cheat on you. Aye, she might get a bit narked at you now and then but she's not the sort to go in for hanky-panky."

The brothers had reached the lane that linked Canada Road with Kingdom Road. In scalloped shadow between the gable of a tenement and the wall of a paint warehouse a girl and boy hugged and kissed with a desperation that defied modesty, while a small dog, collared and obedient, squatted close by like a guardian. Sounds of hymn-singing from the mission hut on Scutter Street hung tinny and triumphant in the Sabbath air.

Craig stopped and faced his brother. "Go back t' your friends, Gordon. There's nothin' you can do. It's only a matter o' time until Kirsty leaves me."

"Craig, what – ?"

"True, though – an' I can't say I'd blame her." He put the cigarette into his mouth and left it there, dug his hands into his trouser pockets, shuffled his feet. "If I can't hold her then I deserve to lose her. Anyway, there's better men than me on offer to her now. I just wish to God I'd never brought her to the city. I could have held her well enough in Dalnavert, maybe. But here in Greenfield – " He shrugged, resigned.

"I can't believe my ears," Gordon said. "These men, these other men are only friends. Are you tellin' me she shouldn't have friends? Good God, Craig, she's not your bloody slave. She's your wife."

"Aye, but she's not."

"What?"

"We're not married, not kirk wed, not wed under the law."

"Jeeze!" Gordon exclaimed. "Why didn't you marry her? I mean, why don't you marry her now?"

"She won't do it."

"I thought – I mean, I had a suspicion that somethin' was wrong," Gordon said, "but never for a minute did I guess that Kirsty wasn't legally your wife."

"Common law, I suppose, would give me somethin' to hold on to." Craig spat the cigarette delicately from his lips, without removing his hands from his pockets. "At first it was me. I was careless, too bloody careless. I just wanted her, easy as possible, an' then – Greta, you know. Then Kirsty wouldn't let me make her my wife. She saw no reason for it, didn't want to change things, so she said."

"You do still want her, don't you?"

"More than I ever did," Craig said.

"Fight for her then, for God's sake."

"I'll not do that," Craig said. "I shouldn't have to do that, damn it."

"So you'll just let her go?" Gordon said. "Worse, you'll drive

283

her away."

"Sometimes I think she'd fare better without me."

"You're mad. You're loopy!"

"I can't give her what she wants."

"How do you know *what* she wants?"

"Apparently other men know it without havin' to ask – Lockhart, Frank Tubbs – men more like her than I am."

"Rubbish!" Gordon said. "Kirsty's just like us, out of the same barrel, Craig. Dalnavert, Hawkhead – "

"Out the Baird Home?" Craig said. "Aye, who *is* she? Where did she *stem* from? Who *was* her bloody father? There's always been somethin' different about Kirsty Barnes, somethin' I've never been able to understand."

"This is nonsense," Gordon said. "It was you she ran away with, remember."

"Because there was nobody else, no choice," Craig said. "Now there is an' I can't hold her."

"Because you'll not bend. Because you'll not even try."

"I shouldn't have to try, should I?"

Anger mingling with pity for his brother, Gordon puffed out his cheeks impatiently. "You could start by comin' back with me now, back to the house."

"What for? To apologise?"

"You don't have to apologise. Just come."

Craig shook his head and, removing his hands from his pockets at last, assumed the upright stance of a burgh constable. "I'll not go to the dogs, never fear about that," he said. "No bloody woman will ever do that to me, wife or otherwise."

"Glad to hear it," Gordon said, thinly. "Now, if you'll pardon me, *I'm* goin' back to one-five-four to finish my tea."

"Wi' your fancy friends," Craig said.

"Yes, with my fancy friends," said Gordon.

Later that night, much later, Gordon stole into Lorna's room to tell his sister what he had learned about the true state of Craig's marriage. It was the evening of the following day, however, before Lorna had an opportunity to tell Ernest, but only hours after that when Ernest reported to Frank the welcome news that might, just possibly, change forever the course of his life, and Kirsty's.

*　　*　　*

Once before, long since, impetuosity had brought Frank Tubbs close to ruin. Now, older and wiser, he conducted his relationship with Kirsty Nicholson with a patience that precluded disaster. It would have been a comparatively simple matter to persuade the girl to become his lover. But that was not his objective. It was undeniable that he desired her, though, and if he could have separated sexual longing from all the other emotions that Kirsty roused in him then he might have been content to allow things to jog on as they were, but this he could not bring himself to do. Ernest was engaged to Kirsty's sister-in-law, his mother was dependent upon him, he was Kirsty's partner in business and, most important of all, his good name was vital to his career. Eventually, Frank realised, he must change the nature of the relationship, or terminate it.

Frank was puzzled by Kirsty's willingness to put herself out to meet him in Glasgow; not once had she offered an excuse to avoid a rendezvous, a luncheon in the dining room of the Art Club. For several weeks he suspected that she was being charitable, showing gratitude for small favours by indulging an aging, unthreatening gentleman, and then, grudgingly, he acknowledged that she liked his company as much as he liked hers. After Ernest delivered his startling news that Kirsty was not, after all, legally beholden to Craig Nicholson, Frank's whole attitude changed and he knew that he must act, act soon before he lost his nerve and with it the first woman in years with whom he had permitted himself to fall in love.

*   *   *

Kirsty liked the Art Club. It boasted the most comfortable lounge in Glasgow and had a dining room at the rear to which women were admitted at an hour normally sacred to hungry males. It hid behind an unprepossessing façade in Bath Street, which, being the home of umpteen doctors, was lightly referred to as the Valley of the Shadow of Death. Inside, a mixture of painters, poets, craftsmen and journalists disguised the club's essential conservatism with hints of Bohemianism. Kirsty was introduced to several of Frank's writer friends. They seemed quite struck with her, not at all 'leery' of the fact that a young married woman and a crusty bachelor might choose to lunch *à deux*. Conservative men of letters they might be, with not a velvet jacket or hand-painted cravat among them, but they were also sufficiently urbane to acknowledge that one must not judge a book by its cover or a banana by the colour of its skin. After three or four visits to the Bath Street club Kirsty felt very safe and unimperilled in its big, deep recesses and its snug dining room.

As November advanced, cold weather crept across the country and stealthy frosts brought in first traces of a harsh brown fog to shorten the winter days. Noon, however, was a bright time and Kirsty walked briskly from the railway station. She took pleasure in the crisp, crinkling feel of cold air on her cheeks and even the faint burnt paper taste of city smoke on her lips. She wore the first of her winter outfits, a stylish outdress in pastel blue cloth, with a long lined skirt, stiffened at the hem. Her hat was high at the back, ornamented by a vertical bow of wired ribbon that made her seem quite conspicuously tall, a feeling she rather enjoyed.

The porter at the door recognised her and showed her at once into the dining room where Mr Tubbs was already seated at a table for two in a corner beyond the room's huge stone fireplace. A selection of new paintings hung in ostentatious frames around the walls; Kirsty did the decent thing and paused to give each a second's study. Frank, no doubt, would discuss their merits at some point during lunch and impart discreet instruction on the painter's art.

Frank rose to greet her, smiling but somehow, she sensed, a little less warmly than usual. It was nothing she could put her finger on, however, and the progress of ordering and eating lunch was as smooth and effortless as ever. Frank's conversation was perfectly natural and unforced. He talked diffidently of the writing of his latest serial story, asked after Bobby, Lorna, and affairs related to the shop. Talk was gentle today, a shade guarded, without the personal revelations that had on occasion drawn them so close together that time had flown and half the afternoon had been lost over the coffee cups.

Kirsty had just begun to think that he was anxious to be rid of her, that some professional matter which he had not introduced was lying on his mind. She did not feel in the least resentful. She had business to conduct at the bank in St Vincent Street and did not want to rush in at the last minute before afternoon closing.

About half past one, lunch over, she said, "Well, shall we go now, Frank?"

Carefully he laid the little cigar he was smoking in the furrow of the ashtray, reached across the table and cupped one of her hands in both of his. She was startled by the unexpected gesture. He had touched her not at all, except in circumstances when she needed comforting.

"Not yet, Kirsty," he said. "If you'll bear with me a bit longer, I've something to ask you first."

"Of course," she said.

"Kirsty," he said, "would you consider becoming my wife?"

It was all gone, all in that moment. She felt suddenly lost, not confused or angry but removed, as if she had become a spectator to the scene. The curious thing was that if any other man had asked such a question Frank was the one and only person in the world with whom she would have discussed it. For a second she was on the point of asking *him* how she should answer his question. She heard herself give a queer, nervous laugh and say, "How can I marry you when I'm already married to Craig?"

"But *are* you married to Craig?"

"What do you mean? He's my — my husband."

"In law," Frank said, "or just by habit?"

"How dare you suggest — "

"Kirsty, tell me the truth, please."

She withdrew her hand now. Her fingers were trembling and, ridiculously, the big vertical bow on her hat quivered on its wire and reflected her nervous distress.

"You've no right to ask me that."

"I'm in love with you, Kirsty. I wish to make you my wife."

"For God's sake, Frank. I'm — I'm — not free."

"It's true, isn't it? There's no record, nothing legally binding? Nothing to prevent you leaving Craig Nicholson if you choose to do so?"

"Bobby, for one thing."

"Craig would never dare bring you to law over custody of the child."

"What is this, Frank? What's put all this into your head?"

"I like Bobby. You know, don't you, that I'd take the best care of both of you? I would treat Bobby as if he were my own son. And I love you, Kirsty, more deeply and tenderly than you can possibly imagine."

"Who – who told you?"

"Craig. Indirectly."

"Frank, I – I can't leave him. He took me when nobody else would. Whatever his faults, he's given me a good home."

"He took you when there was nobody else *to* take you, Kirsty. He's done no more for you than any decent man would do for a woman he pretended was his wife – an' in my opinion, a deal less than you deserve." He reached for her hand but she would not give it to him. "Look at me, Kirsty. Do you doubt that I'd love and cherish you for the rest of our lives?"

"No."

"Am I too old, is that it?"

"No, Frank, not that."

"I can give you what you *should* have, Kirsty. You would be loved, always."

It was on the tip of her tongue to ask him to define his sort of love, to justify his conviction that she was not loved in another, different way. But held it. She felt sorry for him and, more than that, suddenly sorry for herself.

"I know all that's true," Kirsty said.

"What then is your answer?"

"I – I don't know what to say."

"Are you telling me it's no, Kirsty?"

"Please, Frank. I need time to consider – "

"If I've no hope at all I'd be grateful if you'd come straight out with it."

He had drawn away from her, back in the chair, one arm draped over the spar. His jacket was thrown open, waistcoat creased over the beginnings of a paunch, the gold watch chain that he sometimes wore drooping. He studied her intently, not letting her evade him. He required her to see his hunger and it both frightened and excited her. He spoke in the soft, dry tone that she had grown used to over the months of their friendship, said again, "Straight out with it."

"I haven't said no, Frank."

"You *aren't* legally married to Nicholson, are you?"

She shook her head.

"He was never the one for you, Kirsty. It's not too late to change, you know."

She got to her feet, not hurriedly, showing no sign of the appalling confusion that his words had created in her.

She said, "I would prefer it if we didn't see each other for a while, Frank."

"Oh, God!"

"No," she said. "No, it's not a refusal. But what you ask, what you offer me – I have to consider carefully before I give you an answer."

He got up too. "Have I a chance, Kirsty?"

She smiled faintly. "What if I don't love you, Frank?"

"Don't you?"

"I don't know," she said. "Honestly, I don't know."

"How long before – ?"

"Soon," Kirsty said. "Soon, I promise you."

* * *

The hall of the Bank of Scotland's branch in St Vincent Street never failed to impress her. Today, heels clicking on marble, pass-book in hand, thin wisps of evening fog trailing behind her, Kirsty was suddenly struck by the position that she had attained in life and the fact that she was no longer awed by its appurtenances. She stopped, literally, in her tracks. In one of the long, yellowish mirrors on the hall's left wall she could see herself reflected against hazy electrical light. Cheeks glowing, hair with a heavy, auburn sheen to it, she was clad in the sort of fashionable clothes that any woman would be proud to wear.

It was less vanity than surprise that brought her up short, however. All around were businessmen, senior clerks, accountants and company secretaries, the low, confidential hum of money being gathered and distributed, of financial transactions both petty and profound. And here she was, Kirsty Barnes, not so long out of the dormitory of an orphan home, not so long escaped from the dirt of Hawkhead, with a pass-book of her own and a cheque for fifty pounds to enter into it. And, most important of all, no timidity, no feeling that she did not belong here in the enclaves of the rich. At that moment all the implications of Frank Tubbs' proposal of marriage struck home. She went forward to the teller's counter in a daze, entered into her private account that quarter's share of shop profits that had accrued to her and, still in a daze, emerged from between the bank's

Athenian columns and descended once more to the street.

Hawkers and newspaper vendors were out to catch end-of-the-day trade. At the junction of St Vincent Street and West Nile Street horse traffic surged around one of the new electrical tramcars that had slipped its rail, the city all hoarse and raucous under the cold, blue canopy of sky that hung above the smoke. Kirsty paused. For some reason her heart was beating frantically in her chest. She did not feel ill or distressed, however. She was flushed with such energy, such excitement that she could hardly contain it. She hurried towards the railway station at a speed that was not quite ladylike, that caused gentlemen who should have known better to turn and look after her with wistful smiles or little nods of approval. Apprentices did not chirrup at her, however, carters did not crane from their boards and croon inviting tom-cat calls. She had grown away from them, had acquired a status that debarred such vulgar familiarity and put her beyond the reach of their aspirations. Kirsty strode on, skirts swinging, purse tucked securely under her arm.

Smoke and the bellow of trains in the tunnel below the street — she would soon be there, soon be snug in a carriage, riding out of Glasgow, riding back to Greenfield, to the apron, the kitchen, the stove, to Bobby, to Craig. Except that she did not have to go back there. She was under no constraint, no obligation to return early to Canada Road. She was not held, as her neighbours were held, by the threat of hardship or the settling of domains that drew a wife close to a husband yet, mysteriously, kept them separate and apart. She could escape at any time, step effortlessly upward. She did not have to do as Joyce McAlpine had done, flee for her life, steal away to some foreign country. She had money, a business and, most generous of all the gods' gifts, she had a man ready and eager to marry her, to give her that last hitch up from the gutter. She had no doubt at all that Frank would carry her into a comfortable world of drawing rooms and servants, of Christmas parties and summer fêtes, that his talent and her acumen would provide well for them, and for Bobby. With David there had never been that hope to cloud the issue; the untenability of it had kept her love for him pure, pure but unreal.

If she left Craig there would be scandal, ripples and gossip and malice in the close at 154. But she would be far away, untouched by it. Her friends, the only ones she cared about, might be stiff and awkward at first but she was sure that adjustments would be made in time. Lorna and Gordon would not abandon her. Perhaps even Craig would have what he wanted, reason to march, proud and scowling, martyred and happy, on the spot where circumstance and prejudice had placed him and from which he could not bring himself to move.

"Where to, Ma'am?"

"Pardon?"

"Destination?" said the clerk at the ticket window, patiently.

"Oh!" Kirsty came down to earth.

"Where, Ma'am, are you goin' to?"

"Greenfield," Kirsty said without thinking and, a moment later, went soberly through the gate to the concourse that led to the platform and the waiting train.

Nine

The Road to Resolution

The letter was contained in a cheap brown envelope whose gummed flap had come tantalisingly unstuck at the edges. It was propped against the metal barrel of the Koffee Kanne that had been Johnnie's sole legacy to his successor, not off to one side but smack-bang in the centre of the desk amid a litter of invoices, purchase slips and stock orders. Gordon, a cigarette in his mouth, elbows propped on the desk, stared at it, stared and stared and stared at it as he had been doing off and on since the damned thing had arrived with the noon delivery.

Three times he had reached for the horn-handled, steel-bladed paperknife. Three times he had put the knife down again. Twice he had had the letter in his hand, thumbnail under the little bubble in the sealing flap. Twice he had resisted the temptation to tear the envelope open and had placed it back against the coffee maker. Once he had even filled the kettle and set it to boil on the gas-ring on the table in the office's back corner. But when steam was up and all he had to do was hold the letter against the hot, moist plume, he had shown the white feather, put the letter down unopened and brewed himself a cup of strong black Java instead. Now all he seemed capable of doing was staring at the bloody letter as if he might wear away the envelope by will power alone, read without guilt the thin little missive within and, crucially, extract from it the return address.

By then Gordon was no longer even sure that his initial identification of the handwriting was accurate, that John Whiteside's name and the address of Adair's warehouse had been penned by Greta Taylor at all. Indecisiveness was compounded by fear of what he might discover in the letter itself, what confessions, what final revelations would turn his longing for Greta inside out, transform love, in an instant, into hate.

Breezy had not been around since mid-morning or Gordon might have been tempted to ask his stepfather's advice. On the other hand, in the matter of Greta's past and present welfare, Gordon still harboured a niggling suspicion that Breezy had been less than candid with him, though Breezy had assured him, hand on heart, that he had no knowledge of where Greta had hidden herself away. Now here was a letter addressed to Johnnie which had strayed by chance his way. Greta could not have known of Johnnie's marriage or his disgrace or she would not have written to him at the warehouse. What did she want from Whiteside? What sort of liaison was there between them and had the letter been forced from her by some early communication from Whiteside, some threat? All he had to do to gain peace was open the bloody letter and to hell with conscience. And he couldn't do it.

Gordon was still seated at the desk when, unexpectedly, Josephine arrived. She knocked and entered, smiling as he started back from a posture that seemed to her more dozy than contemplative. "God, it's you!"

"Aren't you glad to see me?" Josephine said.

"Of course, but – "

"Came round to drag you away." Josephine came around the desk and kissed him on the mouth. "Supper?"

"I – I – "

"Do I detect a certain reluctance, sir?"

"No, it's – it's not that. It's not you, I mean. It's somethin' – something else."

"What?"

He hesitated, then pointed with his thumb. "That."

He had known what she would do, what she would say, but wasn't as relieved as he thought he would be when she plucked up the brown envelope and studied it closely.

"It's addressed to Johnnie."

"I know."

"An Edinburgh posting," Josephine said. "From one of his

293

fancy women, I expect."

"I think," Gordon said, "it's from Greta."

Josephine's mouth opened but for once she found no ready opinion, no question on her tongue. She glanced from the letter to Gordon then cocked her head, squinting at him with an enigmatic expression that, he realised, did not quite disguise an element of hurt.

"What does she say?" Josephine asked, at length.

Gordon shook his head. "How would I know? It isn't addressed to me."

"Good God!" Josephine exclaimed and thrust the letter back at him. "Open it."

Again Gordon shook his head. "Can't go interferin' with somebody else's mail."

"Ridiculous!" She wagged the letter at him. "Take it and open it."

Gordon noticed, with a trace of disappointment, that Josephine did not volunteer to commit the little crime for him. She was, he guessed, almost as scared of what the letter might contain as he was. He had never made any bones about his feelings towards Greta and now, in a way, Josephine's rival had returned. "Won't *you* open it?" he said.

"Not up to me. Not my lover."

She was angry, angry at him for keeping her on the string too. She was even more anxious to know what the letter said than he was, what it portended. It was as if she thought that he was using the letter as a female might, to tease and taunt and gain a mischievous power over her. At that moment Gordon realised that Josephine might be seriously in love with him. All avowals to the contrary, declarations of 'independence' notwithstanding, she wanted him not for a friend or even a lover but, after all, as a loyal and steadfast husband.

"We shouldn't have seen it," Gordon said. "It came to me by accident only because Greta doesn't know about Whiteside an' what's happened to him, how things have changed here."

"Damn it, Gordon! Damn it! Won't you open it?"

By way of answer he slid the letter from her fingers and, in the same motion almost, tugged open a drawer of the desk. He extracted a large cream-tinted envelope from it, slotted Greta's unopened letter into it and, with a great slavering lick and a punch with his fist, sealed it tightly away. He groped for a pen and the ink bottle, bent over the desk. He did not even hesitate when Josephine touched his back, brushed his hip with her skirt and said, "Why are you doing this, Gordon?"

He finished the address with a flourish, rolled the blotter over it and flung the pen aside. He turned then, cramped against the desk by Josephine's weight. He had never seen her look so perplexed, so sad. He said, "Greta didn't write to *me*. She wrote to Johnnie. It's none of my business what she needs from him, not now."

"Don't you want her to come back to you?"

Gordon said, "I have what I want right here."

"Meaning?"

"Meaning you, of course."

When she sighed he could feel her breasts against his forearm and warmth from her neck and face. She clasped him in an embrace that was almost painfully grateful. It was all Gordon could do to reach around her and press the electrical bell that summoned Bert Ramsden, whistling, from the storeroom.

Gordon handed the old man the letter and a shilling.

"Stamp an' post, Bert. Fast as you can."

"Aye, Mr Nicholson."

After the office door had closed, Josephine sniffed and said tearfully, "Do you know what?"

"What?"

"Supper's on me."

*   *   *

Towards the middle of the week a strange little wind sprang up, sufficiently brisk to chase away the fog that haunted the shores of the valley of the Clyde but not brisk enough to prevent frost falling in a rime at dawn and dusk. Soon after sunset the weird wee wind became so keen that you could feel the cutting edge of it against your lips and inside your nostrils, taste its cold prickle on your tongue and see, against the street-lamps' glow, the frost dust swirling down and gathering, visibly, on metal, slate and stone. By Thursday the wind had found its voice. It moaned a wintry dirge up closes and through backcourts, plucked at cowls on chimneyheads, creaked across boards and rubbed resinously against window panes. On the fourth floor of the Claremont

Model lodging house, just under the roof, you could hear the squeak of tiles, the arthritic creak of beams contracting and watch, if you were daft enough, frost materialise in drafty shapes above the stairwell, like lodgers long dead still searching for a billet and a bed.

Sammy, though, could not see the stairwell and, now that he was safe upstairs, Hog had no interest in it. He was snug with his chum, his pipe and his bottle. Dark rum, tobacco and an old brown blanket would keep out the cold. His voice was lowered to a soft, grating bark that told you how much pleasure there was for him in the prospect of winter and its sufferings. He was discussing with Sammy the proposed demolition of the ancient tenements that formed the slums of the Madagascar, railing against landlords who would grow fat on profits ground from the bones of the homeless poor. He knew folk there, he said, good folk; folk like Prue Alston and her daughter Angela who now and then gave him womanly consolation, folk like Mr Galletti, the hunchback, who lived in the pig mews and eked a living from playing music in the street.

"*Brrr-Brrr-Broom-Broom*," said Sammy, with a daft grin and an erratic motion of the elbows.

Hog had worked six days last week on the Merkland cattle dock, watering beasts and sluicing slurry from the cobbles. He had earned enough to keep him in drink for a fortnight. He had been tossed out of three bars and escorted back to the Model by unfriendly coppers on two occasions and, if the weather had been warmer, would have been ejected from the shelter for a night or two to teach him a lesson in discipline and sobriety. But Mr Black was no brute and had adjusted to Hog's indiscretions. He had contented himself with slinging the wee man upstairs into the big, empty attic which, without heat, was used now only to accommodate a passing trade in tinks and navvies. It was hardly punishment had Mr Black but known it. Among the dusty cubicles of the attic Hog and Sammy had long ago secured refuge from the rules of the establishment. They went there silently after curfew to tipple and smoke and talk, until sleep or stupor claimed them, and they were wakened only by the clanging of the breakfast bell far down below.

Even if drawn and quartered Hog would never admit that Sammy was more to him now than a source of petty income. In fact, Sammy had had the hems put on him at the People's Mission. So ardent a watch was kept on his moral welfare now that he only had to think about pilfering from the Orphans' Box or the tray for the Aged and Infirm and some horse-faced lady or scowling gent would pop up as if by magic at his side and, forefinger raised, would say, "Nah, nah, Samuel," and remind him that bad boys went to hell and not to heaven when they died.

Sammy didn't care about that. Sammy didn't care about much any more except Hog's companionship and the bottle the old man shared with him. What he received from Mr Moscrop was a different kind of attention from that given him by his pals in uniform. In fact, under Hog Moscrop's tutelage he had come to regard coppers less as friends than enemies; if not enemies at least as part of that great force of restrainers whose aim in life was to stop a lad enjoying himself. Sammy no longer waited for a policeman to escort him back to the Claremont. He found his own way to the lodging house the instant work was done. He would meet with Hog in canteen or community room and they would sit, hunched together, over tea and bread. Hog would talk, Sammy would listen, both would wait for Lights Out and an opportunity to creep into the building's upper reaches and settle down to be soothed and refreshed by rum and tobacco in lieu of sleep.

Under separate brown blankets they squatted in the dusty cubicle and drank from their separate bottles. Hog had had enough savvy to find a bottle of his own for the boy, gill-sized, so that he could ration Sammy's greed for booze and ensure that Sammy never became perilously drunk. Hog was wary of the warning he'd received from Nicholson and confined friendship and drinking to the Claremont. Even so he liked the midnight confabulations, monologues, really. He tried to pretend that Sam understood every word he said, every boastful utterance, every long-winded tale of persecution and injustice. He even grew, in his way, quite fond of Sam, responding to trust and affection as you might to some gangling, half-grown pup.

On that December night there was an easy air to Hog. He had silver in his pocket and the promise of more work at the Merkland before Christmas. He had drunk just enough to bring on a festive glow to go with the cold outside and the soft banter of the odd little wind around the roof and through the rafters. So mellow was the old man, in fact, that he soon gave up complaining about the destruction of the Madagascar and talked instead of the wife that was dead and the sons that were gone. He even sang Sammy a funny wee song, clean and innocent, that he had sung long, long ago when his own lads were young and cradled: *"List to the curlew cryin', fainter the echo dyin'. Even the birdies an' beasties are sleepin', but my bonnie bairn is weepin', weepin'."*

The bottle in the boy's hand was almost empty but he held the neck to his mouth like a soother. Big, distorted head rested against the partition, blanket wrapped about him. He was too sleepy to join in, eyelids drooping, a smile on his face. Aye, a handsome boy, really, Hog thought, seen in the dark, lit only by the glow from the coal in his pipe, a wee red gem in the bowl in his palm: *"Dreams t' sell, fine dreams t' sell, Angus is here wi' dreams t' sell-oh. Hush ye my babbie an' sleep wi'out fear, Dream Angus has brought ye a dream, my dear."* Hog wondered vaguely if Sammy did dream or if, for him and his kind, all of life was just that, no nightmare but one long waking dream.

He leaned over, gently detached the bottle from the boy's grasp and tucked the blanket about his chest. "Sammy, Sammy, are y' sleepin'?"

There was no answer but a snore.

"Huh!" Hog snorted and, turning against the wall, pulled up the blanket, let the bottle and pipe slip from his fingers and, within seconds, was snoring serenely too.

*   *   *

Gentlemen and ladies inhabited the West House in Gartnavel's Royal Mental Hospital. The building, like the grounds, was stately and elegant as any of Scotland's famous hydro-pathic hotels and just as comfortable within. Breezy had made play of the fact that it was the first time his father had ever been mistaken for a gentleman. It was worth the annual payment of one hundred and sixty pounds to visit Daddy Adair in such grand surroundings, to sit with him in the airing court when the sun shone, even if they did not exchange two sensible words and the old boy did not seem even to know who the devil he, Albert, was.

Humane attendants helped Mr Adair about, saw to it that he

sat nice at dinner table and was present at every concert, every piano recital, every billiards tournament, ensured he participated in all the purposeful activities that kept the institution humming and disguised the fact that half the inmates were blown by senility or inherent mental disease. Moral management was the best that staff and doctors could manage and, on the surface, everything was thoroughly well organised and almost civilised – except, that is, for the noises. It might be as peaceful as Eden in the garden courtyard or well-appointed drawing rooms yet fox-barks, crying, distempered howls and oscillating wails were all around. The sounds were so distressing that at first they would make you squirm with loathing and then by their sheer persistence would break your heart. You saw nobody with an open mouth, only the polished oak doors of locked bedrooms, or barred windows above you and, now and again, a scurrying attendant or a glimpse of a shambling figure at a corridor's end. And the billiard balls would go on clicking and the grand piano tinkling as if nothing at all was happening.

Now, on a late night in December, with trees and buildings stark, the noises were even more disturbing.

"God, I'm glad you're with me, son," Breezy said.

The hackney cab had dropped them at the top of the drive. The cabby had turned tail and got himself out of there as fast as he could. The West House towered, ill-lighted and sinister. A solitary gas lamp burned in the doorway and the building seemed to be alive with noise as if the wind had gathered within an invisible chorus to accompany its lamentations.

It had been half past eleven when a policeman had turned up at the door of the mansion on Great Western Terrace. Breezy, in dressing gown and slippers, had been partaking of a nightcap before joining Madge in bed. His heart had given a leap and a gulp when he'd seen the uniform on the step and had received from the man the handwritten note that had been telephoned down from Gartnavel to the station at Maryhill. He supposed that the authorities at the hospital had failed to realise that he was connected to the telephone too and had just followed their usual procedure. The note was as cryptic as it was unexpected. His father was dying. It was not anticipated that he would last the night.

Even as Breezy stood shivering at the open door with the slip

299

of paper in his hand, Gordon had arrived home by cab. The cab had been held. There had been a whispered conversation. Breezy had informed a startled Madge of the turn of events, had dressed and been out of the house all within ten minutes.

"Do you want me to contact the rest of the family?" Gordon had asked. "Polly an' Heather, for instance?"

"No," Breezy had answered. "I'll go on my own."

"I'll come with you, if I may."

"Aye," Breezy had said. "I'd appreciate that."

Now they were ringing the bell at the hospital door. Now they were being admitted by the Night Attendant and Deputy Superintendent, a woman. Now they were being led along a corridor, through one locked door, then another, along an avenue of awful, sourceless sounds.

Gordon walked by Breezy's side, silent and scared. When they entered the long drawing-room and were met by a doctor, he stood respectfully back to let Breezy hear the word in private. The conversation was brief and, as it ended, Breezy turned towards him and shook his head. Gordon gave him a sign, a wave of the hand, watched the oak door being unlocked and saw Breezy follow the doctor into the darkened bedroom. Gordon did not know how long the visit would last, or what might be its outcome.

He asked the Deputy Matron, a thin pleasant woman with gold eyeglasses perched on the end of her nose and a dressing robe that smelled aromatically of herbs. She answered without prevarication. "Grave," she said. "It's a galloping pneumonia."

"But Breezy – my stepfather saw him yesterday afternoon an' he seemed fine then."

"It came upon Mr Adair suddenly in the form of a slight cold which worsened rapidly as the night progressed. Doctor Munro felt it would not be prudent to move the patient to the infirmary."

"Will he die?"

"Oh, yes." The woman touched Gordon's sleeve gently as if to take the sting out of her prognosis. "Would you care for a cup of tea?"

"Please."

The woman went off and Gordon seated himself in one of the armchairs. He lay back, hands in his overcoat pockets, and closed his eyes. The noises had abated but he could still make out weeping, sobs, somewhere deep within the shuttered house. He opened his eyes. He studied the light fitting. Three frosted globes to each fitting. He had boxes of identical globes in stock in the warehouse. He wondered who did the purchasing for the hospital and from what source they bought their appliances. The woman returned, bearing tea things on a tin tray. She touched him again, sympathetically, as Gordon leaned forward to pour tea from the pot. He was tempted to ask about the light globes but decided against it. He tried to express courage in a strained smile and the woman retired again almost immediately. Gordon leaned back, sipped tea, lit a cigarette, listened to an uninformative silence from behind the bedroom door, and waited.

Some ten minutes later Dr Munro slipped out of the bedroom. He did not, Gordon noticed, lock the door behind him. Gordon got to his feet. The doctor was quite young, not above forty, and had a fine set of curly brown side-whiskers which he stroked sombrely as he broke the bad news. "I'm sorry to have to tell you that your grandfather has breathed his last."

"What?"

"Mr Adair has departed this life."

"God! That was quick," Gordon said, before he could censor himself. "I mean, a mercy that he did not linger in sufferin'. Where's Bree . . . my father?"

"He is taking his last farewell," Dr Munro said. "You may go in if you wish."

Gordon hesitated. He had not corrected Munro in the matter of relationships and realised that the doctor expected him to go forward to view the corpse. He steeled himself, crossed to the big oak door and touched the ornate handle.

The door creaked open an inch or two and Gordon, swallowing, entered the shadowy room. He had no impression of furnishings for the light was centred around a small lamp on a bedside table, and white sheets and a pale coverlet absorbed his attention completely. Breezy, still in his overcoat, was seated on the side of the bed, slumped, a hand over his face, the other lightly touching the knuckles of the old man's fists which had been folded neatly together and placed, as in prayer, against his breast.

301

"Albert?" Gordon whispered.

"Yes," Breezy said. "Yes, I'm here."

"Do you want to be alone?"

"No, no, son. Come forward, see this."

Gordon had never before seen a corpse. Madge had kept him from the room where his father had been laid out, and the coffin had been sealed before the funeral service. He had an echo of that terrible day in him, though, as he moved to Breezy's shoulder and stood there, looking down at the husk in the bed.

"Do you see him?" Breezy asked.

"Uh-huh."

"Look at his hands," Breezy said. "They're just like my hands now. Huh! An' I haven't done a stroke of manual labour in forty years. Huh! I'm the old man now, it seems. Do you think he's at peace?"

"I think he is," Gordon said.

He was not frightened by the features of the corpse, nor was he dismayed. The old man's face had sunk in on itself but many of the wrinkled lines had gone. There was no peevishness, no hostility printed there now. The eyelids were lightly closed as if at any moment they might spring open again, express surprise that all his grievances had been taken from him, that dying had not been more difficult.

"Do you believe there's such a place as heaven, son?"

"Yes," Gordon answered.

Breezy got up stiffly, drew his hand lingeringly away from the folded fists. "I'll see him there, then."

Self-consciously Gordon put an arm about his stepfather's shoulders and led him away from the bed but, before they reached the door, awkwardness passed and a strange tender rapport possessed the younger man. He pulled Breezy to him, hugging him tightly. "There," Gordon said, chokingly. "There. I'm with you, you know."

"Aye, I know you are, son," said Breezy and, with eyes squeezed shut, let himself weep without shame.

*   *   *

Day shift had never really suited Craig's temperament. He had little patience with impudent schoolchildren, heavy traffic and dour hordes of working men all of whom needed guidance and shepherding. He preferred the hard edge of the back shift when pubs were thronged and the promise of trouble hung ever-present in the air. Best of all, though, he liked Greenfield's streets at night, when he could walk alone and undisturbed and nurture the illusion that the burgh belonged to him. He had been on day duty since Monday, however, and had taken his disgruntlement out on Kirsty. He had groused at her for the least wee thing, almost as if he were colluding with Frank Tubbs by demonstrating that he, Craig Nicholson, was not best option and that she would be better treated by a gentler man.

Kirsty did not rise to the bait. She had grown tired of Craig's rough, argumentative games. She let him snipe away at her with apparent indifference and remained calmness itself, not patronising but distant.

"Is there a shirt for the mornin'?"

"In the drawer, where it always is," Kirsty said.

"I hope the collar's not too starchy."

"The collar's perfect."

"It's a fine bloody thing when a man has to put himself out at the crack o' dawn on a winter's morn."

"I'll be up to see you off."

"You weren't up on Monday."

"You never wakened me."

"I shouldn't have to waken you. Other men don't have to waken *their* wives."

"What'll you want for breakfast?"

"Oh, so I've a choice, have I?" Craig said. "What'll it be, then? A dish o' scrambled eggs, poached haddock, some devilled kidneys, maybe? That's what they'll be havin' up at Breezy's house."

Kirsty said, "Kipper or bacon?"

"Bacon."

She had done the day's wash, had hung it to dry on the pulley by the ceiling. He had castigated her about that too, about the fact that she did not take her turn with the other coppers' wives in the wash-house in the backcourt, that she had a different laundry arrangement, that his house was full of wet clothes and steam, that she spent her evenings at the bloody sink when she should have been attending to him. She'd said nothing to any of this.

Beneath Craig's petty criticisms lay darker discontents, guilts

303

and fears that Kirsty could only vaguely discern and of which she preferred to remain oblivious. Deliberately she disengaged herself from his tantrums. Though she was tired after a day in the shop, she worked through her chores quickly and efficiently, thinking less of Craig than of Frank, of the answer she must give him before long.

"I could do with a cup of tea," Craig stated.

"I'll make one in just a minute."

Newspaper discarded, he was seated forward in the armchair, a Gold Flake in his mouth. He had taken off his shoes and socks and wiggled his bare feet towards the fire. He had removed his collar too, had unbuttoned his shirt and disconnected his braces as if to prepare for bed. She thought that he seemed tense, all coiled within himself. For a moment she was tempted to go down on her knees by his side and cajole him out of his blue mood. But she would only be mocked for it, rebuffed, accused of trying to rob him of his sleep. Instead she made tea and buttered toast.

"Are you not havin' any?" he asked.

"No."

"Why not?"

"Because I don't feel like it."

He chewed over this response to see what substance it contained to fuel further argument. Finding none, he finished his late supper, rose and bade Kirsty a curt good night.

The instant he'd gone from the kitchen, Kirsty abandoned her sewing. She spooled up cotton thread, sheathed her needle, closed the lid of the mending box and sat back in her chair, sighing.

It was peaceful in the kitchen. Bobby was fast asleep in the front room and the sounds that Craig made as he prepared for bed were comfortingly subdued.

Curiously, Kirsty was not tormented by indecision. She knew where she stood with herself. She did not love Frank Tubbs. She could not, however, deny that, measured by any criteria, she would be better off separated from Craig Nicholson. Besides, she had never been the bargain that Craig had thought she would be. She had never given him what he had expected of her. Even so, she was less afraid of committing herself to Frank than of parting from Craig. She closed her eyes and sought out the best words to use. In this instance there were no 'best words'. She would have to come straight out with the truth: "Craig, I'm leaving you."

Far away a bell clanged, harsh and brassy. She listened, waiting for it to recede, to veer away from Canada Road and carry its threat elsewhere.

At that moment the kitchen door opened, Craig confronted her and Kirsty, rising guiltily, cried out, "What?"

*   *   *

The cab stance at Churchill Drive was deserted when Gordon and Breezy emerged from the hospital grounds. They had both recovered their emotional stability and were, if not cheerful, at least relieved to leave Gartnavel behind them. Tobacco and a long walk down the gusty avenue had cleared their heads. On seeing the cab stance empty, Breezy suggested that they walk home and had set a brisk pace along Great Western Road towards Hyndland.

It was not so late that all lights were out. The drawing rooms of one or two mansions still blazed cheerfully, as if in rehearsal for the festive season. The air was cold and mobile and you could see stars here and there among the wafting clouds and, Gordon thought, a trace of moonlight in the sky over Partick. Tomorrow would be a busy day for Breezy. He had been relieved from undertaking any duties that night, sent home with the assurance that the staff would see to temporary care of the body. What official sanctions would be required before a funeral could be arranged even Breezy could not imagine. He did not suppose that it would all be plain sailing but prayed, silently, that a post mortem would not be demanded by the circumstances of his father's death.

Gordon respected Breezy's wish to keep his thoughts to himself and stepped it out by his stepfather's side, all trace of tiredness gone from him, his mind alert. At first he had thoughts of death and its meaning but, unlike Breezy, the loss had not been severe in its consequences. He found himself thinking not of old Donald Adair but of Greta and of Josephine. It seemed that he could not think of one in isolation from the other these days, could not separate memory from opportunity.

The cab came past at a fast lick. Breezy, though he showed no sign of fatigue, raised his arm and shouted after it as the vehicle rounded the corner at Hyndland Road on one wheel and, lurching, clattered away towards Partickhill.

"Taken, I fancy," Gordon said.

"Damned fool, drivin' at that speed," Breezy grumbled and paused on the corner to scowl down Hyndland Road in the wake of the demon driver.

At the sound, Gordon swung round. He barely had time to snatch Breezy back onto the pavement before a second hack thundered down from Cleveden Road, shot across the cobbled junction and on down Hyndland Road too.

Mourning put aside, Breezy planted his hands on his hips and yelled after the driver. "What the hell's your hurry?"

The cabby, swinging round, shouted, "Fire. Fire in the Greenfield," and cracked his whip over the horse's ears to urge it away from the runnels of the brand new tramlines.

"Fire *where*?" Breezy called, but the hack was well out of earshot by then. "Did he say Greenfield, son?"

"Aye, he did," Gordon answered and, hesitantly at first, wandered down Hyndland Road to the railings that overlooked the railway track. On tiptoe, he peered over them, over rooftops and black leafless boughs to the quadrant of the sky where, minutes before, he thought he'd glimpsed moonlight. No moon glowed with such fluctuating radiance or in such angry colours.

He watched, frowning, for half a minute, Breezy at his back now, and then, through his teeth, said, "It's a big 'un, all right."

"Couldn't be the warehouse, could it?"

"No," Gordon said, "too far to the west for that. It's Greenfield, though, or the tail end of Partick. Might be a tenement, like Kirsty's tenement?"

Flame tinted the glow russet and, for an instant, sprinkled sparks like tiny falling stars against the racing clouds.

"I think we should get down there," Breezy said.

"I think you're right," said Gordon.

*   *   *

Hog Moscrop was a heavy sleeper, well used to the wayward behaviour of his body. He had learned to ignore coughs and chokings, episodes of wheezing and the cramp that often gripped his legs in the wee small hours. He would rise but one level towards consciousness, growl drowsily, perhaps pound a fist on his thigh to bully nerves and tendons into passivity, then wallow over into sound sleep once more. Thus it was that smoke had half filled the cubicle before the tearing in Hog's throat became too rapacious to put down to phlegm, and the little man awoke with a jerk.

Hog's first thoughts were that he would be obliged to pay for the old brown blanket that had turned to char and would surely suffer expulsion from the Claremont for being caught up here at all. Smoke was thick but, apart from minor patches of smouldering cloth, there was no sign of flame and not enough light to define the extent to which fire had taken hold of the wooden door and outer wall. Spluttering, Hog groped for his bottle and his pipe. He found only stinging heat. He yelped and stuck his hand into his mouth.

Sammy was snoring, a bundle, dead to the world, safe enough in his curl of blanket in the corner. Hog hopped to his feet and stamped daintily upon the burning cloth. Red and gold petals floated upwards, settled on Hog's chest and shoulders and, to the wee man's astonishment, burned.

Reaching, he swept the smouldering blanket from the floor and tried to fling it over the top of the cubicle. Rusty wire netting pawed at the remnant and it fell, dripping fire, across his forearm. Hog yelled, shook it off and, with eyes streaming and lungs clogged with acrid smoke, groped for the door handle behind him. Old varnish had turned hot and waxy and had just begun to blister, adhering to Hog's flesh like tar. He yelled louder. He hauled open the door and, blinded by tears, stumbled out into the attic and fell gasping to his knees on the boards.

Hog did not intend to push the door of the cubicle behind him. The motion was instinctive, the reflex of a man rushing to leave the scene of a crime. He had no thought for Sammy, no thought for anyone but himself. He crawled away from the reeking cubicle on all fours, quite unaware that the air he had admitted to the room had fanned the smoulder and that, with a sudden *phaff*, flames had blossomed within. He retched, then rose and, with hands to mouth, ran for the stairwell to get himself back to his own floor, his own bed so that Mr Black and the governors could not hold him to blame for anything.

"Mister Hog?" Sammy, still drunk, sat up.

He had seen fire before. He knew what it was but not what it signified. He could not associate it with the attic. He had no notion what it was doing here. He wondered if this was one of the dreams he sometimes had about the Fiery Pit. He could never remember the dreams, only the cold crawl that came to his skin when he awakened. And this wasn't cold but hot. Hot!

Sammy kicked at the burning thing that clung to his feet. He kicked and slithered and pressed back against the partition, roaring in incomprehensible pain, "Haw . . . Haw . . . Haw . . . Haw . . . " a roar that changed to childish screams as the wind found space above the little cell and sucked flames upward in delicate spirals that Sammy thought were alive.

He rushed at the door to escape.

Smoke had gone shooting up too, and the sounds it made were like the rifles of the Volunteers when you heard them from far away.

He tore at the door with burnt fingers.

Pain was dense and penetrating. He remembered the feel of the birch, punishment, sharp pain not blunt, not like a kick or a blow from a fist. He remembered the men in the uniforms, and the stuff they put on his bare back and the scalding feel of it.

Terrified by the fact that he did not know what he was being punished for, he screamed louder: "*Mister Nicholson, Mister Nicholson, Mister Nicholson!*"

When no answer came, no rescuing hand to snatch him away, he did the only thing he had wit left to do. He fumbled for the tarnished police whistle, cupped it in his hands and blew and blew, silently, until all breath was gone.

*　　*　　*

Craig reached Scutter Street minutes after the engines. The steamer was already being connected to its hoses and the new 45-feet-long escape ladder awkwardly run out. The horses, a pair to each vehicle, were snorting and stamping and Station Officer Kelso was striding this way and that in his tall, brass-crested helmet, cream-coloured gloves and oilskin leggings, bellowing commands.

Six firemen were being assembled under a firemaster to enter the burning building by the front door as soon as the hoses were ready to pump up water from the fire cock. Beat constable John Boyle, assisted by Ronnie Norbert, had blocked off the street's ends. Somehow they held at bay the crowds that had gathered at the first blood-stirring clang of the bell. Urchins and men, some younger women too, overcoats and shawls flung carelessly over their nightshirts and petticoats, were all agog and set to cheer when the first spurt of water emerged from the steamer's jets.

Craig had flung his tunic jacket over flannels. He had stuffed his bare feet into old canvas tennis shoes and, bare-chested, had run like the wind from Canada Road to Scutter Street. He was spurred not by concern for public safety but by the thought of daft Sammy Reynolds.

Lodgers, herded out of the Claremont, had gathered in a great uncertain group some fifty yards east of the building; a sorry lot, bemused and draggled, some carrying boots, others little bundles of soiled clothing, toolboxes, a saucepan or two, one with a broom over his shoulder, another with a china plant pot cradled in his arms, another still with an excited terrier wrapped in a blanket and held tight to his chest. Mr Black was among them, talking, calming them down, his gaunt, craggy features ruddy in the glow from the Claremont's upper floors.

"I want it under control. I don't want to have to evacuate the whole street," Officer Kelso was shouting. "There's enough confusion as it is. Where's the water? I want to see water."

The Claremont seemed to have grown larger, to loom like some huge cliff over them all. Craig dived into the crowd of lodgers.

"Where's Sammy? Where's Reynolds? Have you seen the daftie?" Craig snapped. "You – have you seen the boy anywhere?"

"Nah."

"You?"

"No' me, sir."

Craig grabbed the Superintendent's arm, spun him round.

"Are they all out?"

"I – I – "

"Have you counted them?"

"No, Craig, I . . . "

"For Christ's sake! How many were in tonight?"

"I don't – "

"Where's the bloody register, man? Check the bloody register."

"I left it. It's inside."

"An' Sammy?"

Mr Black shook his head.

"Hog Moscrop?"

"He's here. He's out. I'll swear I saw him."

"Where did the fire start?"

"Upstairs. I told the fireman. The attic. Nobody was up there tonight, thank God."

Mr Black struggled to compose himself, to shake off his bewilderment. Craig had no more time for the man. He gave him a shove with his shoulder and pushed past him.

Cheers rose from the gatherings at each end of the street as water vomited from the nozzles of the hoses and the steamer, blowing smoke, chugged violently and sent the first jet flying high. A fine haze of spray blew back on the draught from the building and wetted Craig's cheek. It made the lodgers step back, some laughing, others disgusted at the touch of cold water on their flesh, covering themselves as if it, not sparks, might burn. Craig emerged from behind the steamer cart. He looked this way and that and saw Moscrop some twenty yards away.

Hog was fully dressed, boots laced, the cap firm on his head. He had his hands in his pockets and was staring up at the building with an expression of fierce interest on his face. But Craig knew that Moscrop had spotted him and as he began to edge towards the man, Hog sidled away and endeavoured to hide himself in the crowd.

"Ronnie, nail that wee bastard," Craig shouted.

There was no escape for Hog. Ronnie had him by the collar before he could escape. Urchins cheered and swayed as Ronnie spun his baton, locked it tightly across Hog's throat and held him fast until Craig arrived.

"Where is he, Hog?" Craig demanded.

"I dunno what the hell ye mean?"

"Sammy – where is he?"

"Never saw him. Ye telt me t' leave him . . . "

"Look at him," Ronnie said. "He's burned black! Look at his bloody hands, Craig."

Hog Moscrop began to struggle. He flailed at the air with

blistered fingers and, in desperation, shook loose from his trouser hems little tadpoles of charred cloth.

"God! You left him," Craig said. "You were up there an you left him behind."

"Never, never saw him, never, never," Hog jabbered. "It wasnae me. It wasnae me."

"Boozin', you were boozin'."

"NAW, NAW."

"Damn you, Hog, where is he?"

"Last I saw – upstairs."

*   *   *

It had taken some little time for the women in No. 154 Canada Road to organise themselves. Firemen's wives, of course, were far too sensible to want to watch their husbands at work but the novelty of a big blaze had a certain appeal for the others. In the end, after some negotiation, older children were distributed to look after younger children and Jess Walker and Mrs Swanston set off for Scutter Street. Sensing Kirsty's anxiety, Mrs Piper took pity on her and offered to mind Bobby and, minutes after the older women had left, Kirsty too was hastening towards the aurora that lit up the night sky.

By the time she reached Scutter Street a dense crowd had gathered. Policemen had been mustered from all over the burgh to control the multitude and firemen had hoses functioning and escape ladders extended, and the great red circus was in full swing. Wild rumours circulated forth and back among the onlookers; fifty dead already, thirty trapped in the basement; blind men and cripples were being brought out through the roof to be carried down the ladder. Lack of visible evidence of any such horrors did not deter the scaremongers and there was drama in plenty to keep the crowd on its toes. Firemen grappled with hoses and bathed the front of the Claremont with puny jets while the rescue ladder, one brave soul clinging to its tip, was cranked up towards the building's cap of smoke and flames.

It had been decided to evacuate the tenements on either side of the lodging and Sergeants Byrne and Walker were directing this difficult operation while, in the backcourts, veteran firemen aided by coppers were stationed to ensure that burning debris did not ignite the middens.

Scutter Street, Banff Street and part of the Windsor Road had become a vast arena from which to watch the spectacle. Kirsty did not share the general enthusiastic excitement. It took her several minutes to elbow her way through the crowd. She was frightened by the din, the stench, by the hot, overwhelming glow of fire reflected in windows, on slates and in the slivers of water that slicked the cobbles and rushed, gurgling, down gutters and drains.

She recognised many of the policemen, of course. Archie and Peter, a heavy rope taut between them, were marking off the limit of the gallery while Sergeant Drummond steered milling spectators back from the danger area. Now and then he would glance apprehensively behind him as if he expected the Claremont to explode. The fire, however, seemed to be confined to the roof and the lodging's north-west corner. Veiled by blackened glass the flames within had no definite shape and only casual animation.

Craig was nowhere to be seen. Common sense told Kirsty that, if Sammy was safe and well, Craig would be enjoying every minute of the big event and that she had no reason to fear for his safety. She could not, though, still her nagging anxiety and called out to Sergeant Drummond, *"Where's Craig? Have you seen Craig?"*

Hector Drummond gave her a wave and then, realising the point of her question, began to hand his way along the rope towards her.

At that moment a cry from the crowd caused every head to turn and every face to tilt up and a great *Oooooo*, like a sigh, to go up.

A man had become visible in the third-floor window.

A second later glass shattered and fell like crystal rain as the window broke outward.

The crowd swayed and surged and Kirsty was catapulted against the rope and might have injured herself if Hector Drummond hadn't pulled her beneath it. The sergeant, though by nature a modest man, took her into his arms and held tightly as together they watched Craig clamber from the broken window and edge his way along a narrow ledge high on the building's face.

Craig's features showed ruddy in the glow of the fire within.

Now that the window was gone flames could be clearly seen, livid sheets that snarled and crackled in the wind. The fireman on the ladder covered his face with his forearms and yelled down to inform Officer Kelso that the fire had possession of the whole of the building, then, as the hoses jerked to bathe the façade, the ladder swooped away and left Craig, seemingly abandoned, clinging to the narrow ledge.

"Ah, God!" Drummond groaned. "He went upstairs after all."

"What do you mean?"

"We heard a story that Sammy Reynolds was inside."

"How can you possibly . . . "

"Not now, lass. Later will be time enough."

The sergeant was holding her so tightly that she could hardly breathe. It was as if he feared that she too would be taken by an insane impulse and might rush into the burning building to rescue her man.

Kirsty had no such inclination.

Her immediate reaction was to hide her face in the sergeant's shoulder. She could not bear to watch her husband squander his life on such a foolhardy gesture.

She recalled daft Sammy only too well. His plight had roused her sympathy when Craig had brought him, orphaned, to her house. But there her pity dwindled, measured against the cost that would accrue if Craig slipped and fell.

She leaned against Hector Drummond's stout belly and silently watched Craig flirt with death for no good cause.

No motive in the world would excuse his madness and, she vowed, she would never forgive him for it, come what may.

*   *   *

Craig couldn't have explained to Kirsty just why he was convinced that Sammy was still alive and trapped within the building. He had only Hog Moscrop's word for it that Sammy had been left on the attic floor. But he could sense somehow the piercing blast of the silent old whistle that Sammy had dug up years ago from the ashpits west of the Madagascar. In his mind's eye he could see Sammy's scarlet cheeks puffed out with effort as he blew and blew for rescue and redemption. He couldn't explain to Kirsty and he certainly could not use intuition as an argument on Firemaster Kelso. He had to be logical and persuasive.

"Pardon me, sir," he had said. "But I believe we should try to get the lodging's register."

"Haven't we got that? I thought we had." Kelso was a very tall man of about forty, bearded and moustached and with high, black, arching eyebrows that gave him an air of surprised severity. "Didn't the Superintendent bring it out with him?"

"No, sir, apparently not."

"Very well, I'll send a man in."

"I know exactly where it is, sir."

"And who the hell are you?"

"Constable Nicholson, sir, from Ottawa Street station."

"I see. The Claremont's on your beat, is it?"

"Aye, sir."

"Where is this register? Is it handy?"

"In the Super's office just to the right of the door."

"I have no authority over you, Constable. On the other hand, I am in charge of this operation and I can't allow anyone to enter ... "

"I can be back with it in sixty seconds, sir."

Kelso hesitated, then said, "Go then, dammit – but take care."

Attracting almost no attention, Craig entered the doorway. In the stone-floored foyer, heat and smoke were quite supportable but from above came strange boomings and a noise like a scrubbing brush being rubbed over canvas.

At first he had no idea what the sounds signified but when he went to the foot of the stairs and peered upward he realised at once just what he had let himself in for. It was like hell turned upside down. Above the second level he could see nothing but flames embroidered with black where handrails and galleries had once been.

"SAMMY?" When he opened his mouth heat turned his throat and tongue pricklingly dry. "SAMMY?"

Craig stepped on to the staircase and shouted again, "SAMMY, ARE YOU THERE?"

Bits and pieces of red-hot debris fell, splashing sparks, on to the angle of the stairs. Craig was no longer without fear. He trod carefully, one step at a time, towards the corner where the firefalls landed.

"JESUS, SAMMY – ANSWER ME."

314

Hopeless; he knew now that it had been hopeless from the start. If Sam had been asleep, drunk perhaps, and Hog had not wakened him then the boy would surely have suffocated. All optimistic conjectures about empty rooms and possible rescue had been foolish. Nothing could come down the staircase, nothing above the second floor could possibly have survived.

Craig covered his face with his hands and stepped hastily back as the object fell from above. Black, not red, it was outlined against the flames for a split second and when it struck the staircase it bounced and skittered and spun downward with a strange little clinking sound.

Craig stooped, licked his fingers and picked up the rusty police whistle.

*   *   *

Brickwork on the back stairs was warm and a thick, fat-smelling mist hung on each landing as Craig leapt up the steps two at a time. He regretted his impetuosity. He had brought no torch, no axe, no protection for his head. He was ill-clad too for such a venture and, above all, he had wasted far too much time in getting here.

The fire, he calculated, had been burning for twenty minutes or more and would surely have eaten into the rafters of the attic. He had only been up there once and could not recall how the roof was braced. He remembered only too well the wooden cubicles, set out like gigantic matchboxes. Even within the confines of the end staircase smoke was acrid enough to constrict his lungs and throat. He felt as if he were inhaling white spirit, a substance simultaneously wet and dry.

When he reached the door of the second floor he found that it was bolted from the inside. He hammered on it with his fists, kicked it in frustration then went on again. He bounded up the stone stairs towards the oppressive, sweating heat and the dense clouds of smoke that filled the staircase's upper reaches. Already he was sapped by exertion, drenched with perspiration, weakened by the lack of air. He had trapped himself here, separated from Sammy.

He could get out again, could turn and dive down the staircase again, make it to the street in seconds. But the whistle in his pocket would not allow him to surrender so easily. He leapt past the landing to the door that gave access to the Claremont's long third floor. It opened, unimpaired. Craig confronted the fire at last, a thick, fierce wall of orange and red that filled the main stair and bent itself wickedly along the ceiling.

Combustion had already occurred in several of the cubicles. By the outer wall a beam burned furiously, flames coaxed and stretched by draught from a broken window. He had a sense of where he was now, however, where the fire had settled temporary limits. What frightened him was the great snarling sound that came from above. Spumes of creamy-coloured smoke seeped through the ceiling, bits of lathe and mortar cracked and tumbled down about him.

The open door was creating a through draught, Craig rammed his shoulder against it, slapped shut the bolt. He was badly frightened now, and clung to his purpose with all his will. He pushed himself forward towards that wall of fire out of which, miraculously, Sammy's old steel whistle had fallen or had been hurled.

And then a voice said, "Haw, Mr Nicholson."

It did not seem like Sammy Reynold's voice at all. It was quiet and conjectural, intelligent in its inflexion.

Sammy was lying in a heap, belly down. His face was turned towards Craig, his cheek crushed against dusty boards. He was burned, horribly burned, hair scorched from his head, eyebrows vanished. His flesh was blackened and his clothing, especially about the head and neck, had turned to tar. So far gone was he that he seemed to feel no pain at all.

He showed teeth like a dog when he squeezed out the words. "Find ma whistle, did you, Mr Nicholson?"

Craig crouched. "Aye, Sam, I have it right here."

"Gi'es it back then."

Sammy was lying close to the third cell. He hadn't been here when the fire had started. He had been to the north, beyond the stairwell. How he had got here, when he had revealed himself and how the pain of the burning had affected him, Craig had no idea. It was all without point, without consequence. He took the whistle from his pocket and turning Sammy's hand, gently laid the barrel against the blistering palm, cocked the blistered knuckles round it.

"Can you feel it, Sammy?"

"Aye."

Craig made no offer to remove the boy. He had been liberated at last from false promises, from impulsive gestures. He was aware of the ferocity of the sounds overhead and of the heat on his exposed flesh but he experienced no urgency, no fear for himself.

Sammy's voice was only a whisper now, so faint that Craig had to go down close to the floor, like a tracker, to hear it at all.

"Will ye be stayin' wi' me, Mr Nicholson?"

"Oh, yes, Sammy, I'll be stayin'."

"Good," Sammy murmured, and died.

*   *   *

Staggering under its sticky weight, Craig carried the boy's body to the stairwell door. He still felt compelled to get Sammy out of the Claremont, somehow, but when he tugged open the door he saw immediately that escape by that route was impossible. Roof timbers had thundered down the well and the smoke was impenetrable. He slid the body from his shoulders and placed it in a sitting position against the outer wall.

The heat was furnace-like, he could hardly breathe. He was torn between an irrational loyalty to the corpse and the necessity of saving himself. He hesitated only for a moment then he opened Sammy's palm and removed the old steel whistle. He patted Sammy's head and left him to the flames.

He scuttled along the narrow avenue between the burning cubicles and the building's outer wall. Blue flames painted the skirting and the ventilator panels belched smoke.

He realised that he was trapped. Both ends of the loft were blocked by fire and fire was moving rapaciously through the Claremont, consuming it from within. He had no time to waste. He found a window, braced himself and lashed out at it with his foot.

The rubberised sole had no effect.

Flame, like burning oil, slid across the planking. The ceiling boards creaked and bulged overhead. Craig cowled the tunic jacket over his hair and drove at the glass like a bull, cracking the pane. He backed off and lashed out once more with his foot. The glass broke and fell away from him in jagged shards. He climbed through the frame and on to the narrow, wet ledge outside.

To be in the air was a relief, however perilous his position. He sensed rather than saw the crowd below, cluttered equipment, cobbles washed by rain from the hoses. He felt the strenuous little wind tug at his jacket as he crabbed along the sandstone ledge that provided a holding for drainpipes and rones. He felt dangerously safe. All he had to do was hold his position for sixty seconds and a fireman would surely rescue him.

He watched the metal ladder sway, wires sag, big wheels swivel, and the fireman — his neighbour McGonigle, as it happened — cinch the rope around his waist and reach up, reach out for him. The ladder was close to full extension. Two solid steel wheels struck and bounced from the sandstone. The ladder yawed away from Craig again.

Below, Officer Kelso was shouting so loudly that Craig could hear him even above the bellow of the flames.

Legs had begun to tremble, arms turn to lead. Buttocks ached as if he'd been kicked. His head sang with the force of his attack upon the glass. He glanced up. The guttering of the roof hung like gaudy bunting, piled with red-hot slates, ready to tear loose at any second and pour down upon the firemen.

He must hang on. Hang on. He must not let go.

The ladder, and McGonigle, came in close again, swooping towards him, braking. The ladder flexed and twisted. McGonigle's little blackened face was split by a grin, all white teeth and a red-leather tongue as if he were enjoying the wild ride. Back it came, steadied, and McGonigle was reaching out to him with both arms.

For an instant Craig was immobilised by uncertainty.

"Come on, Craig. Jeeze, come on."

He danced on the ledge, let go his hold and flung himself outward like a cat.

McGonigle caught him by the tunic, grabbed, pawed, hooked him by the armpits and dragged him in hard against the ladder's narrow shelf.

One steel wheel jabbed into Craig's side but he had no breath to cry out with the pain it caused. The ladder was sliding away, not retracting but rolling back from the wall of the building.

He thought: there'll be nothing left of the Claremont, nothing left of Sammy. Thought too how safe it felt, airy but secure, with his neighbour's arm around him and his face buried in McGonigle's shoulder. He could smell the wet flannel jacket, the stink of oilskin. He felt alive, more alive than he had ever done as the ladder whipped back and forth in a great irregular arc above Scutter Street. He was cut, bruised and scorched, aye, but he had survived. He was safe, safe and alive after all.

Too close to McGonigle to hear the roar from the crowd below, the first Craig knew of the cascade from the roof was when he was struck by a flame-sheathed lathe that tore across his shoulders and lodged against his face.

He cried aloud then, as a hail of slates whistled past his head and raw, red, searing pain possessed him.

*   *   *

She had been in the cold waiting room of the hospital all night long. She had watched the dawn come up over the trees in the Kelvin groves and the wind, the same wind, scutter and play among the leaves. She had watched breakfast lights go on in the tall mansions that overlooked the park, had seen the University's cleaners and janitors trudge up the steep paths from Dumbarton Road.

She had spent much of the night on her feet; it was warmer that way. Without protest, she had let Gordon coddle her, fetch tea and biscuits, and, when she grew too weary to stand, had let him lead her to a bench and sit with his arm about her. He told her again and again how it was that Breezy and he had arrived in Scutter Street, and had talked and talked and talked in a low, confidential voice about Breezy and Lorna, old Donald Adair's passing, about Josephine and Greta.

Kirsty had not attempted to silence him. She'd found comfort and consolation in his presence, in the lifeline of words, of ordinariness, that he'd offered to prevent her drowning in an ocean of worry.

It was after eight o'clock before Kirsty was summoned. She left Gordon reluctantly and followed a prim nurse down a corridor to the ward where patients with burns were housed. She was not to be permitted to visit Craig, even to see him. She was ushered into a small side room where a brusque young doctor waited to give her information on Craig's condition.

The news was not as grim as it might have been, not as final as

319

Kirsty had expected. Burns to Craig's face, neck and left upper arm were of the third degree. He had been treated under general anaesthetic, burnt areas cleansed to prevent contamination. If toxaemia was resisted and when the effects of shock lessened, treatment by application of tannic acid solution would begin. The healing period would be prolonged, however, and some scarring inevitable.

Kirsty listened to the medical litany with strange detachment. She had been along this road before, with Bobby. The doctor remained brusque, as if he had business elsewhere in the hospital and could not spare time to soothe mere relatives.

Damage had been inflicted to the retina of Craig's left eye. It was too soon to predict if sight would be impaired. Inflammation of the bronchial tract and lungs was not, apparently, serious. Two broken ribs; an affliction quite minor compared to burning but an added complication in the rendering of effective treatment. Strictly no visitors would be allowed for at least four days, possibly longer.

The doctor asked her if she had any questions.

Kirsty shook her head.

The doctor nodded, bade her a good morning and departed at once, leaving a nurse to escort Kirsty back through the tiled corridors to the waiting room.

To her surprise, and chagrin, Breezy and Madge had arrived and waited now for news, together with Sergeant Drummond and an officer she recognised as Lieutenant Strang. Both policemen wore uniforms, were spick-and-span in appearance and had applied an air of solemn gravity that could not quite disguise their physical weariness.

"Oh, dear, dear!"

Tearfully, Madge rushed forward to wrap her fat arms about Kirsty.

Kirsty did not resist. She patted her mother-in-law dutifully and looked across the woman's shoulder at Gordon.

"What's the word, Kirst?" Gordon said.

"He'll live," said Kirsty.

*   *   *

She resisted every blandishment, all Madge's weepy pleas to return with them to Great Western Terrace, let them take care

320

of her until such time as Craig was released from hospital. She was polite but firm. She wanted, needed to return home. She had Bobby's welfare to attend to and, she said, the shop.

The last statement was cynical, cruel almost, but it stifled Madge's protests and demands. Kirsty was aware that her mother-in-law was being kind but she resented such charitable gestures, saw in them only subtle and selfish manipulation.

Gordon offered to accompany her back to Canada Road but she rejected him too. She paused only long enough to speak with Lieutenant Strang and Sergeant Drummond who had a practical purpose in being there, as well as personal interest in the welfare of an officer. She listened to their explanations of procedure, their assurances that Craig's wage would be paid in full until such times as he was restored to health, that the burgh would ensure that she did not suffer hardship.

She listened, nodded, murmured appropriate responses – and resisted the temptation to remind them that she was no ordinary housewife, that she needed no burgh council hand-outs to survive.

It was almost nine o'clock before Kirsty managed to shake them off and step into a hack to carry her the short distance back to Canada Road.

Hector Drummond had given her news about the fire. He had told her that Craig had gone in to rescue Sammy Reynolds, that the boy's remains had been found on the second floor of the building, and that Sammy, poor laddie, had been the conflagration's only victim. Enquiries of various kinds were under way. A certain Mr Moscrop had been taken into temporary custody, though later, in the light of strenuous denials of involvement and a total lack of evidence to connect him with the blaze, had been released. Resident lodgers from the Claremont had been found temporary accommodation in the People's Mission where they would remain until other arrangements could be made to house them. Nothing was said of Craig's courage. No praise, or blame, was heaped upon him by the officers. For that, at least, Kirsty was thankful.

There would, however, be no escape from talk for a day or two, from the extravagant gossip of neighbours and the lauding of Craig's name. He was no reprobate, like Andy McAlpine. All the bitterness and reserve that the Nicholsons had engendered would be instantly lost in reflections of Craig's glory, and the rediscovery of his sterling qualities.

Praise, rumour and sympathy would all seem equally trivial to Kirsty in the days to come. She had herself to think about, her future and Bobby's future. The rest was distraction, a hazy pall of words that hung over her as the residue of smoke from the Claremont's burning hung over Greenfield. Whatever she did, however she behaved, she would be cast as villain, Craig as hero. Simple minds would find reasons for condemning her. But she had learned to live without concern for neighbourly opinion and she was willing, just, to believe that they meant well, and to let it go at that.

That afternoon, depleted though she was by lack of sleep, she dressed Bobby in his Sunday best and took him round to Gascoigne Street.

She had tried to explain to him what all the excitement had been about, and why his father would not be coming home for a week or two.

"Hospital?" Bobby had glowered.

"Yes, hospital. But he's all right. Daddy just needs to have a good long rest in bed."

"Bad leg?"

"No."

She had him on her knee and he'd waited. He had not been at all distressed at having to spend a night in a strange bed in Mrs Piper's house, curled up by the side of her sons. Bobby's childish adaptability was, for Kirsty, one of his less endearing features. He had been fed and entertained, and his security, it seemed, had not been challenged. His concern for his father was distorted by selfishness.

"No' go swimmin'?"

"Not for a while, a long while, Bobby."

"Huh!"

Kirsty understood perfectly that he was only a young child whose responses had not yet been tuned, that he did not truly understand what had happened to his Daddy or what the consequences might have been, might yet be. Even so she was cool with him, and he was sulky as they walked through streets still reeking of smoke to the shop in Gascoigne Street.

Bobby did not in fact thaw out until his Aunt Lorna, hiding

sentimental tears, made a great fuss of him and Uncle Tubby –
who had cancelled all his appointments – offered to take him out
for a tramcar ride with a dish of raspberry ice-cream at the end
of it.

Kirsty was less easily appeased.

She followed Ernest and Bobby out into the street. The man
was wrapped in a long woollen overcoat with his scarf thrown
casually about his throat. Bobby, in a neat blue coat and long,
buttoned leggings, was impatient to be off on the afternoon's
adventure. He clung tightly to Ernest's hand and scowled at his
mother for having the audacity to delay Uncle Ernest in conversation.

"Does Frank know what's happened?" Kirsty asked.

"Oh, yes. Lorna came to the house before breakfast to give us
the news. Besides, it's all over the *Glasgow Herald*."

"I require to talk to him; Frank, I mean."

"All right," Ernest said. "When and where?"

"If Lorna will look after Bobby for a while, I'm going back to
the Western Infirmary tonight. I won't be permitted to see
Craig, of course, but perhaps somebody will tell him that I
called. In any case, I need first-hand information on Craig's
condition before I – " She paused. "At the hospital gates, tell
Frank, at eight o'clock."

"I'll tell him," said Ernest. "I expect he'll be there."

"I'm sure he will," said Kirsty.

*   *   *

That afternoon the aggravating wind dropped and, with dusk,
came the first heavy rain that the city had seen in weeks, a cold,
straight, glassy downpour, more wintry in its way than snow.
Wards and waiting rooms echoed with its drumming and the
splashing of swiftly flooded eaves. It was a night to be home by
the fire, not there in the Western Infirmary.

Kirsty wondered if Craig was conscious enough to hear the
rain from his bed in the ward, and where his ward was situated.
She had no notion in which of the long, dimly-lighted rooms her
husband lay. She wondered if his eyes were bandaged, if he
could only hear the rain and not see it, or if, with the remnants
of a countryman's instinct, he had sensed the weather-change
earlier that day and had been alert for it.

She had no hope of being allowed to visit Craig's bedside, to exchange even a few brief words with him. He was being kept – the doctor's word – 'sterile' for his own protection. She felt separated from him and lonely among visiting relatives who came and went from the waiting room, speaking in whispers, some sad, some jovial, some just plainly bored.

She was kept waiting for a half-hour before being treated to a curt interview with a Matron who, reading from a written note, informed Kirsty that Mr Nicholson had shown no signs of crisis of the blood so far and was as well as could be expected under the circumstances. Stiffly, Kirsty asked when it would be convenient to call again. She was informed that there would be no further news until after doctor's rounds tomorrow and that it would be the beginning of the week, at the earliest, before Constable Nicholson would be in any fit state to receive bedside visits from his next-of-kin. Kirsty left the Infirmary with the distinct impression that her presence was nothing but a nuisance and that she had no right to express interest in her husband's welfare.

Under a black umbrella that seemed oddly in keeping with her mood of anxious irritation, Kirsty hurried down the avenue towards the lights of Dumbarton Road and her rendezvous with Frank Tubbs.

Frank was waiting in the shelter of the arch of the hospital lodge, hat pulled down, collar of his overcoat turned up, hands dug into his pockets in a manner that made him look as miserable as a mendicant. Without a word of greeting, he took Kirsty's arm and, ducking the ribs of the umbrella, led her across cobbles and puddles, over the Partick Bridge into the nether end of Argyle Street; not to the cool, marble-tabled café that sold the best ice-cream in Glasgow but to a small, ply-panelled supper shop. It was clean enough in spite of an odour of frying fat and stewed tea. Each table was covered with a chequered cloth. Gaslight filtered through rose shades. Best of all, at that in-between hour on a wet weekday night it was deserted.

Frank took Kirsty's overcoat, her hat too, shook out the umbrella and draped them, with his own coat and hat, on the antlered stand by the door. Then he seated himself and, without preliminary, said, "Now tell me – how is he?"

"I'm not sure. They were very uninformative. I don't think

324

he's going to die or anythin'. But – " Kirsty shrugged. "I don't know."

"How are you?"

"I'm all right. Tired."

Frank reached across the little table and took her hands in his. He did not release them when a young girl in a long apron came gliding from the rear of the shop and showed them a menu. Without taking his eyes from Kirsty's face, Frank told the girl to bring them tea and toast and she went off again.

"Why did you ask me to meet you tonight?" Frank said.

"I wanted to see you."

"Is that the only reason?"

Kirsty hesitated. "No."

In the dim, rose light he looked younger, softer. But sadness was still in his eyes and no cast of light would ever, she realised, eliminate it. She also realised that he knew why she had asked for the meeting, what her decision would be and that, being Frank, he would make that easy for her too.

"You won't leave him now, will you, Kirsty?"

"How can I?"

"Oh, you could, you could," Frank said. "But then I wouldn't have fallen in love with you if you'd been that kind of woman."

"I'm not being a martyr, Frank, if that's what you think."

"No, nor a saint either." He gave a wry laugh and, using it to cover the gesture, lifted his hands from hers and sat back in the wooden chair. "It's a pity we are as we are, isn't it?"

"So – so tied, yes."

"That isn't what I meant," Frank said. "I love you, Kirsty. I wanted to make love to you. I still do, for that matter."

"It isn't – "

"I know it isn't," Frank said. "I'm not having a try at that, Kirsty. Compensation or consolation, call it what you like. No second-bests. You don't love me, do you?"

"Not as you mean it, no."

"How do I mean it?"

"You don't make me hurt," said Kirsty.

"Is that the hallmark of loving in your book? Hurting?" Frank said. "Surely not!"

"It would hurt me to leave Craig."

"Yes, I know."

"Even before, even if nothing had happened – the fire, his injury," Kirsty said. "I don't know what he's going to be like, Frank."

"The same, probably, only worse."

"Perhaps you're right," Kirsty said.

"But you'll put up with it for always?"

"I imagine I will."

"Do this for a man who was too careless to be bothered with marriage," Frank said, "who, I gather, almost left you at one point?"

"But he didn't," Kirsty said. "He's still with me. We're still together."

"Now he'll need you. Is that what you've been hoping for, Kirsty, that one day *he* would need *you* ?"

"I don't think you understand," Kirsty said.

"I don't think I do," Frank said.

Kirsty said, "Craig's always needed me."

She sat back too as the girl in the apron brought the order of tea and buttered toast. It was her turn to look at Frank. But he would not meet her eye. He had already begun the process of separation that would allow him to retreat with pride intact. He glanced away, half-turned and stared out over the lace half-curtain to the rain-drenched street, to the rain falling straight out of the arc lamps, white rain, less gentle than snow.

Frank said, "Have you told anyone about my proposal?"

"Of course not."

"That's always something, I suppose."

"Ernest?"

"No, no. He may have guessed that I was stuck on you – not difficult to do, really – but as for a proposal – "

"What will happen now, Frank?" Kirsty said. "I hope we can go on bein' friends."

"That's asking a lot," he said. "Too much, in fact."

"I didn't mean to hurt you, you know."

He nodded bleakly, shifted position and reached for the teapot. Together they watched the golden brown stream from the vessel's spout fill two cups. Toast on the plate oozed yellow butter and a faint, appetising steam. Frank pushed the plate towards her with a little open-palmed gesture.

Kirsty looked at him, frowning.

"I can't," she said.

"Aren't you hungry?"

"Yes, but – "

"Damn it, Kirsty," Frank told her, "eat your toast, drink your tea, and then I'll find a cab to take you home."

"You don't mind?"

"Of course I mind," Frank said.

"But – "

"But nothing. Eat your toast."

She left him twenty minutes later, alone on the pavement outside the supper shop, and rode home in the cab he'd hailed for her.

*   *   *

Craig was propped up in bed by three big hard bolsters at an angle that gave him relief from the stabbing pain in his left side. By moving his head he could scan the length of the ward through his right eye. He wore only a singlet, like a baker or a stoker, only his was spotlessly white. The only dressings on the burned portions of his upper body were a light gauze covering over his left eye and a pad of medicated paraffin bandaged to his left hand.

Since they had allowed him out of bed to attend to calls of nature, he had glimpsed his reflection in window glass and the lavatory's white tiles – and did not dare ask for a mirror. If his face was anything like his left arm and shoulder then he was a sorry, shocking, ugly mess. He could see with the tail of his working eye black crusting and brown scaling and the hideous wormcast scars that the blisters had left. Tannic acid treatment, he was told, caused the discolouration, but he did not believe the doctor or the nurses who thus consoled him. He had seen in the eyes of his few visitors the shock and disgust that his wounds engendered, had seen Hector Drummond bite his lip, and Kirsty's tears.

God knows, the arm was bad enough, black and wasted and scabbed with dead tissue. The itch was growing worse by the day too, and his hands were tied into soft cotton mittens every night to stop him scratching involuntarily in his sleep.

Sleep! Huh! Precious little sleep he got, except for cat-naps in daylight hours when, for five or ten minutes at a time, he would find a position that would ease the pain in his ribs, and the itch would cool and his back would stop aching, and for precious seconds he would feel as if he were floating, floating upward, drifting away on fluffy white clouds.

"How are you faring today, son?" Sergeant Drummond said.

Craig opened his eyes. The left eyelid stuck, as usual and, though it was discreetly veiled by a gauze lid, he worked at it with his muscles until it came unglued.

"Fine," he said.

"I brought you some tangerines."

Craig nodded at the three pieces of fruit wrapped in red paper. He had forgotten that it would soon be Christmas and that provision merchants would be stocked up with seasonal fare.

"Thanks, Sergeant."

"I also brought you this – from the lads."

Drummond held out the square of cardboard and Craig read the letters, printed large and simple in green crayon: WE ALL HOPE YOU ARE FEELING BETTER AND WILL BE IN THE DEEP END WITH US SOON. It was signed in pencil by Archie, Peter and Ronnie Norbert.

"Aye, thank them too, will you?"

He felt little or no gratitude. He had no desire to see his pals right now. He endured Hector Drummond's afternoon visits because he knew, without being so informed, that the sergeant was the burgh's assigned representative, instructed to report on the constable's progress and, when the time came, to break the bad news. Craig had no illusions on that score. He'd had endless hours upon which to brood about his future. He knew he'd been lucky, if you could call it lucky, to survive the blaze at the Claremont and had McGonigle's bravery to thank for it. Fireman McGonigle had also been injured; a head wound, not too serious.

Sergeant Drummond had been Craig's first visitor. He had come again late the same night accompanied by Lieutenant Strang, and had jotted down Craig's personal account of the fire. They were after Hog Moscrop, Drummond told him, but could prove nothing conclusive against the slippery wee sod. In death as in life, Sammy Reynolds was being saddled with the blame. From all of that, even grief over Sammy, Craig felt distanced. He understood what had happened to him, what his injuries would mean. It was only a matter of time until Hector Drummond told him the truth. And when Drummond appeared, that quiet, grey afternoon, Craig knew that the time had come.

The sergeant said, "I hear you are mending well, Craig, and that you will be let out of this place quite soon."

"Where did you hear that?"

"From the doctor himself." Drummond's dry Highland accent had become even softer. He was seated on a wooden chair by the bedside, back to the half-screen that he had moved on its rubberised wheels to provide a modicum of privacy. "I have spoken with him just ten minutes since. He has every hope that you will be discharged before Christmas."

"Like this?" Craig pointed a forefinger at his face.

"It will, of course, be necessary to convalesce. And you will have to be calling here at the infirmary for treatments for a while. But, no, you are sound, so I'm told. No damage done to lungs, kidneys or heart. You will be fit to go out in a week."

"When will I be 'fit' to work again, Mr Drummond?" Craig said. "When will I be 'fit' to put on my uniform an' get back on the beat?"

Hector Drummond let his weight sag, forearms on his thighs. He looked, Craig thought, venerable now, with his helmet off and the trappings of the police station stripped away. He was past it, had given his service. Soon he would be put out to pasture in some dreary boarding house down the coast. For an instant Craig's self-hatred was mellowed by sympathy for the old sergeant and he did not press the man.

At length, Drummond said, "The Police Committee has considered your case, Craig. It is the Committee's opinion that you should be paid in full until you are completely recovered."

"An' then?"

"A suitable pension."

"What!"

Hector Drummond stared down at the polished floor, at one tiny grain of dust that whispered about beneath the edge of the bed.

"Craig, you have taken your lickings in the past," the sergeant said. "The pension will be a recognition of all that you have done, all that you have given . . . "

"What the hell are you tryin' to say?"

"Ten shillings a week seems to be the sum settled upon."

Craig stirred – the ribs stabbed him like two daggers – and struggled to sit up straight. Drummond's big hand gestured to him to be still. "Ten bob a week, eh! What about the house?"

"Och, there will be no need to vacate your apartment for a long while yet, not until you are well and are settled."

"Settled?" Craig said. "What's this you're tellin' me? I'm sacked, is that it? Dismissed, discharged, paid off, booted out?"

"Och, no. No, no, not at all."

"So I will be back in uniform?"

"Craig, you'll be scarred."

"Jesus, we're all scarred in Ottawa Street. Half of us, anyway. John Boyle's got a scar a bloody mile long on his chest."

"That is different."

"It's my face, isn't it? I won't be 'pretty' enough to be a burgh constable any longer." Craig let himself slump back against the bolsters. "How bad will it be, Hector?"

"Bad enough," Hector Drummond told him.

"Couldn't the bastards even wait until – ?" Craig shook his head. "I suppose not. Get at me now, when I'm feelin' bad; right?"

"I should not be the one to be telling you these things," Hector Drummond said; a statement not an apology. "But I have known you longest. For what it is worth, I've always thought you were . . . "

"Stuff the flattery," Craig said, "just tell me the bloody truth. How bad is it goin' to be?"

"It is not up to me to – "

"How bad, Sergeant Drummond?"

"Impaired sight in the left eye. Some disfigurement."

"The doctor told you this?"

"Yes. It's the partial loss of sight that's the problem for the Police Committee. A constable has to have – "

"I know – eyes in the back of his head," Craig said. "Perhaps I could grow a beard."

"What good would – "

"Pensioned off." Craig rubbed his fingertips over the crown of his shoulder, brushing pinkish scales from the fringes of the crust. "Have I an alternative, Sergeant?"

"Perhaps you could be found a job inside Percy Street."

"Doing what?"

"Helping to keep the Records."

"Naw, that's a job for women an' old men. Civilians."

Drummond said, "Or in the stables?"

"The stables!" Craig exclaimed in disgust then, squinting, said, "Would I get to keep the house at one-five-four if I worked in the stables?"

"No."

Craig rubbed his shoulder hard. He could feel blood beginning to ooze from the surface, sticky against his fingertips, and made himself stop. He stuck his right hand firmly behind his head and contemplated the ward ceiling, the grey triangle of light shed by the long grey window.

"How long do I have?" Craig said. "I mean, before the Police Committee starts to get strappy?"

"Six months."

For half a minute Craig lay motionless. He had both eyes open and could see the ceiling's patterns and, oddly, the coarse weave of surgical gauze, each imposed upon the other, though one was distant and the other very close.

"Tell them," he said at last, "I'll take the pension, an' be out of Canada Road before spring quarter day."

"Och, now, there's no need to – "

"Oh, aye, there is," Craig said. "And, Sergeant – "

"Hmmm?"

"Don't come here again."

*   *   *

Visiting time: a necessary evil for nursing staff, a bare half-hour during which chairs were moved out of position, flowers required water, fruit needed to be washed, candy made the furniture sticky and the shining floor, Matron's pride and joy, was dulled by footprints. Kirsty had never learned the art of standing up to authority and, like the other wives and sweethearts, crept apologetically past the starched figure at the ward door and tiptoed across the floor as carefully as if she were following a line of stepping-stones. Conscious of a protesting squeal from the linoleum, she moved a chair and put down upon the rigid

331

coverlet the box of cakes that she had brought to stimulate her husband's appetite.

She was sure that Craig had heard her coming, had been aware of her approach since the moment she had entered the ward. He lay quite still, however, feigning sleep. The sheet was bound tightly across his lean belly, one arm folded across it, the other down by his side. She eased the cake box towards the foot of the bed and, seizing the opportunity, closely scrutinised his damaged face.

"What're you lookin' at?"

She started guiltily, the chair legs squeaking loudly beneath her.

"I was just – " She hesitated. "It's gettin' better, I think. There's new skin growin'. Is it still sore?"

"Nope," Craig said.

"Itchy?"

She reached for his unbandaged hand but he drew it away, not quickly but deliberately, and folded it in a fist against his breastbone.

He said, "What's in the box?"

"Chocolate buns an' two Lucky cakes," Kirsty said. "I see you've got tangerines. Did Sergeant Drummond bring them?"

He did not turn his head, did not move a muscle.

"Aye, but fruit's not the only thing Drummond brought today," Craig said. "I've been given the boot, Kirsty."

At first she did not understand and Craig, now that truth was out, struggled and sat up. Leaning forward, he glanced up and down the ward at bowed backs and black hats, bandaged hands and burned faces. "The boot, the heave," he hissed. "Sacked, dismissed, pensioned off. Out."

"Ah!" Kirsty exclaimed.

She was not unduly surprised at the news. It had dawned on her some days ago that Craig's facial scars would never completely heal, no matter what the doctors might do, and that the members of the Police Committee would not want a man so marked in one of their proud uniforms.

"Is that all you can say?" Craig demanded.

"Did Drummond – I mean, is it official?"

"As official as it needs to be," Craig said. "The bastards have offered me ten bob a week as a pension."

"What about the house?"

"We'll have to leave Canada Road."

"I see."

"Tied property's for burgh employees only."

"When will we – ?"

"Spring quarter."

"Craig, what'll you do?"

"Crawl on to the rubbish heap, I suppose. How the hell do I know?" He slumped despondently against the bolsters. "I haven't had much chance to think about it."

She reached again for his hand, persisted, found it and held it, fingers laced with his. "Well, at least we won't starve."

"On ten bob a week? Damned near it."

"There's the shop. We still have the shop."

He wriggled his hand free of hers. "Naw, *you* still have the shop. What I've got is *nothin'*."

"You've got me. You've got Bobby."

"Huh!"

"Is that all we mean to you?" Kirsty said.

The need to speak quietly took the heat out of her words and Craig in turn spoke in a sibilant whisper that, whatever his intention, softened his abrasiveness.

"I didn't mean that," he said. "I mean, what've *you* got? No bargain in me, Kirsty. Look at me. Go on, take a long hard look. How can you stand it, uh?"

"Well, you're no oil paintin', Craig, not right now," Kirsty said. "But I never married you for your looks."

"What did you marry me for?"

"Because I loved you."

"Loved me!" He snorted. "Naw, naw. I just happened to be handy. Come on, admit it. I was just your ticket out o' Ayrshire. Now I think you'd be better off wi'out me."

"That's true," Kirsty said.

"An' since we're not really married – "

"Find a minister," Kirsty said. "I'll marry you tomorrow."

"I don't want your bloody pity, Kirsty," he said. "Look at me! Jesus, who'd ever want to marry this gargoyle, this worthless wreck."

"All the more reason."

"For what?"

"To grab me while you can," Kirsty said.

"Huh! I don't have t' grab you," he said, then, after a pause, "do I?"

"For a worthless wreck," Kirsty said, "you're still an arrogant beggar, Craig Nicholson."

"I can't even earn a wage, not like this. Who's goin' to take me on?"

"I will, I tell you."

Down in the lower wards handbells were clanging to signal the beginning of the end of the visiting period. Apprentice nurses were standing by in closets with dusting mops and polishing cloths at the ready, and the clink-clink-clink of china bed-pans, decently removed for half an hour, indicated that medicine would soon be on the march again.

"I'll talk to Breezy," Kirsty said.

"*Don't* talk to Breezy. I want nothin' from him."

"His father died. Did you know?"

"Oh! When?"

"The night of the fire. He was buried last week."

The news did not impinge to any degree upon Craig's consciousness, though she had no doubt that he had heard her and that, in some part of his brain, he had recorded the fact.

"Your mother wants to come in tomorrow," Kirsty said.

"No."

"Gordon an' Lorna then?"

"*No.*"

"Craig, you've got to see somebody, sometime."

"For what?" he said. "So they can snivel over me?"

Kirsty rose. She lifted the cardboard cake box from the bed by its string and dumped it unceremoniously on the locker top then stood by him, looking down at him with a frown, hands planted on her hips and elbows cocked.

"Look at me, Craig."

"Eh?"

"You've done a lot of shoutin' this past week: 'Look at me. Look at me.' Now it's my turn. I want you to take a good long hard look at me before I go, Craig."

He stretched his neck, thrust out his jaw. "There. I see you."

"Both eyes," Kirsty said.

"What?"

"Lift the lid, Craig. Look at me with both eyes, please."

"Kirsty . . . I . . . "

She glanced up the ward. She could hear the handbell loud in the women's ward beyond the stairhead but the looming figure of Matron was gone from the doorway. Quickly, before Craig could resist, she stepped close against the bed and pinned him down with one hand, taking care not to put pressure on his ribs. She reached out and delicately plucked at the corner of the gauze dressing that protected his left eye, lifted it from the fold of the bandage.

"Easy, easy, easy, easy," Craig pleaded, body tense, fists clenched tight. "You'll hurt it, you'll damage it, you'll – "

She stooped, her face no more than six inches from his.

"Look at me, Craig, an' tell me what you see."

"It's – it's a blur. That's all – a blur. You're just a blur, Kirsty."

"Aye, that's all I've ever been," she said.

With the tip of her finger she cautiously brushed the eyelid of the injured eye. The lid twitched, his cheek quivered, a thin film of moisture oiled the eyeball and trickled against the lashes.

Kirsty said, "Try again."

"No, it hurts."

"Does it?" she said. "Does it really hurt? Or is it just too hard for you, Craig?"

He jerked up his bandaged hand and cupped it over the scarred and teary eye and, in defiance of the pain behind his ribs, turned away from her just as the cry of the handbell broke deafeningly into the ward.

Kirsty stepped back from the bed. She swung on her heel and headed straight for the door. She almost reached it before he shouted, "KIRSTY!"

The porter with the handbell stopped the clangour in surprise and Matron appeared magically by the door again, glaring sourly first at Kirsty and then at Craig. Kirsty turned on her heel and retraced her steps to the bedside.

Craig was sitting up, forearm squeezed against his ribcage.

"What?" she said.

Craig grinned sheepishly, winced, and stretched out his right arm to gather her to him.

"I can see you fine," he said.

Ten

A Little Epilogue

On the surface of things life in the Tubbs household moved across the cusp of winter at its usual even pace.

The parents of groom and bride-to-be met for a lavish pre-Christmas dinner at the Adair mansion on Great Western Terrace, and Lorna and Madge now and then took tea on a Sunday afternoon with Ernest and Phyllis. The mothers got on if not famously, at least well enough not to embarrass their offspring.

Brother Frank, however, was missing from all of these social unions. He offered polite, though somewhat feeble, excuses for his absence. He made amends by taking Breezy to lunch in the Art Club early in January to discuss, as men will, the fortune and the fate of the young 'uns and to make it clear that, come what may, he intended to honour his promises and stand behind his brother financially until such time as Ernest might honestly call himself his own man.

Breezy felt just a shade uncomfortable in Frank's company; nothing you could put your finger on, nothing sinister, just differences in attitude and outlook that could never be reconciled.

"Frank Tubbs is a cold fish, don't you think, dear?" Madge would say; and Breezy would answer, "Well, coolish anyway."

There was nothing cool about Frank's typewriting machine in the weeks that led December into January. The pace of his labours was more feverish than ever. When, early in the New Year, he took himself off to London on publishing business the silence he left behind him in the flat was audible and, for Phyllis at least, depressing.

If it had not been that Ernest was up to the eyes and needed her at home, Phyllis would have packed her bag and travelled to visit one of her other sons, to divert herself by spoiling her grandchildren. With Kirsty Nicholson still very much tied to looking after her sick husband, however, Ernest had had to divide his time between commercial selling and aiding Lorna in the shop and Phyllis did not have the heart to desert him.

According to Ernest business at Gascoigne Street had been more than brisk. Beneath her youngest's exhaustion was a jubilant streak at the scale of the seasonal turnover. The plotting of new lines had apparently paid handsome dividends and the little shop had hummed from morn until night throughout the Christmas month, coining profit enough to pay Frank well on his investment and, if trade continued to be good, to allow Ernest to say goodbye to the warehouse that employed him, marry Lorna and depend on shop profits to support them.

Phyllis tried to put aside her trepidation, to share her son's youthful optimism, his eagerness to be up and at 'em, to take life by the throat. She wished sometimes that a little more of his father's stuffiness had been bred into her youngest's character, yet she could not help but love him for his adventurous nature and his cheerfulness.

Ernest, however, was not alone in planning for the future. Five days after his return from London, Frank broke the news to his mother and brother.

"I'm going away," he said. "Off to London."

"Oh!" Phyllis slipped her tiny feet to the floor and rose from the chair by the fire. "Oh, dear! For how long?"

"A year," Frank said. "I've accepted a contract to edit a brand new magazine for Thomas Eagan's publishing company. It can't be done from here."

"What if it takes?" Ernest said. "What if the magazine's successful?"

"I sincerely hope it will be," Frank said.

"Then you'll be gone for good," said Ernest.

He had moved closer to his mother, unconsciously separating himself from his brother who stood off by the piano in the window bay with his hands behind his back. Phyllis swayed slightly and Ernest put an arm about her shoulders.

"Is it what you want, dear?" the woman asked.

"Yes, Mother, it is," Frank answered.

"To leave Glasgow, to leave us?" said Ernest.

"No, that's the painful part," Frank said, with a strange reflective note in his voice that added sincerity to his words. "That's the price I'll have to pay for my – advancement."

"What – what'll we do without you, Frank?" Ernest cried, with a wobble in his throat. "How will we manage?"

"You'll just have to, old son," Frank said.

"Indeed, we will," Phyllis said.

She stepped forward, steady now, leaned up and kissed her eldest on the cheek. Her tiny hand held on to the lapel of his jacket, lingering, and then she let go and stepped back towards the hearth, and Ernest.

"What you will do – " Frank said. He corrected himself. "What I *suggest* you do, Ernest, is to settle on a date of marriage. March would be about right, wouldn't you say, Mother?"

"Yes, March."

"Bring Lorna to live here, if she's willing," Frank went on. "The house will be quite large enough, once I'm out of it, to afford you a degree of privacy. Mother will have her own room. Besides, Lorna Nicholson's not the sort of girl – "

"But it's *your* house, Frank," Ernest protested. "What happens if things go not well in London, if you hate it, if you want to come home?"

"We'll cross that bridge when we come to it," Frank said. "The shop will support you, will it not?"

"Yes, yes, I expect it will," Ernest said. "But *I* can't take your place, Frank. I'm not ready, I'll never be ready, to take your place."

"Mother?" Frank said.

"He's ready," Phyllis said.

"And you?"

"I just want you to be happy, Frank, that's all. And if London's the place – "

"London *is* the place," Frank said.

"Then you must go," said Phyllis Tubbs and, with a breaking heart, gave poor Frank her blessing.

*   *   *

338

At first, for a day or two, Bobby had been wary of his father's changed appearance. The fact that he had been sternly warned by his mother against horseplay and obstreperous behaviour had chastened him and he went about the house feigning a mouse-like timidity that in due course became a game in itself.

"What's wrong with him?" Craig had asked.

"Nothing," Kirsty had answered. "He's just shy because he hasn't seen you for a while."

"I frighten him, don't I?" Craig had said. "This ugly, twisted mug would frighten anybody."

"Does he look frightened?"

"He's so bloody quiet."

"I think I put the fear of God in him," Kirsty had said. "Maybe I overdid it."

"I wish he'd stop starin' at me."

"He can't help that."

"Naw, naw, you're right. I hate it, though. I hate bein' stared at."

"It'll not look so bad when you can shave again."

The dark stubble that clouded half Craig's jaw was mapped by pink where new skin had grown and by the last, hard, lichen-like crusts of damaged tissue. He had a little brown leather eye patch which he wore over the damaged eye in strong light. A specialist doctor in opthalmic injury who had examined the retinal structures had expressed no firm opinion but merely a set of odds, three to one against complete recovery of sight in the eye.

Discomforts, scattered throughout his body, had made Craig by turns stoical and irritable. He was, however, glad to be shot of the infirmary's barrack room regimes and the boredom of being bedridden. Besides, his appetite had returned and he preferred Kirsty's cooking to the watery wee meals that were served at the Western, and the fact that he could sleep when it suited him and not when it suited the nursing staff.

During his first week at home he had spent half of every day in bed, bolstered against the crabbing ache in his side. For the rest of the time he had mooched about the kitchen or had perched awkwardly on the armchair by the fire. The ribs were knitting and healing, however, and by New Year's Day Craig was fit enough to help his son open the presents that had been bought for him and even, with effort, to get down on all fours on the carpet to help Bobby play with his new toys.

After that Bobby had become his father's boon companion. In a flash he seemed to understand the nature of their common bond in suffering. He would seat himself against Craig's chair, calipered leg stuck out, and now and then reach up and pat his Daddy's thigh and say, "There, there."

The change in Craig's physical appearance had affected Kirsty more than she'd dared admit. She had assumed it would make no difference. But it did. The smooth, regular lines of Craig's face had been destroyed by the burning, and the scars, even when healed, would rob him of his arrogant handsomeness. She could not deny that he had been reduced by his injuries and that, however much she sided with him in his denigration of the Greenfield Burgh Police Committee, she secretly agreed with its decision.

Craig wore cardigans and jerseys with high soft collars and wrapped an old soft woollen cravat loosely about his neck to hide his patched flesh. He was scrupulously careful not to expose his body to Kirsty's gaze, or Bobby's, and took to holding a kerchief casually against his cheek as he lolled by the fire and, at table, would cock his head to present, as best he could, an undefiled profile to his wife and son.

'No visitors' remained the rule.

Gordon alone was granted a personal interview, an hour of his brother's time, and that in the back bedroom with curtains drawn and nothing but the purring flame of the gas fire to give light.

When Archie and Peter came to the door, Craig scuttled into the back room with whispered instructions to Kirsty that he was not to be disturbed. When neighbours, curious as well as concerned, dropped in with a little gift of baking or a dish of cream custard for the invalid, Craig would shoot away into hiding at the very sound of their voices. Only Mr McGonigle was permitted to speak with Constable Nicholson face to face, and for the best part of one Sunday afternoon, fireman and copper exchanged reminiscences about the Claremont blaze and exorcised their nightmares with manly jokes about hair's breadth escapes from death.

Craig left the house only to fulfil his appointments at the Western Infirmary. He refused Kirsty's company, refused

Kirsty's offer of a cab, struggled alone on and off tramcars, muffled up in a balaclava, a scarf over his nose and mouth like a man with toothache. For the rest of the time he remained indoors, as shy and suspicious, as surly as a hermit who fears not ridicule but the contamination of a sinful world.

. "This can't go on," Kirsty had said, eventually.

"What can't?"

"Hidin' like this."

"I'm convalescin'."

"You won't let anybody through the door. Your mother – "

"I don't want her down here, crowin' over my 'poor face'."

"What about the Force?"

"What about it?" Craig had said.

"Hadn't you better go down to the station an' enquire as to the procedure for collectin' the pension?"

"Don't have to. I had a letter."

"When?"

"Last week. It arrived when you were at the shop."

"Why didn't you tell me, Craig?"

"Didn't have to. There was nothin' in it we didn't already know. Expressed sympathy. Assured me of support. No hurry but – out."

"Your eye's – "

"My eyesight's just an excuse. You know that as well as I do. I suppose I should be grateful. I'm not entitled to accident compensation at all."

"Is this final?"

"'Course it's final."

"In that case hadn't you better start lookin' for work?"

"Hah!" Craig had said, bitterly. "Where? In the Gem, maybe? Come an' see the freak. Maybe old man Galetti could teach me t' dance an' play the drum."

"Stop it, Craig."

Later, she'd asked him about the house. But he'd evaded that issue too, throwing the onus back on to her as if, somehow, her ability to pay for a new apartment, in or out of Greenfield, had become the reason for their eviction from the coppers' tenement in Canada Road; and Canada Road a kind of Eden, a paradise that could never be regained.

Craig had asked only one thing from her, a modest sum to

contribute to a fund for a headstone to mark Samuel Reynolds' last resting place, not far from Jen Taylor's little grave in Wolfe Road cemetery. Hector Drummond and Ronald Norbert had, it seemed, undertaken the necessary arrangements, and there had been quite a turnout of coppers from Ottawa Street at the interment, and both Mr Black and Mr Dugdale had been led away in tears.

Kirsty had personally delivered a contribution of five pounds to Ottawa Street and had answered many questions from sergeants and constables as to Craig's state of health. She could tell from their attitudes, however, that they knew of the Committee's decision and, however unwittingly, had already begun to draw away. Craig Nicholson was no longer one of them and never would be again.

That very afternoon, Kirsty journeyed into Glasgow to call upon Mr Marlowe, her solicitor, to seek not just his advice but his assurance that whatever she did now would be legal and binding and would work out, in the long run, for the best.

*   *   *

Frank had hired a porter to bring his luggage in through the side arches from the cab rank and load it into the guard's van of the Glasgow-to-London sleeping-car express. With an indifference to the fate of his possessions that Ernest could never emulate he had then abandoned all interest in his trunk and cases and had strolled across the St Enoch concourse and, after acquiring a platform ticket for Ernest, had entered straight through the gate in search of his berth.

It was no night to bid farewell to anyone, let alone your eldest brother. The Glasgow sky had obligingly opened and sent down a deluge of sleety rain that, Frank predicted, would turn to snow on the moors beyond Thankerton and cause delay in the long pull up to the Beattock summit. Frank spoke like a seasoned traveller, though, in truth, he had visited the capital only a half dozen times in his life. He would not arrive in London like a homeless waif, however. In their eagerness to acquire his services the Thomas Eagan Publishing Company had agreed to provide him with furnished accommodation, an apartment, adjacent to their editorial offices in High Holborn. He would 'move in' there directly tomorrow morning, be unpacked and at his desk by ten and, he predicted, cracking the old Scottish whip before staff members knew what had hit them.

Ernest had heard all this cheerful stuff before. He had heard it fed to his mother, had known that she was not deluded by it but had gone along with the general family pretence that Frank was at long last doing the right thing.

When Ernest had told Lorna she had cried, "Oh, no. Not Frank. I *like* our Frank," as if there were others in her ken that she would willingly have seen off to London.

Ernest had made a point of telling Kirsty face to face. He had observed her reaction with particular interest. She had uttered no cry of protest, had not even appeared taken aback, had merely pursed her lips for a moment and nodded as if, somehow, she had expected it.

Kirsty had asked for details of the job, the magazine, the company for whom Frank would work, expressed intelligent interest in other words. But not one syllable of regret that Frank was leaving Glasgow had passed her lips, an omission that Ernest resented and that, for a week or two, coloured his opinion of Kirsty unfavourably.

Now Mother had done her weeping, Frank had taken his farewells and Ernest had him alone at last on the long platform that stretched away to the south, rails curving and diminishing into the sleety sky and darkness beyond the station arch.

They stood outside the sleeping car and looked right towards the locomotive making steam, and left towards the platforms.

Ernest, who had waited for this moment, could delay no longer.

He said, "Are you still hoping that she'll come?"

"Who?" Frank said.

"Kirsty Nicholson."

"No, old son, it's too late, far too late for Kirsty to be out and about."

"I told her the train time."

"Yes, I thought you would," Frank said. "But there's no point in searching the concourse, Ernest. Kirsty will not be here. There won't be a tender farewell scene."

"She *is* the reason you're leavin', though?"

Frank uttered a wry little '*huh*', and shook his head, not in denial but at his brother's naivety.

"She turned you down, didn't she?" Ernest said.

"I should never have asked her."

"What *did* you ask her?"

"God, but you're inquisitive!"

"I'm sorry."

Ernest shuffled his feet and gazed into the gloom of the station again, squinting as if he still hoped that, by some miracle, the woman Frank had fallen in love with might appear out of the smoke to redeem the situation. He gave a little start when Frank put a gloved hand on his shoulder.

"Nobody knows, Ernest. And I'm sure you won't ever tell," Frank said. "I asked her to marry me. I knew at the time that it wasn't on but I couldn't – " He shrugged. "I had to try, didn't I?"

"Perhaps if Nicholson hadn't been injured – "

"No, no," Frank said. "She's *his* wife, even if they aren't legally married. She'll *always* be Nicholson's wife. The fire and the injury had nothing to do with it. She'll never leave him. I should have been perceptive enough to realise it from the first."

"I can't understand it. You're so much better than he is."

"No," Frank told him, "you can't measure character against a moral scale."

"I can," said Ernest.

"The fact is that Kirsty didn't love me," Frank said. "How can I possibly hold that against her?"

"You're far too reasonable for your own damned good, Frank."

"Perhaps London will change me, hm? Perhaps London will toughen me up."

"I don't think I want that to happen," Ernest said. "I just wish – "

The guard's warning whistle pierced the emptiness. The soft, punchy sounds of carriage doors being slammed and a sudden voluminous blast of steam from the locomotive added a final urgency to the parting.

"You'd better get on board," said Ernest.

"Yes."

Frank stepped to the door and hoisted himself on to the wooden step that hung beneath it. Holding on with one hand, he offered the other to Ernest but Tubby would have none of that. He gave a little, sentimental shout and hugged his brother to him.

"Don't you dare burst into tears," Frank said.

"Never," Ernest said, thickly.

"Look after Mother."

"Yes."

"My love to Lorna."

"Yes."

"Unless you're coming to London, you'd better let me go."

"What? Yes."

Ernest released his brother and stood back while the door slammed, and the window rattled down.

The platform now was empty, except for the guard who with whistle and flag gave the signal to the driver that it was time to begin the journey.

As the locomotive throbbed and chugged and couplings clanked and the sleeping car carriages began to roll, Ernest glanced once more towards the platform's end, hopeful to the last that Kirsty would appear, waving, blowing kisses – anything.

"No," Frank called out. "No, Ernest."

Ernest crabbed to the right, side-stepping to keep abreast of the sleeping car as it gathered pace. He raised his hand. "Write, Frank. Don't forget to write."

"I won't. Tell Kirsty – "

"What?"

" – I won't be far away."

An iron pillar barred Ernest's progress to the platform's end. He stopped. He dug his hand into his overcoat pocket and brought out the large linen handkerchief that his mother had thoughtfully put there. He flapped it out and waved it, and watched his brother's face at the sleeping car window swiftly become invisible as the train hauled out in the grey-white night.

Ernest put the handkerchief to his nose and blew, sighed, blew again. Then he walked down the length of the platform towards the concourse and the city arches, feeling, to his surprise, less melancholy and more mature now that his brother had departed and he was finally, if unfortunately, on his own.

*   *   *

The Knowe that Sunday afternoon was as grim and uninviting as a bastille. Josephine had requested that the driver of the hired carriage wait for her and, not grudging the expense, had paid him generously in advance. She expected no warm welcome from her cousins and wanted a ready excuse to leave, the means of a quick getaway to hand whenever she had obtained what she came for.

Snow plastered the face of the Campsie Fells and the breast of the moor above Blanefield but in the hollow where The Knowe huddled trees dripped black in a landscape as scraped and napped as a mezzotint. Only the lawns held snow, wasted and wet as washed lace and too scant to catch the glimmer of gaslight that hazed the villa's drawing-room window.

Within the drawing-room green boughs smouldered in the grate and even Dolphus, seated upright in a narrow chair like the guardian of the coal scuttle, shivered from time to time in spite of the brown wool cardigan and great, tattered housecoat that were swaddled about him. Amanda, vain even in pregnancy, had chosen a day-dress that exposed her forearms, thin and pale as the snow on the lawn, each little dark hair raised by the chill. Only Johnnie looked moderately comfortable in the dank and frozen room. He was garbed like a gamekeeper in layers of thick tweed and hairy wool that made him appear not so much countrified as coarse. He smoked, defiantly, one of Dolphus's rusty cigars and had by his hand a bottle of Old Deerhound and a crystal glass from which he sipped as he padded conversationally around his cousin Josephine and sniffed for the purpose of her call.

"Where is Aunt Olive?" Josephine said. "I trust that she is well?"

"As far as we know," Johnnie answered, "she's bloomin'."

"My wife," Dolphus put in, "spent the festive season with her aged aunt in Duddingston."

"And took the girls," Johnnie said. "And hasn't returned."

"Mama will be back," said Amanda.

"Will she?" said Johnnie.

No tea had been ordered and Josephine had naturally refused Johnnie's offer of whisky.

"Mama will be here when my time comes," said Amanda.

"Perhaps, to save Mama the inconvenience we should pack you off to Duddingston too," Johnnie said. "How would you like that?"

Amanda did not reply but her cheeks turned scarlet and she held a lace handkerchief to her nose and, Josephine noticed, there was a trace of tears in her eyes, probably not for the first time, nor the last.

Johnnie Whiteside stretched his legs and removed his gaze from his wife's mute suffering. "Stop blubbin', dearest. Of course we won't send you to Duddingston. How could we possibly manage without you?" He looked at Josephine. "What do you want, Josephine?"

"I would prefer to have a word with you alone."

"Amanda," Johnnie said, "why don't you take your Daddy down to the kitchen and make sure the fowl's bein' boiled properly?"

"No."

"No?"

"No."

Heavy, weary and listless though she might be, Amanda still retained a stubborn streak. She refused point blank to leave her husband alone with his good-looking female cousin. It was as if she feared that somehow he would do to Josephine what he had done to her, imagined that Johnnie still carried an aura of irresistibility. Josephine could have informed her otherwise but sensibly held her tongue.

"Dolphus," Johnnie said, "will you favour us with your absence for a moment or two? You may take the coal scuttle with you if you wish."

The man put up no defence and ignored the jibe completely. Hugging the housecoat about him, he rose and shuffled out of the drawing-room without a word, closing the door quietly behind him.

"Now, Josephine, the purpose of your visit?" Johnnie said.

"I require Greta Taylor's address."

"Do you, indeed! Why?"

"To pass on to Gordon."

"Did he press you to come here?" Johnnie asked.

"No. I came quite of my own volition."

"Why?"

Josephine did not hesitate. Archness had never been in her character. She said, "Because I must know where I stand with Gordon, and I never will while this woman is – what? –

347

unaccounted for."

"What a curious way of puttin' it," Johnnie said.

He stroked his hand across his hair then smelled his palm as if, like Gordon, he feared that he carried the stench of brew-wash about with him.

"Will you give it to me, please?" Josephine said.

Johnnie smiled, slyly. "What will I get in return?"

Amanda cried out, "Stop it. Stop it. Give her the woman's address. I know you have it."

For an instant Johnnie was taken aback by his wife's shrill vehemence. He shifted position uncomfortably and took a couple of puffs on the rusty cigar before tossing it into the fireplace. Even Johnnie Whiteside, Josephine realised, had been dragged down by The Knowe's drabness. Amanda's shrewishness hinted at things to come, at who might eventually gain the upper hand when there were children, nannies and inheritances to arm her against his cruel indifference.

Josephine said, "Do you have it, Johnnie?"

"I think I might be able to recall it, if I really try," Johnnie said, his casual insolence thinned by Amanda's ire, his arrogance now just sham. "How did you find out that I was in possession of such information?"

"The letter that came to the warehouse," Josephine said.

"Ah. Of course!"

"Give her what she wants, John," Amanda snapped.

"For little Gordon's sake, hm?"

"For *her* sake," Amanda said.

"Oh, my, my!" said Johnnie. "You are quite a little viper today, Amanda, aren't you?"

"She was your lover too, wasn't she?" Amanda said, accusingly. "It might have been your child that died."

"Don't be ridiculous!" Johnnie said, angrily. "Greta Taylor was nothin' but a street tart who did what she did for money, strictly for money. My lover? God!"

Amanda, leaning forwards, shouted, "Give Gordon her address."

Johnnie slapped his hands to his tweed-clad thighs and leapt to his feet. He pointed a forefinger at Josephine. "See the trouble you've caused. I just hope you know what you're doing, girl. I warn you, your sweetheart's just liable to choose Greta over you. He's been infatuated with her ever since he *slept* with her. She's exactly his type, don't you realise, out of the same damned gutter."

It was Amanda's turn to fling herself, unsteadily, to her feet. Her fingers balled into fists. She raised them, shook them and cried childishly, "Give it to her. Give her what she wants."

Johnnie sighed loudly and tried to force his old, conceited smile. But it was gone. All that remained of it was a bitter grimace that showed how thoroughly he had been defeated by the circumstances he had created for himself. Sighing again, he said, "Oh, very well then, very well. To keep you all happy I'll do as you ask." He turned, opened a drawer in a table, took out a tablet of paper and a pencil. Bent over, he scribbled for a moment, tore the top leaf from the tablet, turned again and thrust it towards Josephine. "There!"

Josephine stood up, smoothed her dress, and took the paper slip from his fingers. "Why did Greta Taylor write to you, Johnnie – you, of all people?" she asked.

"She needed me to do something for her," Johnnie said.

"You?"

"Ironical, isn't it? In the end, I was the only one she felt she could trust."

"To do what?" Josephine enquired, softly.

"She insisted on payin' for the child's headstone," Johnnie Whiteside said. "Quite adamant about it. I saw to it that the money she sent me by instalments was spent to that end."

"But," said Amanda, "Uncle Albert paid for the headstone."

Johnnie shrugged, said nothing.

"What happened to the money?" Amanda demanded.

Johnnie shrugged again, sheepishly this time.

"You *pig!*" the girl shrieked. "You kept it, didn't you? You kept the money for yourself. You greedy, selfish, disgustin' *pig* ."

They were still shouting at one another when, seconds later, Josephine let herself out of the front door of The Knowe and climbed into the waiting carriage. It was not until she was half-way to Glasgow, however, that she realised that, for all her vehemence, Amanda had not thought fit to insist that Greta Taylor's payments be returned.

*   *   *

Memory was the queerest thing. It played the most shocking, underhand tricks and had, of itself, no conscience. When Kirsty saw Jess Walker at the door of her house in the close of No. 154, she was transported back to that sad afternoon when she'd returned from Walbrook Street, from loving and parting – the last time she'd seen David. Since then life had flowed on, had taken David from her. Death had put him where he was safe and secure forever. She did not think of him often these days. It was half a year since last she'd removed Nessie Frew's album of photographs of China from its hiding place and slipped from the pages the letters that David had written to her. Nothing now, really, but scraps of the past.

The sight of Jess Walker waiting at the door with Bobby on one side of her and her son Georgie on the other was totally unexpected, however, and brought not just a rush of panic but a sudden revival of guilt and loss.

"What is it, Jess, what's wrong, what's happened?"

The woman's severity eased. "Nothing, nothing at all." She placated Kirsty in a charitable manner, setting aside their differences, for a while at least.

"Mammy," Bobby said, as if to put Kirsty out of her misery, "Daddy's gone tae see a friend."

"What friend?"

"Craig asked me to look after the wee one," Jess explained. "He said you'd be home early."

"Yes, Ernest – Mr Tubbs – is in the shop today," Kirsty said. "Did Craig tell you where he was goin'?"

"Tae see a friend," Bobby insisted.

Jess Walker shook her head. "Craig didn't look well, Kirsty. He was all muffled up. Does he feel the cold badly?"

"No, he – yes, he feels the cold."

Kirsty glanced out into the street as if she expected Craig to come striding in, dour and handsome and whole in his uniform. Bobby broke that silly spell, that drifting sense of disorientation. He crabbed towards her and pressed the calipered leg against her, murmuring, "Georgie willn't play wi' me."

"Will so," said Georgie, gruffly. "Cannie play wi' you when you cannie run, but."

Georgie was old enough now to feel the sting of his mother's palm against his ear, the blow drawn since this was warning, not punishment. "You, get inside," Jess Walker said, and, with her elbow, projected Georgie back into the narrow hallway behind her. The boy was not reluctant to go. He was too old now, too tough to be a companion to the crippled child upstairs, was embarrassed by Bobby's eagerness for friendship.

"Did Craig say who he was meetin', who this friend might be?" Kirsty asked.

"No. He just said he wouldn't be long," Jess Walker answered and again remarked, "He didn't look well to me, Kirsty."

"Sammy." Bobby pressed his face into Kirsty's coat. "Daddy said since it was a nice day he'd go an' see Sammy."

"Oh!" Jess Walker said. "So he's gone to Wolfe Road. I expect he'll be wantin' a look at the new headstone. He was always fond o' the daftie."

"Wouldn't take me," said Bobby.

Though she now knew where Craig had gone and why he had braved the stares of neighbours and passers-by, Kirsty was none-theless disturbed by the morbidity of his mission and, perhaps, by the mood that had driven him out into the raw, cold after-noon. She detached Bobby from her side and, stooping, held him by the shoulders. He was pouting even before she told him what she wanted of him, as if he'd guessed what was coming.

"Will you stay with Mrs Walker for another wee while?" Kirsty glanced up at the sergeant's wife who, without smiling, gave a nod of sanction. "I'm goin' to find Daddy, an' then we'll come home an' make the tea."

"Daddy not gone t' the hospital?"

"No, no, son." Kirsty eased him towards Jess Walker who offered her big, motherly hand and sensibly waited until Bobby took it before she drew him on to the doormat.

"Georgie play wi' me?"

"Oh, aye, Bobby," said Jess Walker in a tone that must have made Georgie quail. "He'll play with you – or I'll know the reason why."

A few minutes later Kirsty was out again in Canada Road, heading not towards Gascoigne Street but west towards King-dom Road and the inhospitable territory beyond the tenements where the burgh's new graveyard was situated.

Already the afternoon was gathering towards dusk. After days of rain, dry weather was welcome and the gloom of the suburb was cheered by lighted windows as folk steered through the streets, well wrapped against the cold but at least dry-shod. Kirsty had sensed a similar forenoon bustle in Glasgow's St Vincent Street, and as she'd returned to Gascoigne Street to make sure that Tubby had kept his promise to help out in the shop.

Ernest's recent coolness towards her had been understandable. Though she had not actively encouraged Frank to fall in love with her, there had been times when she had needed him, had used him, she supposed. Guilt in her stemmed from the fact that she had driven him out of Glasgow too. Something in her prevented her finding a love that she could hold on to. Stubborn pride was her failing as much as it was Craig's even if it made itself apparent in ways less obvious, less male and austere.

Kirsty had never been to Wolfe Road before. She had no inclination to go there now. Ahead of her, she could see wrought-iron railings, leafless saplings, monumental stone gates and, extending in a long strip into the dusk, an avenue of tablets and memorial stones, no friendly clutter here, only emptiness, and a smoky sky beyond.

Craig wore an old donkey jacket, one of the first items he'd bought in Glasgow. He'd furled the balaclava over his ears and had unwound his scarf. He was leaning against the sandstone post at the cemetery's padlocked gates, doing nothing, except smoking. The cigarette was cupped furtively in his palm – copper's habit – and when he drew on the tobacco the coal made a tiny hot glow in the gloaming.

He did not seem in the least surprised to see Kirsty. He did not move to greet her but waited for her to come to him.

"Did you find it?" Kirsty asked.

"Aye."

"Is it nice?"

"Aye, it's nice. It has an angel on it. Can you imagine – an angel for Sammy Reynolds, an angel with its – its wings folded." Craig lifted his hand to his mouth and sucked on the cigarette. "An' his name, just – just his name, engraved on granite."

She put an arm out and waited and, after a pause, he pushed himself away from the post, dropped the cigarette, and took her hand in his.

"Aw, but I'm tired, Kirsty," he admitted. "I'm so damned

tired."

"It's been a long walk for you. Are you sore?"

"Uh-huh!"

"Come on, we'll go back now. I'll see Sammy's stone another day." Kirsty held him as close as she dared.

They walked, without speaking, away from the cemetery, out of the end of the Wolfe Road and towards the mouth of the lane in the wall of tenements. Greenfield seemed distant, though the sounds of its labours hung in the calm, wintry air, mingled with the growl of machinery from Glasgow and the Govan shore. Craig moved closer, adjusted her arm so that it lay across the top of the strapping that bound his tender ribs. He put his other arm about her shoulders and tickled the soft springs of hair on the nape of her neck.

"Did Bobby tell you?"

"'Course he did," Kirsty said. "He was cross at bein' left behind."

"I didn't want to bring him," Craig said. "It's no place for a wee chap. Anyway, I've seen it an' I won't come again."

He steered Kirsty away from the area of broken cobbles that led to the lane, and veered towards the river's oily lights. Kirsty did not ask where he was taking her for she thought that she knew.

It was not quite the same vantage that Craig and she had discovered one Sunday afternoon almost five years ago but a similar platform of sand and ash that protruded out over the Clyde. Tonight Craig did not grip the black iron railings as he had done then, nor did he kiss her and rub his body against hers in an amorous byplay that had led them swiftly home and swiftly to bed. He had made love to her often since that sunny afternoon but she had never forgotten her first experience as a wife. To her surprise, Craig remembered too. He did not have to explain the whim that had brought him here on a dark, cold, working-day evening.

Across the water arc-lamps lit the lading docks and wharves, the ribs of ships and warehouse walls, travelling cranes and booms and jibs. She leaned against him with the water at her feet, tenements ranked behind, and felt within her a shift in the tide and waited, as it were, for the current to strengthen.

"Look," Craig said.

The tugs came past, one, two, three in a line. Wash from their bows was proud and crested, funnels set back, long brown billows of smoke blowing low across the water. Kirsty watched the little boats pass, slipping away out of the city as if nightfall had released them and sent them off with a nudge towards the estuary and the open sea.

Craig sighed. "Ach!"

"What is it, dear?"

"Look at us," Craig said. "I'm marked, an' Bobby's marked. It's all gone wrong, Kirsty. Sometimes I reckon we're marked by all the promises I never managed to keep."

"But when you made those promises they were meant, Craig, weren't they?"

"Aye," he said. "They were meant."

She heard the wavelets slap against the stone-faced embankment below, and tasted the tugboats' dry smoke.

She said, "If I made promises to you, would you believe that they were meant to be kept?"

"I suppose I would."

"What if I made them come true?"

"What promises?"

"You'll see."

"What promises? Tell me."

"It's gettin' cold," Kirsty said. "I think we should be gettin' back."

He pressed his arm more closely about her and hugged her. When he grinned new skin, wrinkled against old, ravelled his cheek, an expression somehow impudent, as if injury had revealed a mischievousness that had been hidden before.

"What promises, woman? Tell me," Craig said. "What the hell are you up to now?"

"All in good time, Craig Nicholson," Kirsty told him and, wrapping her arm about his waist, walked back with him towards the Greenfield, paired at last like ponies in a game.

*   *   *

Gordon found it difficult to concentrate. Upon his desk he had accumulated four bulging files stuffed with records of invoiced stock that Johnnie Whiteside had never got around to balancing against sales; he had too a pile of catalogues from manufacturers that Breezy, by letter and by telephone, had stirred up again. The Kaffé Kanne, Whiteside's only legacy, bubbled on the gas ring and the ashtray, even by noon, was heaped with stubs of Gold Flake cigarettes and burnt match-ends.

Collar unfastened, pencil in mouth, Gordon did his best to bear down on the work on hand. All he could think of, however, was Josephine – missing Josephine, who had gone he knew not where and who had left no message where she might be found or when she might return.

She had been missing since Sunday, three days. He had called each evening at her flat in Park Gardens, had on each occasion found the door locked and the windows unlighted. None of her friends at the Temperance office had seen her. She had failed to show up at the monthly meeting in the Glassford Street halls on Monday night. Gordon was reluctant to barge into her place of work but, so nagging had his anxiety – and his desire – become, that he'd decided to take that drastic step tomorrow.

Every time the office door opened, Gordon glanced up from his notations with an air of expectancy. Every time he saw only old Willie or young Billy there, and felt his concern increase.

It was about noon when the door flew open and the youngest member of the warehouse staff, a red-haired lad of fourteen, stuck his head in and announced, "Got a letter here, Mr Nicholson. Special delivery."

Gordon stretched across the littered desk and snapped his fingers. "Give it here."

Josephine's handwriting, bobbing vowels and tall tees, an unfamiliar Ayrshire postmark; he ripped open the envelope with a brass paperknife and tugged out the letter. Address embossed in burgundy, ink pea-green; he scanned the communication hastily and then, still reading, sank back into his wooden chair.

Walter, Jo's father, had not been in the best of health. She had returned to the family home to be with him. She might be gone from Glasgow for some little time. Meanwhile, if Gordon was interested, she had stumbled upon the whereabouts of the girl, Greta Taylor, about whose welfare he seemed rather concerned. She hoped he might find some use for the information.

She signed herself 'Affectionately, Josephine'.

Gordon read the letter again, murmured, "Oh, Josephine,

Josephine! Dear God, what have you done?" then scrambled to his feet, grabbed his scarf, overcoat and hat and, stuffing the letter into his pocket, set out for Edinburgh at once.

*　　*　　*

None of the servants would go near the instrument that hung, black and threatening, on the wall in the hallway of the Adair mansion on Great Western Terrace. The electrical bell might ring all day long and obtain no response from kitchen quarters except frowns, pursed lips and hands clapped to ears. Breezy had remonstrated with his domestics and had conducted classes in the operation of the device but all to no effect. Superstition, fear of disembodied voices, overcame obedience. The women remained in awe of the telephone.

Breezy could hardly blame them. Though he'd die before he'd admit it, the dashed thing gave him the shivers too. Being a man of the world, however, he forced himself to put out an occasional call to his broker and to accept the occasional call in return.

When the telephone rang that morning, filling the house with its persistent trill, Breezy had hurried, grumbling, from ten o'clock breakfast, had plucked the earpiece from its bracket and, with more annoyance than awe, had snapped, "Yes, Mr Rogers, what is it now?"

It hadn't been Mr Rogers, however. For a good ten seconds Breezy had been thoroughly disconcerted to hear Kirsty Nicholson's voice on the wire.

"Kirsty?" he'd asked. "Is that our Kirsty?"

Yes, it was indeed Kirsty. She was telephoning from the newly-installed public instrument in Glasgow's central post office building to enquire whether it might be convenient to invite herself to tea that same afternoon.

Of course it would be convenient. He would see to it that it was convenient. Would she be coming alone, or accompanied by her husband?

Alone.

"It's Craig," Madge had said. "It can't be good news. She'd never have used that machine for good news. Craig must have had a relapse."

"Kirsty didn't say anythin' of the sort."

"She wouldn't, would she? Not on that thing." Madge had gone ranting on, "I wouldn't use one o' those things unless it was desperate. Perhaps it's Bobby. Perhaps he's been taken ill."

"Kirsty's comin' for tea, that's all."

"Bad news, mark my words," Madge had said and then, voice deepening with perplexity, "What'll I wear? What will I wear?"

In the end, after half a day of indecision, Madge had stuffed herself into one of the new 'S' corsets and a suitably sombre tea gown in black satin and chiffon. Thrust out fore and aft like a mourning kangaroo she greeted Kirsty in the upstairs lounge. By contrast Kirsty looked slim and lithe in a small-waisted dress with a close fitting skirt and trained back, and a hat with a feather and bow that was just a shade too springlike for the cold February afternoon.

Breezy didn't notice the flaw in fashion. He was again smitten by the thought that his stepdaughter-in-law was as pretty a girl as he had ever seen and that if he'd been twenty years younger – no, thirty – he would have been tempted to sweep her up and away, like a proper scallywag.

Tea was formal and elaborate; brown bread and white, freshly-baked scones, great creamy meringues and, naturally, the full silver service. It was taken at a table before the blazing fire and, though it was not yet dark, Madge had had the curtains drawn.

Kirsty seemed a little on edge, just toyed with a slice of bread and butter, sipped tea from her china cup, and went through the first half-hour of the visit politely but vaguely. She answered all Madge's queries about Craig's health, Bobby's welfare, even about the shop. No disasters were revealed or even hinted at, mainly because Madge hadn't grasped the implications of her son's injuries and failed to ask quite the right questions.

To avoid distractions Kirsty waited until tea had been consumed, the table cleared and removed to its place by the window, before she lifted her suede-leather purse and, unbuttoning it, took out a large brown envelope which she placed in Breezy's bewildered hands.

"What's this?" Breezy said.

"It's a banker's draft," Kirsty said.

"Why are you givin' *me* a banker's draft?" Breezy said. "If you require goods for stock, then Gordon's – "

"Not goods," Kirsty said. "Property."

"The shop? I don't own the – "

"No, but if I've heard right, you *do* own the farm at Old Garscadden?" Kirsty said.

"Old Garscadden?" Madge swayed.

Breezy did not open the envelope. He held it, like a guddled trout, across both palms and stared at it. There was nothing upon it to hold his attention except his name printed in black ink. For a moment he frowned, then an eyebrow rose, and he laughed.

"He lost the job," Breezy said. "Of course he did. The burgh wouldn't keep him on. That's what all the sulkin's been about. Craig's been given the damned sack by the Burgh Police Committee. Am I not right, lass?"

"That's it," said Kirsty. "Craig's contract of employment will terminate on March thirty-first."

"How badly is he disfigured?" said Breezy.

"Badly enough to make him shy of meetin' people," Kirsty said.

"And the rest of him?"

"In sound workin' order," Kirsty said.

"Albert, will you please tell me what's goin' on?" Madge said, testily. "I don't appreciate bein' treated like a piece of wall-paper."

"Craig, dearest," Breezy said, "is out of work and," he glanced enquiringly at Kirsty, "out of a house too?"

The girl nodded.

"That's – that's – a crime!" Madge exclaimed. "How can they do such a thing to a hero? Breezy, you'll talk to Mr Organ about this, first thing tomorrow."

"No, Madge, I will not," Breezy told her in a tone that brooked no argument. "It's not Organ's decision. It's the members of the Police Committee who have made up their mind."

"They said it's the damage to his eye that's made Craig unfit for duty but I think it's his poor, burned face," Kirsty said.

"Of course it is," Breezy agreed. "Can you blame them for not wantin' a policeman to show his scars? Wouldn't look right, would it?"

"Albert, how can you say that?"

Breezy ignored his wife's protesting question and put one of

358

his own to Kirsty. "Pension?"

"Aye, ten shillings a week."

"Not bad," said Breezy. "God, when I was Craig's age I could have lived like a lord on ten bob a week. But that wasn't yesterday. Still, it's better than nothing. The burgh isn't obliged to offer any form of compensation, you know."

"It isn't the money," Kirsty said. "I can support us all on what the shop brings in. But that won't do for Craig."

"I'm sure it won't," Breezy said. "Does he know what you have in mind – offerin' for a farm, I mean?"

"No, I haven't told him yet," Kirsty said.

"Goin' back to farmin'," Madge said, with a little wail. "After all I did to drag him out of it."

Neither Breezy nor Kirsty saw fit to challenge the accuracy of Madge's self-centred statement.

"How did you find out that I was just about to put Old Garscadden on the market?" Breezy asked. "I've even drafted the advertisement."

"Lorna told me," Kirsty said. "She also told me what the price would be. I calculated ten percent as a holding offer, the sum of the banker's draft exactly."

"What if Craig doesn't want to become a dairy farmer?" Breezy said.

"Then I'll think of somethin' else," said Kirsty. "If Craig agrees, though, will you sell me the farmhouse and the land at the current askin' price?"

Breezy stroked his moustache with a corner of the envelope and looked sly. "Well – I'll have to think about it."

"Al-*bert!*"

"Right, I've thought about it," said Breezy. "Once it's been viewed and approved, Old Garscadden is yours if you want it, Kirsty."

"Will ten percent be enough?"

"Ten percent is generous," said Breezy. "Who's your agent in the matter?"

"Mr Marlowe."

"Thought it might be." Breezy put the envelope, unopened, into his vest pocket and buttoned his jacket again.

Madge said, "Old Garscadden's a midden of a place. It's been run to rack an' ruin. The herd's worn thin an' probably diseased.

It'll cost you a pretty penny to nourish the pastures an' restock before you can find regular customers for the milk." •

"It's not money that'll be needed," Kirsty said. "It's time an' effort."

"I don't know what Craig'll have to say about all this," Madge said, "when you eventually see fit to tell him."

All three were now on their feet, grouped on the Indian rug that fronted the hearth. Madge still wore a peevish expression but her tone had softened a little, mollified by the fact that somebody had at last brought her elder son to heel, even if that 'somebody' just happened to be his wife. She watched Albert offer his hand to Kirsty Barnes and saw the young woman take it as if it were the most natural thing in the world for an orphan brat to buy property from a gentleman.

"When will you make your first inspection?" Breezy asked.

"Sunday, if the weather's dry."

"With Craig?"

"All three of us," said Kirsty.

"I hope you're not disappointed," Breezy said.

"Not this time," said Kirsty.

*   *   *

In the weekday half-dark Edinburgh was strange and sinister to anyone unfamiliar with its closes and wynds. The old town in particular, towering like cliffs above the gardens and railway station, seemed redolent not so much of history as bloodshed and violence. The Royal Mile, strung between Palace and Castle, had a crooked, narrow oppressiveness that a shoal of lantern-lit pubs did nothing to dispel. The Janus face of the splendid capital did not appeal to Gordon one little bit. Wreaths of east-coast haar clung dankly to the housetops and slunk up from the gutters, and Gordon shivered as he navigated a route, by fits and starts, to the steep, twisting street known to all and sundry as the West Bow.

Here, in the shadow of the Castlehill, a spit from national colleges, law courts and the great cathedral of St Giles, he found at last the entrance to Monks' Close and, at its nether end, the square of stumpy tenements that formed the slum where, according to Josephine's letter, Greta Taylor could be found.

Gordon was seriously disorientated. A couple of hours ago he had been at his desk in friendly old Partick, thinking only of Josephine. Now here he was in the capital, with smoke in his lungs and the inimitable reek of brewers' industry in his nostrils and the walls of buildings, seeping stench, hemming him in. There was an impression of life all round. He could hear it but not see it. Only skulking cats, or rats perhaps, brought movement to the scene. Shadows in the stairwells, shadows against the faint, phosphorescent sheen of windows. Childish cries, wailings and snarling shouts, the splash of ancient drainage. He had once supposed that Benedict Street was close to the barrel-bottom. How little he had known. Monks' Close was ten times worse, a place as haunted and frightening as a sepulchre.

It was not just the physical lineaments of the place that frightened Gordon but the realisation that, if his information was correct, he would find Greta here, would know if he had sustained nothing more substantial than an illusion in his heart or if reason and romance, guilt and desire, were really the stuff out of which love fashions itself. Thinking of Greta, he felt stronger. He removed his hands from his overcoat pockets, squared his shoulders and picked his way over garbage and mud towards the arched doorway that gave access to a spiral staircase.

One light, a gas-flare, burned high on the wall of the second landing. The stair's only water closet had a broken door and a cracked pedestal, slimy puddles about it. One bent, iron tap provided water. On each of the landings were two doors, varnish long peeled away, woodwork pitted. Gordon chose the middle landing, the door to the left, rapped upon it.

The door opened a quarter of an inch. He looked down into an urchin's face, into one visible eye. He could not decide whether the child was girl or boy; the ragged smock gave nothing away.

"I'm looking for Greta Taylor. Do you know where she lives?"

He might have been speaking a foreign language for all the answer he got. The door closed instantly and, within, he heard a slap and a shriek and a male voice barking furiously as if the androgynous child had been at fault for his, Gordon's, intrusion.

Hastily he moved on, upward.

The topmost landing was unlighted. It had a lighter feeling to it. Broken skylights gave glimpses of the haar, and an iron railing protruded outward over the curved stairwell. Gordon hesitated. He could smell the stench of fish, hear a scrabbling sound from behind the door to his right. He dug out his match-box and cautiously struck a match.

Relief and apprehension gripped him. The door was just as scarred as the neighbouring door but had upon it a plain, clean postcard, stuck in with a thumbtack. Printed upon the card was a single word – *Taylor*.

Tentatively, Gordon knocked.

For a full minute there was no reply, no tell-tale sound from the other side of the door. He knocked again, gently, and he heard a voice he hardly recognised ask who was there. He gave no answer but rapped with a shade more insistence.

The door opened a little and he saw again a pale cheekbone, and an eye.

"Greta?" he said. "It's me."

She gave a little cry. She tried to close the door upon him but he would have none of it. He put out an arm, a foot, blocked the door and, finding no resistance now, pushed it open and entered.

There was no hallway. The room was a single apartment with a sloping ceiling inset with one canvas-covered window; a truckle bed in the corner, a table, two wooden chairs, a tiny fireplace of black iron upon which, apparently, all her cooking was done; jug and basin, kettle, clothes-rack, two big wicker baskets filled with dress fabrics. From a rope strung between two nails was suspended a line of garments whose alteration and repair, Gordon guessed, gave Greta employment and a meagre income. The bedsheets, turned down, were clean, floorboards scrubbed and the room had a fresh, laundered smell of soap and the pressing iron that reminded him of the house in Benedict Street.

Greta wore a patched shift, a shawl about her shoulders, legs and feet bare. She had obviously been in bed. When he looked again, by the flicker of an oil lamp, he saw that the garment she had been stitching had been laid neatly across the blanket, threads and needles, braid and lace placed to hand. He saw too, on the shelf by the bedhead a green bottle, mug and spoon and, even before she spoke, he blurted out, "God, you've been ill."

"What of it?" Greta said.

The phrase was defiant but shock and illness had strained her and her voice was husky and weak. She had lost much weight, her sturdy figure reduced almost to skin and bone. Her dark eyes, because of it, had a hugeness that suggested not just astonishment but a stunned sort of innocence.

"It's freezin' in here," Gordon said. "Get back into bed."

"Is that what you came for?"

"For God's sake, Greta. Get into bed."

"How did you know where to find me?"

"I'm not answerin' any damned questions until you're tucked up under the blankets. Jeeze, you could catch your death just standin' here."

"I've not died so far."

"No," Gordon said. "By the look o' you, though, you're halfway there. Into that bed, Greta, this instant."

She hesitated. She was weaker than she would ever admit. Gordon's sudden appearance here in Monks' Close had drained the last of her resistance. She turned from him and, gathering the shawl about her and hugging it to her breasts, clambered into bed and, wheezing, sat back against the bolster.

"Pull up the blanket."

"Who're you to give me orders?" Greta said.

"Pull up the damned blanket, an' stop arguin'."

Furiously she snatched the blanket's corner and switched it over her thighs and stomach, folded her arms and sat back.

"Satisfied?" she demanded, her voice still too weak to carry real hostility.

"Why's the fire not lit?"

"Because I've no coal."

"Can't you afford coal?"

"None o' your business."

"Can't you carry it upstairs, is that the trouble?" Gordon said and, not waiting for an answer, rattled on. "How long have you been like this, Greta? Ill, I mean?"

"Who says I'm ill?"

"Jeeze!"

"It's only a cold I can't shake off," she said. "It'll go away when the summer comes in."

"Have you seen a doctor?"

"I've a bottle. There," Greta said. "Anyway, my health has nothin' to do wi' you, Gordon. If it was curiosity brought you here, I hope it's been satisfied, an' you'll go away again. Right now."

"Not a chance," said Gordon.

Whatever romantic notions of a generous and tearful meeting he had nurtured had vanished completely. He was flummoxed by her debility, disturbed by her appearance. He might have expected an abrasive greeting, however, and when he thought of it, would perhaps have been disappointed if she had lost all her self-assertion. He moved to the bed and seated himself upon it, reached for her hand.

Tensing, she tucked it further under her arm.

"Whiteside told me," Gordon said. "He gave me this address. I was hopin' you hadn't moved on."

"Moved on to what?"

"Bet you can't guess who our old pal Johnnie married?"

"Married? Johnnie's married?" She was unable to disguise her interest in this piece of news.

"Hitched to Amanda, he is."

"Amanda? Your fiancée?"

"Johnnie's wife now."

"How did that happen?" Greta asked.

"It did, that's all," Gordon said. "He was so guilty about it that he gave up your address. Not to me, actually, but a friend of mine."

"The blonde, the tall woman?" Greta said.

"What do you know about her?"

Greta shrugged. "I saw you, a while ago, near St Giles."

"Hoh!" said Gordon. "An' you ran away an' hid? Oh, Greta, why did you do that?"

"Look at me," she said, without self-pity. "You wouldn't have thanked me for steppin' out o' the gutter when you were arm-in-arm with your sweetheart, an' her such a fine lady."

"She isn't my sweetheart," Gordon lied. "She's just a friend, a very good friend."

"Do you sleep with her?"

"Yes, of course I do."

"In that case why have you come here?" Greta said. "So you can have us both?"

"She sent me here. Josephine, the blonde woman, sent me to find you."

"What for?"

"To choose."

"God, she must be mad t' suppose you'd choose – "

"I'm here, aren't I?" Gordon interrupted.

He put out his hand and gripped her elbow. After a moment, she slackened her upright, indrawn pose, allowed him to find and hold her hand in his. He leaned forward and made to kiss her, but she balked at that, turned her face away.

"Don't," she said.

He touched her hair, let his fingers linger on her cheek, then he rose with a sigh and stood by her, hands thrust into his overcoat pockets. He said nothing for a while, waited quite deliberately until she found within herself one tiny vestige of hope, so faint as to be beyond foolishness. He waited until she glanced up at him and then he spoke.

"I'm manager of Adair's warehouse, Greta. I've a bit of money put by – not much, but not bad. It isn't Josephine I want, and she's clever enough to know it. That's why she sent me here, why she helped me track you down."

"Gordon," Greta murmured. "Don't."

"You know what's comin', don't you?"

"Please, no. It's not right. After all I've done. Men – Johnnie – your brother . . . " She put a hand to her face, not to hide shame but tears. "You know what I am."

"I know what you used to be," Gordon said. "But I know why too. Remember that, Greta. I know why."

"She was all I had."

"No," Gordon said. "Jen was all you thought you had. You had me too, only neither of us really knew it."

She began to cry, quite loudly. He had heard her cry only once before, on the night that Jen died. She had cried in his arms and he should have held on to her then, not let her go until the pain had eased, the wounds had begun to heal. He had slipped into betrayal then, had been drawn into it by his naive association not with Breezy but with the other Adairs. He had tried to ignore the niggling guilt and, if he had not been betrayed in turn, might never have understood what it was that troubled him and clouded his love for Greta.

He didn't touch her, didn't comfort her.

He let her cry, rocking, alone in the narrow bed.

For a second he thought of Josephine, her fine, wholesome

blondeness, her laughter, her appetite, and her independent spirit. When had Josephine recognised that he was one of life's natural protectors, realised that they were too akin ever to be comfortable as man and wife? He felt a generous gratitude towards Josephine and, perhaps in emulation of what she had taught him, he let Greta find her voice again.

She wiped at her tears with a corner of the sheet, and said, "I can't be the same again. I never will. I can't be your mistress, Gordon."

"Is that what you think I'm here for?" Gordon said. "I'm not lookin' for a mistress. I'm lookin' for a wife."

"I can't, Gordon, I can't go back to Glasgow."

"Fine," he said. "I'll come here to Edinburgh."

"But your job?"

"T' hell with that. If you haven't got the courage to square up to the past then I'll square up to the future – right here. I'll even move into Monks' Close, if you like. Start by sellin' rat traps door-to-door."

"Don't be bloody daft," said Greta.

"Come with me then. Come back with me to Glasgow."

"What'll they say, what'll they all say?" Greta protested. "We'll be shunned."

"By whom? Not by Breezy, not by Kirsty, not by Lorna. An' the rest don't matter a tuppenny damn. I'm not afraid o' anyone's opinion now."

"But the stuff, the clothes. I can't just leave."

"Who gives out the work?"

"His name's Rice."

"How much does he pay you?"

"Three or four pence a garment."

"Leave it, leave it all. We'll lock the door, post him the key. An' if he wants to have the law on you, he'll have to find you first," Gordon said.

"You've changed," Greta said.

"I hope so," Gordon said. "By the way, there's a train at eight o'clock. We could catch it if we're nippy."

She hesitated and then folded back the blanket and swung her feet to the floor.

"I'll get dressed then," she said. "Be a gentleman an' don't look."

A Little Epilogue

"As if I would," said Gordon.

* * *

The day was beautifully hard and cold. In the shadow of the hedgerows and along the back of the ramshackle byre frost lingered far into the afternoon, bristling and glittering on weeds and withered grasses and the fronds of old bronze bracken. The sky downriver and north across the Kilpatrick hills was clear as isinglass and did not take on the tint of rose until some time after three when the rays of the westering sun found the haze of chimney smoke that lay over the valley of the Clyde and deepened the blue-pearl hue of dusk on the fields that fenced the farm. In that light Old Garscadden seemed marginally less ragged and run down. Instead it assumed an indomitable and ancient patience, like the tiny Roman fort which had been dug from a knoll on its northern boundary and whose stones had been used to shore and shape the grasslands' dry-stone dykes.

The track was bone-hard, the ditches glazed with ice and the Nicholsons walked dry-shod through Garscadden's yards, around its grazings and into the farm house that quietly waited to be occupied again.

Breezy had seen to it that the steading had been cleaned, decayed furniture removed for burning. He had worked through the offices of the Duke's estate agent who had appointed a retired cowman to tend the beasts that remained on Old Garscadden's acres. Byre, dairy and milking parlour held the strong, shaggy odour of cows and the pungency of the disinfectant which was added to sluicing water, smells that reminded both Kirsty and Craig not of Hawkhead or Dalnavert but of Bankhead Mains.

It had been in Kirsty's mind to invite Gordon and Greta to accompany them on the outing. But Greta was unsettled yet, not quite at ease as a guest in the mansion on Great Western Terrace, not quite accepted by Madge. Besides, Kirsty was wary enough of the effect of change on Craig and did not want him to feel that the presence of the woman who had once been his mistress was intended as a threat. Craig was not at all reluctant to visit Old Garscadden. He had raised an eyebrow when Kirsty had suggested to him the possibility that a farm not far from Glasgow might provide them with a roof and an income.

He'd said, "I thought you were a shopkeeper, born an' bred?"

Kirsty had shaken her head. "Not born, an' certainly not bred. I was a farm lassie when you took me away, Craig, an' it's still in the blood."

"Aye, with mud an' muck an' cold early mornin's." He'd spoken without bitterness or heat, his head cocked as he'd regarded her, blinking the damaged eye. "Do y' really want to go out an' look at this place?"

"Yes."

"Well, it can do no harm, I suppose," Craig had said.

She'd realised that she must not lead him too eagerly, too quickly, must make it seem as if the decision were his, even if the idea had been hers at first.

In addition to Breezy and Mr Marlowe, however, she'd had words with Lorna and Ernest, for, like it or not, they would inherit the management of G. A. Nicholson's Emporium, though she, Kirsty, would keep a financial stake in the enterprise.

"Huh!" Lorna had said. "Going back, retracin' your steps; is that such a good idea, Kirsty?"

And Ernest had said, wistfully, "Perhaps it's the best thing to do when things go wrong and plans don't work out."

Gordon was too taken up with Greta to pass much of an opinion on anything. He had spoken at length with his stepfather about his own future and Greta's and explained that he did not intend to let the grass grow under his feet now that he had responsibility. In response to Kirsty's news about the farm, Gordon had merely grinned, "You'd never catch me goin' back into the byre of my own free will. But him, my dear old brother, he was always on the odd side. Aye, I think it might suit him just fine."

Kirsty had planned the outing with care. They had travelled by train to Milngavie where she'd had a trap waiting, the vehicle hired without driver for the afternoon. Craig had climbed up on to the board and clicked the reins and the sturdy little pony had gone off at a fair lick along the road, much to Bobby's delight.

The boy had sensed adventure, the best kind of adventure, shared only with his mother and his father, just the three of them, on a bright, sunny day setting off for a new place, with new things to see and to do.

"Burds?"

"Rooks," Craig had said. "See their nests."

"Cows?"

"No, son, they're not lady cows, they're gentlemen bullocks."

Bobby had thought that explanation highly hilarious and even Craig had smiled at his son's laughter, though he was the cause of it. Kirsty had sat at the back of the trap, an arm about Bobby's waist and had watched Craig's shoulders straighten as villas and cottages dropped behind them and the road ran between thorn hedges and pastures at last.

It had been years since Kirsty had seen Craig so brisk and alert. He was still pained by the damaged ribs but, putting that minor discomfort aside, walked smartly about the yards, paced out fencing and clambered up into lofts with much of his former energy.

"My Daddy would've liked it here," he said, in passing.

And Kirsty had said, "It's not near as big as Dalnavert."

"Thank God for that," Craig had told her just as he vanished round the back of the byre.

The afternoon had gone and there was just the first faint nip of night frost in the atmosphere, before the woman, the man and the little boy came together again at last by the high gate at the yard's end. Craig, his work done, lit a cigarette, leaned his elbows on the cracked spar and looked out over the russet hills. Kirsty stood by him, not touching, waiting, while Bobby, unchecked, dabbed in the shallow ditch and, with satisfaction, broke the membranous ice into shards and particles with the heel of his shoe and the rod of the caliper.

Kirsty said, "What do you think, Craig?"

"It's in damned poor state," Craig replied.

"The price seems reasonable, though."

"I want no special terms, you understand; no favours from Breezy Adair," Craig said.

"No, I've made that clear. If we do decide to take it we pay the askin' price in full," said Kirsty.

"You've been into it thoroughly, haven't you?" Craig said.

"If you mean about stock – "

"I mean about money."

"Aye, I have."

"It'll take the best part of your savin's, just take them an' burn them up. If we don't make a go of it, Kirsty, we'll be back where we started – only worse."

"I'm not concerned about the money," Kirsty said.

"You'll have to work hard," Craig said. "Aye – but that never frightened you, did it?"

"It'll not be my hard work that'll make Garscadden tick," said Kirsty. "It'll be what you do, Craig."

"What we do together, is that what you mean?"

"Aye, that's what I mean."

He lowered his elbows from the gate, flicked away the cigarette. Below him his son knelt on the hard ground and crawled under the lowest spar into the big, wide, empty field. Kirsty and Craig watched him, let him explore unchecked, within their sight.

In the cool, red angle of sunlight Craig's facial scars were clear to see. He did not attempt to hide them from her, or the eye that watered in the cold. She did not find them anything but ugly; and yet, already, she had begun to feel that they were part of the man, a characteristic that would fade in time into the whole.

She put out her hand and touched his cheek.

"Not pretty, eh?" Craig said.

"Oh, no, not pretty," Kirsty agreed.

"We're stuck with it, though," Craig said. "I'm sorry."

She moved closer and put an arm about his waist, slipped her gloved fingers into the pocket of his old, black donkey jacket.

"What do you say?" she asked. "Do we take it?"

"Aye, we take it," Craig said.

"There's just one condition."

"What's that?"

"I want you to marry me," Kirsty said.

"Aye, I knew there'd be a catch," Craig said.

She frowned at him, wondering if this was cynicism, words uttered by the young, proud, angry, ambitious, discontented boy who had led her to Glasgow and had, for better or worse, shaped her life to his. But Craig was smiling. He even managed a mischievous wink.

"In kirk," she said.

"How will you manage that?"

"Pull strings," Kirsty said.

Before Craig could answer the couple were interrupted by

their son's cry of discovery.

"Heeeeeeh!" the boy called out.

Bobby stood with arms akimbo staring in wonder at the creature that had risen from the grass some yards in front of him. The hare, a buck, was large and half in white. Poised and upright, nose and ear tufts twitching, it contemplated the little red-coated stranger with wary interest out of its keen brown eye while Bobby, no less wary and alert, regarded it in turn. Finally he could resist no longer and took a pace towards it, reaching to stroke its soft, appealing fur. And the hare was gone, not racing, but limping away in a zig-zag path, with Bobby, limping too, following in pursuit.

"He'll never catch it," Craig said.

"No," said Kirsty, "not yet."

"I'd better fetch him back before he falls."

"Aye."

Craig swung himself on to the gate, dropped over it, then, involuntarily, turned and, leaning over the bar, kissed Kirsty on the mouth.

"All right," he said, "in kirk."

Then he strode off to chase his son across the brow of the hillside and down to the drifting stream.

*   *   *

The Reverend Harry Graham, minister of St Anne's church in Walbrook Street, was none too pleased at the young woman's request. He made it clear, as sternly as he could, that he did not approve of out-of-wedlock liaisons, hinted too that he was aware that there had been some jookery-pookery with Practice and Procedure in the matter of Bobby's baptism. He was, however, willing to be persuaded that a marriage finally blessed before God might make up much of the moral ground that had been lost in a common-law union or to put it another way – better late than never.

Nominally Kirsty was still a member of St Anne's and the Reverend Harry, in his heart of hearts, felt that he owed a little debt, if not to his martyred assistant, David Lockhart, at least to the memory of Nessie Frew.

For whatever reason, Mr Graham finally agreed to perform the marriage ceremony. He did not insist on conducting the service tucked away in the vestry, though he did lay down some conditions, framed as suggestions, to make the event a bit more comfortable for all concerned. To these Kirsty willingly acceded.

It was a month before spring quarter day, before the house at No. 154 Canada Road would be vacated and Sergeant Byrne's brother's cart would haul the Nicholsons' possessions through the streets of Greenfield and out to the wilds of Old Garscadden. Kirsty had already begun the process of sorting and packing and a pyramid of cardboard boxes stood against the wall in the front bedroom.

Craig was seldom at home. Indeed, he camped out two or three nights a week now, sleeping on the floor before the fire in the farm kitchen at Old Garscadden, gradually 'taking possession' by subtle degrees. Legal details, shop matters and the practical business of stock buying and the replenishment of damaged gear kept both Kirsty and Craig occupied but, oddly, also brought them closer than ever before, bonded at long last in common purpose.

In the midst of all this activity, weddings, in the plural, were endlessly discussed and not just by Craig and Kirsty. Lorna and Ernest had decided to wait until May, in which month, with luck, Frank would be able to free himself from his duties in London for a day or two and would travel north to stand by his brother's side at the hitching rail. Gordon, of course, had no such sentimental niceties to stay him and declared his intention of marrying Greta by civil ceremony just as soon as he had found a suitable place for them to live.

Greta had changed. Grief and neglect had taken her down. Now it was up to Gordon to restore her health and good spirits and, by cherishing and love, make amends for the hurts that had been inflicted upon her by the careless egotism of the rich. In this Breezy was right behind his stepson and, while with Kirsty, Greta soon re-formed the orphan bond in a relationship that gave her comfort and assurance.

Of all the difficult and awkward situations that Gordon had had to learn to cope with since he came to Breezy's house, none compared to his meeting, face to face, with Josephine Adair. It was an obligation that he could not shirk. A plain, unvarnished letter of farewell would not do at all, not for the gentleman he aspired to be. He wrote to her at her father's house and requested a rendezvous in Glasgow. He met with her one drizzling afternoon in her rooms in Park Gardens, where he drank tea, ate coconut buns and told her that she had been right to distrust him, that he had not had the gumption to be true.

"Not to me," Josephine had said. "But true, nonetheless."

He'd felt small in her presence, as if she'd grown larger in stature in the weeks since last they'd met. He had not asked her what her plans might be for she, he knew, had none except a calendar of rallies and conventions. Her attitude to Temperance seemed to have become listless as if through the chatter of committees she had discerned some other voice, quite small and tender, that would lure her, in time, away. Gordon had eventually kissed her on the cheek in the hallway, had murmured his thanks and had left with the knowledge of her hurt upon him to add to his store of experience.

At half past four on a gloomy afternoon witnesses and guests gathered in the empty church on Walbrook Street. Reverend Graham could not help the furtive hour; those who came to God out of a wilful darkness deserved no better. He had seen to it that there were flowers in a vase in the hall and that the clerk had turned up the heat in the pipes. He'd even found an organist who, for Nessie's sake, would play a hymn and, in muted tones, put out the triumph of the Wedding March. It was very quiet in the kirk. There was no sun to tint the glass in the arched windows and the gasoliers were lit only over the table and the open pews. Robed and alone, the Reverend Graham entered from the vestry door to find the groom attired in police uniform, constable's blue worn proudly for, the minister suspected, the very last time.

Harry Graham had kept abreast of Craig Nicholson's chequered career. He had learned from Kirsty that that career was now over. He had not been prepared for the burned face, however, for the extent of the scarring, for the watering left eye. He felt a rise in sympathy that had not been there before and pondered for a moment, what Nessie would have to say about her dour, handsome lodger now. Then, as the strains of the organ sounded softly, he looked up to see the bride arrayed in a gown of soft, pink cotton-sateen, come towards him on the arm of Albert Adair.

Kirsty was glad of Breezy's support. She had not been at all nervous throughout the course of the day. She had raked and reset the fire, had made breakfast, had bathed Bobby and massaged his leg. She had even washed a tub of shirts and underclothes while Craig paced and smoked and glanced at the clock and waited for Gordon with a restlessness that had at first amused and latterly irritated Kirsty.

She had been relieved to hear her brother-in-law's knock upon the door, even more relieved when Craig, dressed in uniform, went off with Gordon to the warehouse from whence they would walk the short distance to St Anne's. Then Lorna had arrived and, to Kirsty's surprise, Greta and Madge with her. Bobby had been royally entertained by his aunts, old and new, while Kirsty had been groomed and dressed and, in general, done up like a dish of fish, all with one eye on the clock on the mantel.

Bobby was left in the care of Mrs Piper, as arranged. The women travelled by carriage to Gascoigne Street where Tubby and Breezy were waiting. The shop had been shuttered and locked, and a second carriage had arrived – and Kirsty was almost alone at last, except for Breezy who rode with her in his role as the Man Who Would Give the Bride Away.

It had been a strange mishmash of a day, comic and silly, and at the same time quite serious, almost grave. She had stared out at the streets of the Greenfield as if she would never see them again, had ticked off in her mind each incident and episode that had brought her, out of girlhood and into womanhood, to this hour of this March day at last.

Breezy was too downy a bird to intrude upon her reverie. In fact, he spoke only twice.

As the carriage rolled into Walbrook Street, he glanced at Kirsty and said, "I'd offer you a penny for them, chookie, but I suspect they're worth a whole lot more than that right now." And, as St Anne's came into view and the carriage halted, he leaned forwards, kissed her on the brow and said in a voice that had the merest sentimental tremble to it, "Brave girl."

Even Breezy's blessing, with its witting ambiguity, had not shaken Kirsty from her unemotional state. She felt as if she were cruising on a stream that held no threats, gliding forward to a destination that had been thoroughly mapped and charted.

It was not until she entered the darkened church, heard the

organ notes, saw Craig ahead of her and felt Breezy's arm leave hers that breath checked in Kirsty's throat. A peculiar tension gripped her midriff and a sudden wave of uncertainty threatened to engulf her. She was only vaguely aware of the witnesses, those folk for whom she cared and who cared for her – just six of them, a neat half dozen, gathered in the pew close to the front – Madge's big dominating hat, Greta's plain new gown, Ernest's elegant collar and Ascot cravat. She reached Craig's side and stood by him. He inclined his head but did not smile. Nervousness had gone from him, all trace of it, and all his fretful pride. It was not just the pinched embroidery of scar tissue that made it seem so. He was with her at last. Even so, as Kirsty listened to the minister's voice, she could not help but feel the presence of others in the kirk. It was as if they had come silently into the balcony; Nessie, Nessie with David by her side.

The sensation that she was watched in what she did grew and became overwhelming. Even as she spoke the words of response, answered aloud the questions that were put to her, it was all Kirsty could do to stop herself turning, turning swiftly, to catch a final glimpse of them there in the darkness.

And then it came upon her that she did not have to look round at all, for if they were with her now, they would be with her always, not to chide but to comfort her in the years that lay ahead. She felt the knots of tension loosen, and was possessed of a certainty stronger than anything she had ever known before.

She heard herself say, "I do."

Behind her Madge was weeping, Tubby too perhaps, but there was no other sound in church, and the shadows behind her were still.

"Kirsty?" Craig whispered.

"Hmmm?"

He smiled at her daftness, took her left hand in his and, as gently as any man could, slipped on to the outstretched finger her brand new wedding ring.